BETTER LUCK
next time

Other books by A.R. Casella and
Denise Grover Swank

Asheville Brewing Series
Any Luck at All
Better Luck Next Time
Getting Lucky
Bad Luck Club

BETTER LUCK
next time

A.R. CASELLA AND
NEW YORK TIMES BESTSELLING AUTHOR
DENISE GROVER SWANK

To Sean, whose charisma, business smarts, and inability to keep a secret inspired Finn. We miss you always. —ARC

To Jenna, I love you, girl. Never let anyone break your spirit. —DGS

CHAPTER

One

"It's going well, don't you think?"

Adalia Buchanan glanced over her shoulder, smiling at the tremor in her sister's voice. Only Georgie would worry that an event with a full house might be going badly. Adalia had been to art showings that had a grand total of four guests and Two-Buck Chuck in plastic cups. As far as she was concerned, the grand reopening of Buchanan Brewery was a major success.

"Georgie, stop worrying. There are people lined up outside, waiting to get in. Everyone loves the new brews. That guy from the Best Brews website is losing it over the Cesspool of Sin ale—"

Georgie's eyes flew wide. "Losing it how?"

Adalia rolled her eyes. "In a good way. River made it, so how could it be anything short of amazing?" She leaned in closer and grinned. "And if you tell him I said that, I'll deny it until my dying breath."

While Adalia liked River Reeves well enough and thought he was the perfect man for her overachieving sister, she didn't want to get his ego out of whack by giving him too many compliments for free. No one liked a man with an outsized ego.

Georgie nodded, anxiety still filling her eyes.

Adalia wished her older sister would learn to relax, but Georgie's name might as well have been Georgie Perfectionist Buchanan. Relaxing wasn't in her wheelhouse, especially on a night like tonight. To be fair, it *was* a big deal, especially for Georgie. Buchanan Brewery might now belong to all four Buchanan siblings, but Georgie was the only one who'd put in the capital to refurbish the decades-old facility and pay the staff during a nearly three-month shutdown.

So yeah, Georgie had a lot riding on a successful relaunch.

"Don't *worry*, Georgie. Everyone is loving everything about the place, from the beer to the updated décor, and even the new merch." Adalia gave her a smug smile as she listed that last item, since she was the one who'd designed it. "And they love that you've still kept some of the past too, from Beau Brown ale to Dottie herself."

Georgie's eyes flew wide in horror. "I would never get rid of Dottie!" Then she added, "Even if I could."

The Buchanan siblings had inherited the brewery from their paternal grandfather, Beau Buchanan, but the gift had come with a few stipulations, the least outrageous of which was that Beau's longtime girlfriend, Dottie Hendrickson, couldn't be fired.

"Why would we ever get rid of Dottie?" Adalia scoffed. "The woman is a national treasure." She saw the older woman making the rounds, and Dottie looked up and smiled as if she knew she was being discussed. Maybe she did, actually. She seemed to have an uncanny way of knowing things.

Adalia felt a rush of warmth. Dottie was a hoot to have around, and she'd been around a lot. It seemed she'd decided to take the wayward Buchanan children under her wing. If she'd treated them like projects, it would have been insulting, but Dottie wasn't like that. "Is it just me, or does Dottie's hair look more lavender than usual?"

Georgie laughed. "She told River she used a new rinse. It looks good on her, I think."

"Anything would look good on her," Adalia said. "She could pull off bright orange without looking like a clown."

Georgie gave her a soft smile, emotion practically oozing out of her pores, and Adalia restrained an eyeroll. She knew her sister was happy she was making connections in Asheville. Over the past few months, Georgie had poured her worry into two things: the brewery and Adalia. Which, to be fair, Adalia had shown up in Asheville a sobbing mess back in June.

Was it weird that the only friend she'd really made here in Asheville was the eighty-two-year-old great-aunt of her sister's boyfriend? Probably, but Adalia either stayed at home or went to the brewery with Georgie, so it wasn't like she'd had a lot of opportunities to socialize. Normally, that would have bothered her. Normally, she was the social one of the three Buchanan siblings—oops… *four* Buchanan siblings, but Adalia knew absolutely nothing about her newly discovered half-brother, Jack Durand, other than he didn't seem to have a sense of humor. Or at least he didn't display one in the video business meetings he'd participated in with his sisters. Still, he was somewhat useful, and he'd played a big role in the opening party, even though he'd made all of the arrangements from Chicago.

Adalia had learned of his existence at the reading of Grandpa Beau's will, and at first she'd had no interest in getting to know him. It had felt almost like a betrayal of her mother. Now, as of today, she was his roommate. He'd gone back to Chicago shortly after the will reading for undisclosed reasons—packing did *not* take three months; Adalia had done it in an afternoon—but he'd shown up at Grandpa Beau's house this morning in a small moving van towing a Prius.

Up until a couple of weeks ago, Adalia had been sharing the house with Georgie, but her sister had spent so much time at River's apartment that he'd finally asked her to move in. Georgie had done some more worrying about Adalia, not wanting to leave her alone with their inherited devil cat, Jezebel, but Adalia had encouraged her to be happy and take her lovefest elsewhere. Something she'd regretted as soon as Jack set a move-in date. He'd dragged his feet for so long she'd kind of hoped he'd forgotten about it. Although she'd lived with plenty of Craigslist strangers, none of the others had been her brother.

"He's not a stranger," Georgie had admonished when Adalia had voiced her irritation. "You've talked to him in our video meetings."

"Where he's all business. Nothing personal. He's like a robot. And besides, I've never met him in person."

"He was at the will reading," Georgie had reminded her.

"And we never said a word to each other." But Adalia had flinched at the reminder. She wasn't proud of the way she'd acted that day. She'd talked about him right in front of his face, like he wasn't even there. Like he was an inconvenience rather than a person. She of all people should have known better, and she couldn't help wondering if he held it against her.

She definitely would have.

Bright and early that morning—had he driven all night?—Jack had dropped off some of his belongings in Georgie's old room. He'd said all of thirty-two words to Adalia (she'd counted), most of them conveying the message that he was dropping the rest of his stuff off at a prearranged storage facility. Then he'd promptly disappeared until a few hours before the opening, which had irritated Adalia to no end.

"Why couldn't he have come into town yesterday?" she'd asked her sister while they were going through the final preparations. "He should be here helping."

"He set a lot of things up remotely, Addy, and you know it. I don't know why he couldn't come to Asheville sooner, but he's here now. Be nice."

Be *nice*.

Nice better not be in any description of Adalia Elizabeth Buchanan. Feisty. Loud. Even obnoxious, but *never* nice. Her mother had been nice, and all it had gotten her was an overbearing, cheating husband, who treated his children like fleas on a dog.

Except that wasn't entirely true. Adalia had come close to being nice with the last man in her life, and it had cost her more than she was willing to contemplate.

She shook away the bitter memories, searching for Jack in the crowd. She watched him for a moment, impressed by how well he fit in with the staff, something she wouldn't have expected since most of them hadn't been privy to the awkward video chats. But he'd introduced himself to everyone before they opened their doors, and she had to admit he'd done well. He apologized for showing up a few months late— which had gotten a few chuckles, mostly because he'd delivered the line in a self-deprecating tone—and said the

11

kinds of things people wanted to hear in a tone that implied he meant them (open door policy, no issue too big or small, yada yada). She'd listened more closely when the speech turned personal. Apparently, he'd gotten his start as a busboy when he was fifteen, then worked his way up the ladder at a few restaurants before taking over as manager of a bar. He'd delivered every line with an air of humility that had softened Adalia toward him—just a little—and instantly won over the staff.

She was a little jealous that he seemed more inclined to talk to them than he was to her. Then again, she hadn't made it easy.

"At least Jack is here," Georgie said. "Lee couldn't be bothered."

It was true, their full-blooded brother had sent his sisters a group text, not a congratulations but a warning.

Dad and Victoria are keeping an eye on your relaunch. Don't screw it up, or I'll never hear the end of it.

Rude, to be sure, but then Lee had been rude to Adalia ever since she'd up and moved to Asheville. Although Lee had given Georgie his approval to rehab and run the brewery, he'd appeared to immediately regret it. Whether it was because he really wanted nothing to do with their inheritance or because their father wouldn't let him hear the end of it (Dear Old Dad was clearly super bitter to have been skipped over in Grandpa Beau's will), Adalia couldn't be sure, but she suspected it was a combination. She'd initially planned on taking a hands-off approach too, but then she'd gotten into trouble and abruptly moved to Asheville. Lee had seen it as a personal betrayal. Especially since he didn't know the real reason she had moved. They'd gotten closer recently, and she hated to lose that, but she'd hate it even more if she had to see the look of disappointment in his eyes. She couldn't bring herself to tell him what had happened.

She glanced back at Georgie, who was biting her lip, and decided there was one thing she could do. Her sister was on the ledge of anxiety, and she knew there was only one person who could talk her down. River was moving around the room, talking to the customers. At least half of them already knew him from when he was the brewmaster at Big Catch Brewing, the brewery he'd started with his friend Finn. The customers were greeting him with big smiles and offering congratulations on a successful reopening. Adalia knew they were also (rightfully) praising his beers. Georgie needed to be in the middle of that. Not stuck on the periphery like a wallflower.

Before she could drag her sister over there, Dottie wove her way through the crowd and stopped in front of them. "Addy, I need you to come talk to a young man about the T-shirts you designed with Hops and Jezebel."

Adalia shot a glance at her still-anxious sister. "I'd be happy to, Dottie, but I need to take care of my sister first. I'll be right there."

Without waiting for either of them to respond, she wrapped an arm around Georgie's back and started pulling her across the tasting room.

"What are you doing?" Georgie asked, trying to resist without creating a scene.

"River," Adalia called out as she tilted to the side to get a look at him in the midst of the crowd.

He turned to face her with a question in his eyes.

She dragged her sister around a couple and practically thrust her at him.

"I'm done babysitting her. It's your turn."

Georgie gasped in horror, but Adalia threw her arms around her sister and whispered in her ear, "You've done an amazing thing here, Georgie. Now *please* let yourself enjoy it."

Georgie gave her a surprised look, but Adalia winked, then turned to River and said in a deep voice, "Young man, I expect you to make sure my sister has a good time tonight, or there will be hell to pay."

River grinned, probably in part because she'd needled him plenty of times about the fact that she was older than him by a few weeks, especially since Georgie was three years older than both of them.

Her work done, she set out in search of Dottie, only to plow into the broad chest of a very handsome man, or so she thought for the split second before she recognized him as Finn Hamilton. His hair was longer, the curl more apparent, and his blue-green eyes were the sort that kept a person guessing: blue with one outfit, green with another. Still, his looks didn't matter. She and Finn had gotten off on the wrong foot when they'd met, and even though they'd seen each other a couple of times since, they were still apparently on the wrong foot. Literally. He'd been holding a glass of beer, and it sloshed over his hand and onto her shoes.

"Oh, Adalia," Finn said, grabbing her arm with his free hand. "Sorry about that."

"It's a crowded room. Bound to happen." Sure enough, one of the tasting room employees was Johnny-on-the-spot with a rag to help clean up the spill. She stepped to the side, pulling Finn with her.

He let her go abruptly as though realizing he was still holding on.

"I saw the article," she blurted out.

He made a face she couldn't interpret. "Which one?"

Fortune had written a piece about him and his sale of Big Catch to Bev Corp, a national distributor. They'd praised the move and called him a "self-made man," but a good portion of the citizens of Asheville were pissed at Finn for selling out to Bev Corp (River included, though they'd mostly made up), and *The Asheville Gazette* had countered the article with a piece of their own, alleging that Finn's parents—who were mega wealthy—had made a substantial donation to the Duke business school right before Finn had been accepted. So his reputation was deep in the crapper. In fact, Adalia was surprised to see he'd come out and risk a public tarring and feathering. Even more so because he'd clearly come alone.

"Both." She flashed him a smile. "Plus all of the comments. They really paint a picture."

His eyes darkened.

Oh crap. She'd only meant to tease him—wasn't laughing about something the best way to blunt the sting?—but obviously he'd taken it the wrong way. She of all people understood what it was like to be judged based on the success of your parents. She'd lived not only in her father's shadow, but that of her two older siblings. The expectations could be so smothering. So limiting. The one thing she'd always been able to count on was the look of disapproval in her father's eyes, because she would always be a disappointment to him. Was Finn's family supporting him, or had they tossed him to the wolves?

"There you are, dear," Dottie said, sidling up to them.

Adalia started to respond, but then she realized Dottie was talking to Finn.

The older woman lifted her hand to his cheek and patted lightly. "Did you go see Lola as I suggested?"

Lola? Who was Lola? A therapist? A prostitute? A rabbit who could play the flute? With Dottie, there was no way of knowing.

He gave her a sheepish look. "No, but…"

Dottie shook her head and clucked. "When will you young people learn to trust me? Lola is a good friend, and she's exactly the person who can help you"—her gaze shifted to Adalia—"help *both* of you figure out what comes next."

Finn seemed to stumble over his words before saying, "Dottie…"

"I'm teasing," she said with a grin. "Mostly. Just know I care about you."

Adalia knew that part was true. Dottie cared about a lot of people. Soon after Adalia had come to Asheville, Dottie had invited her over for tea and brought her on a tour of the art studio in her detached garage. Adalia had wandered around in awe of the woman's talent. Later, over tea, Dottie had given her a key and told her to use it anytime she pleased. If she wanted privacy, all she needed to do was tie a scarf around the door handle.

Adalia had protested, saying she refused to kick the woman out of her own studio, but Dottie had been persistent—one of her superpowers—and before Adalia knew it, she'd agreed to come at least once. She had been nearly a dozen times now, although she didn't have anything to show for it.

Dottie had known what she needed without being told, and from the way Dottie was staring into Finn's eyes, Adalia had a feeling Finn had his own intervention in store. Sure enough, Dottie said, "You must come to my house for tea. And soon. Promise me."

He nodded. "I will."

"Good boy," she said, patting his cheek again. "Let Aunt Dottie help you set things right."

If only Dottie could set all things right, but Adalia knew firsthand it wasn't that easy, at least not for her. There were too many fresh wounds, too many scars. Some injuries never healed, especially wounds to the heart.

CHAPTER Two

It wasn't supposed to be like this.

The article in *Fortune* was supposed to be Finn's victory lap. He deserved it, damn it. He'd built Big Catch Brewing out of nothing. No, that wasn't quite true. He and River had done it together. Without the beer, a brewery was just a building, and making beer hadn't mattered much to him. It was the idea that had excited him. He liked selling. Marketing. Building. *Doing.* And sure, his father had given him part of the seed money, but he'd paid it back after the first year.

Except apparently everyone had thought he should hold on to that golden goose for the rest of his life, because no one in town seemed happy about the sale. He couldn't go for a drink or a meal downtown without getting scowled at by someone. And when a pretty girl approached him, it was just as likely that she wanted to yell at him as proposition him. They thought he was a sellout, that he'd invited sharks into their tank. But he didn't see it that way. Finn's father had always told him that fish didn't learn to swim half so fast if there wasn't something with teeth chasing them.

Of course, Finn's father's response to the *Fortune* article was that he could finally leave "that Podunk town" behind.

He couldn't understand why Finn hadn't left yet. Charlotte was big and getting bigger—the kind of place where young people moved to become somebody.

"Time to grow up, Finn," he'd said. "Set your sights on something bigger than a brewery." If he knew about the local coverage, he hadn't said anything. Neither had Finn, although it made him feel like a coward that he hadn't confronted his parents about the whole Duke thing. He already knew what they'd say. They'd done it to help him, to be supportive, and no one had been *obligated* to accept him.

In truth, his father wouldn't understand why the public vitriol was getting to him. His dad had always said that earning hatred was an earmark of success, but Finn had never felt that way. His mom wouldn't have either. He'd inherited her desire to be liked—and until now, people always had liked him. That mattered to him, and this town mattered to him too. He wasn't going to move on like it had been some stepping stone. His life was here.

But it sucked that he couldn't talk it out with anyone. Most people weren't sympathetic, it turned out, when you complained about the fallout of selling your company for millions. He'd made up with River, mostly, after screwing up their friendship by selling the brewery without consulting him (to be fair, Bev Corp *would* have paid him a bundle to stay), but things weren't the same, and River didn't have much time on his hands. He had his relationship with Georgie, and both of them lived and breathed Buchanan Brewery. And for the first time in his life, it seemed Finn had nothing but time.

Three days after the grand reopening of Buchanan Brewery, he was sitting in his house in sweatpants— *sweatpants*—at two p.m. on a Tuesday, willing himself not to think about everything. Trying specifically not to dwell on the way Adalia Buchanan had treated him—like he was a sad sack, like she should be nice to him because he was *that* pathetic. Somehow he would have preferred it if she'd been more cutting.

His phone rang, jolting him out of the doldrums.

It was Gretchen, the Bev Corp exec who'd handled the sale.

Warily, he picked up the call. "Let me guess. You saw the article in *The Asheville Gazette*, and you want to give it back."

She laughed. "Well, I did see the article, but no, we're still happy with the sale. Even if it was disappointing to see River Reeves…jump ship."

From the pause, he understood she was nodding to the nautical theme of the brewery, a joke he and River had cooked up because of their names—River and Finn.

"Yeah, but the guy you brought in from Charlotte is the real deal." Which was true, but he was still being treated as an outsider. If Bev Corp had thought they were playing it safe by choosing a North Carolinian, they'd miscalculated. Finn was from Charlotte too, and it had been commented on a time or two in their early days.

"We're very happy with him. The problem is one of publicity. We didn't foresee this much pushback from the locals."

"You and me both," he muttered.

"Yes," she said, "I'm aware you've had your own…difficulties, so I'll cut straight to the point. We're hoping to hire you as a consultant. We need a community liaison. Someone who can help us improve our image and reclaim a space in the local beer community."

Finn actually laughed at that, genuine, unfiltered laughter. He couldn't remember the last time that had happened. "You want to hire *me* to rehab *your* image?"

"Yes, I can see why you might find that amusing," she said. "We don't want to necessarily publicize the fact that you're the one helping us. But you built Big Catch, Finn. You know business. You found your niche in that community as an outsider. You can help us strategize."

Somewhere in the middle of her pep talk, Finn felt his no turn into a yes. It wouldn't take up much of his time, and what the hell else was he doing with his life? He'd been hoping for the next big thing, the idea that would help him find success a second time and not be a flash in the pan, but instead he'd become a hermit. If anyone knew how he spent his days, they'd stage an intervention. Besides, if he agreed, he'd be helping the community too, wouldn't he? Rehabbing the brewery's image would involve raising charity dollars, for sure. His old employees would benefit as well. He didn't like to think people might hold a grudge against them for decisions he'd made.

"I'll do it."

———————

He hadn't really intended to take Dottie up on her offer of tea, but after talking to Gretchen, he felt the need to share his news with someone who wouldn't judge him off the bat. So he showered and got dressed in real clothes—a button-down short-sleeve shirt and khakis—and found Dottie's number on his phone's contact list. While he knew Dottie shared River's distaste for big corporations, his friend's aunt wasn't judgmental. She wouldn't hate him for it.

Can I take you up on tea? he texted.

Her answer was almost immediate: *I'd already set out another cup for you.*

He suspected that was just Dottie trying to sound mystical, but it still gave him the chills.

As he drove to her house, he found himself whistling, feeling pepped up.

When he got to Dottie's place, her car wasn't in the drive, but there was a real clunker in its place—the kind of car that looked like it wouldn't get you to the gas station. It might be a faded yellow, or perhaps it was just a really dirty white, the kind where the dirt had seeped into the paint and could no longer be cleaned off. The bumper was secured in one corner with mechanical tape. He would have wondered if her car was in the shop, but this wasn't the kind of vehicle a rental place would give out. Did she have other guests? She hadn't mentioned anything, but Dottie was notorious for holding impromptu gatherings.

He got out and knocked on the front door, grinning a little as he took in the bright yellow trim. God, his mother would hate that, but he liked the look. It was sunny, and it screamed that the person inside didn't care about convention.

No one answered, so he tried the knob. It opened.

"Dottie?" he called.

Still nothing. He let himself in, shutting the door behind him, and made his way to the kitchen. Two empty teacups sat across from each other on the table, but there was no sign of Dottie. She'd left a short note. *Help yourself, dear. I'll be back shortly. I ran out of cream, so I walked to the corner store.*

So much for Dottie being psychic. But the note didn't mention anything about the other car.

Someone screamed in the back yard, and Finn flinched as if he'd been struck. Was it Dottie? Had someone maybe, what, mugged her? The thought didn't fit—both because

Dottie was the kind to befriend muggers rather than scream at them and because the sound was so angry.

He walked to the closest window and looked out at the back yard. No one was there, so he left the house and circled around. A fluttering scarf caught his eye from the door of Dottie's studio. Then he saw that the door was cracked open. The cry must have come from inside.

Maybe he should mind his own business, but he'd never been particularly good at that. Besides, for all he knew, the driver of that whacked-out car could be trying to carry off Dottie's art. He didn't pause to think about it. He was already moving.

He opened the door a few more inches, but he didn't get any farther, because the person inside wasn't a stranger. It was Adalia Buchanan. She was always pretty, with those bouncy curls he wanted to touch, but right now she was magnificent. Her hair had been swept back into a messy bun that barely contained it, her cheeks were streaked with paint, and she had a ferocious look in her eyes that reminded him of a Valkyrie. It took a moment for him to notice what she was working on.

Finn wasn't an art connoisseur, but he hadn't been a beer connoisseur either. He'd known genius when he'd tasted River's home brews, and he knew it now, looking at that canvas in front of Adalia. He didn't recognize any of the shapes as objects or people. But the bright colors slashed and swirled together in a way that expertly conveyed a mood. Sadness. Despair. Anger. So much anger.

Seeing her with that painting, it felt like an awakening. Like he'd finally found something else worth getting behind. Worth fighting for. So he wasn't prepared for what he saw next. She pulled a utility knife from the pocket of her cargo pants and slashed the painting, wet paint staining her fingers and the drop cloths spread out beneath her. The anger had faded from her, and even though she attacked the painting with violence, a deep, deep sadness had permeated her gaze.

He wanted to stop her, to take the knife from her fingers, to soothe her, but he felt immobilized. He couldn't do anything but stand there and watch her in the grip of whatever powerful emotions had made her destroy something she'd made. Something beautiful. It would feel wrong to interrupt such a private moment.

But he must have shifted or something because the next thing he knew, she turned toward him, her eyes wild, that knife still in her hand. She saw his eyes on it and dropped her hand, her expression that of a woman who'd been caught naked by a Peeping Tom.

And he was the pervert in this scenario.

"I…I'm sorry," he blabbered. "Dottie invited me over for tea, but she wasn't inside, and I heard you scream. I worried there might be a burglar out here stealing her art or—"

"Get out," she said, her voice ice cold. He wouldn't have known she was embarrassed, that she was affected by what had just happened, if not for the slight flush of her cheeks. Part of Finn knew he should just leave, but he felt the need to say something else, if only to help himself process what he'd seen.

"Why would you destroy it?" he said softly. "Your work is magnificent, Adalia. I've never seen anything like it."

Something flickered in her eyes, and for a moment he thought she was pleased, that his words had moved her, but then she grabbed the slashed canvas from its stand and handed it to him, the wet paint slopping on his fingers. "Then you keep it."

And she walked out and left.

CHAPTER *Three*

"Come on, Bessie," Adalia coaxed as her car pulled into the inclined driveway of her house. "You can do it."

Bessie was a hunk of junk, but she was *Adalia's* hunk of junk, purchased here in Asheville. She knew Georgie had practically chewed off her tongue to keep from offering to buy her a car, especially after learning just how little she had in her savings account. Her sister had settled for forcing "bonus" money on her for designing the merch and bottle labels for Buchanan and a "stipend" for her work on social media. Adalia had considered turning it down—she was one-fourth owner, which meant she should only make money when the brewery made money—but in all honesty she needed it. It had made her feel like she'd earned the car.

Besides, Adalia's father had given her enough lectures over the course of her nearly thirty years that it had sunk deep into her skin—there are no free rides. Only losers accept handouts. *When will you ever live up to your family name?*

When pigs learned how to fly, and she hadn't seen a winged pig yet, although if she were being honest with herself, occasionally she looked.

Jack's car was already in the drive, so Adalia steeled her back as she walked toward the front door. To say things were awkward between them was an understatement. Jack had been in the house for three nights, and while they were polite to each other, somehow that made it weirder. If Jack had been a normal roommate, Adalia could have ignored him and hung out in her room, but she felt an obligation to at least make some kind of effort to talk to him. Too bad he seemed to be struggling with what to say just as much as she was.

She dumped her purse on the bench in the small entryway, then headed for the staircase, eager to shower and remove the dried paint smeared all over her hands and lower arms. Red seemed to be her favorite color in Asheville, and she'd already gone through several tubes. She kept meaning to buy more, but the pull toward Dottie's garage was sometimes so strong it nearly possessed her. She'd find herself in Dottie's driveway…and a fresh tube of red acrylic paint would be waiting for her next to the palette and brushes Dottie had given her.

Thank God, since Adalia had left anything to do with art in her New York apartment, as well as everything else that hadn't fit into her suitcases. Georgie had offered to pay for her things to be packed and moved, but Adalia had left the remains for her roommates to pick through.

When she'd left New York, she'd intended to leave art behind too, but it turned out her soul needed art as much as her body needed oxygen. She'd tried to deny it the first month, hoping that doodling with the Buchanan Brewery logos and merch would satiate that unquenchable hunger to create, to pour every bit of her feelings into some medium outside herself. But she'd been a fool. Other than her mother's death, she was at the lowest point of her life, and her soul begged for release.

Once Adalia had finally acquired Bessie—the salesman had raised his brows and asked, "Are you sure?"—the very first place she'd driven to was Dottie's garage. She hadn't even stopped in to say hello, not that she'd needed to. Dottie had told her no greetings were necessary. Somehow she understood that Adalia's art was a private thing right now, and she respected her privacy as she worked through the tangled emotions consuming her.

She hadn't painted on canvas in years, but Dottie had left her a stack of sixteen by twenty canvases along with the paints and other supplies. Waiting, as if she'd known that Adalia would be by sooner rather than later. A note had sat beside them:

Georgie told me you worked in mixed media, but the choices for those pieces are such a personal thing—the choosing as tied to the artist as the creation itself—and I would never presume to know your artist's soul. Start with this or anything else in my studio—what's mine is yours!—and if you'd like to begin collecting materials that grab you for your mixed media, you can put them in the bin in the corner. Let your heart guide you, Addy. It won't steer you wrong.

Adalia had laughed bitterly at the last line. Her heart had brought her nothing but pain. Her art too. She still hadn't put anything in the bin.

Her first painting had been for Alan Stansworth, the man who'd hurt her heart and slashed her soul.

It was Alan who'd driven her to leave New York for Asheville, wounded and broken. Her mentor turned lover had used her in the worst way a person could. He'd stolen her art—her heart's creations—and claimed them for his own. The pieces had been in an exhibit under *his* name.

And so she'd destroyed them. Now she couldn't seem to stop.

She'd sobbed and sobbed as she poured her heart out onto the canvas that day, ending with a piece so full of chaos and yearning it had stolen her breath. It was good. No, it had been more than good. It had been her best piece yet. But the irony twisted something in her heart, and before she even knew what she was doing, she'd slashed the painting with a utility knife Dottie had left on a workbench, putting as much effort into the slicing as she had into the brushstrokes.

At the end, she was covered in paint and the canvas was shredded into so many pieces it was unrecognizable. An emotion she couldn't name—although she was sure there was probably a German word for it—swept through her, a mixture of relief and emptiness. Like she'd just dumped every last bit of pain onto the canvas, leaving her heart a shell. She cleaned up her brushes and her palette, dumped the canvas into Dottie's dumpster and went home, scaring Georgie half to death when she saw all the red paint covering her body and thought Adalia had had a run-in with a serial killer.

But the emotions had built back up again, and three days later, Adalia was back out at the garage, doing it all over again. And again.

Only Dottie had known the truth. Until today. Adalia's face flushed at the reminder of having been caught by Finn as she hurried up to her room, grateful Jack didn't pop out. She stripped her clothes and stepped into the shower in the adjoining bathroom. How long had Finn been watching her?

She'd gone over to Dottie's studio after receiving another wheedling text from Alan, one in a series of texts and emails that had started weeks ago. After a discussion with Georgie, who was certain he was just trying to get back into her good graces so he could use her again—Georgie had, thank God, tricked him into dropping the charges against her—she had ignored them. But they still kept coming, and for some reason, she hadn't blocked his number like her sister had suggested. It was as if part of her wanted to punish herself. So she'd gone to Dottie's thinking she'd paint out her emotions about Alan. Instead, she'd found herself painting her relationship with her father, how he'd always been so disappointed in her. How he'd given most of his attention to Lee, and what little was left for Georgie, who had been so desperate for his approval too. That look of appreciation in Finn's eyes, of wonder tinged with sadness, had strummed something inside of her—and then unleashed a fresh flood of anger that had her handing him the wet painting, slopping red paint on his designer clothes. Alan had admired her work too...and look where that had gotten her.

But being caught in the act, as it were, had thrown her. How long could she go on like this? What if other people discovered what she was doing? She could hear her father's voice in her head: *Mature people don't throw temper tantrums with paint and knives. Grow up, Adalia!*

What if he was right?

After her shower, she went downstairs, wearing a pair of pajama pants and a cami with a built-in bra (only because Jack was there) and raided the fridge for something to eat. Sure enough, there were two casserole dishes in the fridge with notes: "Jack, eat this for a slice of home," and the other, "Addy, you need more protein."

Dottie.

She still had a key to the house and often left food in the fridge, even more so since Georgie had moved out.

Adalia reached for the dish addressed to her.

"You found Dottie's food," Jack said behind her as he walked through the back door.

She nearly dropped the heavy glass dish. "God! You scared me!"

"Sorry," he said, still standing in front of the door with his phone in his hand.

She set her dish on the counter and lifted the foil. "Enchiladas?"

She grabbed a fork to poke inside and saw they were stuffed full of black beans.

"Mine is goulash," he said, moving closer. "Help yourself."

She cocked an eyebrow. "Goulash is a slice of home? I thought for sure that Dottie had figured out how to make a casserole deep-dish pizza."

A rare grin stretched across Jack's face, and for the first time Adalia could see his resemblance to her brother Lee, especially in the eyes. Jack's were brown and Lee's were hazel, but they had a similar shape to them. "My nana used to make it for me."

Adalia's eyes flew wide. "How did Dottie know that?"

He laughed. "I know Dottie tries to convince everyone she's psychic, but there's an explanation for this one. I mentioned it to her during a video chat."

Adalia couldn't help but feel a small wave of disappointment. Dottie might not be psychic, but she *was* intuitive. In a weird way, it would be nice to think there was more to it. "Missing home?"

Jack looked caught off guard by her question, but to her surprise he answered. "Yeah."

Something told her it wasn't a place he was missing, more like a *who*. She nearly peppered him with questions, but it occurred to her that Jack had spent thirty-plus years without knowing any of the Buchanans. He'd shown up at the will reading with a trunk full of baggage. She'd hate for him to start peppering her with questions about her massive issues, so instead she asked, "Have you eaten?"

"No, but I'm sure it's good."

She laughed. "No, doofus. I'm inviting you to eat with me. Apparently, we're family, and we're living together, so we might as well start doing some things together."

His eyes widened in surprise. "Like having family dinners?"

She shrugged, trying to pretend it was no big deal, but she and Georgie and, more often than not, River used to eat dinner together most nights. They still invited her over more than they should, but it wasn't the same as the casual pattern they'd developed. She missed it. "We don't have to…"

"No," he said quickly. Then, as though realizing he'd seemed too eager, he said more deliberately, "I'd like that."

"Well, okay then," she said, pulling out the goulash for him. "Let's fill our plates and sit at the table."

"Okay," he said, "but I'm a little nervous about those enchiladas."

Adalia laughed again, relieved to see Jack loosening up. "Last week Dottie told me that I looked pale and was worried I might be anemic. She knows I don't eat meat, so I guess she thought beans would do the trick."

"Got any Beano?" he joked as he pulled two plates out of a cabinet. "We've got a meeting with Georgie first thing in the morning."

"No, but now you *really* have to eat some. Then she won't know who to blame for the stench."

He smiled, a genuine smile, and Adalia was surprised how happy it made her to know she'd been the one to put it there.

"I think our first family dinner needs to be celebrated with alcohol. Beer or wine?" she asked, then shot him a teasing grin. "What wine goes with goulash and bean enchiladas?"

He started to answer, then stopped himself, his smile stretching wider. "Isn't it sacrilege to drink anything but Buchanan beer?"

"I won't tell if you don't."

"I think there's a cab on top of the fridge, although that's the worst place to keep wine." He made a face as he glanced up at the small foldable six-bottle wine rack.

"A cab sounds great, and move the wine rack anywhere you see fit." She paused and looked him square in the eye. "I know this is awkward for both of us. We barely know each other, and—surprise!—suddenly we're family, but this is your house too. Move things around if you want."

He studied her for a moment, then said with a deadpan face, "You feel awkward with me?"

Oh crap. Adalia tried to figure out how to smooth this over, but he broke out into another grin.

"You asshole," she said, but her laugh softened the words.

"There's the woman I met in the conference room."

She made a face, then said in a defensive tone, "Okay, I was a bitch. There's no excuse. I'm sorry. I've always been the outcast Buchanan, and suddenly I had someone else vying for my spot."

He grinned. "Well, you apologize like a Buchanan, so I think I'm currently holding the title for biggest outcast."

Putting her hand on her hip, she gave him the side-eye. "I think I'm gonna like you, Jack. We can be outcasts together."

He reached above the fridge and grabbed the bottle of wine. "Let's drink to that."

They fixed up their plates and heated them in the microwave while Jack opened the wine and poured two glasses. They carried their plates to the dining room table and fell into an easy conversation as Adalia gave him a very abbreviated, glossed-over retelling of growing up with Prescott Buchanan as a father.

"You were lucky not to have him harassing you," she said, pointing her fork at him to prove her point.

"Maybe," he conceded. He hadn't told her much about himself other than mentioning his grandmother. Apparently she'd watched him while his mother worked. She'd been his entire world before she died while he was in middle school.

"I'm sorry," Adalia said softly. Jack hadn't said his mother was difficult, but she heard it in his voice. If he'd been close to her, wouldn't he have mentioned her with the same affection he'd used for his nana?

He shrugged, pushing a couple of beans around on his plate with his fork. "I'm sorry that you lost your mother."

The way he said it made her think he'd reached the same conclusion about her as she'd come to about him: they had a lot of similarities. Both had wished they'd had a father in their life—or a loving father in Adalia's case—and they'd lost the person who grounded them right around the same time.

She poured the last of the wine into their nearly empty glasses and lifted hers. "To the youngest Buchanan siblings. We might be the outcasts, but we're a scrappy lot."

His eyes lit up, and he clicked his glass with hers. "To us."

A knock rapped at the door, and Jack shot a look in that direction before glancing back at her. "Are you expecting anyone? Is that Georgie?"

"No, and Georgie would just walk in." Adalia got up from the table and walked to the door, worrying it was one of the neighbors, like the woman with the frizzy hair and wire-rimmed glasses from down the street, who was forever complaining about Jezebel. Come to think of it, the cat hadn't been skulking around the kitchen while she and Jack heated up their food—which meant she'd probably gotten out again.

Sucking in a breath for fortitude, she opened the front door, saying, "I'm sorry for Jezebel. I'm not sure how she got out again, but I'll be happy to pay for the damage…"

Her words trailed off when she found herself face-to-face with Finn.

He gave her a sheepish look and started to say something, but she slammed the door in his face.

"Who was it?" Jack called out.

"No one."

Oh. God. Why was he here? What did he want? Was this some sort of wannabe intervention?

Finn knocked on the door again. "Adalia. Open up. Please."

"Is that Finn Hamilton?" Jack asked in surprise. He'd followed her into the entryway and was looking out of one of the sidelight windows flanking the door.

How did Jack know Finn? No, that wasn't important. What *was* important was that Finn had seen her in her most vulnerable state and now he was here. On her front porch.

Jack narrowed his eyes as he studied her. "Is there a reason Finn's on the porch pounding on the door while you're standing on the other side not letting him in?"

"Tell him I'm not home."

Jack smirked. "I think that ship has sailed." But when she didn't smile back, he turned serious. "Is this where we move to phase two of family bonding and I step into my role as big brother? Do you want me to send him on his way and tell him to leave you alone?"

Maybe it was Adalia's humiliation that was making her emotional, because Jack's offer brought tears to her eyes.

Jack's eyes darkened, his body tense. "So that's a yes?"

What was she doing? She didn't let other people fight her battles. Or at least she tried not to. Georgie had helped her out of her legal snafu only a few months ago.

She really *was* pathetic.

Finn knocked again. "Adalia. Please. If you'll just listen to what I have to say…"

Jack reached for the doorknob, but Adalia put her hand on his. "Stop. I'm just being ridiculous. I'll talk to him and send him away."

"You sure?" Jack asked, his brow lifted.

"Yeah, but I definitely could have used you a few months ago." Before he could ask questions, she pulled the door open.

"You have ten seconds to tell me why you're here—then we'll pretend like this never happened."

Finn looked surprised, then turned serious. "I guess I better get started."

CHAPTER

Four

Dottie had come back to find Finn holding that wet, ruined painting, feeling both lost and found.

"Oh," she had said, nodding. "I wondered if you two would run into each other." She hadn't commented on the painting.

And while she really had gone out to get some cream, or at least she'd gone to the trouble of buying some while she was out, he couldn't help but wonder if she'd set this up. If she'd known, somehow, that seeing Adalia out in the studio—releasing her soul onto that canvas—was exactly what he needed.

He hadn't ended up telling Dottie about the whole Big Catch thing, if only because the Big Catch thing was now very much at the back of his mind. He had a new idea, and he was nearly bursting with it.

If not for Dottie's gentle admonition—"Dear, give her some space. And *do* take a shower. If people see you out on the streets looking like that, I shudder to think what the next article will say."—he might have left for Beau's old house then and there.

Instead, he had gone home and showered. Because it was a fair point.

Now, standing on Adalia's doorstep, it occurred to him that Dottie had probably meant that he should give her more than a few hours.

Still, he was nothing if not dogged. He wasn't going to give up just because she was frowning like she'd caught him leaving a flaming bag of dog poop on her porch.

"I have a proposition for you," he said.

"Oh boy, you're not off to a good start," Adalia commented. It was only then he noticed the big, dark-haired guy looming behind her. Jack, doing the whole big brother thing. They'd met in person a few days ago at the reopening of Buchanan, and he'd been perfectly friendly then. Not so much right now.

"Explain yourself," Jack said flatly.

"When I saw you—"

Adalia's scowl deepened, and she turned to Jack. "Can you give us a minute?"

"Did I just get upgraded from ten seconds?" Finn asked. And immediately regretted it when they both glowered at him.

"I'll be upstairs in my room," Jack said as if he thought Finn might take advantage of his sister in some way. Had he met her?

Adalia just nodded, but when Finn tried to come inside, she blocked his path. Moving her index finger back and forth, she said, "Nuh-uh-uh. To the back porch with you."

He was happy enough that she'd agreed to talk to him that he didn't push his luck. Even if it would have been much quicker to cut through the house. He started walking around, figuring she'd follow him, but he heard the door shut behind him.

Was this her way of getting rid of him?

He circled around anyway, his mind buzzing, and found her waiting on the chair that her grandfather used to favor. Did she know that, or had she just felt drawn to it?

She pointed to the other chair, which was unnecessary—there was only one—and he sat.

It was obvious from the look on her face—and, well, the fact that she'd made him tromp around the house—that she was still angry, so he did what he should have done in the beginning. He apologized.

"I'm sorry about earlier. I swear on all that's holy that I didn't know you were there. Dottie invited me over for tea the other day, and I wanted to talk to her, and then I heard you scream. I was worried that someone might be—"

"Stealing Dottie's art," she said, something in her softening. "Yeah, you said. And I suppose I do have the car of a would-be art thief." She rubbed between her eyes. "I'm sorry I've been so snappy. I guess I'm a little embarrassed. Dottie lets me use the studio, and it's a bit of—" her lips tipped up, "—art therapy. They say it works wonders, right? Anyway, I'd appreciate it if you didn't say anything about this to Georgie or River. I don't want to worry them. They're so busy right now, and…"

Her words trailed off, like she'd maybe run out of them.

"I meant what I said," he said, seeking out her gaze. She wouldn't look him in the eye. "Your talent…it's *magnificent*. Look, I've been feeling lost lately." Somehow it was easier admitting that to her after what he'd seen. Like maybe she understood. "I thought the world would open up to me after I sold the company, but it didn't work out like that. The ideas all dried up."

"Because of the article in the local paper?" she asked, as if drawn in despite herself.

"No," he said, admitting something to her he'd barely admitted to himself. "Before that. It almost felt like there were too many opportunities. I couldn't focus on anything."

She huffed a little at that, not that he blamed her. He'd heard it before. Poor little rich boy. And the people who had said it to him—or thought it of him—were right.

"My parents have been after me to leave Asheville. My father says I need to find a bigger pool. But I like *this* pool. Even if it no longer likes me." He couldn't help but let a little of his hurt leak into his tone.

"Oh, they'll get over it," Adalia said, waving a hand. "People love gossip. Just you wait. Someone's going to do something totally cracked in a week or two, and no one will remember."

"But I'll remember," he said. She lifted her gaze then, looking at him. Looking into him, it seemed. She had lovely, deep hazel eyes—hadn't some old, dead English guy said eyes were the window to the soul?—and he felt a strange longing to touch her cheek. But that was beyond foolish, and he ignored it. "I've been lucky for as long as I can remember. Except I've realized it wasn't luck at all. Or not just luck. My parents have been boosting me up the ladder for so long that I didn't even realize it was happening. It just felt normal. It was my life."

He'd done a lot of introspection after finding out about the endowment his folks had given to Duke. Thought of at least a dozen other instances of them "helping." Hell, the building they'd landed for Big Catch had been owned by an old golf buddy of his dad's. *Uncle* Carl.

"And now?" she said softly.

"And now I want to do something without them." A corner of his mouth ticked up. "Something they wouldn't like."

She smiled back at him. "Now you're talking."

"This city has done a lot for me. Even if the people here aren't so fond of me right now, it feels like home. More so than my own home ever did. I want to give something back." And because he had trouble shutting his mouth sometimes— River had told him he couldn't help himself—he added, "And I want people to change their minds about me. I want them to realize that I might not have been born here, but I care about this city too. I'm part of it."

She mimed checking off an invisible list, one item at a time. "So this new enterprise you're thinking of is inspired by one part revenge, one part ego, and one part genuine emotion. Gotcha." She tilted her head. "No offense, but what does this have to do with me?"

He got up, feeling so much energy thrumming through him he needed to be on his feet. "Adalia, your work inspired my new idea. I want to put on an art show, featuring little-known artists, for charitable causes benefiting the city. It can be a biannual thing. Maybe we'll even let people vote on the cause in one of the local papers."

"Like the *Gazette*?" she asked.

He couldn't read the look on her face, but he definitely had her attention now.

"Sure," he said, "I don't hold a grudge."

"And I'm sure it wouldn't hurt if they published something that made you look like a saint," she said, challenging him.

He shrugged, not denying it. "We'll rent a warehouse for the opening, and whatever hasn't sold by the end of the first

41

month can be part of a traveling show. We'll let breweries and whatnot display them. They'll want to, because it'll be a good blast of publicity. In fact, we can have them bid on who gets to host the pieces. The artists will get their portion of money from their sales…" He felt the need to mention that upfront; he'd seen her car. "… but any profit above that will go to the cause."

"We?" The look in her eyes was an open challenge now.

Hadn't he made himself clear? She was the person who'd inspired this. He couldn't do it without her. Dottie had already agreed to participate, and she'd indicated she had a few friends who might be interested. But it all fell apart without Adalia. She was the lynchpin for his plan. The reason for it.

"Yes," he said. "You have a talent that deserves to be seen. To be experienced."

She laughed again, although this time there was no hint of real humor. "Oh, is this performance art, then? You want me to make pieces and destroy them in front of an audience?"

He frowned. She'd been right earlier—this *wasn't* going well. He'd hoped that by explaining himself, by telling her his reasons for wanting to do this, she'd be more open to participating.

"No, that wasn't exactly how I was envisioning it," he said. "Maybe you could leave the utility knife at home."

She got to her feet, and even though she had to be more than half a foot shorter than him, it felt like she was staring down at him.

"Look, Finn. You don't know me. I'm sorry you've been through a shitty experience, but that doesn't mean you're in any special position to understand me and what *I* have been through. Which you haven't even asked about, by the way. Believe it or not, normal people, who are stable enough to show their art, don't destroy their own things. Besides, in case you haven't noticed, I have a job. I'm helping at Buchanan."

"Yeah," he said, "I saw the shirts you came up with. And the labels. They're brilliant. And River told me that you've been handling the social media accounts."

He paused, knowing he shouldn't say what he was going to say next, and already aware that he was going to say it anyway. Because she was wrong. Because she was, for some reason, denying herself something she needed as desperately as she needed air. He'd seen it in her eyes. In the sorrow that flashed through them as she slashed the canvas with that knife. And even though he *didn't* know her and had no right to confront her like this, he refused to give up on her. He didn't want her to give up on herself. It would be a tragedy if she did.

So he slashed with words, which had always been his knife of choice. "How many hours of your day will it take up? One? Maybe two? Is that going to be enough to satisfy you?"

Her eyes gleamed fiercely, and he wondered for a moment if he'd gone too far. Were those tears?

"If my designs are as good as you say, maybe I'll become a graphic designer. It's harder to smash a computer than it is a painting. I might just be able to make it work."

"Do you really believe that, Adalia?" he asked. "Because I don't. There's a fire in you that won't be put out, and stylizing some words and photos and doodles won't even throw a thimble of water on it. Please, just think about it. I want to do this. With *you*. I have the resources to make it work."

Her expression twisted, and he instantly knew he'd said the wrong thing.

"Get out," she seethed, just like she had in the studio. "It's never, ever going to happen."

CHAPTER

Five

"Are you *sure* you're feeling okay?" Georgie asked.

Adalia pushed back a wave of loose curls from her cheek as she sat up at her makeshift desk in the corner of Georgie's office. She loved her sister with every fiber of her being, but sometimes working with her was like living under a magnifying glass.

"For the tenth time, I'm fine."

"It's just that you're so quiet today."

Adalia heard the worry in her sister's voice, and while she appreciated that she cared, right now it felt stifling.

"I'm fine. Really, Georgie. I didn't sleep well, just like I told you the previous nine times you asked." She'd tossed and turned, finally drifting off at around four. Finn's discovery of her secret had made her do some serious reevaluation of her life.

Maybe her father was right. Maybe it was time to grow up.

It had come as no surprise when Adalia's father had disapproved of her going to art school, but his refusal to pay her tuition had come as a shock, especially since he'd paid for all of Lee's and Georgie's college expenses. Nevertheless, she'd gone anyway, to a very respected—aka *very expensive*—school at that. But the loans had gotten out of hand, and even though she hadn't finished school for that very reason, she still had to repay them. They ate up the vast majority of the money Georgie was paying her. She knew her sister would pay off the loans in a heartbeat, but Adalia would never let her.

Still, pride didn't pay the bills. Maybe she really should get a graphic design job.

In the back of her head, she heard Finn telling her it would never satisfy her inner fire, that it would be like trying to douse a blaze with a thimble of water, but who did he think he was, anyway? It had given her the chills, hearing him say that, but anger had chased them away. He didn't get to tell her who she was.

Even if he wasn't far off. Even if he saw her more clearly than the people she'd known her entire life.

"Things are going well with Jack?" Georgie asked.

There was a topic Adalia could latch on to. Anything to keep Georgie from poking at her feelings. She sat up in her rickety chair and turned in her seat to face her sister. "Actually, we had a family dinner last night."

Surprise flashed in Georgie's eyes, and Adalia thought she saw a hint of pain, but her sister shook it off quickly and smiled. "Really?"

"Yeah," Adalia said with a shrug. "Dottie dropped off some food in our fridge, so we made plates, opened a bottle of wine, and sat at the dining room table and talked."

Her eyes flew wide. "Jack opened up?"

"The conversation was pretty superficial, but…I like him." The memory of Jack coming to her defense filled her with fondness and gratitude. "I'm honestly glad he moved in."

Georgie took a moment, then said, "That's great." She lowered her voice. "Is that why you're so tired? You two stayed up late?"

"Georgie." It would have been easy to say yes, but that would have been a lie, one that might easily be caught, and she refused to say anything about Finn.

Because you know what she'll say, a traitorous voice inside her insisted. *You know she'll encourage you to start making things again. Things you don't destroy.*

"I just worry about you, Addy."

"I know, but I'm fine."

Georgie's lips pressed together, expressing her obvious doubt.

Groaning, Adalia snapped her laptop shut and stood. "I'm going to go work at Brown Beans." The coffee shop down the street had a horrible name and subpar coffee, but the internet was fast and the employees left you alone.

"Addy," Georgie protested, dismay filling her voice.

Adalia snagged her purse, slipping the strap over her shoulder, and grabbed the closed laptop. "Just to give you fair warning, I've decided to look for a graphic design job."

Georgie was out of her seat in an instant. "*Why?*" she said, coming around the desk. She sounded as concerned as if Adalia had just expressed interest in joining a cult.

Releasing a sigh, Adalia held her gaze. She hadn't planned on having this conversation yet, but now that she'd brought it up, she might as well push through with it. "There's not enough work to keep me busy." Finn had been right about something else too, damn him. "You know this is a part-time position, and I want to keep it, but I need to do more." Then she steeled her back and said, "I need to make money. I have bills to pay."

Georgie's face fell. "Your student loans." She grabbed Adalia's upper arms. "Let me pay them off, Addy." She shook her head before Adalia could protest. "Now, hear me out. You can pay me back if that makes you feel better, but you won't be stuck with all that interest, and we can lower the payments so it's affordable."

Adalia stepped back out of her sister's grasp. "Why should you bail me out at all? Going to art school was *my* choice. You and Dad and Lee were against it, so why should I expect you to help me now?"

"I was wrong," Georgie said with tears in her eyes. "You're so good, Addy. Of course you should have gone."

"How do you know I'm good?" Adalia countered. "Because the arrest warrant valued the art I destroyed at over one hundred thousand dollars?"

Because she'd been arrested, and Georgie had bailed her out via a bail bondsman.

Her sister started to say something, but Adalia cut her off. "You didn't see the value of my art until someone else did?"

Georgie's cheeks flushed. "Dad paid for me and Lee to go to school. It's not fair that he didn't pay for you."

"That's between *me and Dad*," Adalia snapped. "Not *you*." She headed for the office door, not surprised to see River and Dottie standing outside the office, along with several other employees. They'd raised their voices, and sound carried in the industrial office area.

"But we have a meeting in ten minutes," Georgie called after her.

"Have it without me. We all know airhead Addy isn't good for anything except for fluffy designs and social media posts."

That wasn't fair, but Adalia realized that was how she felt about herself. That she'd been given a pity job. One whose scope kept shrinking until soon there'd be nothing left.

She expected Dottie or River to say something. Or for Georgie to maybe vault out of her office with a cape on, intent on rescuing her. But no one tried to stop her as she made a beeline for the exit, blinking when she hit the bright sunlight.

It was a beautiful day, but Adalia barely noticed as she stopped to shove her sunglasses on her face and stuff her laptop into the oversized purse.

No, Georgie's laptop. The one she'd bought for the brewery so Adalia could work on the graphics. Sometimes it felt like she had nothing of her own anymore, that the independent person she'd been—the artist—was shrinking and shrinking until there'd be nothing left of her either.

Adalia started walking, and even though she'd told Georgie she was going to the coffee shop down the street, she found herself heading downtown.

Downtown Asheville was nothing like New York City, but it had an appealing vibe of its own. Creative and more laid back than the hustle and frenetic energy of New York. Truthfully, it fit Adalia like a glove, and as she mindlessly walked, she felt her stress ease a bit. Her problems were still there, but they didn't feel so overwhelming.

Stopping at a coffee shop, she ordered a latte and treated herself to a chocolate croissant. She took both out to a table for two on the sidewalk, feeling herself relax further as she sipped her coffee and nibbled on her pastry. She set her laptop on the table and started to create a résumé, but she ended up people watching. In art school, she'd made a game of observing passersby, trying to figure out who they were and where they were going, making up stories about them in her head. Sometimes she'd even sketch their stories in her book.

She'd been lonely back then. Although she'd always had a large enough circle of acquaintances, something inside of her had quailed from letting herself get too close. Except with Alan. She'd let her guard down with him, and look where that had landed her. Here she was once again, inventing lives for strangers on the street because she couldn't bring herself to have a difficult conversation with her sister.

She was focusing on a mother pushing a stroller when she heard a familiar voice say, "Mind if I join you?"

Finn. He stood next to the table, gesturing to the empty chair across from her. Was this an unhappy accident, or had he come looking for her?

Her back stiffened. "If you're here to talk to me about—"

He lifted his hands in surrender. "Not a word. I promise."

With pursed lips, she gave him a slight nod, wondering why he wanted to sit with her if not for his charity idea. Wondering why she was a little disappointed he didn't intend to push it.

"Working outside of the office?" he asked once he'd lowered himself into the other chair.

"Sort of." She didn't feel like telling him what she was really up to. Not after what he'd said to her. She was worried she'd see disappointment in his eyes, although for the life of her, she couldn't figure out why his opinion mattered. "But mostly playing the 'Who are you?' game." She was slightly embarrassed to admit it, but it felt safer than talking about the résumé. Or her art.

He leaned back, his upper shoulder pressed against the railing around the small seating area, his arms crossed over his chest—did he always wear button-downs or polos?—and an amused look lit up his eyes. "Okay, you've got me. What's the 'Who are you?' game?"

"It's simple," she said, leaning forward, sure this would scare him off. He might talk like a poet, but he was still a rich boy businessman. His name was Finn Hamilton, for God's sake. "You find someone walking by and come up with a story about who they are and where they're going."

He cocked an eyebrow.

"I'll start." She scanned the street and found the mother pushing the stroller as she emerged from a store. "That's Willow. She's a former executive of some BS company from Charlotte—they probably made toilet paper or something. Then her husband got a hair up his butt to move to Asheville. She was reluctant at first, but see that yoga mat sticking out of the bottom of the stroller?"

Finn turned slightly, nodding when he caught sight of the woman.

"She joined a Mommy and Me yoga play group and she's considering becoming a yogi."

His slight smile turned into a full-blown amused grin. "And her baby's name?"

"Fig Tree, Tree being the middle name, of course."

"Of course," he said, still smiling. "But you never said where they were going."

"Home. The baby's about to go down for a nap and she's eager to try the tantric sex method she learned from the instructor while they sipped organic oolong tea after class."

Adalia had said it to shock him. She was pretty good at catching people off guard, and she'd come to recognize it for what it was—a defense mechanism to keep others at a distance. And she definitely needed to keep Finn at a distance. Only he didn't look as taken aback as she'd expected. Instead, he pursed his lips as though giving it some thought. "Interesting how you jumped right to sex."

A slow smile spread across her face. He'd surprised her, and she delighted in surprises. *Good* surprises. "You disagree?"

He let his arms drop to his sides and sat up slightly. "No, quite the opposite." He turned slightly to glance at the woman before turning back to Adalia. "I'm sure her husband is already waiting at home, ready to strip her naked the moment she walks through the door."

The way he said it made Adalia shiver with anticipation, but she mentally shook herself. This was Finn. The man who'd betrayed River by selling Big Catch to one of those mega conglomerates with so many product lines the people who ran it probably only knew about half of them. Finn Hamilton was much too good-looking, rich, and cocky for his own good. He was used to getting anything and anyone he wanted, and she wouldn't be one of his conquests. Not her and not her art either.

Then again, he wasn't coming on to her.

"Okay," Adalia said with a mischievous grin, picking up her coffee. "Your turn."

His eyes lit up and he rubbed his hands together. "Okay."

He scanned the area, waiting for someone to catch his attention.

"I understand if you're intimidated," she teased, then took a sip from her mug.

"You underestimate me," he said with an evil chuckle.

She perked up an eyebrow and tried to suppress a grin. Who would have thought Finn had a playful side? Granted, she barely knew him, but he hadn't made a great first impression. She'd met him the night she'd flown back into Asheville, which was when he'd dumped an ice-cold bucket of hard truths on River.

Grandpa Beau had worked as many twists and turns into his will as a spy novel. If the Buchanan siblings failed to place in the top five in a national brewing competition next year, the brewery would go to River. Something Georgie had known about but hadn't yet had the heart to tell River. Finn's revelation had split them up, and even though the breakup had been brief, it had caused Georgie pain. She shouldn't forget that, yet her opinion of Finn kept bouncing back and forth so fast it was giving her whiplash.

"Okay," he said, casting her a playful look. "That guy at ten o'clock."

She glanced around. "I don't see a clock."

"No," he said with a groan. "I'm the center of a clock and he's at my ten o'clock."

"Why are *you* the center of the clock?" she asked, biting back a smile. She shouldn't encourage any playful banter between them, but she was finding it hard to resist. "Why can't *I* be the center of the clock?"

He groaned longer. "Fine. You can be the center of the clock. He's at your four o'clock."

Her mouth twisted to the side. "I prefer twenty after, thank you very much."

She kept a straight face for all of a second before she burst into giggles.

His expression seemed to ask, *Are you for real?*, but it slid into a grin. "Okay, you got me."

"I couldn't resist," she said, then turned slightly to see a man walking past them on the sidewalk. "Him?" she whispered as an elderly man in a Hawaiian shirt walked by with a leashed miniature poodle.

He nodded, leaning closer. "Merv Singleton. Age sixty-two. Divorced."

"Divorced?" she countered. "He has a wedding ring."

"It's still fresh," he added hastily. "He can't bear to take it off."

"Well, at least you didn't make him a widower," she groused with a grin. "That would be morbid."

"Hey, I'm new to this."

"Why the Hawaiian shirt?" she asked.

He glanced over his shoulder for another look, then turned back to her. "Their honeymoon was to Hawaii."

"And he's been wearing Hawaiian shirts ever since? No wonder they're divorced."

He laughed, a full-throated laugh that brought a smile to her face.

"And the dog?" she asked.

"Fluffy belonged to his wife, Nancy. Merv won her in the divorce."

"He stole her dog?" she asked in mock dismay. "He's a monster."

Finn sat back in his seat, accepting his defeat. "Yeah. You're right. Merv deserved to be left."

She laughed. "And you left off the other part. Where's he going?"

"To his one-bedroom apartment so he can feed Fluffy lunch." He thumbed behind him. "He's returning to his miserable, lonely existence."

"Wow," she said, shaking her head. "Remind me to never play this game with you again, Debbie Downer."

"At least my mind wasn't in the gutter," he teased. "Poor, poor Merv. I don't know if he'll ever get laid again."

"Oh, I think he will," she said, nodding past him.

He turned and they both watched as an older woman walked out of a knitting store, carrying a bag that read *Knitters Come With Strings Attached.* She gave "Merv" a saucy grin, and he swatted her behind. A woman came out behind her just in time to see it, and it was obvious she was swallowing laughter. With long, curly black hair and a bold red and blue skirt, she didn't fit Adalia's image of a knitter. Not that she had anything other than respect for knitters, but this woman looked like she should be dancing flamenco in the streets of Barcelona, not sitting with a cup of chamomile and a lap full of yarn. Sure, she was thinking of her mother's knitting habits—for all she knew some people knitted to death metal—but she couldn't help herself. The bulging bag the woman held said her habit was serious. Adalia was tempted to use her for another round of the game, if only because she was interesting, but she held back for some reason, her gaze returning to Merv.

"I want to be like them when I get old," she said wistfully.

"And have as many knitting supplies as your heart desires?" Finn asked, his eyes dancing.

She glanced at him, wondering if he'd noticed the lovely woman—hadn't Georgie told her he was a well-known womanizer?—but his gaze was firmly on Adalia.

"Maybe that's *your* dream," she countered. "And besides, Merv had Fluffy, so he wasn't *really* alone. Dogs are man's best friend, you know. Have you spent much time with

Hops? He's adorable. Who could be lonely with a little guy like that around?"

"What, Beau's cat doesn't strike your fancy?"

"Don't get me wrong," she said. "I respect a lady who knows her own mind, but sometimes it feels like that house is too small for two ladies who fit that description. Dogs are different. Besides, she's on another walkabout. River says the neighbors are blowing up his phone again."

He looked a little chastened, probably at the memory of the last time Jezebel had come home after an extended leave of absence. It had happened the night he spilled the details of the will. He opened his mouth to say something, but a buzzing sound came from his pants pocket. Pulling his phone out, he glanced at the screen, then stood.

"I've got to take this call, but I'll concede this round to you." He tipped his head to the side. "Rematch sometime?"

She stared at him like he'd grown tusks. Was he asking her out on a date?

No…she didn't get that vibe. Just a casual *sometime if I run into you* kind of thing.

"Yeah, sure."

He grinned, his blue-green eyes lighting up. "I'll take you up on that."

Then he turned around, answering his phone as he walked away.

She was surprised by how much emptier her table felt without him.

CHAPTER
Six

Finn had spent half the night thinking about all the ways he'd screwed up with Adalia, only to find her in his path. Dottie would call that fate, he was sure, and he had to admit he liked the idea. He'd approached her table thinking he should apologize and maybe take a different tack, the kind where he didn't attack her life choices and act like her self-appointed guru. The thing was, seeing her in Dottie's workshop had done something to him he didn't fully understand, and he didn't just care about Adalia accepting his offer—he also wanted her to do what was best for her. And there was no denying she was an artist, through and through.

Sometime in the middle of the night, he'd looked her up on social media. Not the Buchanan account, hers. And the pieces she'd created were all nearly as evocative as the one he'd watched her tear apart.

But it had taken him all of five minutes to realize the direct approach wasn't going to win him any favors. And another five minutes to discover he liked sitting and talking to her too much to fight with her. Yet. Because he hadn't given up.

Truthfully, the reason he was downtown in the first place was because he'd met with a realtor friend to discuss which warehouses were available for lease in the next few months, something he'd known better than to mention to her. It wasn't that he intended to strong-arm Adalia into the idea—clearly she was not the kind of person who could be strong-armed—but his plan had grown on him enough that he intended to follow through even if she'd meant it when she'd said, "It's never, ever going to happen." Plus, a part of him thought the temptation might be too great for her to stay away if the show was already a go.

No appropriate spaces were available, which had brought him to his next idea: Gretchen wanted an image rehab for Big Catch. Why not open there? They had an event space, which would eliminate the need to pay rent, plus the charity angle would do wonders for their rep. So he'd texted her to call him, saying he had something good for her.

But then Adalia had mentioned Jezebel, and it had propelled him back in time a few months to that awful night he'd broken River with some hard truths and a handful of supposition.

What the hell was he thinking? River had only just forgiven him (mostly) for making the decision to push forward with the sale without first discussing it with him. There was no way Adalia would jump on board the Bev Corp train, and truthfully, River wouldn't be pleased either. No, if he was going to open the show anywhere, it should be at Buchanan. Maybe the suggestion would even be enough to get Adalia on board. Dottie would certainly be pleased.

But first he had to think fast and throw another idea at Gretchen.

"Hello," he answered, striding away from the coffee shop. He'd been heading back to his car, parked in one of the public garages, when he'd spotted Adalia.

"Slay me with your brilliance," Gretchen said. "Your former employees woke up this morning to a spray-painted wall. 'Big Catch STDs.' Real smart."

Well, that one was easy.

"There's your first opportunity for some good community engagement. Why not hire a local artist to paint a mural? Something that beautifies the street."

She made a *hm* sound. "Okay, not bad. Not that they deserve it. Do you have anyone you can recommend?"

Not off the top of his head, but he could ask Dottie.

"I'll send you a couple of recommendations later today."

"Good deal."

An old man sitting at an outdoor table at a restaurant, about the age of "Merv" from earlier, scowled at Finn like he'd trampled his daisies. He grinned at the guy, and the man threw a half-eaten dinner roll at him. That was a first. He kept right on walking like nothing had happened.

"And this idea you wanted to talk to me about?" Gretchen said. There was an eagerness in her voice, and he knew a moment of panic. What was he supposed to tell her?

He flashed to River again—to the devastation on his face the night he'd learned about the bizarre terms of Beau's will. The outright fury that had bloomed in his eyes after being informed of the sale of Big Catch. And it was River who made him think of what to say next.

"How about holding a beer festival? Heavily discounted tickets for locals. You can give tents to all of the breweries in town without charging them. It would send the message that you're not here to shut them down. You just want to peacefully coexist." He'd met River at a beer festival, and Bev Corp certainly had the money to put on a good one.

"Interesting. As much as I hesitate to reward these ingrates for their behavior, you might be on to something. Put together a proposal for me and get it to me by early next week. Tuesday would work. Monday would be even better."

"Will do," he said, lingering outside the car garage in case the signal died when he entered it.

"Good work, Finn."

She clicked off, and he felt a rush of warmth. Handing the art show over would have been a mistake—maybe on par with not telling River about the sale. He was glad he'd thought of another idea on the fly, and hell, it was a good one. Maybe it would even help River and Georgie.

He shot off a quick text to Dottie: *Know of any muralists? Got a job down at Big Catch.*

She replied immediately: *Ah, yes. I heard about the STDs. Come over for lunch.*

And since he was hoping he'd also be able to talk to her about Adalia, he sent her a thumbs-up.

"I took the liberty of making you an appointment with Lola," Dottie said as soon as he entered the kitchen. As always, she had set out more food than any two people could reasonably eat. Some sort of vegetable something, mac and cheese, and fresh cornbread. He suspected she'd selected the menu especially for him and whatever problems she thought he was having. Probably some of it would end up in River and Georgie's refrigerator. She always stopped by and left River things, like some kind of good food fairy.

"The fortune-teller?" he asked. She'd been after him to see her since the whole fallout from the Bev Corp sale. "When?"

"Tomorrow afternoon at two," she said. "I had a sense you wouldn't be busy."

Likely because he hadn't been busy for months. He wasn't going to compliment her foresight on that one. His father was actually passing through town tomorrow night, which meant he *did* have dinner plans, but his dinner plans wouldn't interfere with a two o'clock appointment. Although, to be honest, he was more inclined to try skipping the dinner than his unsolicited appointment with the psychic.

We're going to figure out your next step, Son, his dad had said, as if he were a wayward child. He had no intention of going along with whatever plan his father had cooked up, but he respected him enough to hear him out.

Just like he respected Dottie enough to go along with the whole psychic thing.

"Fine," he said grudgingly. "I'll go. If you give me a few good recs for a muralist. I know you know everyone in this town."

"Of course," she said, retrieving a slip of lilac-colored paper from the kitchen counter. "I already wrote some ideas down for you. Now, help yourself to some food. I worry about how you eat."

Probably because he always ate like a starved person whenever he was around her. Something about homemade food did that to him. His parents had never cooked at home, and he'd never really learned how either. He subsisted off of takeout and easy-to-fix meals. It felt nice, being around Dottie. Letting her spoil him like he was her own. Like she did with all of the people in her circle.

He accepted the paper and then served himself some food. By the time he sat down, there was a cup of hot tea in front of him. He wasn't really in the mood for it again, to be honest, in the heat of summer, but he knew better than to turn it down. She probably wanted to read the leaves or something.

Dottie sat across from him, having served herself.

"She said no, didn't she?" she said conversationally.

"Did Adalia talk to you?" he asked, his brow furrowed. He took a bite of food and nearly moaned. God, Dottie was a good cook.

"No, dear, and I suspect she didn't talk to anyone else about it either. Art is very personal."

He was beginning to realize that.

"Yeah," he admitted, "she said no—a hard no—but I was hoping you might talk her around." A corner of his mouth ticked up. "Turns out she's not amenable to my type of persuasion."

"Did you try to seduce her?" Dottie said eagerly.

"What?!" His fork clattered on his plate. "No!"

"Pity," she said. "That girl needs some loving."

Despite his protest, dangerous images popped into his head. Of Adalia's soft lips. Of her chest splattered with paint. Of those bouncy curls, barely held back by anything she used to try to contain them. Of the way emotion lit up her hazel eyes, bringing out different colors.

Then, as if she hadn't just thrown a grenade into their conversation, Dottie continued, "I'll see what I can do to help. In the meantime, I have a few friends who have expressed an interest in the show, and if you intend to follow through, I expect we can spread the word quickly."

Happy to change the subject, he said, "Yes, I fully intend to follow through. In fact, I'd like to have your thoughts on something. I talked to a friend about warehouse spaces for the show, and it doesn't sound like anything appropriate will be available in the next few months. I know Georgie worked a big event space into the redesign of the brewery. Do you think she'd be open to hosting the show? I figure we can make opening night a big event, and any pieces that didn't sell can be on display in the brewery for the following month. Available for sale, of course. It'll be a good promotion opportunity for the brewery and for the artists."

She nodded sagely. "I like the way you think. What if we do it before the holidays? Maybe early November."

It would be a quick turnaround, so the artists would largely have to use pieces they already had. Unless they worked fast. Would that eliminate the possibility of including Adalia's work?

"But Adalia…"

"Doesn't have a stockpile of work. Yet. But if we consider the number of paintings she's destroyed, I believe she'll have time to make one."

Hearing it felt like a stab to his gut. How many had there been? He hated to think of her feeling that angry, that desperate.

"Have you chosen a charitable cause for the first show, or do you plan on crowdsourcing it?"

It was a little funny to hear Dottie say "crowdsourcing," and he couldn't help but think of his own grandmother, who'd passed away several years ago. She'd been such a prim and proper woman, always dressed in long skirts that almost looked Puritan, and she'd had a look of horror reserved for kids who ran around with raspberry jam on their faces and touched her antique furniture. He couldn't imagine her ever using a word like that.

Maybe it was weird that he came to see his friend's great-aunt by himself, without River, but Dottie had told him that he should consider her family too, back when he and River were working together. And after the whole mess with Bev Corp, she'd told him they were *still* family.

Family doesn't change with the weather, boy. Either you are or you aren't.

His family had never really been like that. He didn't have any siblings, and while his parents cared about him, they weren't warm in the way Dottie was. Their kind of caring came with expectations and in the form of unsolicited five-year plans.

"No, I haven't gotten that far yet."

"Might I suggest that you talk to Maisie? From what I understand, one of the shelter's regular sponsors fell through."

Maisie was River's best childhood friend, someone Finn counted a friend as well, even though he'd been too embarrassed to reach out to her after the whole Bev Corp mess. She was loyal to River first and foremost, and like Adalia, she was not the kind of woman to mince words. She would have totally eviscerated him. He would have deserved it, of course, but he'd already felt pretty low at the time.

It had lifted his spirits a little when she'd texted him after seeing the article in the *Gazette*, pointing out that the author, who'd attacked him for his parents' donation to Duke, had gone to a school that had a building named after his family. *Takes a bro to know a bro*, she'd said with a wink emoji. And because he knew Maisie meant the "bro" thing somewhat fondly, at least where it concerned him, he'd laughed.

He'd hoped to see her at the reopening of Buchanan, but she hadn't shown. Maybe because her business was suffering. She ran an independent, no-kill dog shelter, a labor of love.

Suddenly, he remembered how Adalia's eyes had lit up when she talked about Hops, plus the fact that Buchanan Brewery had used Hops on some of their new labels. It fit with their relaunch, didn't it? Maisie could even bring in some of the animals to make a whole thing of it. Maybe that, plus the inclusion of Buchanan Brewery, would be enough to convince Adalia to take part.

"Good idea," he said. "I'll talk to her after I discuss this with River."

They continued eating and talking, although the conversation veered away from the art show. When they finished their lunch, she reached out her hand expectantly. Did she want to sing "Kumbaya" or something?

Before he could wonder too hard, she said, "Your teacup, please."

He'd drunk all of two sips, so he gulped down the now tepid tea and handed it over.

"Oh dear," she said, her eyes sparkling. "Yes, I'm glad you're going to see Lola."

He waited, but she didn't explain.

"You're not going to tell me what you saw?" he asked.

"If I did, you might not keep your appointment."

He rolled his eyes. Given how many times she'd urged him to visit this Lola, he couldn't help but wonder if she was trying to set them up.

Why did his stomach give a weird lurch at the thought?

The answer made him feel even more off course.

Because part of him wished that if she were setting him up, it would be with Adalia.

CHAPTER

Seven

By the time Adalia left the coffee shop, she'd created a résumé and uploaded it to a job site, but she hadn't mustered the will to actually apply for a position. Not yet. Baby steps.

She nearly didn't go back to the brewery. She was embarrassed about how she'd handled things, even if everything she'd said was true, and this mess with Finn and her uncertainty about her job had created a whole tempest of emotions straining for release. She was dying to go to Dottie's garage, but her previous safe space now felt tainted.

So she did the right thing—the grown-up thing. She sucked up her pride and went back to the brewery, because she actually had some work to do for the social media accounts. Might as well face Georgie and everyone else. It wasn't like she was quitting; she was just going to put in the appropriate amount of hours given the work she had to do. No more handouts or pity work.

She caught some of the staff watching her when she strolled through the tasting room around two, but they quickly turned back to their work.

Georgie was sitting at her desk, her forehead scrunched as she studied her computer screen, but she glanced up as Adalia walked in the room.

"Addy," she said, her face a mixture of concern and contrition. "Are you...do you..."

"I'm not going to blow my stack again, if that's what you're worried about."

"No," Georgie gushed. "That's not what I was going to say. I—"

"I'm fine. Let's just let it go." She scooped up a basket of props she'd been gathering for a photo shoot, plus a couple of collapsible light reflectors, and headed out the office door.

The tasting room had great afternoon light, it was all updated and shiny, and it held a ready supply of Buchanan Brewery bottles. She quickly got to work setting up several still shots, but then she noticed the handful of customers in the room, some of them watching her with open curiosity, and a new idea popped into her head.

She noticed a couple at a table against the wall embedded with windows. The lighting was perfect and the couple was adorable. They were cute but not overly so. They looked like people you could sit next to and strike up a chat with instead of getting the cold shoulder. If she and Finn were still playing the 'Who are you?' game, she'd have whispered to him that they were Walt and Fiona, and it was the beginning of a beautiful friendship over two pints of Beau Brown.

That was when it struck her... River had mentioned more than once that Grandpa Beau's brews hadn't lived up to their potential because he'd let things slide over the past few years. The brewery had lost distribution business, but their tasting room had often been full. It was because the people who showed up were friends with Beau and Dottie and all the

67

other employees. They felt like they belonged there. The Buchanans only needed to extend that feeling into their brand.

The Buchanans weren't just selling beer. People gravitated to the brewery because it felt like home—not the kind of home people had, granted, but the kind of home everyone *wanted*, with a warm family, a sweet gathering space, and a fridge full of beer. They needed to convey that feeling in their marketing.

Adalia hurried over to Jack's office and popped her head in the door. (He'd meant it about the open-door policy, it turned out.) "Jack, got a minute?"

His attention had been buried in some papers on his desk, but he glanced up without any sign of impatience. "Sure, what's up?"

"I have an idea, and I need your help."

"Okay," he said, pushing his chair back from his desk. "I'm listening."

She quickly explained her line of thinking, and his face lit up.

"That's brilliant, Adalia. What did Georgie say?"

"Well…nothing yet. I haven't told her."

"Why on earth not?"

Good question. Because she was worried it would crash and burn? Because she didn't want Georgie to feign enthusiasm just to bolster her? Or was it because she felt like she'd lost her secret space in Dottie's garage and this was its replacement? She didn't want to analyze it. Not right now.

"Let's just keep it between us for now, okay?" she said.

His brow furrowed. "I hate to keep things from Georgie. I've already got a few strikes against me here. I showed up later than I said I would, and I'm not a full-fledged Buchanan."

She nearly told him that no one was holding those things against him, but there was probably a grain of truth to what he'd said. He just didn't have as much history with Georgie, Lee, and Adalia as they had with one another. Adalia could blow her top at her sister and know she could come crawling back, and even though Lee was being a total butt, she knew he'd get over it eventually. They didn't have that level of trust with Jack…yet.

She settled for giving him a warm smile. "You're gonna be fine, and I'm not going to put you in an awkward position. But can I get you to do me one little favor?"

"What?" he asked warily.

"Will you do a quick internet search for a media release? I want to take some candid photos of some of the patrons in the tasting room, but I need releases." When he hesitated, she added, "It's for the social media accounts. That's all. It's not a campaign. Let's see what kind of traction the posts get. Then we can figure out if it's worth taking to Georgie."

He hesitated, and for a moment she worried he'd say no. That he'd refuse to help unless she got Georgie to sign a permission slip. But then he turned to his laptop. "How many do you need?"

"I'm not sure," she said. "Print me ten to start and bring them out to the tasting room." She hurried back to her spot from earlier, hoping the couple hadn't left.

Walt and Fiona were still there, so Adalia dragged a chair over, and introduced herself, and asked if they would be open to having their photos taken and posted on the Buchanan Brewery social media accounts. When the woman hesitated, Adalia said, "You'll get free beer out of it. I know you're drinking drafts, but I'd like to bring over some bottles so the labels will be in the photo. If you like, I'll let you see what I'm posting before I put it up."

"So we get to keep the bottles you bring over?" the man asked with a hopeful look.

"You bet," Adalia said. "And we'll top off your glasses while we're at it."

"You've got a deal," he said, and his girlfriend agreed.

"I'm Adalia, by the way. What are your names?"

The man introduced himself as Grayson, and she sputtered out a laugh when the woman said she was Fiona.

Fiona tilted her head, as if asking what was so hysterical about her name.

"Sorry," Adalia said. "Just thinking of an inside joke."

She'd totally have to lord this over Finn the next time she saw him.

By the time Adalia got them set up with the bottles and full glasses of Beau Brown and Hair of Hops, Jack had come out with the release forms. Before he had a chance to refuse, Adalia recruited him to hold the reflective screens while she snapped photos with her phone. She made a grouping of the images she liked and let Fiona pick her favorites, which Adalia then posted to Instagram. She tagged the customers and included their quotes about why they'd come to Buchanan that day and what they were drinking.

Georgie walked into the tasting room and did a double take when she saw Jack holding a reflective screen.

"Jack was helping me with some photos," Adalia said. "For social media."

"Oh," Georgie said, all wide-eyed like she was caught off guard. "Actually, I'm happy I caught both of you together. I was hoping we could have dinner together tonight—if you don't already have plans, that is."

Jack looked uncertain.

Adalia wasn't sure she wanted to be in close proximity to her sister after her blowup this morning, but then the Buchanan way was to shove negative emotions into the corner and ignore them. Adalia would rather have a day or two to let it simmer before moving straight to the ignoring phase, but if Jack was there, it would ease the tension. It would also help the sisters get to know him better. Besides, the whole hiding from emotions thing didn't really work for her, anyway. Clearly. She looped her arm through Jack's. "We'd love to. Got any place in mind? Because if not, I do."

Georgie blinked, looking between Adalia, who still had her arm looped through Jack's, and Jack, who hadn't attempted to remove it. "I didn't. Whatever you suggest is awesome."

"Great," Adalia said, a huge smile spreading across her face. "No takebacks."

———

Several hours later, Adalia couldn't help but be amused by the fear on her sister's face. Jack looked a little nervous too, but it was the straightlaced, prim and proper Georgie who had Adalia nearly bursting with glee.

"You know I hate karaoke," Georgie hissed across the table. "And you lied when you said everyone who comes in has to sing. The waitress just confirmed it."

"Come on, Georgie. It'll be fun. Besides, you loved to post yourself singing One Direction songs on Facebook back in the day. This will be a lot less embarrassing."

Georgie's eyes flew wide as she turned to Jack. "I *never* did that. And One Direction came out *long* after I was in high school."

"That's what made it so embarrassing," Adalia said.

71

"I never did that!"

Jack grinned, then shot a glance at Adalia. "Methinks the lady doth protest too much."

Horror washed over Georgie's face, and Adalia decided to end her sister's misery. "Okay, Georgie never posted videos of herself singing One Direction songs, but we do have some home videos of her singing Beach Boys songs for Mom."

Georgie's face softened. "I forgot about that."

"You don't have to sing by yourself," Adalia said, "but we're all singing one together before we go." She gave her a huge, cheesy grin. "You can't say no to family bonding."

Her sister started to protest, then sank back into her seat. "Okay. Fine. But no video. I am *not* letting you show this to River."

Adalia laughed. "Okay."

"I'll agree to this on one condition," Jack said with an uber serious face. "I refuse to sing 'We Are Family.' It's a total cliché."

Georgie cracked a smile. "I totally agree."

"Well, that's unanimous," Adalia said. "I hate that song."

"So what do we sing?" Georgie asked.

"Let's hang out and eat for a bit and maybe it will come to us," Jack said, picking up a menu.

"Words of wisdom from my wise older brother," Adalia said in a deep voice.

"Which means you're still the baby," Georgie said, picking up her own menu.

Adalia gave them both a saucy grin. "You say that like it's a bad thing."

Of course, in most families it probably wasn't, but in the Buchanan family, it had ultimately meant being all alone.

But she shoved the bitter memories away and focused on the present, because she was having fun with Georgie and Jack, and she *did* want to get to know him better.

They ordered their food and discussed superficial things, like their favorite bands and movies. Then they moved on to college (Jack had gone to community college but hadn't finished), first jobs and, after a couple of drinks, first crushes—Georgie and Adalia learning things about each other that they hadn't known.

Jack seemed to share freely, but Adalia couldn't help thinking he was holding something back. She had no idea what it could be, and she didn't plan on interrogating him. Heaven knew she had plenty of secrets of her own. He had to wonder why she'd abruptly moved to town in June, yet he hadn't asked. And he still hadn't asked about Finn showing up last night, or why there was a red footprint next to Bessie in the driveway. He knew she was an artist, but there wasn't a hint of her art in Grandpa Beau's house. He had to have questions. His reserve, which had initially put her off, made her respect him more. Jack Durand was the kind of man who respected other people's secrets.

By the time they all shared a slice of cheesecake and a brownie sundae, the three siblings were laughing and enjoying one another's company. Of course, that was when the announcer called out, "Next up, we have Adalia, Georgie, and Jack."

Horror filled Georgie's eyes. "We haven't even picked out a song. And how did they get our names?"

"Lucky for both of you," Adalia said mischievously as she slid out of her seat. "I submitted our names and our song when I went to the bathroom right before we got our food. You can pick next time."

"There won't be a next time," Georgie said in a tight voice.

Adalia grabbed her hand and dragged her to the stage. "You say that now…"

There were only two mics, so Adalia shared one with Georgie and let Jack have the other. He shuffled his weight back and forth as though he was on the defensive line of a homecoming football game and his home team was being slaughtered.

Adalia couldn't help laughing. She hoped he brought that energy to the song she'd chosen.

"Don't *worry*," she told them. "Just have fun." Then the music to Bruno Mars's "Uptown Funk" started playing and she darted a glance at her siblings. "I hope you remember how to dance."

Jack challenged her with a look that smacked of *bring it on*, and she beamed, making a big show of brushing off her shoulders.

The lyrics kicked in on the screen, and Adalia burst into song. While she never hoped to have a singing career, she knew she could carry a tune. She sang loud and moved to the music, because who could stay still while listening to or belting out this song?

To her surprise, Jack could sing too, and he met her challenge, singing and dancing with her. Georgie sang a little more softly than the two of them, but she began to lose some of her inhibitions as they went along, especially since the crowd had started cheering them and singing along. The two sisters started dancing around their brother, and when they got to the line about Saturday night, Adalia shouted out "Wednesday night" instead, and they kept it up for the rest of the song.

When they got to the bridge, Adalia called out, "Take it, Georgie!" then nudged her sister closer to the microphone. Georgie looked terrified again, but she started to hesitantly sing, "before we leave…" and the crowd shouted her name, encouraging her to own it. By the time she got to the end of the bridge, Georgie *was* owning it, belting out the words while Jack and Adalia danced next to her, snapping to the beat.

Adalia motioned for the crowd to get to their feet and sing along even louder. The entire restaurant was full of energy, and Adalia was lapping up every bit of it as they brought the song to a close. When the last note played, everyone was whooping and hollering and applauding, and Adalia gave her sister a quick hug.

"I'm so proud of you, Georgie!"

Before her sister could say anything, Adalia stepped in front of the microphone beside Jack and called out, "My brother, Jack Durand! New to Asheville and very single, ladies!"

Or so she thought, anyway. Cheers rang out, along with a few wolf whistles.

"I'm Adalia Buchanan—Yes! Of the notorious Buchanan Brewery!"

Jack wrapped an arm around her, taking control of the mic, and said, "Also very single."

There were more cheers and whistles, and one man shouted, "I like 'em wild!"

"Hey!" Jack said in a semi-playful tone as he pointed into the crowd. "That's my sister you're talking about."

Adalia broke into laughter. "And the shy one of our group is Georgie Buchanan, who is taken, boys. Her sights are set *very* firmly on River Reeves, so don't bother wasting your time."

There were a few groans but plenty of laughter and cheering as Adalia gave them a mock salute. "And our work here is done. Good night!"

The crowd shouted and clapped as they walked off the stage. The poor woman who got on stage next and sang "Total Eclipse of the Heart," slightly off key, didn't stand a chance.

The manager came over and comped their desserts and invited them to come back on the weekend. "I haven't seen the crowd this excited since those rodeo clowns came to town."

"We'll definitely give it some thought," Georgie said in a rush, probably hoping to keep Adalia from accepting the offer. "Thank you."

When they walked out the door shortly afterward, they stood on the busy Asheville sidewalk for a moment, the three of them suddenly unsure of what to say. They'd been in a bubble, and now it felt suddenly fragile, as if it were on the verge of bursting. Finally, Georgie said, "Thank you, Addy. That was fun, and I think I actually needed that."

"Good," Adalia said smugly. "And I won't even say I told you so."

Georgie cocked an eyebrow, but she was grinning as she turned to Jack. "How's that for a welcome to the family?" She gave him a hug, then took a step back. "I'll see you both tomorrow morning."

She glared at Adalia, as if challenging her to disobey.

No worries there. Adalia needed the money, and she was actually eager to work more on her branding project. She'd already come up with the look she was going for with the photos, and maybe Jack would be open to helping her with the copy, which seemed more in his wheelhouse than hers.

Maybe she really could marry her art to the brewery and still be satisfied. Or maybe this was just another thimble full of water.

Only time would tell.

CHAPTER

Eight

Finn had felt weirdly nervous about texting River. It had occurred to him—belatedly, as things often did—that he should have already talked to him about the art show, which had sent him down a path of wondering *why* he hadn't talked to him about it. They weren't as close as they'd been, and it was Finn's fault. If River reacted badly to his plan, or perhaps his continued efforts to include Adalia in said plan, Finn worried it would strike another blow to their wounded friendship.

So he'd put off contacting him until after he got home that afternoon. And then he found himself looking up the muralists Dottie had hand-selected for Gretchen. One had a portfolio that included a couple of graphic sex murals, which were artistically pleasing, although perhaps not what they were going for given they'd be covering up the STD graffiti. He recommended the other two but made himself a note to contact the third painter about the show. (She had other work that would be a little more appropriate for a wide audience.) So he texted Gretchen the information and started his proposal for the event he'd conceived for her on the fly, only to realize he was still avoiding what he'd set out to do.

Just like he'd avoided telling River about the whole Bev Corp thing.

A quick glance at his watch told him it was somehow already five forty-five.

More likely than not, River was at home with Georgie, and the two already had dinner plans—a thought that made him feel a strange ache—but he'd text him anyway. And if River invited him over, which he did sometimes, Finn would accept. Even if he still felt a little weird around Georgie on account of he'd broken them up and all.

I have an idea I'd like to run by you, he wrote to River. *Free for dinner?* And then, because he still felt a little nervous, he added, *Nothing to do with Bev Corp.*

He immediately cursed himself. Why'd he mention them at all? He fully intended to tell River about the thing he was doing for Gretchen, but it would be better to explain in person, and he was also more interested in talking to him about the art show than the beer festival.

Sorry, that was weird, he added, because he couldn't help himself. *Want to go to that place we like that has Taco Tuesday?*

Another pause, and he saw the three dots indicating River was writing something. Which was when Finn realized it was Wednesday.

I mean, it's Wednesday, he added. *Obviously. But they're still open.*

He waited for those dots to form words, pushing forward and back in his office chair.

Finally, River's message came through: *Good God, Finn. Give me time to respond. Yes. Tacos sound good. Meet at 7?*

Finn grinned at that, grateful he'd said yes. Grateful, too, that he wouldn't have to go over to their loft and explain the whole art show thing in front of Adalia's sister, who probably didn't like him and definitely wouldn't approve of him.

Not that he needed her approval, of course.

He sent a thumbs-up to River, then decided he should invite Maisie too. She'd always joined them for Taco Tuesday. Sure, it was Wednesday, but he felt bad that he'd gone so long without seeing her, plus he liked Dottie's suggestion about donating the first show's profits to her shelter. Adalia would probably think he was being manipulative—that he was just asking her because it would twist River's arm—and to be honest, he wouldn't mind if that happened (a little), but he really did just want to see her. There was nothing wrong with that, was there?

Hey, stranger. It's the bro. What are you doing for dinner? he texted her as he pulled on his docksiders. River always laughed at him, but he didn't like to wear sandals, even in the summer. He hated getting his feet dirty .

I'm currently looking at a frozen dinner covered in two layers of ice. Do these things go bad? Also, do you have a better option?

Anything goes bad if you put enough effort into it. Know it's Wednesday, but are you up for that Taco Tuesday place? Seven?

Make it six thirty. I'm almost hungry enough to roll the dice on this piece of brown and red ice.

He wasn't exactly hungry, having eaten a huge plate of food at Dottie's (she'd given him enough leftovers to take home to feed him for at least two days), but he'd had more company than usual over the last few days, and it had felt good. He craved more. So he sent another thumbs-up.

When he got to the restaurant, Maisie was already sitting at a table in the back. She had a view of the door, and she grinned and waved at him as he came in. Her red hair was down, and it struck him that it was longer than when he'd seen her last.

He headed toward her, ignoring a couple of dirty looks, one of them from a toddler, which, to be fair, might have had nothing to do with the whole public infamy thing.

Before he could sit down, Maisie got up and wrapped him in a hug.

"It's good to see you," she said, letting him go and sitting back down. "I was bummed to miss the whole Buchanan reopening."

"Yeah," he said, taking a seat, "I was surprised not to see you there."

She shrugged, but before she could say anything else, a waitress came by.

He nodded to the enormous margarita sitting in front of Maisie. "One of those, please?"

"Any food?"

He shook his head. "No, I think I'll wait until the rest of our group gets here." Turning to Maisie, he added, "I'm sure River won't mind if you don't want to wait, Maisie. He knows how hangry you get."

Maisie was always pale—it was the Irish in her, she'd say—but she lost what little color she had.

"You invited River?" she hissed.

The waitress lifted her eyebrow and stepped away, wisely assuming she didn't want to get in the middle of…whatever this was.

"Um, yeah," he said. "This is our Taco Tuesday place."

"So what," she fumed back. "It's Wednesday, and the three of us haven't hung out in months. It's no longer a thing." Her gaze shot to the door.

"It's okay," he said, feeling like he'd messed up again, although he didn't understand why. Maisie and River had been best friends since they were teenagers—something Finn had

81

felt the weight of sometimes, since River was the closest friend *he* had ever had. So what the hell was going on? "He's not going to be here until seven. Sorry. I thought I'd mentioned it." Or maybe he'd just assumed she wouldn't care.

"Well, you didn't, or otherwise I wouldn't have come."

She flagged down the waitress, and the look on her face must have scared the poor woman half to death, because she was there in an instant.

"I'd like my food to go, please," Maisie said. "And the check."

The waitress hurried off.

"What happened?" Finn asked.

Maisie looked away, but not before he saw the hurt in her eyes. Oh crap. Were those tears? He'd never, ever seen her cry before.

Finn was dense sometimes, but he wasn't stupid.

"Oh," he said. "I never… I didn't know how you felt."

"Yeah, well, neither does he," she said bitterly. "No need for both of us to be miserable about it. He's been so busy in Loved-Up Land he's barely noticed." She shook her head, as if chastening herself. "Which is the way it should be. I'm glad he's happy—really I am—and I don't want to ruin it. Every time he texts, I text back. I tell him I'm busy, which is true. I was out of town for half the summer getting some dogs rehabbed at the Moon Barn and visiting my sisters. Beatrice and Dustin have been holding down the fort. The *crumbling* fort. But River and I haven't seen each other in months."

"Shit," he said, feeling like the worst kind of scum. The waitress showed up with his margarita, and he took a big gulp. "Well, I guess this isn't the greatest time to tell you, but I'm putting together a charity art show, which I'm hoping to launch at Buchanan Brewery…" He shrugged a little as he said it. "I want to donate the proceeds to the shelter." And, because he could imagine Adalia telling him he was trying to act like Saint Finn, he added, "Dottie's idea."

Maisie brightened a little, but it was like she was on a dimmer. "Well, I want to hear how *that* came about sometime. That's so generous of you, Finn. We could really use the help. What would we need to do?"

"Well…" He paused, uncertain of what he should say, but he admitted, "I still need to talk to River about it to see if they're open to hosting it there. We might want you to come in for the event, talk a little bit about what you do. Maybe bring some of the dogs."

She nodded. "I'll send someone."

"Maisie," he said slowly, worrying how she would react. "Are you going to talk to him about it?"

"What's the point? I just need to get over it. Fully over it. And then we can pretend nothing happened."

"But he won't be pretending if he doesn't know. He just…won't know."

The waitress returned, hurrying over to the table with Maisie's takeout bag and the check.

Maisie glanced at her watch again, then slapped some cash down on the table.

"We'll talk about the show later, Finn. Thank you. And please, please don't say anything to River."

Then she was gone, and Finn was sitting in front of two margaritas.

"See, I told you he was a drunk," he heard a woman say in a stage whisper to her friend. Finn raised the drink as if toasting her, winked, and took a big sip. Her scandalized gasp put him in mind of Adalia and her game.

God, being around her this afternoon had made him feel so good, as if his worries had suddenly been lifted off his shoulders. He wished she were here now so they could come up with a story for Karen at the other table. So he could tell her about the weirdness with Maisie, and she could help him figure out what the hell he was supposed to say to River.

Nothing was the appropriate answer. But he was terrible at keeping secrets. Sure, he'd kept the whole Bev Corp thing mum, but that was business, and business had always been something different for him. Something separate.

By the time River showed up, Finn had started in on Maisie's margarita and the basket of chips was down to the dregs.

They hugged, and River seemed genuinely glad to see him, but Finn felt weighed down by what he knew. Maybe it would be better if he told? If River knew, he and Maisie could have an honest conversation at least, and that would be for the best, right? Keeping secrets certainly hadn't done any favors for him in his friendship with River.

"Something wrong?" A corner of River's mouth tipped up. "I mean besides the whole being tarred and feathered thing."

"Um…"

Maisie was supposed to come, but she ran away because she found out you were coming. She's in love with you, I think.

"No," he said slowly. "But I do want to proposition Georgie's sister."

Wait, that hadn't come out right.

River raised his brow. "Say what?"

Finn fidgeted. "Sorry. I meant, I do have a proposition for Georgie's sister." River was still looking at him funny, so he hastened to add, "A work thing."

He spent the next several minutes explaining his idea, Dottie's contribution, and his hope that Adalia would play a role, the conversation only halting, briefly, when the waitress came by to take their orders.

"I think Georgie will be pumped," River said. "It'll be great for the brewery, plus I know she's been worried about Adalia. Other than the stuff she's done for Buchanan, which is amazing, she hasn't picked up a paintbrush or made as much as a magnet since coming here."

Finn wished there was such a thing as jaw glue. Did River really not know that Adalia had been working in Dottie's studio? Did that mean Dottie hadn't told him?

If not, then this was yet another thing Finn was supposed to shut up about. It felt a little like torture, knowing things you shouldn't.

You kept the Bev Corp negotiations secret. You're capable of shutting up if the situation requires it. And ding, ding, the situation requires it!

River frowned. "How'd you know about her art, anyway?"

"Something's up with Maisie," Finn blurted out.

Shit. It was like all of the various secrets he knew had vied to come out of his mouth first, and that one had won.

"What?" River asked, in genuine shock. And no wonder. He hadn't known Maisie was in on the whole dinner invite, so Finn's comment must have seemed like it had come out of nowhere.

"I asked her to come to dinner, and she showed up, but she left when she found out you were coming," he said in a rush of words.

River cursed, his expression darkening. "I thought she was avoiding me again, but I guess I didn't want to believe it."

85

Finn didn't want to betray her further by saying anything else—hadn't he already made everything worse?—so he just said, "I think you should talk to her. We're going to donate the proceeds of the first show to the shelter. Which means we should probably get her to come."

"Oh, I'll talk to her," River said. "I'll tell her Hops is sick or something. She might turn me away, but she'd never refuse to help a dog."

There was something a little bitter in his tone, and Finn wanted to tell him he was getting it wrong, that Maisie was staying away out of self-preservation, but he'd already crossed enough lines. He'd do best to stay silent.

Right?

Right.

"You never did answer my question about Adalia," River commented, giving him a look. The kind of look that said River knew he'd deflected that earlier question, because *of course* River had noticed.

Oh, he was in for it, all right.

CHAPTER
Nine

If Adalia had thought family bonding night would make Georgie chill out, she was wrong. Thursday morning, Adalia caught her sister watching her several times with even more concern than before. She'd asked her more than once if she needed more coffee or if she wanted donuts from the shop down the street. Something was up with her, and it was getting on Adalia's last nerve.

After offer number four, Adalia glared at Georgie. "I think I need to move my desk."

"Why?" she asked, then frowned. "I know Jack has an office and you don't, and I know you got here first, but—"

"Georgie. Stop," Adalia said with a sigh. "Jack's the events coordinator. Of course he needs an office. It's just that I need more...space."

"We'll find it." Giving Adalia her full, undivided attention, she added, "You just tell me what you need."

Adalia narrowed her eyes. Something was definitely up. "Why are you acting so weird?"

Her sister's eyes flew open. "Am I acting weird?... I'm not acting weird."

"Yes. You are," Adalia said, turning in her seat to study her sister. "You've been treating me like I was told I only have forty-eight hours to live. Like I'm some delicate, fragile glass bottle that's about to break. What the hell is going on?"

Georgie's eyes filled with tears.

"What?" Adalia pressed, wondering for a split second if she and River were having some sort of fight, but no, Georgie wouldn't react this way. She'd be more likely to retreat into herself. "What is it?"

"I know about Dottie's studio," Georgie said softly, her eyes full of concern.

It took Adalia a half second to realize what she was talking about. Then horror washed over her. "What? How did you…"

But she didn't need to finish the question, because she already knew.

Finn.

Her dismay was just as quickly replaced with anger. "I'm going to *kill* him."

Georgie got up and closed her open office door, dragging a guest chair over to Adalia's and grabbing both of her hands. "I know we haven't talked much about what happened right before you moved here—"

"I don't *want* to talk about what happened!" Adalia started to get to her feet, but her sister tugged her back down.

Worry etched her sister's face. "You don't have to talk to me, but I think you should talk to *someone*. River thinks so too."

"*You talked to River about this?*" Adalia snatched her hands free as humiliation heated her cheeks. Then she understood. River had known first, and he'd told Georgie.

Oh, my God. How many people knew?

"I know money's tight," Georgie rushed on, desperation on her face, "but River and I are more than happy to pay for your visits."

Adalia shook her head, sure she'd heard her sister wrong. "You and your boyfriend want to pay for me to see a *therapist?*"

"There's no shame in seeing a therapist, Addy. Trust me. I did it for years."

"No, but there is a heaping amount of shame when you can't pay for it yourself."

A tear slid down Georgie's face. "I can't stand the thought of you creating art and destroying it. River said that Finn told him your work is breathtaking."

"Did he now?" Adalia asked in a snotty tone, but she was in self-preservation mode. *Red alert. Batten down the hatches.* "I know Finn Hamilton *thinks* he knows everything, but I didn't realize he was an art connoisseur."

"Addy, this is all coming out wrong."

"Actually," she said in a deadly calm voice, "I think it's coming out exactly right." She turned in her seat and snatched up her purse from the floor. "I've got to go." Then, as an afterthought, she snapped the laptop shut and cradled it to her chest as she stood.

"Please don't go," Georgie pleaded. "Let me help you."

"You want to help me?" Adalia asked in the coldest voice she could muster. "Then leave me the hell alone."

She left Georgie crying in her office, and she had to admit that she felt like a world-class bitch for that, but she knew what Adalia was like in self-preservation mode. They said a wolf would bite off its own foot if it were in a trap. Adalia was more the type to bite off someone else's. She was leaving for Georgie's benefit, not her own. If she hadn't left, Defensive Adalia would have eviscerated her.

Only she didn't know where to go, once she left. Her clunky car hadn't started that morning, so she'd gone in with Jack. Of course, their house couldn't be more than two miles away, which made it walkable, but she didn't want to go there. Not yet. Instead, she shoved the laptop in her purse and just started walking. She found herself downtown, aimlessly walking in circles around the city blocks, letting the anger bleed out of her. There was an itch at the base of her head, a craving to go to Dottie's garage, but she didn't have a car, and she knew that what she created would only be destroyed. Then Georgie would have even more ammunition to call her crazy.

She didn't call you crazy.

No, but Adalia had seen the fear and worry in her eyes. *Maybe she didn't say the words, but she's thinking them all the same.*

She wasn't sure how long she'd been walking, but it was long enough that her anger had burned off, leaving irritation and disappointment. Only she couldn't figure out who she was disappointed in—Georgie? Finn? Herself?

Maybe Adalia should leave Asheville and go somewhere no one knew her. She could start over again, but doing what? She wasn't exactly qualified for much. She dug out her phone and checked the job site app—no requests for an interview.

Perhaps if you actually applied for a job, you'd get an interview request.

She wanted to kick her inner voice in the shins.

But the question of whether she should move on wouldn't leave her mind, so when a storefront across the street caught her eye—Psychic Readings by Lola—she stopped.

Didn't Dottie have a friend named Lola?

She remembered the name, and it was such a Dottie thing to have a psychic friend. Was this the universe telling her that the answers to her questions could be hers if she simply walked across the street? Possibly she was just nuts, but she found herself jaywalking. A car came to a halt as she walked in its path, and she held up a finger of warning after the driver laid on the horn.

"Not today, Merv!" she shouted in warning, for some reason using Finn's name from the 'Who are you?' game.

The older man snapped out of his momentary shock and shouted out the window, "It's Herv, not Merv!"

Whatever. Finn would probably get a kick out of that. Plus the Fiona thing.

If she were speaking to him.

Adalia stopped in front of the door and read the hand-painted sign: *Appointments encouraged, but walk-ins welcome. If you were meant to see me, I'll have scheduled an appointment for you.*

She snorted. "I bet."

She'd never been to a psychic or had her palm read or sat down for a tarot reading. Some of her friends were into that kind of thing, but Adalia had always told them that she was in charge of her own future, not some woo-woo person with a deck of cards. It tickled Adalia to pretend Dottie's waves of intuition were something more supernatural, but this was a bunch of hocus-pocus nonsense.

God, what was she even doing here? She was confused, for sure, feeling like she was standing at the center of a crossroads with a target on her back. Part of her wanted to put down roots in Asheville, but the rest of her was ready to run anywhere that would protect her from the humiliation of facing her sister, River, and most of all Finn.

But did she want to resort to *this*? She had better ways to spend her money. Like her next student loan payment.

Yet she found herself unable to walk away. Neither could she get herself to enter. It was a harmless thing, she rationalized, and Dottie would be pleased she'd come to see her friend, yada-yada. What could it hurt?

Then again, what if she didn't like what Lola told her? Therein lay the crux. That itch at the base of her neck pushing her to enter—it was the same feeling that kept sending her back to Dottie's garage. But what if this visit to Lola could put a stop to that?

Did she actually want it to go away? If Adalia didn't have art, then who was she?

Maybe it was time to find out.

Before she could change her mind, she opened the door and walked into a small waiting room filled with thrift-store chairs and a loveseat. A door on the back wall opened, and a young woman with brown, chin-length hair and bangs appeared. Adalia had expected someone much older. Lola looked like she couldn't be more than a year or two older than her.

"I've been waiting for you."

Adalia stopped in her tracks, trying to disguise her surprise. "I don't have an appointment."

"I know, but I knew you were coming."

Narrowing her eyes, Adalia thumbed to the door behind her. "Because you mystically book appointments for those who need them?"

A smile lifted the corners of the woman's mouth. "That, and I have a security camera pointed at the front door. I've been watching you try to decide if you were going to come in or not."

Adalia's cheeks flushed. "Let's just say I'm a skeptic. I only decided to come in to see if you're Dottie's friend Lola. She's mentioned you."

The woman's face lit up. "Oh! I love Dottie! Any friend of hers is a friend of mine." She took a step back from the doorway and motioned for Adalia to enter. "Come in. Have a seat on the sofa."

Adalia walked into the back room, surprised that it looked more like the stereotypical therapist's office than a psychic's parlor. There were plants and soft lighting in addition to a plush sofa. A couple of stuffed chairs sat opposite the sofa with a worn coffee table with water rings between the pieces.

Had Dottie used some kind of reverse psychology to get Adalia to see a therapist?

Now she could add paranoia to her list of psychological issues.

"Shut the door behind you," the woman said softly as she sat in the floral armchair. "I'm Lola, by the way."

Adalia shut the door as requested and took a seat in the center of the sofa.

"And you are?" Lola prodded.

"Shouldn't you know that already? Didn't you psychically pencil in my appointment? What name did you use?"

Lola laughed, obviously not offended. "It doesn't work like that, but if you feel better with anonymity, I'm fine with that."

"Yeah," she said with a firm nod. "Let's go with that." She glanced around. "Where's your crystal ball?"

Lola shook her head slightly. "I don't have one. They're more useful for talking with the dead, and if that's what you're after, you'd be better off visiting Deidre and her daughter down at the New Age crystal shop a few blocks over." She paused. "You know, Asheville is surrounded by crystal, which is a great conductor of energy."

"Huh, is that why Dottie collects so much of it?"

Lola smiled fondly. "Yes, not that she needs it to read people's energy. Dottie has her own form of intuition."

Wasn't that the truth. "So what form does your intuition take?" she asked. "Palm reading?"

"Tarot cards are usually better for truth-seekers looking for more direct answers. I'll tell you what I see, and we can talk it out to interpret what it means." She pulled open a drawer in the table between the chairs and pulled out a worn deck of cards. Closing her eyes, she began to shuffle them. "I'm sensing a lot of negative energy rolling off you."

"What was your first clue?" Adalia asked. "My attitude or my sharp tongue?"

Lola's mouth lifted into a patient smile as she continued to shuffle. She opened her eyes and held out the deck. "Lay your palm on the cards."

Adalia was a hair's breadth away from getting up and walking out, but something told her to shut up and play along. Still, she couldn't help but smirk as she placed her palm on top of the deck.

Lola placed a hand on top of hers for a couple of seconds before pulling the deck away and shuffling some more. "Are there any specific questions you want answered?"

"Let's just see what the universe shows you," Adalia said, already regretting this. How much was it going to cost her, anyway? Why hadn't she asked for Lola's rates?

The "psychic" stopped shuffling and began to set out the cards, faceup. "Oh," she said as she placed a card with a skull and crossbones. "That's usually not the first one."

Adalia just nodded, her eyes on the skeleton, and watched as the rest of the cards were lined up in a neat row.

"Wow," Lola said when she finished. "There's *a lot* of upheaval in your life right now."

Adalia pointed to the skeleton card and joked, "So when I leave here, should I head on over to the funeral home to prearrange my burial?"

"It *is* a death card, but it likely doesn't mean what you think it does. It usually represents the death of an old life." She glanced up at Adalia's face. "Are you thinking about making a big change? Leaving a relationship? Moving to a new city?"

It took Adalia a second to answer. Her gaze was locked on the card, tears filling her eyes. She was so shocked she didn't even think about disguising her reaction. "Uh…a career change, actually. And moving."

Lola gave her a look and said, "It'll be easier for us to figure out the specific meaning if you tell me why you walked in today."

She shook her head. "General is fine. Keep going."

Lola told her that someone from her past would reappear soon, causing her heartache, but someone else would be there to support her. The person she least expected.

But all Adalia could see was that death card.

"Like I said, it rarely means death," Lola assured her with a worried voice. "It means a very significant change, and since it's inverted, that usually—"

"That's okay," Adalia said, grabbing her wallet out of her purse. "How much do I owe you?"

"I really hate to see you upset like this," Lola said. "I can help you work this out if you'll give me some background."

"No, that's okay," Adalia said, shaking her head, and pulled out two twenty-dollar bills and held the bills out to her. "Does forty cover it?"

Lola put her hand over Adalia's and searched her eyes. "No. This one is complimentary. I'll charge you next time."

There wouldn't be a next time.

Adalia got up and rushed out into the waiting room, closing the door behind her. Her phone buzzed in her pocket. She nearly ignored it, but she pulled it out anyway, feeling faint when she saw Alan's name on her screen above a text.

Addy. Baby. I miss you. We need to talk. Please call me.

He'd left her alone for a couple of days. She'd dared to hope that maybe he'd forgotten about her. That he'd lost her number. But here he was again. Hadn't Lola said something about a person from her past reappearing? If she was right, Alan wasn't going to back down like she and Georgie had hoped. He was going to keep turning up like a bad penny.

Time to block his number.

But he'd just find a different way, wouldn't he?

A sob bubbled up, but she swallowed it back down. She needed to go home. She needed…she needed to address the possible meaning of that death card. Was she supposed to give up her art?

Glancing down at the text on her screen, she reached for the door to the sidewalk and plowed into a firm body.

Strong hands grabbed her upper arms, holding her upright. "Adalia, are you okay?"

She recognized the voice before she even looked up into his worry-filled blue-green eyes. She'd run straight into the devil himself.

Finn.

CHAPTER Ten

Finn sincerely hadn't intended to tell River everything. He'd started off by admitting that Adalia had been painting in Dottie's studio, and the rest had unfurled from there. Somewhere in the telling, he'd realized just how much the situation had been weighing on him. The need to *do* something, to help her through whatever was haunting her, had been a constant companion. He'd carried it around with him all day long, gone to sleep with it. Telling River had felt like an unburdening in more ways than one.

Finn and River had met with Jack Durand for a breakfast meeting this morning to discuss the show—Jack being the new events coordinator for Buchanan Brewery—and although he and River hadn't explained the whole *Adalia's been destroying her own paintings* thing to him, they'd let him in on an idea they'd tossed around the night before. And the three of them had spent the morning working on it. After they discussed the show, of course. The plan was to hold the as-of-yet unnamed event toward the beginning of November, just when people started considering holiday gifts. That gave them a little under two months to gather everything together, but he figured they could pull it off. He didn't have a whole lot else going on at the moment.

It remained to be seen what Adalia would do when she found out he'd spilled her secret. He had to admit the odds were pretty good she'd pour a bucket of red paint on him. Or go all in and use pig's blood. Maybe she'd just refuse to see him again.

The last thing he had expected was for her to run into him—literally—as he was walking into the psychic's...could it really be called an office?

Her eyes flew wide. "What the hell are you doing here?"

"I'm so sorry," he said, because obviously she knew. "I met with River last night to talk about the show. I mentioned how much I love your art, and he asked me what I'd seen because you haven't been doing art..." He paused, not really sure what else to say, and ended with the obvious. "I'm not very good at keeping secrets. I didn't know it *was* a secret. From them, I mean." Which wasn't quite true, so he amended. "I figured they at least knew you'd been coming there. Not necessarily what you were doing to the paintings. With the knife."

She shook her head in disgust. "You really don't have a filter, do you?"

"Not most of the time, no. Trust me when I tell you I wish that I did."

A pretty woman with short dark hair had opened the door to the back, he registered, although he wasn't sure when it had happened. She was looking at them with interest.

"Finn?" she asked.

"Hey," Adalia said, as if affronted. "How come you guessed his name?"

The woman—Lola, surely—glanced at her. "Because he *did* have an appointment. One your friend Dottie made."

Seeing Adalia here, he'd assumed Dottie had arranged this intentionally. Like maybe she'd decided a psychic's office was the best place for him and Adalia to hash things out and discuss the show. He wouldn't have put it past her. But Lola's reaction suggested otherwise. Was this another chance meeting…at a psychic's?

He believed in fate—to an extent—and it felt like it was throwing them together. But even if that was true, what was he supposed to do with the opportunity he'd been given? How could he get Adalia to trust him after all the dumb mistakes he'd made?

"Well, at least I'm somewhat encouraged that you're not stalking me," she said, pushing away.

She was about to leave when he found himself saying, "I think you should stay."

"What?" she asked. She sounded like she thought he was a fruitcake, but at least she'd stopped walking.

"I didn't mean to, but I witnessed something very personal to you," he said. "I know one of your secrets. It only seems fair that you should know some of mine."

She shot a dubious look at Lola, but he thought he saw something else in it. Anger, and maybe a little fear. Suddenly, Finn found himself wondering how Adalia's reading had gone. What had the psychic told her?

Whatever it was, it had sent her running out of the building.

"No offense, but that only works if I buy that Lola here is a psychic. I'm not sold. Besides, you don't just know my secret, you shared it with my sister's boyfriend, and thus my sister. You'd need to give me free rein over who I tell."

"Scout's honor," he said, making the sign.

"You *would* be a Scout," she said.

"Not to interrupt," Lola said, "but I can give you an accurate reading if you'll provide me with some background. Details like what brought you here, other than Dottie, and what problems you're dealing with right now." The glance she gave Adalia indicated she had been less cooperative.

"Whatever you need," he said, looking at Adalia as he said it. "I'm an open book."

He was prepared for Adalia to say no. The look she'd given him at the door...

But something shifted in her eyes, like maybe she'd decided she didn't want to go wherever it was she'd been heading with such purpose before she rammed into him. She walked back into the adjoining room, glancing over her shoulder at him. "Oh, this is going to be good."

Finn followed, feeling a prickle of misgiving for the first time.

What if Lola told him that he was fooling himself? That the whole art thing was a distraction from the fact that his life had crumbled around him? That he was destined to be lonely for the rest of his existence because he couldn't make a good decision if his life depended on it? That he was already a has-been at thirty-two.

He wasn't so sure he wanted Adalia to witness that, but then again, she hadn't wanted him to see her pour her emotions out onto that canvas before she tore it to pieces. Fair was fair.

Lola gave him a glance.

"Are you okay with this?" he asked. "I guess it's not...traditional to have someone else sit in on a reading."

"Oh, I've seen all kinds," she said, and he believed it. She was a friend of Dottie's, after all.

He made his way into the room, which looked like the office of the therapist he'd gone to see after his falling-out with River. He'd gone to one appointment. The only person who knew was Dottie, who'd told him, "Dear, no need to be so ambitious. Most people don't resolve their issues in a single session."

Which he knew, of course, but it had been an afternoon appointment, and the office had smelled strongly of egg salad. Something that had prevented him from focusing on anything but the egg salad.

Adalia sat in one of the two chairs, and since the other was clearly intended for Lola, he settled onto the couch. As Lola sat down across from him, Finn found himself wondering what he'd signed up for. It felt like he was about to be interrogated.

"Tell me a little about yourself," Lola said. And he couldn't help but glance at Adalia. He made eye contact for a second, which was enough to tell him they were thinking pretty much the same thing: what exactly did psychic mean if it didn't mean, well, psychic?

But Lola was onto them. "Like I told your friend," she said patiently, "I don't know everything. If I did, I'd have won the lottery years ago. But some of us are more...intuitive. More capable of tapping into deep truths. I'm not sure I can help you, but I'd like to try."

Point to Lola.

"Do you know who I am?"

Adalia snorted, and he flushed a little, knowing exactly what she was thinking.

Pompous much?

"I... I'm just trying to figure out where to get started."

"I know you founded Big Catch with Dottie's nephew," Lola said. "And I know about the sale and some of the fallout."

"So what do you want to know?" he asked uncertainly.

"You're at a crossroads," Lola said. It wasn't phrased as a question. "Do you find yourself torn between two paths?"

Did he ever. But he only wanted one.

"Yes. I guess one road would be to leave Asheville. To accept that I'm not wanted here. That would probably be the more prudent thing to do. It's what my parents would like me to do. But it's not what I want." He glanced at Adalia. *Go big or go home, Finn.* "I've felt lost lately. Like nothing makes sense anymore. I thought it would be easy to find the next big idea after the sale went through, but I felt empty even before the blowback. Because I let down the people who matter to me."

He ran a hand through his hair, which was longer than it had ever been in his life. His usual stylist, whom he'd considered a friendly acquaintance, had written a comment on the *Gazette* article. *I know this guy!!! Good tipper, but he wouldn't stop talking about himself. SO conceited.* Finn had wanted to tell her that he was just someone who liked talking…that he'd thought you were *supposed* to talk to a stylist. That she was the one who'd asked him questions. But he'd turned off his computer instead. And let his hair grow.

"I guess I was a little depressed," he admitted. "I wasn't leaving the house much. I didn't know how to feel in my own skin anymore. Then I saw something I shouldn't have seen—" He looked away from Adalia, not wanting to reveal her secret again. "Anyway, it made me realize I wasn't the only person feeling that way. It…unleashed something in me. I realized that I don't need to start another multimillion-dollar business right away." Okay, he shouldn't have said that part. He could practically feel Adalia rolling her eyes. "I can do something meaningful. Something that makes people's lives better. Something that matters. And I want to help that other person too. The one who feels like I do."

"What if the other person just wants to be left alone?" Adalia asked, the question lacking any of the heat he might have expected.

"Then I'll do my best to give *him* space," he said, smiling at her. "Sometimes my eagerness gets away from me."

"You need to let other people make up their own minds," she answered. "Even if you don't like the answer. There may be things you don't know about this *exceptionally* handsome and charming young man."

He glanced back at Lola again. Her eyes had rounded. Probably she felt like she was in the middle of something, because she was. But her presence was pretty much the only reason Adalia had agreed to stick around, so he was grateful she was there. Grateful, too, that Dottie had unwittingly—or maybe not?—sent him Adalia's way again.

"Shall I take out the deck?" Lola asked, her tone kindly. As if she felt sorry for him.

"Sure," he said, embarrassed. The psychic thought he was a hot mess. Great. He shot another glance at Adalia. She was looking at him, but he couldn't read her expression. At least she wasn't staring daggers of hate at him. He'd take it.

Lola went through the song and dance of shuffling the cards. Then she asked Finn to touch them so he could infuse them with his essence or whatever. So he held his hand against them for a moment, feeling Adalia's eyes on him. Feeling an uncomfortable throb of self-consciousness.

But he reminded himself this was nothing compared with what he'd witnessed Adalia doing. Worse, he'd shared her secret with River, and by proxy Georgie, which had clearly filled Adalia with shame.

He'd expected Lola to chant, or roll her eyes back, or something equally dramatic, but she just shuffled again, letting his energy guide her or whatever. She frowned as she laid out the cards, so that probably wasn't good, especially since the first one had a skull and crossbones on it. Was this what Dottie had seen in his tea? Maybe she'd figured it would be best if someone else passed on the sorry news.

He glanced up at Adalia, but her eyes were on the cards. She shifted her gaze up to Lola, her expression accusatory.

"What, do you pick the same draw for everyone?"

"No," Lola said, glancing from one of them to the other. If she was acting, she was a good actress, the kind who'd win awards. "But you're right, they're exactly the same. You're both in the middle of transitions, so it's not surprising there would be some overlap, but…well…I've been doing this since I was a teenager, and that's never once happened."

"Lay it on me," Finn said, joking but just barely. "Are we both going to die? Is a semi going to barrel down on us as soon as we leave?"

"Trust me, I already asked," Adalia said in an undertone.

"No," Lola said, her gaze darting over the cards. Then she gave them another look, first Adalia and then Finn. "No, I think it means you're meant for each other."

CHAPTER

Eleven

Adalia burst out laughing. She wasn't sure why she'd agreed to stay for the reading, but she had, and something had kept her there too. Maybe it was the look in Finn's eyes whenever he darted a glance her way. That look told her she was his lifeline, and what he'd said to them…he felt just as messed up as she did. Sure, he'd caused his own problems, but couldn't the same be said of her?

Then Lola had said they were meant for each other, which was so obviously bogus, and now she couldn't help but wonder if Dottie had somehow manipulated this into happening. Maybe she'd snuck into Georgie's office and hypnotized Adalia.

"I doubt it," Adalia said, glancing at Finn. He looked shell-shocked, but she thought she saw something like hurt in his eyes. "Nothing personal. I'm not exactly looking for a relationship."

"Maybe I misspoke," Lola said quickly, as if sensing she was losing her audience. "It might not be a romantic connection, but there's no denying your futures are intertwined. I've never seen a stronger indication." She gestured for them to look at the cards as she said it, and it struck Adalia that it wasn't just the same spread: it was in the same order.

Maybe Lola wasn't totally full of it. There was no denying Adalia kept running into Finn, and he'd already had an impact on her life.

If Lola was right—and that was a *big* if—what exactly did all of this mean?

Was Finn freaking out at the thought of his future being hitched to hers? Or was he just as desperate to get out of this nightmare as she was?

"Do you smell something burning?" Adalia asked, wrinkling her nose.

Lola's eyes widened in alarm. "What?"

She turned to Finn. "You smell that, don't you?"

He gave her a confused look.

"It smells like burning plastic." She leaned forward, locking eyes with him. "Don't you smell it?" She lifted her eyebrows as high as she could.

Understanding filled his eyes and he sat up straighter. "Yeah. Definitely." He bobbed his head and got to his feet. "We should get out of here so you can figure out what it is, Lola."

"But I don't smell anything," she said, looking worried.

Adalia felt guilty for scaring her, but not guilty enough to stay seated. "Maybe it's just my nose." She shrugged as she grabbed Finn's wrist and dragged him to the door. "I burned a Pop-Tart this morning, and I haven't been smelling right ever since."

Finn glanced back at Lola. "How much do I owe you?"

"Just send the bill to Dottie!" Adalia called out, dragging Finn behind her. "He's good for it!" She didn't slow down until they were out the door and halfway down the street.

"Where are we going?" he asked, but she noticed he wasn't giving her any resistance.

"I'm hungry. You're buying me a late lunch."

"I am?" He gave a slight shake of his head, looking only slightly less dazed than he had on Lola's couch. "Yeah. Okay. Let's do lunch."

"Let's *do* lunch?" she asked, walking slower now but still holding his wrist. "You make it sound like we're about to film a porno."

His face turned red. "*Adalia*, I—"

"Relax," she said, coming to a halt at the street corner. "I make inappropriate comments when I'm nervous or uncomfortable." She gave him a direct look. "The more uncomfortable, the more inappropriate. For the record, I dialed it back so I wouldn't scare you off."

She spotted a Mexican restaurant and started to drag him toward it. "I hear they have a great Taco Tuesday night...and yes, I'm well aware of the fact that it's Thursday." She was babbling, which was totally unlike her, just further proof of how shaken she was.

He made a face when he saw their destination, like maybe he wasn't in the mood for Mexican food. She might have asked him about it, but then he tried to lace his fingers with hers, and she stopped and jerked her hand away. "What are you *doing*?"

He gave her a blank look. "I thought you wanted to hold hands."

"What? No!"

He studied her for a long moment and then slowly reached out and grabbed her hand anyway.

For some reason, she didn't resist. She told herself she was doing it for him. From what he'd said in the weird psychic/therapist room, he clearly needed a friend. The fact that she hadn't pulled away had nothing to do with the fact that his touch made her feel grounded and slowed down the spinning in her head.

They were silent as they walked the rest of the way to the restaurant. He opened the door for her, still holding her hand, and part of her couldn't believe it. She wasn't one of those people who held hands while walking down the street, not with anyone, but life had a way of laying to rest personal rules and preconceived notions.

The hostess showed them to a booth right away, likely because it was well after the lunch rush. Finn released her hand before sliding into one side, muttering something about déjà vu, but he didn't explain, and she didn't ask. The hostess placed a basket of chips and two containers of salsa on the table, then headed back to her stand at the front of the restaurant.

Adalia took the seat across from him and set her purse down next to her.

"What the hell happened back there?" Finn asked, running a hand through his hair. He had nice curls now that it had grown longer, the kind she would have liked to paint if asking him wouldn't have stoked his ego.

If she was ever going to paint or sculpt or screen-print again.

"Which part?" she asked, flagging down a passing waiter. "We're gonna need a pitcher of margaritas." She turned to Finn. "Anything for you?" Then she hastily added, "Just kidding…maybe."

"The pitcher and two glasses," Finn said, looking up at the waiter. "There's a bonus twenty-dollar tip if you can get it here in less than five minutes."

The young waiter practically sprinted to the bar.

"Frozen!" she called after him.

"Back to what happened at the psychic's," Finn said, leaning his forearms on the table. "Did Dottie send you there so we'd run into one another? Is this one of her elaborate schemes?"

"Trust me. I considered it. But this wasn't her doing unless she hypnotized me," she said, giving it another moment of consideration before dismissing it. Dottie *was* capable of many things, but it would have taken a master of manipulation to pull something like that off. "It was just like Lola said. I was a walk-in. After Georgie talked about having me committed, I took off and started walking around. That's when I saw her storefront." She tilted her head. "Does a psychic have a storefront or an office?"

He leaned even closer, his eyes wide. "I was wondering the same thing, but go back to the part about Georgie having you committed. Are you kidding me?"

He seemed outraged on her behalf, which felt kind of nice, but she couldn't let him think that of her sister. "Okay, no," she said with a sigh. "Not committed. But she and River want to pay for me to see a psychologist." She started to drum her fingers on the table, trying to expel some of her pent-up nervous energy. "Do you think seeing Lola counts? Psychic. Psychologist. They're practically spelled the same. There's just a lot of extra letters after the C-H in psychologist. Plus, you saw her space."

He reached over and covered her hand with his, applying pressure when she tried to pull away. "Adalia. Take a breath. Just breathe."

If any other man had tried to tell her that, there was a good chance she would have slapped him, but for some reason she didn't understand, Finn's touch grounded her again. It stopped her from spinning out of control.

He looked just as surprised as she was that she hadn't decked him. She liked that he'd been willing to roll the dice.

The waiter appeared next to the table with a sloshing pitcher and two margarita glasses. "Four minutes and three seconds."

Finn removed his hand from hers and pulled out his wallet, then handed the waiter a twenty-dollar bill. "A deal's a deal."

The waiter picked up the money and headed back to the kitchen, licking spilled margarita off the back of his hand.

"Did he just do what I think he did?" Adalia asked, turning at her waist to watch him walk away.

"Waste not want not," Finn said, pouring a frozen margarita into one of the glasses and handing it to her before filling his own glass. "So Georgie and River want you to see a therapist.… How do you feel about that?"

"I'm sure it's a good idea for some people, but I have my own way of dealing with things."

He gave her a lopsided grin. "I can see that."

She smacked his hand on the table. "If therapists are so great, then why aren't *you* going to one?"

"I tried one a month or so ago, and let's just say it wasn't a good fit."

"So you went to a psychic instead?"

"That was Dottie's doing." He narrowed his eyes at her. "Did Lola really pull the same cards for you?"

"Right down to the skull and crossbones and the card with the guy lying on the ground with a bunch of swords sticking out of him. Who knew tarot cards were so morbid? But at least she told me the death card didn't mean I was going to bite it. She said it signified the end of something or some major change in my life." She gave him a tight grin. "At least you already know what yours is—selling your brewery." Her smile faded and a heaviness filled her chest. "Mine…"

The thought of giving up her art stole her breath. Could she do it?

"No, Adalia," he said, his eyes burning with an intensity that made them look greener than blue. "Not that."

She took a generous sip of margarita and he took a drink too, eyeing her as though he was trying to read her.

"Maybe it was about leaving New York. You've started a new life too."

She shrugged.

"I really am sorry about telling River," he said. She could tell he didn't feel comfortable talking about it, yet there was a determination in his eyes that told her he felt the need to apologize properly.

She shrugged again. "I guess they were going to find out at some point." Then, before he could prod her about possibly giving up her art, she said, "So, about your charity art show…"

"River and I discussed it last night, and I guess he talked to Georgie. Buchanan's going to host the first one."

Georgie hadn't mentioned that. She'd gone straight to the matter of Dottie's garage.

"Did you pick a charity?" she asked, keeping her eyes on the chip basket as she reached for one.

"Yeah," he said, sitting up a little. "My friend Maisie's animal rescue. One of her big donors flaked on her, and they need the money."

"The one River's known since he was like thirteen?" she asked, then gave him a knowing grin. "Good choice. Hard for

River to say no when you're raising money for his childhood friend and puppies."

"It wasn't like that, Adalia," he said defensively.

She gave him a knowing look. "But it kind of was." When he didn't say anything, she said, "It's a compliment, Finn."

"Is it, though?"

Lifting her glass, she said, "To knowing what you want and going for it."

"I'm not sure I should drink to that," he said, but the corners of his lips twitched, like he wanted to smile, and he clicked his glass into hers. She drained her margarita, then put the glass on the table with a thud. "Hit me."

He refilled the glass as a waitress walked over. The woman gave Finn an odd look, like maybe she recognized him, and said, "Oh, you already have drinks."

"Friends in low places," Adalia said. "Do you have shrimp tacos?"

"Yeah, but I can bring you a menu…"

"Not necessary. Just bring me that," Adalia said, challenging Finn with a raised eyebrow. "Live on the wild side with me."

He rolled his eyes, but that smile was finally escaping. "Bring me the special of the day."

"Do you want me to tell you what it is?" the waitress asked in confusion.

"Nope," he said, grinning at Adalia.

"Okay…," she said as she walked away.

"Look at you, Finn Hamilton," Adalia said appreciatively as she sipped more of her drink. The tequila was already making her head fuzzy, but she didn't care. Her plan was to get shit-faced. "I'll help you with your charity thing."

His eyes brightened with excitement. "You will?"

She held up her hand. "Yeah, but not how you think. I'll help you pick the artists and set things up the night of the event, but I won't be displaying any of my own art."

Disappointment flickered in his eyes, but it was gone just as quickly. "I'd be grateful for any help you're willing to give. Dottie has made a bunch of suggestions, some of them great, but we both know her taste runs on the eccentric side."

Adalia grinned. "I love that woman, but agreed." She finished off her margarita and shook her empty glass. "Again."

Finn gave her a long look, but just as she was starting to wonder if he was about to get all withholding on her, he refilled her glass. "How are you not getting brain freeze?"

Her body felt deliciously warm, now that he mentioned it. "It's one of my many talents. Tell me more about yourself, Finn Hamilton."

He hesitated, studying her. "What do you want to know that you don't already?"

"First of all, how is a cute guy like you still single?"

His face flushed. "Just what every man wants to hear, a beautiful woman calling him cute like he's a purse dog."

"You are the furthest thing from a lap dog," she teased, letting herself take a good look at him.

Funny, she'd never given him much consideration as a potential love interest, maybe because the very first time they'd met, she'd thought him a prowler, and as soon as that impression had faded, he'd gone and broken up Georgie and River. But looking at him now…how had she not noticed how he filled out that button-down shirt? Or how observant his gorgeous eyes were? Or how beautiful those curls were now that they'd grown a bit? Her fingers were itching to touch them. And his lips… Finn had lips that looked soft yet firm, and she suddenly wondered what it would be like if he kissed her.

Where had *that* come from?

Lola. She'd done this. She'd insinuated the idea of Finn in her head, and now she was thinking crazy thoughts.

She needed to change the subject, yet she couldn't help asking, "Why don't you have a girlfriend?"

He looked her straight in the eyes. "Maybe I'm just waiting for the right woman."

Now it was her turn to blush, and she took another sip before changing the topic. They talked a little about his time at Duke and hers at the Lanier School of Fine Art. The waitress brought their food and Finn made a face when he realized the special was chili rellenos, so Adalia gave him one of her tacos and ordered nachos and another pitcher of margaritas.

Finn looked like he was about to stop her, but he must have thought better of it.

She'd always taken him for a smart man.

The nachos came out around the same time the new pitcher arrived, and Adalia giggled as she poured some into her glass, spilling a little on the table.

"Why'd you move to Asheville?" Finn asked quietly.

She held up a finger, waggling it back and forth. "I'm not drunk enough yet to tell you that."

"Then why did you go see Lola?"

"I told you already."

"But did you?"

She grabbed a chip from the nacho pile. "Lola told me that something from my past would come back to haunt me. Since we had the same cards, it must be true for you too. Do you know what that could be?"

He pursed his lips. "I guess it could be a number of things. The Duke mess. My parents' money. My decision to sell Big Catch. What about you?"

She narrowed her eyes, wondering if she should tell him. Part of her couldn't believe she was considering it, but the whole psychic experience had created an unexpected bond. Grabbing her phone out of her purse, she unlocked it and pushed it across the table.

Hesitating, he picked it up, his eyes darkening when he saw the unread text on the screen.

"Who's Alan?" he said, handing back the phone.

Was that jealousy she heard in his voice? No, that had to be the margaritas talking. Finn hardly knew her and knew nothing about Alan. "My former mentor."

His jaw set, hinting at a side of Finn she hadn't seen before. "A mentor who calls his protégé *baby*?"

She nibbled on a chip.

"What's he so eager to talk about?"

"Beats me," she said. "Surely he knows I'm smart enough not to let him use me again, but he won't leave me alone."

"What do you mean, use you again?"

When she didn't answer him, he set down his fork slowly, as if working to control a burgeoning anger.

"Adalia. What did he do?"

He wasn't angry at her, she knew. It was a protective anger.

So she relented, and told him everything, even more than she'd told Georgie. "He was one of my art school professors. I wasn't even sure he knew who I was, but then he dropped by this small show I had last year. He seemed impressed and introduced himself. I reminded him that I'd been in a couple of his classes. He played it off like he really did remember me, but I wasn't so sure. It didn't matter. He was this amazing artist, one of the most sought-after professors, and he was interested in *my* work. I was awestruck. He asked if I had any more pieces he could see."

Finn watched her with dark eyes, making her feel self-conscious, and she vaguely wondered if he was mad at her, but then he reached across the table, covering her hand with his own.

"So you let him see your work?" he asked, prodding her to continue.

Was he remembering what he'd seen in Dottie's garage? Somehow she knew he was.

She nodded. "I had a small studio space I was renting with a few other artists, and he started coming by once a week or so to look at what I was working on and give me advice. After a couple of months, he suggested I work in his studio. My mixed media pieces are—were—fairly large, and I didn't have much room in my existing space. I was thrilled. He rented part of a warehouse and the light was great. He seemed excited to have me there, and I basked in his attention. It was no surprise when he kissed me." She paused. "I'll admit that I had a crush on him, but I never suspected he was interested in me. Not like that. Plus, he was letting me use his studio space for free."

Finn's hand tightened over hers. "Did he take advantage of you, Adalia?"

She glanced up at him, surprised at the concern on his face. "I wasn't some underage fool."

His eyes darkened. "That doesn't answer my question, does it?"

"No," she said with a sigh. "It was consensual. We started sleeping together, and although I didn't move out of my apartment, I spent most of my time at Alan's. But then my pieces started disappearing. Alan said the studio was running out of room and he was having them moved to storage. Around that time, he started treating me differently, making me feel like I was stupid. That his opinion mattered more than mine did. I broke up with him, but he chased me, showering me with gifts and attention, and convinced me to take him back. He promised things would change. And they did for a bit, but then they got worse. He started insulting my work, telling me I was a hack and that I'd be nothing without him. He alienated me from my friends. I told my brother Lee what was going on, and he offered to help me, but only if I agreed to leave Alan. Around that time, Alan told me that he was having a show, but I'd hardly seen him work on any pieces, and the ones I had seen were honestly not worthy of a show at Michael Roe."

She picked up her glass and finished it off, her head swimming, but everything else felt numb. It occurred to her that she'd purposely gotten this drunk so she'd find the courage to tell him the truth. So that he'd understand why she'd destroyed that piece and why she couldn't, no matter how much she wanted to, create anything for his show. She'd done it so she wouldn't fall to pieces when she explained how Alan had stolen her soul.

"What happened?" he asked so quietly she could hardly hear him.

"He wouldn't let me watch him set up for the show, which was weird. He told me that he was being superstitious, that he was afraid I'd jinx it, but things weren't adding up. I dropped by the gallery the night before the exhibit opened, and then I realized why he hadn't wanted me to come—they were all my pieces. Every last one of them. He'd stolen my work and put his name on it."

"Adalia," he gasped.

She ignored him. "I was so *furious*. Furious with him for gaslighting me and stealing my art all while tearing me down and making me question my talent, but I was even angrier with myself for letting him get away with it. He used me in every way imaginable, but most of all, he stole the deepest part of me and claimed it as his own. I lost it. I found a couple of gallons of paint in the back and started tossing it on the pieces—every last one of them. Someone at the gallery called the police, and I was arrested for felony vandalism. Alan had shown up by then. I guess someone had called him too, and he stood by and just let them put me in cuffs."

Finn didn't say a word, but Adalia could see the fury in his eyes.

"I called Georgie, and she and River arranged to have me released on bail. After I got out, I packed up as much of my stuff as I could fit into a few suitcases, then hopped on a flight to Asheville." She grinned. "That was the night I threw a crystal at you and bruised your pretty face."

He didn't grin back like she'd expected him too. Instead, he looked like he was about to murder someone.

"And now you destroy your art before anyone else can steal the innermost part of you," he said, holding her gaze.

Even drunk, she knew that he could see deep into her soul, much deeper than Alan had ever cared to look.

He cleared his throat. "He dared to send this text after he had you arrested? What happened to the charges?"

"Georgie convinced him to drop them. She made him realize it was in his best interest to make this go away." She finished off her glass. "She can be very persuasive when she wants to be."

He nodded slightly. "Trust me, I know."

Adalia was sure he did.

"This isn't the first time he's tried to get in touch either. He's been doing this for weeks."

"Do you want to talk to him?"

Apparently, she wasn't drunk enough to dull the pain, because tears stung her eyes. "No. I never want to hear from him again."

Finn didn't ask why she hadn't blocked Alan's number. Instead, he got out of his seat and slid in next to her. Without a word, he wrapped an arm around her back and snuggled her into his side, letting her cheek rest on his chest.

They sat like that for longer than Adalia would have expected, Finn holding her while letting her just be. Part of her wanted to tease him for not talking, but the rest of her was too afraid to ruin the moment. Somehow he had known exactly what she needed.

And *that* was a dangerous thing indeed.

CHAPTER Twelve

I think it means you're meant for each other, Lola had said. And damn if Finn hadn't found himself thinking back to that teacup Dottie had taken such an interest in yesterday. Was this what she'd seen?

Running into Adalia at the coffee shop yesterday and outside Lola's shop today…it felt like it meant something. And the fact that she'd chosen the exact same restaurant he'd gone to with River last night? That only added to the feeling of weirdness. The feeling of fate tugging at him.

Because, if he was being honest with himself, he didn't just have a casual interest in Adalia Buchanan. Nor was he on some martyr's mission to convince her to embrace her art. He was *interested* in her. Enthralled by her, in a way he couldn't remember feeling before. And Finn had dated a lot of women. But he'd never thought about any of them the way he did Adalia.

Didn't matter. That Alan asshole had hurt Adalia in a deep way. It was going to take her time to bounce back, and to his surprise, he cared more about her bouncing back than he did about having her in the show. More than he did about giving in to the consuming desire to touch her curls. To kiss her. He longed to tell her that she was somebody of worth—deep worth—whether or not she ever made another piece of art. But he wanted to encourage her to express herself anyway, because it was clearly part of who she was, even if she chose not to show it. Even if she felt compelled to destroy it.

Maybe Adalia thought he was the kind of man who took what he wanted, whatever it cost, but that wasn't totally true. Other people mattered to him. He couldn't be happy if he raked in a big prize at the expense of someone he cared about. This whole Big Catch situation had taught him that, if nothing else.

"Let's get out of here," he said softly, still holding Adalia.

"But we didn't finish the margaritas," she objected, slurring her words slightly.

"I think it's time for me to get you home," he said.

"No," she said, pulling away. "I don't want Jack to see me like this."

"It's only three o'clock. Jack's probably still at work," he said wryly. "I can sneak you up to your room, and he'll be none the wiser."

Of course, Jack might have chosen to stay home after finishing their little project earlier, and he probably wouldn't be grateful that Finn had helped her get soused.

There was also the logistical problem of getting there. He wasn't confident he could get her to walk that far, and while he wasn't as drunk as she was, he was in no condition to drive.

"Let's just stay here," she said.

It was tempting. He didn't want to let go of her. He didn't want her to snap out of it and remember that he was the bigmouth who'd spilled her secret. That he was someone unworthy of her trust.

But her eyes were fluttering in a way that suggested she probably wouldn't be awake for much longer, plus the waitress was already giving him looks that indicated she thought he was a weirdo for coming back for lunch eighteen hours after he'd left for dinner. If his companion fell asleep in the booth, she'd probably assume he was angling to move in.

So he called the person who'd always been there for him, with the exception of those several weeks after he'd screwed everything up.

By the time River showed up, Finn had paid the bill, and Adalia was snoozing against his shoulder. The waitress's eyes bugged out a bit when she saw River had returned too.

"I'm glad y'all like our food so much," she said, "but we're closing for the two hours between lunch and dinner. Maybe you can come back for dinner service?" The suggestion seemed to pain her.

"I'm just here to get them," River said, gesturing to Finn and Adalia. He didn't look as pissed as Finn had feared, but he didn't seem exactly pleased either.

"Okay," the waitress said, her tone indicating she still had plenty of questions that she'd happily keep to herself so long as they left.

"I told Jack to distract Georgie," River said. "She's intent on cheering Addy up, and if she sees her like this…"

"She'll assume the worst," Finn agreed. "But I think this was what Adalia needed, in a weird way. She told me why she's been tearing up her art."

"You know about the arrest?" River asked, surprised.

Finn just nodded, because he didn't want to risk telling him anything he didn't already know. He felt protective of what Adalia had shared, enough so that he didn't feel the usual compulsion to let the information leak out of him like he was a faulty balloon.

"She hasn't even told Jack or their other brother, Lee," River commented, and Finn felt a warm glow inside of him. Despite everything, she'd chosen *him* to trust. Him to tell. He couldn't betray that. He wouldn't.

"Well, let's get her home," River said. "Dottie already left for their house to fix her a hangover cure."

"Don't you need to stop being drunk to be hung over?" Finn asked.

A corner of River's mouth kicked up. "I guess we're about to find out."

River offered to help carry Adalia out to the car, but Finn shook his head and cradled her in his arms. She only stirred once, but she didn't say anything, just made a satisfied sound, like a cat in a patch of sunlight, and settled in deeper. It was like he was her safe place, and he felt the glow inside of him grow a little bigger and brighter. They laid her out in the back seat, securing the middle belt around her, and River set off at a slow speed, careful not to jolt her.

"So," River said after a while. "You finally went to see Dottie's psychic, huh?"

Finn might have overexplained a little in his (multiple) texts, telling River about the random run-in with Adalia, her decision to sit in on his reading, and the fact that the reading had driven them both to drink.

"Do you know her?"

"No, but Dottie's mentioned her about a hundred times." He shot a quick smirk at Finn. "She met her in line at the DMV."

"Of course she did."

Silence hung between them for a beat. Then River said, "So what did you think?"

"She wasn't like I'd expected. I figured since she was one of Dottie's people she'd be more…"

"Loud? Eccentric?"

"Those two words did come to mind." He paused, trying to put the experience into words. "But it wasn't like some vaudeville fortune-telling tent."

"Oh, you mean like the one I ran?" River asked, huffing a laugh.

At the last Buchanan staff party, River had found himself running the fortune-telling tent for a while as part of a ploy to romance Georgie. It was mentioned at least once a day in Buchanan Brewery, or so Dottie said, and Finn had heard the story multiple times. He always felt a little stab of guilt, knowing he was the only reason River and Georgie had been on the outs. Well, him and Beau, who'd written what had to be the strangest will in the history of Asheville.

"I'm still sorry I missed that," he said. "But yeah, I guess it surprised me how legit this felt. I mean, it was practically a doctor's office. Not a scarf or crystal ball in sight. I almost believed her."

"Who's to say?" River said with a shrug. "I give Dottie a hard time, but you know she's right as often as she's wrong when it comes to the mystical stuff." He was quiet for a second, as if weighing something. Then he said, "I don't want to come off all big brotherish, but what are your intentions toward Adalia? I don't need to be an actual psychic to tell there's something going on with you two."

He couldn't blame River for asking. He'd been Finn's wingman dozens of times, and vice versa.

"I don't know," he said honestly. "I care about her, though. I want to be there for her."

"Good," River said, "because she needs a friend like you."

That statement of trust from River meant the world to him, and he would have said so if River hadn't pulled into the driveway of Beau's old house just then.

Jack and Dottie were sitting on the front porch, talking.

"What happened to stalling Georgie?" Finn wondered out loud.

"Guess we'll find out. The fact that she's not here means he must have met with some measure of success." River shook his head slightly. "Looks like my aunt's gotten to Jack too. I wondered how long it would take."

"What do you mean?" Finn asked.

"Let's just say he's been one of the holdouts when it comes to Aunt Dottie. I was starting to think he was afraid of her."

"Well, to be fair, I was afraid of her the first time we met."

Dottie had just been so unlike everyone he knew. So much louder. So much *brighter*. At first he'd suspected being eccentric was some kind of game to her, but then he'd gotten to know her, and it had become clear that she was one of the few people who never tried to dissemble or pretend. Dottie didn't put any thought into trying to please the people she met. All of her concentration was poured into existing, and into helping the people around her achieve what was so effortless for her.

"I still am afraid of her," River quipped, popping his door. "Let's get Sleeping Beauty."

Finn wanted to carry her again—he ached to—but Jack beat him to it, hopping down the porch and hurrying down the hill toward them. He gathered Adalia up in his arms in a way that made it obvious Finn wasn't the only new person in her life who cared about her.

"What happened with Georgie?" River asked.

"Turned out I didn't need to do anything," Jack said. "The new bottling machine is acting up, and she's been handling damage control. It was manufactured in Europe, and it's after hours for all of the call centers. Last I heard, she'd been on hold listening to 'Greensleeves' for over an hour."

"So she'll come home in a good mood then," River commented.

Jack huffed a laugh, but then his gaze shot to Finn, standing helplessly at the side of the car. For a moment, Finn worried the camaraderie they'd achieved this morning would slip away. That Jack would go all big brother again and tell him to leave.

"Let's hope Dottie's cure works," Jack said simply. Then he carried her up to the porch, Adalia stirring as he climbed the steps.

"Jacky! My brother!" she crooned, throwing a sloppy arm around his neck. "You're the one who likes me."

Except Lee liked her too, Finn was fairly certain. And if he could help her heal whatever had happened between them, he would. River was right. She needed friends right now, all of the good ones she could get.

"I sure do," Jack said, "but you're not going to like me after I make you drink this."

Finn and River followed him up the stairs as he set Adalia on the chair he'd just vacated. Dottie grinned at them from her seat, not in the least bit perturbed by the situation. Sure

126

enough, there was a glass cup on the little table between the chairs, its contents a somewhat alarming shade of red.

Jack handed it to Adalia, who gave the contents a big sniff and cringed. "Is that…fish?"

"No, dear," Dottie answered. "With your brother's permission, I've set up a few sardine traps to lure our girl home."

Our girl being Jezebel. A quick glance revealed there were indeed open tins of sardines on either side of the porch. Huh. Jack might have taken a while to come around to Dottie, but he'd already gone to extremes to please her.

Jack shrugged self-consciously. "I don't mind the cat. Besides, she's our mascot for the sours. We need her."

"My brother, the cat whisperer, ladies and gentlemen," Adalia shouted.

A woman on the porch of the house next door flinched upon hearing the word "cat" and hurried inside.

"Adalia, you'd better drink that," Finn said, putting a hand on her shoulder.

He hadn't meant anything by the casual touch…or maybe he had. Either way, Dottie's eyes instantly fixed on it.

"I take it your visit to Lola went well?" she asked.

"She basically told us we're soul mates, so it went swimmingly. Swimmmmingly," Adalia said, grinning.

River shot a look at him, and Finn realized he'd never told him what, exactly, Lola had said. Only that it had seemed legit.

Which meant River now knew Finn considered it possible that he and Adalia were meant for each other. He was surprisingly okay with that. At least his friend knew he was serious.

"Oh, that's not news to me," Dottie said, sweeping the air in a dismissive gesture. "Now, down the hatch, as they say."

Adalia scrunched up her nose and gulped the red drink down.

"Is that the one I've had?" Finn asked Dottie in an undertone. The memory made him shudder. Tomato juice, a raw egg, and other "secret" ingredients Dottie had refused to divulge.

"With a twist," she said.

"Dear God," Adalia said, putting the glass down with a resounding click. "Is it supposed to cure me by making me puke?"

"No, but it is sometimes an unintended consequence," Dottie said.

Adalia hung her head between her legs for a few seconds, but then she sat back up, and her eyes already looked a little clearer.

"Can someone please get me a Sprite or something? Pronto? I might actually die if that taste stays in my mouth."

"Coming right up," Jack said, disappearing inside.

Except several minutes passed without any sign of him, and Adalia seemed like she was in legitimate pain.

"I can go check on him," Finn offered, after what seemed like Adalia's sixth groan.

"It's an eighteen-hundred-square-foot house," she said. "I doubt he's lost. But yes, please God. My kingdom for a Sprite."

He knocked a couple of times before walking in, figuring it was the least he could do given it wasn't his house, and made his way into the kitchen. He could see Jack through the plate glass door, an unopened can of Sprite in his hand, his cell phone pressed to his ear as he leaned against a support post.

He had an intense look on his face, nothing like the relaxed guy who'd been chilling on the porch with Dottie.

It didn't look like he was going anywhere in a hurry, so Finn continued on to the fridge and grabbed another can of soda. But before he could turn back, he heard Jack say, "I wish you were here with me now." A pause, then he added, "I know you wanted this. And so do I, but a few months feels like a long time right now… I don't trust her."

The words were a bit muffled, but someone had left a window open, and the screen didn't block noise.

He exited as discreetly and quietly as he could, Sprite in hand, feeling the weight of knowing one more thing he probably wasn't supposed to tell anyone. For someone who wasn't much good at keeping secrets, Finn had a hell of a knack for collecting them.

Jack Durand clearly had some sort of secret girlfriend he'd left back home. One he wasn't, for whatever reason, telling anyone about. And he'd also said he didn't trust someone, possibly someone here in Asheville.

But he needn't have worried about the compulsion to tell what he'd heard, because moments after he handed over the Sprite to Adalia, he heard a shriek from the neighbor's yard.

Jack called back to them, "Jezebel just leapt over the fence!"

"Look at that," Adalia commented after gulping down half the can of Sprite. "We didn't need the sardines after all."

She got up, looking a lot sturdier than she had any right to given the way she'd been mainlining tequila earlier, and started to circle around the house. Finn, River, and Dottie exchanged looks before they followed her.

They all knew what she was liable to find back there, but they had no idea how she'd react to it.

If only Finn had thought to ask Lola more questions, like whether he'd drawn the death card because Adalia was about to kill him for orchestrating this.

CHAPTER

Thirteen

Adalia had no idea what Dottie put in the nasty concoction, but the fuzziness in her head was clearing, and the events of the afternoon were rushing back in vivid and not-so-vivid detail.

The tarot reading—both of them—ordering her liquid lunch (had she eaten *any* of her tacos?), and then telling Finn about Alan. The last recollection brought a fresh round of shame. She'd decided to tell him, in the end, hence all of the tequila shots disguised with lime juice and sugar, but now...

What did he think of her?

She wasn't sure *why* she'd wanted him to know. She hadn't told anyone other than Georgie, and River by default. Lee was hardly speaking to her, mostly because he knew she was holding something back. Her explanation for her last-minute relocation—that she'd wanted to escape the Alan situation and, *hey, we have a brewery!*—hadn't convinced him. Maybe she should have been honest, forthright, but Lee was too much like their father. He wouldn't understand, and if he found out, he'd almost certainly tell Dear Old Dad.

Nope. Not opening herself up to that.

But why had she wanted to tell Finn? Because Lola had said they were tied together?

Adalia had never been a big believer in destiny. She refused to believe some unseen force was controlling her life. Because if it existed, it was a real dick for taking her mom from her. No, she'd opened up to Finn for a different reason. It was weird they'd had the same cards, but freaky coincidences happened every day.

She'd told him because of what he'd witnessed. He'd watched her wrench something out of her soul and attach it to a canvas, and sure, it had been an abstract, and most people would have just seen a bunch of red and yellow and blue paint on a white canvas, but the look in his eyes, the admiration and the empathy, proved that he hadn't been flattering her. Finn had seen so much more. Then she'd ripped it apart in front of him, and he'd been upset not because she'd destroyed something of monetary value, but because he knew she'd destroyed a piece of herself. The very fact he was horrified by that meant more than every word of praise Alan had ever heaped on her.

And that scared the crap out of her. If Alan could rip out her heart and bring her to the edge of despair, how much worse could Finn hurt her?

There was no doubt in her mind that Finn was interested in her. If the hand-holding hadn't clued her in, then there was the tender way he'd cradled her when he carried her to River's car, something she'd noticed even through her drunken haze. But Finn was a serial dater, and Adalia had no desire to become another notch on his bedpost.

A quick glance over her shoulder confirmed the others were following her into the back yard, which seemed odd. Then again, maybe not. Everyone with the exception of

Dottie was terrified of Jezebel. Apparently Adalia was their human shield. Or maybe they were hanging back in case she yakked Dottie's awful drink.

Jack was sitting on the bench, and Jezebel was beside him, rubbing her head against his chest.

"What the hell?" River said in surprise.

Jack lifted his hand to rub the cat's head, and Finn cried out, "I wouldn't do that!"

But Jack shot the group a confused look as he started to stroke her. "I don't understand why you all keep saying she's mean."

"Did you put catnip in those sardines?" Finn asked. "Or Xanax?"

"No, dear," Dottie said, clasping her hands in front of her as her face lit up with glee. "Adalia's right. He really *is* a cat whisperer." She said it with as much excitement as if she'd discovered he were a wizard. Although, to be fair, it would take a wizard to turn Jezebel into a normal cat.

Taking a tentative step toward the bench, Adalia reached out to pet Jezebel, but the cat arched her back and hissed, taking a swat at her. She pulled back just in time to keep from getting mauled.

"So we've now established that Jack belongs to Jezebel," she said, taking a step back, which was when she noticed everyone was watching her. Narrowing her eyes, she scanned River's and Dottie's faces before landing on Finn's. The man couldn't keep a secret to save his soul, and the fact that he was keeping one now was written all over his face.

"What are you all hiding?" she asked, propping a hand on her hip.

"Maybe we should go inside," Dottie said. "I forgot to mention that sometimes one should stay close to a toilet after drinking my elixir."

"I can throw up outside," Adalia protested, her stomach already churning from the power of suggestion. She should probably try to eat something soon.

Dottie made a sour face. "Oh no, dear. Not *that* end."

"What?" Finn asked in alarm. "You didn't mention that when you practically forced me to drink it a few months ago."

"That's because you got the hangover version," Dottie said, gracing Finn with a warm smile. "Addy got my special batch."

"Dottie's right," Jack said as he scooped up Jezebel and cradled her to his chest. "You should go inside and lie down."

"And maybe we should burn you at the stake," she said, keeping her gaze on Jezebel. She had never seen that cat so docile. Not even when Georgie had given her a double dose of sedatives a month ago before taking her to the vet for her shots. Apparently, she'd revived enough to take a parting swat at the vet tech.

"Don't be silly," Dottie said. "They haven't burned witches for years. People are much more tolerant now."

Adalia whipped her head around to determine if the older woman was joking, but a wave of dizziness washed through her. She stumbled, and Finn was instantly there next to her, grabbing her arm and holding her steady so she didn't fall.

"I agree with Jack," River said, but his answer sounded forced. "Georgie should be here soon. Why don't you rest until she gets home? Maybe Aunt Dottie can make you another cure if you're still feeling off."

"Don't be silly, dear," Dottie said. "It only takes one. If I give her another…" She shook her head. "Let's just say the last girl who drank two of them couldn't get anyone to wax her chest hair."

"What?" Adalia screeched, glancing down at her chest.

"You don't have any chest hair," Finn said. "I promise."

"What are you doing looking at her chest?" Jack asked in a guarded tone. "And why was she so drunk anyway?"

"Here's a better question that might actually be your business," Adalia said in a dry tone. "Why is Georgie coming home early?" She narrowed her eyes even more. "And why are you here, Jack? Shouldn't you and Dottie be at work?"

The three guys were staring at her like she was a cobra about ready to pounce, but Dottie was humming as she held up her hand and examined her nail beds.

"What's going on?" Adalia asked, starting to get nervous. Maybe she hadn't been that far off when she'd told Finn that Georgie was having her committed. Maybe this was some kind of an intervention. She honestly wouldn't put it past her sister to stage an intervention, and River was probably too scared to tell his girlfriend no. Jack, he was still too new to protest, plus he knew Georgie controlled the brewery purse strings, and Dottie…well, Dottie would gleefully attend an intervention and likely pass out weed-filled brownies for refreshment.

There was no way she was sticking around for that.

Her body stiffened as it prepared for flight, but Finn's hand found hers and squeezed.

"River," he said, but it held the hint of a question in it.

River's eyes began to soften.

"No," Jack said. "I say we go inside. Georgie will be home soon."

Adalia looked up at Finn. "What's going on? Just tell me."

She nearly accused him of helping the others set her up, but his gaze was full of warmth and reassurance.

He gave her a soft smile that made her stomach do a little flip that she was pretty sure didn't have anything to do with Dottie's cure. "We have something to show you."

But they were all acting so hesitant that she feared it might not be anything good.

"Finn," Jack snapped. "We need to wait for Georgie."

"No," Finn said, his smile unwavering. "We need to make sure Adalia doesn't feel like she's about to be attacked." They were still hand in hand, and he pulled her around the bench and the tree behind it, guiding her toward a wooden shed at the back of the property.

"You gonna lock me in the shed?" she half teased, getting even more nervous, but Finn's thumb stroked the top of her hand, calming her enough to keep her next to him.

"No," he said, glancing down at her. "You're in charge, Addy."

The rest of the group had followed them over. While Jack still seemed a little pissed, or at least out of sorts, River had apparently come around. He walked over to the shed door and took hold of the handle. "Addy, we know that you haven't had a space at home to work on your art. You shouldn't have to drive across town to do what you love. So Jack, Finn, and I set this up for you."

He opened the door, revealing that all the junk it had previously contained had been cleared out. The built-in back shelves, which had sported rusty tools, were now covered with blank canvases and multiple coffee cans with paintbrushes. There was a small plastic container full of tubes of paint, and wooden and plastic artist's palettes. An easel was propped up against the wall.

There hadn't been any lighting in the shed, but now a string of outdoor lights had been strung around the ceiling and River walked in and plugged it into an extension cord. The lights burst to life, making the room bright and cheery, despite the fact that it only had two small windows, one on either side.

"Dottie said light was important," Jack said, having joined them at the corner of the shed.

"If it's not enough," Finn said, "we can add more."

She shot him a look of surprise. "You helped with this?"

"It was his idea," River said. "What do you think?"

Adalia couldn't help noticing that Dottie had been surprisingly quiet through all of this. She must have helped them figure out what supplies to get, especially since everything was brand new. The shed rehab must have cost hundreds of dollars. River was running short on funds, and Jack was borrowing from his savings until Buchanan was in the black, refusing to take a salary since Georgie was funding everything. Who had paid for it?

"Oh!" Georgie shouted behind her, and Adalia turned to see her running through the side gate. "You showed her without me. I haven't even gotten dinner started yet."

"Adalia knew something was up," Finn called out to her, as if that were explanation enough.

"Is this when you have me committed?" Adalia asked, nervous to face her sister after she'd blown up on her earlier. Again.

"What?" Georgie asked. "No! Why would you say that? After Finn told River about…you know, they decided to create a studio for you."

"But you helped," Adalia said.

"Nope, this was all them. I was stuck at work all day. Some nightmare with the machinery."

"But you paid for…" Her voice trailed off as the truth hit her, and she glanced up at Finn.

He cringed. "Before you cover me with paint, just listen, okay?"

Tears filled her eyes, and she tugged her hand free, then wrapped her arms around his neck, burying her face in his chest. "Thank you."

Before he could respond, she pulled free and turned to face them all. "This means more to me than you know."

"Do you want to get started on something?" Georgie asked, motioning to the open door. "Or go in and look around? I know you want your privacy, so we'll all leave you alone. You can do…whatever you need to do. I'm making you homemade mac and cheese and fish sticks."

"Fish sticks?"

Georgie gave her a sheepish look. "It was your favorite when we were kids. So do you want us to give you some time out here?"

Adalia shook her head. "No, this is enough for now."

They'd gone to so much effort to put this together and give her a space of her own. Their generosity, their wish to help her, it meant so much to her. But even if she gave in to her urges and let herself create, she wouldn't do it here. It made her feel like a bitch given all the effort and money they'd poured into it, but she felt absolutely no draw to this space.

Maybe she would never create again.

Georgie gave her a curious look, and Adalia walked over and gave her a hug. "Thank you."

"Why do you smell like gas station burritos and tequila?"

Adalia laughed as she gave Georgie another squeeze. "It's a long story," she said, pulling free. "Let's go inside, and I'll help you turn on the oven."

"That part isn't hard," Georgie teased.

"Which is why I'm so good at it."

Adalia started to head for the back porch, but she spotted Finn making a beeline for the side gate. She rushed over and blocked his path.

"You're leaving?" she asked, surprised at the depth of her disappointment.

"Yeah," he said, running a hand through his hair. "I have a dinner to go to tonight."

"Oh." The way he'd said it was so vague, like he didn't want to say who he was meeting. Was it a woman?

She felt suddenly awkward and off-balance. "So about the art show…when do you want to get started with the planning?"

Something flickered in his eyes, and suddenly he seemed more guarded. "How about we meet for coffee on Saturday afternoon?"

"Not for margarita pitchers?" she teased. Then her face flushed. "Sorry if I embarrassed you. And I'm sorry if I got…out of hand."

He grinned. "You didn't." He swallowed and lowered his voice. "Thank you for trusting me with your secret. I swear I won't tell a soul. I mean that."

"Thanks."

He started to say something, then stopped, and she almost teased him that the man who could talk about anything now seemed tongue-tied. But he spoke first.

"You're not going to use it, are you?" he asked quietly.

Her pulse kicked up. Was he going to be pissed? But there was no anger or disappointment in his eyes, only understanding.

"I don't know," she answered honestly. "But you all went to so much trouble."

He slowly shook his head. "You have enough baggage with your art without adding any more to the mix, so no guilt, okay?" he said as he reached up and tucked a stray curl behind her ear. "This was about giving you options. You do what you need to do to make yourself feel whole, and to hell with everyone else, okay?"

Tears filled her eyes again. "It's not that easy, Finn."

"But it is," he said insistently. "Alan stole something from you, and you need to do whatever it takes to get it back, Addy." He gestured to the group of people watching them. "They all feel the same way. They'll understand." He gave her a sad smile. "Just like I understand we can only be friends." He leaned over and kissed her cheek before pushing open the gate.

Wait. What? Why could they only be friends?

"Finn," she called after him. "Didn't River bring you here?"

He held up his phone, giving her a cocky grin. "Uber."

It struck her that she'd spent the better part of the last week wishing Finn would go away, that he'd stop hounding her about her art. But now that she wanted him to stay, he was walking away from her.

CHAPTER
fourteen

Finn's father had gotten to the restaurant before him, because of course he had. His dad had once told him it was a power move—a way to keep the other person on their toes.

Too bad his father pulled the maneuver with family as much as he did with his business partners.

"There he is," his dad said, standing and offering his hand for a shake. If Finn's mom had been there, she would have hugged him, but this was a business trip, and even though she could technically travel with his father, she never had.

Oh, I have my bridge club and the gardening society, she'd say.

In reality, though, Finn thought his parents didn't much like each other. It almost felt like they'd had a role in mind and found the person to fit it. They coexisted without much fuss—he'd never heard any explosive fights between them, but he couldn't remember any signs of affection either. The most he'd ever seen was a quick peck on the lips.

That wasn't something Finn wanted, not ever. Some strategies that worked for business didn't work for life. Never would.

He found himself thinking of Adalia—of the look on her face when he'd told her that he knew they could only be friends. It had seemed almost regretful. Or did he just want to think that?

No, he was good at reading people. Most of the time. And if he was totally honest with himself, he'd partially said it to see how she'd react.

After a hearty handshake, he sat opposite his father. A waiter came around and asked for his drink order, and he requested water. It only partially had to do with the margaritas at lunch and at dinner last night. He wanted to keep his wits about him. He had the feeling his father was here to sell him on something, and Reed Hamilton was the kind of man who believed in a hard sell.

"How's Mom?" he asked, picking up a menu.

"Good, good," his dad said dismissively. "She sends her love."

"What are you up here for, anyway?"

"A client likes the golf courses. Has a thing for the mountains."

They made idle chitchat about the weather—the weather!—until the waiter came by to take their orders.

"You know, Son," his father said, finally ready to get down to brass tacks. "Your mother and I would like to see you move a little closer to home. I know you're not interested in investment banking, so I won't ask, but a friend of mine is funding a little start-up in Charlotte that might be of interest to you. Something to do with artificial intelligence and robotics. They have the talent, but they're looking for someone to see them through to market. I told him about what you did with Big Catch, despite knowing nothing about beer in the beginning, and he was impressed. I thought I'd at least pass on the information."

"What applications?" Finn asked. Because damn it, he hadn't expected him to drop something so *interesting*.

"They're going to improve upon those little robots people buy to clean the floors. Put together models to help out at home and whatnot. But it sounds like there'll be applications to other fields down the line. Healthcare. Transportation."

Before Finn knew it, their dinners had arrived, and he'd agreed to at least talk to the team. Not that it would go anywhere. Even if it was the opportunity of a lifetime, he wasn't interested in moving back to Charlotte. Nor did he want to accept yet another boost from his dad.

His thoughts drifted back to Adalia again, and it occurred to him that she wouldn't sit here, across from her father, and fail to mention the whole Duke thing. She probably would have started with that, thrown a bread roll at him like that guy on the street the other day, and taken off. The thought made him smile a little, and he felt the boost he needed to speak frankly.

"You know, Dad," he said, "you don't need to find me a job. And you didn't need to make that contribution to Duke either."

His father cocked his head. "I'm surprised that bothered you, Finn. It was a libelous article in a two-bit newspaper. And why *wouldn't* we have made a contribution? It was your top-choice business school."

Finn let his fork clatter down. "Yeah, I know. And now I'll never know if I got in because I deserved it or if you paved the way."

"What's gotten into you? This isn't like you."

"Well, maybe it should be. I'm going to be doing things a little differently from now on." With the show. With the Big Catch project. With whatever happened afterward.

An ache filled him at the thought, because the future was still so uncertain. Because he didn't know what was supposed to come next. These other things he'd found to cling to were just stopgap measures, weren't they? He needed a plan, damn it.

But Adalia flashed through his head again. Her bravery. Her spunk. And he felt a surge of confidence. He would figure it out, but this wasn't the answer. No more handouts. No more boosts.

Something flashed in his father's eyes. "This is about a woman, isn't it?"

"Yeah, I guess it kind of is," Finn said, grinning.

Finn got to the coffee shop before Adalia, and by the time she came in, he was sitting at a table in the corner with drinks for both of them.

She smiled when she saw him, and something soared in his chest. Her curls had been inadequately contained in a bun, and she was wearing a green shirt that brought out the green flecks in her eyes, along with a boho skirt that kept giving him little glimpses of her legs.

"That for me?" she asked as she got close.

"Yup. A caramel latte, what you got last time."

"The presumption!" she scoffed. "What if today's more of a salted marshmallow, double-foam macchiato kind of day?"

"You made that up on the spot," he accused.

She shrugged and took a sip of the latte, settling in the chair next to him rather than the one across from him.

"Despite your endless optimism for my prospects, art usually doesn't pay the bills. I've worked as a barista, among other things. You'd be shocked by what people order."

"Among other things? Is this where you tell me that you wore one of those giant hot dog suits?"

"Mind in the gutter?" she asked, raising an eyebrow.

He flushed, just a little, and she flashed a victorious grin.

"Point to you," he said. He nodded down at his notebook. "Want to get started?"

"Sure…" She paused. "I'll be honest, I don't know much about the management side of things, so I figured I could mostly help you choose the artists and what to display."

"Sounds good to me," he said. "I was actually hoping you'd be willing to visit a few artists' studios with me after this. I kind of, sort of made a few appointments."

"There's the Finn I know," she said with a wink. "Strong-arming me into it."

She didn't say it like it was a bad thing, but it made him think again of the studio they'd set up—the one that hadn't been right for her.

"I didn't mean to," he said, honestly. "I can go without you if you have plans."

"I know. I want to go with you."

She said it in a way that told him she was more interested in his company than in the outing, per se, and he felt that now-familiar glow inside of him.

"Good." He paused, fidgeting with his pen. "You know, you inspired me to talk to my dad last night…about the whole Duke thing."

"Oh yeah?" she asked, her eyes sparkling. "I'll bet that pissed him off."

He grinned at her. "It did. Especially when I told him the main thing I'm working on right now is a charity art show. He thinks I've gone nuts."

Even more so because he'd admitted it was tied to a woman. He hadn't given his father any details about Adalia, but his dad had seemed flustered by the whole thing. He'd reminded Finn that there were plenty of women in Charlotte too, which Finn had acknowledged, saying the census had estimated the city was over fifty percent female.

"And have you?" she asked, playing a little with the edge of the notebook, her fingers brushing against his hand, the points of contact sending sparks through him.

"Maybe." He gave in to the temptation to take her hand, noticing, as he had before, that despite her skin's softness she had a few calluses, a couple of scars. Artist's hands. He made himself release it after giving it a squeeze. "But I think I kind of like it."

"What are you going to call this art show, anyway? Shouldn't we come up with some sort of name? 'Charity art show' might be accurate, but it doesn't really paint a picture."

"How about Finn Hamilton's Art Extravaganza?" he suggested, struggling to keep a straight face.

She tilted her head. "Or Finn's Not a Jerk, Here's Proof?"

"Ha. Ha. Very funny. How about the Asheville Art Display?"

"Simple but to the point. I like it."

The first appointment he'd made was at three o'clock, so they spent fifteen minutes or so talking about the various arrangements Finn had already made for the show, and then another twenty playing a game of 'Who are you?', although he made Adalia laugh so hard at his story about Bernard, whose wife had left him for a one-legged trapeze artist, that the barista asked them to quiet down.

"You know," Adalia said in a dramatic whisper, "I gave names to a couple in Buchanan the other day, and I was right about the woman. Her name really was Fiona."

"Get out."

"No, this totally happened." She took out her phone and tapped into her Instagram app before handing it over.

But the woman's name wasn't what he focused on. The photos all had a warm glow, a hominess that perfectly channeled Buchanan Brewery. River had always said it felt like a grandparent's basement, but then again, River had Dottie in his life. Finn had never seen his grandmother's basement, and she would have been affronted if he'd asked. To him, Beau's brewery had just felt like a place where he was welcome, a place where there were no expectations. (Admittedly, Beau had gone a little too far with the no expectations thing, but the man had been endlessly stubborn when it came to taking business advice.)

"Wow, did you do more of these posts?" he asked. "They're really good. The copy too. This is the kind of branding people pay consultants to do."

She seemed almost embarrassed when she showed him the other two, both posted yesterday, and he thought maybe he understood why. This might not be the kind of art she wanted to do, but it *was* art. She was putting herself out there after striking out.

Kind of like Finn with this art show.

Hopefully, they'd have better luck this time.

"Each of these already has an insane number of likes," he commented.

"I thought the response was pretty good," she said, her voice softer than usual. "Jack seems pleased too."

Jack.

Finn had run through that phone call a few times since Thursday, but he'd decided he definitely, certainly, one hundred percent was not going to say anything to Adalia. He was already in it with Maisie. She'd texted him at five in the morning—he suspected she'd done it purposefully to wake him up—saying, *What did you do???? River has manufactured some supposed illness for Hops, and he wants to come see me tomorrow morning. You better not have squealed.*

Which he had, of course, so maybe that death card had signified real death after all.

They headed out of the coffee shop at a quarter till three, since the first meeting was at the artist's somewhat out-of-the-way home studio. He didn't really know much, except that Dottie had said the woman's farm animals inspired her work. People liked animals, and it sounded like it would be an ideal fit, what with the animal shelter being the charitable cause attached to the first show.

"Are you okay with taking my car?" he asked as they left the coffee shop. Adalia's car was parked out front, and it looked like it was even more on the verge of falling apart than it had been the last time he'd seen it.

She burst into laughter. "Is that a serious question? I may be fond of Bessie, but she's a workhorse, not a stallion. I won't pass up a ride in your Wunderbus."

More innuendo. She certainly wasn't making the whole "let's be friends" thing easy on him, but then again that was one of the things he liked about her. She constantly challenged him, and she was no easier on herself. It made being around

Adalia feel like an adventure, like anything could happen and probably would.

He led the way to his green Range Rover. "All aboard the Wunderbus."

CHAPTER
fifteen

Finn plugged the address into his GPS and pulled out of his parking spot, giving Adalia the opportunity to watch him without being called out for it.

There was no doubt that Finn was good-looking, and despite his current existential crisis, he had an air of confidence she admired. Still, it was obvious he was floundering. He was trying to figure out who he was without Big Catch, just as she was trying to figure out who she was without art.

He wasn't the usual kind of guy she went for. She tended to shy away from business types—suits, she called them—because usually they were far too much like her father, but Finn was fun when he let his guard down. And he was far from unemotional. He'd certainly surprised her with the gift of her new studio, along with the bombshell that they could only be friends.

That had come out of left field, because if there was one thing Adalia was good at, it was figuring out if a guy was interested in her. Finn definitely was. So why was he holding back?

Because of Georgie and River? That didn't seem like him. Maybe he thought he and Adalia were just too different. He was rich—the Range Rover and his clothing would have proven that even if she hadn't already known—and she was cash poor. Her own car was her Exhibit A. But that didn't track either. He and River weren't on equal economic footing, and they were close friends.

No, he was probably hesitant to cross the friendship line because he thought she was unstable. Heavens knew she'd given him plenty of reasons to think that.

So why had he asked her to help him with the show? Was it because he felt sorry for her? Because he saw her as a project? Maybe, but she suspected there was more to it than that.

He put his car into drive and pulled away from the curb. She watched as his gaze flicked to his rearview mirror before returning to the windshield, his focus complete. She liked that about him. He never seemed to do anything by halves.

Then he took notice of her staring and his cheeks flushed.

He cleared his throat. "How's it going living with Jack?"

"Surprisingly well," she said. "We had a couple of awkward days, but then a family dinner and karaoke seemed to push us over that hurdle."

"Let me guess. You were the one who came up with the karaoke," he said with a laugh.

"What better way to take a man's measure than to make him sing in front of a crowd of strangers? Turns out Jack Durand knows how to wow a crowd. Especially the ladies." A frown stole across her face. "But he was a little off at dinner on Friday night, and when Georgie brought out a cake for dessert, he announced that he was taking a red-eye to Chicago for some kind of personal emergency. I mean, I think he probably had to drive all the way to Charlotte to catch the flight. This time he says he'll only be gone for the weekend, but who knows. Last time a few weeks became a few months. Isn't that weird?"

"Yeah," he muttered, his tone distant.

"I mean, if he'd done it after Jezebel leapt on the cake, I'd be more understanding," she said.

"I overheard your brother talking on the phone," he said in a rush, as if the words were chasing each other out of his mouth. "It sounded to me like maybe he has a secret girlfriend or something in Chicago."

It seemed like he was holding something back, but he left it at that and she didn't press. She'd come to the same conclusion anyway. A secret girlfriend or a life of crime or a hidden identity as a superhero. Whatever it was, he didn't want them to know and she didn't intend to press. Not yet.

"Probably," she said. "From what I've heard, you'd know plenty about secret girlfriends." She said it like she was teasing, but his history bothered her some. After Jack's weird declaration and Jezebel's destruction of the cake, Georgie had pulled her outside to caution her about Finn.

I'm glad you're making friends, Adalia, I am, but don't forget what he did to River. And River says he's dated probably half the women in this town. I'm not saying people can't change, but they usually don't. I don't want you to get hurt again.

She'd brushed aside Georgie's words, assuring her that Finn had made his intentions known—the whole "just friends" thing—but the description had nagged at her. Enough so that she'd called Dottie this morning to pump her for information about him. She'd certainly regretted it after Dottie launched into a long speech about how "an experienced lover was a talented lover."

Finn was no pompous flake. Nor was he the self-centered, egotistical asshole he'd been portrayed to be in the *Gazette* and on social media. (Even his bitchy hairdresser had attacked him!) The jerk they'd portrayed wouldn't have cared so much about a woman he barely knew and claimed he didn't want to sleep with. He wouldn't have taken it in stride when he realized she wasn't going to use the studio he'd gone to such trouble to create for her.

"I've never kept anyone a secret," he said softly, his eyes focused ahead. "But yeah, I guess you can say I've dated a lot. Guilty as charged."

He said that last part like he was making a joke, but she couldn't shake the thought that maybe she'd hurt him. It wasn't what she'd set out to do, so she changed the subject.

"How'd you meet River?" she asked. "When I vetted you with Dottie, she said I should be sure to ask you."

He laughed, the sound genuine and unstudied. "You vetted me with Dottie? Was that before or after our visit to the psychic?"

"After I told you I'd help with the art show." Okay, so it had all kind of happened on the same day. "In any case, she suggested that I ask you about meeting River or, more accurately, how you came up with the idea for Big Catch."

It only then occurred to her she'd jumped from one prickly subject to another, but he took it like a champ, his rich laughter filling the super spacious and luxurious interior of the car. "Dottie loves that story. I'm surprised she didn't tell you herself." His hand shifted on the steering wheel. "We met at a beer competition."

"Like Brewfest?" she asked. That was the competition the Buchanans were supposed to place in next March. If they didn't make it to the top five, the brewery would forfeit to River.

"Actually it *was* Brewfest," Finn said. "River had been job hopping for a few years, but at the time he was working as a bartender at a local restaurant. He'd been making home brews since he was a teenager. We ended up standing next to each other outside of the tent for a popular brewery. Both of us had a tasting glass of their lemon sour, and as soon as we tried it, we gagged at the same time. We got to talking about the different beers we were tasting, and he was so knowledgeable. The guy's got a great sniffer."

Adalia laughed. "Did you mean for that to sound so dirty?"

He chuckled. "Um. No. But there's no doubt his nose can pick out flavor profiles in a beer that other people wouldn't even notice. Which means his palate is pretty sharp too. He just has a built-in intuition, or maybe it's from all that time he spent brewing beer with Beau. I knew within hours of meeting him that he was a genius. The blue ribbon he won for his home brew lager only cinched it."

Adalia smiled at how animated he'd gotten while recounting their meeting.

"We just hit it off. We had this instant connection that felt more like a brotherhood than friendship. Or at least it's what I imagine having a brother would be like. I don't have any siblings."

There was a hint of loneliness in his tone, and she almost commented that siblings weren't all they were cracked up to be, but it would have felt too flip.

"Anyway," he said, tapping the side of the wheel, "I was living in Charlotte, looking for a project. And after hanging out with River for eight hours I knew, deep in my gut, that this could be something amazing. I wanted to start something from the ground up, to be part of building it, you know?"

She was surprised by the passion in his eyes, and a spark of recognition lit in her chest.

He was more like her than she'd realized.

"I do," she said softly. "I use paint or discarded items to make art, and you gather talent and make a business."

He shook his head. "No. What you do is special."

He pulled up in front of a house on what looked like a double lot surrounded by a picket fence covered in peeling white paint.

She wanted to argue with him, to tell him that they were both builders, creators, in their own ways, but it wasn't the kind of conversation they should have outside a stranger's gate.

"So that's how you met him," she prodded. "Dottie said to ask you where the business was born."

He put the car in park and turned off the engine, shifting in his seat to face her. "The official version or the real one?"

"Uh…*have we met?*" she asked, placing a hand on her chest. "Both."

He laughed and his whole body seemed to relax, any residual tension from her secret girlfriends comment draining away. He snuck a glance at the house through her passenger window before turning back to her. "The official version is that we came up with the idea at dinner and hammered out the terms the next day."

"And the actual account?"

He grinned. "I came up with the idea in a porta-potty line. River thought I was pulling his leg at first, because I told him the idea was nothing without him, but I was dead serious, and once he realized it, we just kept bouncing ideas off one another, even when we were in the bathroom stalls, although I admit it was hard to hear each other. We may have been a little drunk. But I knew it was a good idea, and we did officially hammer out the details the next day…while nursing hangovers."

"Why, Finn Hamilton," she said, barely containing her glee. "There's the answer to how we can find your next project. I need to get you drunk on beer." Then she opened her car door and got out, leaving him to follow her to the fence gate.

He caught up, flipping open a nice leather binder, and looked at his notes inside. "This is Stella Price. She's a painter. Dottie says she's, quote, 'extraordinary.'"

"This should be interesting." But then she turned to Finn, suddenly nervous. "What do you want me to do here? Tell you if she's any good?"

"That," he said, his expression softening, "and give me your overall impression. I've been to more than a few gallery events, but I don't know what sells."

"I'm not sure I'll have the answer to that, Finn." The wind blew a few tendrils of hair in her face and she batted them away. "If I did, then I'm not so sure I'd be driving around a car that needs Band-Aids."

He smiled at her and tucked the hair behind her ear. "You don't have to know. Just tell me what your gut says."

She nodded, still nervous. She hadn't given this part much thought when she'd agreed to help him. But contrary to what a lot of people thought, she wasn't flighty and she took her commitments very seriously. She'd asked River about Maisie's animal shelter, and it sounded remarkable. It only made Adalia that much more anxious about everything. She could potentially let a lot of people down, and Finn was the first in line. She understood he needed this to be successful to get back into the city's good graces, and to boost his battered ego.

"Don't overthink it, Addy. Okay?"

She gave him a warm smile. He always seemed to know the right thing to say, like he could see through all of her crap and see *her*.

He reached over the gate and unlatched it, then put a hand at the small of her back to guide her through.

She ignored the warmth that spread from the spot, the way her body seemed more alive when he touched her. Danger lay that way.

"Who's out there?" a woman called out from the back of the property.

"It's Finn Hamilton," he said. "I'm with Adalia Buchanan. I have an appointment with you at three."

"Oh!" An older woman emerged from a thick clump of trees and walked toward them. She was wearing an oversized white button-down shirt, like Adalia used to wear in grade school art class. It was covered in splotches of paint in various colors. "The art show thingy."

"That's right, ma'am, the Asheville Art Display ," Finn said congenially as they walked closer. "Dottie Hendrickson suggested you might be a good fit for us."

The woman couldn't have been more than five feet tall, but she was tottering on platform shoes with three-inch heels. Purple leggings peeked out from under her shirt. Her hair was as white as snow and piled into a messy bun atop her head and her face was covered in wrinkles, likely from too much sun, but her dark eyes were sharp as she surveyed them.

Glancing at Finn, she said, "I know *you're* public enemy number one in Asheville, bringing the big bad wolf to our door. But you're cute, so you get a pass." Her gaze landed on Adalia. "Who are you?"

Adalia's eyes widened slightly. Finn had literally just told her. "Adalia Buchanan."

The woman waved her hand dismissively with an irritated look. "I know that already. What's your claim to fame?"

"Excuse me?" Adalia asked.

"I've heard your name before."

"Adalia's an artist," Finn said, his brow furrowed. "Perhaps that's how you've heard of her."

"Nope. That's not it," she grumbled as a bleating sound came from the trees she'd emerged from. "It was something notorious."

The color drained from Adalia's face. Had this woman heard about her arrest? How? And if she knew, did that mean her father knew? And Lee?

Finn lightly cupped Adalia's elbow and said, "Maybe you've heard of her from Buchanan Brewery. Adalia and her siblings inherited it from Beau."

"That's it," the woman said, snapping her fingers. "You Northerners came down and took over Beau's business. Almost worse than Bev Corp."

"Ms. Price," Finn said, his voice a little tighter now. "The show will be at the Buchanan events room."

"So?"

"You don't have any problems showing your pieces at a business owned by figurative carpetbaggers?"

She shrugged. "I'll deal with it as long as you're there. You'll be there, right?"

Whatever was in the trees bleated again, followed by a chorus of answering bleats. *Were those goats?*

"Uh, yeah," Finn said, his hand still on Adalia's elbow.

"Good, I'll need a date," she said.

Adalia snorted at the woman's presumptuousness, then quickly covered it by clearing her throat. This woman was something else. It was hard to imagine Dottie even being friends with her.

Be the bigger person, Adalia.

"We would love to see some of your pieces," she said evenly and quite maturely, proud of herself for not kicking the woman in the shins. Like a grown-up.

"I bet you would," Stella said, giving her the side-eye.

"I'm sorry," Finn said, sounding just as taken aback as Adalia felt. "What's that supposed to mean?"

She gave Adalia a cold look. "I know your type."

Which still didn't answer the question.

A goat emerged from the trees, chewing on what looked to be a tin can.

Stella spun around and headed back into the trees. "Well, are you coming or not?"

"Why do I suddenly feel like we're Hansel and Gretel?" Adalia whispered to Finn.

"It's a valid concern. What do you think is in there?"

"Obviously a black cauldron over a fire, or a giant oven to cook us in. Probably both."

Finn grinned, his eyes lighting up. "So why are we following her?"

Adalia grinned back. "Don't pretend you're not as curious as I am, but once we get back there, it's every man and woman for themselves. Got it?"

He laughed. "Got it."

But she knew he was lying, just as she knew that his eyes were the color of the Caribbean Sea. He wouldn't leave her to fend for herself.

When they cleared the trees, they found a worn gazebo with a painting on an easel in the center next to a table covered with paints and a plastic tumbler that read, *You have goat to be kidding me.* But it was the scene around the gazebo that stopped them in their tracks. There had to be nearly twenty goats scattered around the tree-enclosed space, which included a couple of broken-down cars, a riding lawn mower, a few rusted bikes, and a moped.

It was then Adalia realized the painting was of a goat standing on top of a car that had a chicken behind the wheel. The car was running over another goat.

"How could a chicken hold on to a steering wheel?" Finn asked under his breath. "They don't have opposable thumbs."

She shot him a confused look as she whisper-shouted, "You see that painting and *that's* what you ask?"

He shrugged, trying to keep a straight face. "It's a legit question."

"I'm sure Stella will be happy to tell you when you escort her to the art show."

"Are you coming?" Stella asked as she clomped across the gazebo's wooden floor.

"Uh, sure. That's why we're here," Adalia said, starting to move closer, but Finn remained in place.

One of the goats was climbing onto the gazebo, and it started chewing on a painting that was resting on the floor against a post. It was of a goat and a pig on a tandem bike that had a chicken trapped underneath its wheel. Stella seemed to ignore the animal as it chomped down on the frame.

Adalia snagged Finn's wrist and tugged, whispering, "You brought me here. You're participating."

They walked into the gazebo, dodging goats, and got a good look at the eight other pieces that were propped up on a handrail on one side—all paintings of goats and chickens, some with a few pigs thrown in. In every painting but one, the animals were using various modes of transportation, and several of them depicted the animals in the throes of violence.

"My art is representative of man and his war against nature."

Adalia thought they had more of a *Planet of the Apes* vibe, minus the human slaves, but art *was* left for the viewer to interpret.

"There aren't any people in those, are there?" Finn asked, whispering in Adalia's ear.

Fighting a smile, she poked her elbow into his stomach. She would *not* laugh at this woman and her work, but admittedly she couldn't believe Dottie had recommended her. Unless her paintings sold for a lot of money…then bring them on.

Another goat had wandered onto the gazebo and started sniffing Finn's pants pocket. He tried to brush it away.

"And the goats roaming around are your inspiration?" Adalia asked. "I didn't know you could have so many within city limits." She and Finn shifted to the other end of the gazebo, but the goat followed Finn, now trying to chew on the flap of his belt.

"I'm sure you can't," Stella said, then cocked her head, "but this is my own sovereign nation. Stellaland."

"You don't say." Then, because Adalia couldn't help herself, she asked, "Do you have your own flag?"

Snorting, Stella said, "What self-respecting country doesn't have a flag?"

But she made no offer to show it to them.

"Uh…" Finn had shuffled to the side in an effort to dissuade the goat, but it just followed him as he stopped in front of a painting that seemed darker than the rest. It showed a chicken lying on the ground with specks of blood, while a dozen or so other chickens were in the process of stabbing it with forks.

"Oh," Stella said, pleased that Finn was studying it. "You've found my favorite. I call that one *Dinner*."

Adalia covered her mouth and fake-coughed to hide a laugh. She had been exposed to all kinds of art and artistic interpretations over the years, but this was by far the craziest thing she'd ever seen.

"Well," Finn said, taking a step back and bumping into another goat that was chewing on a paint-covered brush. "I think we've seen enough."

"So I'm in?" Stella asked as she tried to wrestle the paintbrush from the goat's teeth.

"Well…" Finn shot a panicked look at Adalia, and she decided to ignore the everyone-for-themselves motto and help him out.

As if there had ever been any doubt that she would.

"Stella, while your paintings send *quite* a message, I'm not sure they'll be a good fit for the first show."

"Why the hell not?" Stella asked, propping a hand on her hip as she continued to wrestle with the goat.

Adalia screwed on her best professional face. "The first charity is for a no-kill animal shelter. I'm sure a perceptive woman such as yourself can see how some patrons might find it…slightly offensive."

"What?" she asked with a confused look, then rolled her eyes. "No one appreciates good art these days."

"Ain't that the truth," Adalia said. "Thank you so much for showing us your pieces and we'll definitely keep you in mind for future events."

Stella winked at Finn. "I can wrap that one up for you if you like. All for the low price of twenty-five hundred dollars."

Finn's eyes widened, and Adalia looped her arm through his.

"He's sworn off making impulse purchases. A little too much online shopping." She tugged him, but the goat had a firm bite on Finn's belt.

Trying not to laugh at Finn's panicked expression, she yanked his arm, pulling him free, then dragged him down the steps to the yard.

"You're an online shopper?" Stella screeched, as though it was synonymous with being an ax murderer.

"We've got our work cut out for us with this one," Adalia called over her shoulder.

Then she got them the hell out of there.

CHAPTER
Sixteen

"You saved my life back there," Finn said once they were safely in the car, heading away from Stella's goat farm slash studio of horrors. They'd walked and then run, both of them laughing (once they were at a safe distance), hands linked together. God, he'd wanted to swing her around and kiss her, but he'd silently repeated his mantra—*just friends, just friends, just friends*—and opened the door for her instead. "I won't forget that. We're linked for life now."

"Weren't we already?" Adalia said, referring to the reading. They'd avoided talking about that, like maybe it was bad luck, although he wasn't sure what it was they were trying to skirt around: the possibility Lola could be right or that she might be wrong.

"I guess so," he said. "But now I owe you one."

"Ooo," she said, lifting up her hands and tapping her fingers together in the universal gesture of evil overlords everywhere. "I like the sound of that."

And if that didn't shoot a wave of lust through him...

To distract himself, he said, "Are we really going to risk going to the next appointment?"

"Of course," she said. He shot a quick glance at her and saw a wicked glint in her hazel eyes. They gleamed like gold. "Would you really miss it? What if they only get crazier as we go along? If we stop now, we'll never know."

"There are two left," he said, hesitant. "Let's decide on number three after we see the next one."

"And potentially miss out on the most insane experience of our lives? Never."

He found himself laughing, a near constant with her. He'd never laughed this much with any of his exes. Then again, he hadn't really been friends with any of them. Probably the egg salad therapist would have had something to say about that, about how he was repeating his parents' pattern or something. Except hopefully this whole mess—the articles and his professional slump and his dip into depression—had broken him out of that.

Or maybe Adalia's the one who's helping you do that.

He shook the thought off and reminded himself of the whole *just friends* thing.

"You do have a point," he said. "We ought to give our biographers something interesting to work with."

"You *would* assume someone's going to write a book about you some day." But she said it with quiet amusement. There was no accusation or heat behind it, and he found he didn't mind at all.

"I like that you get me," he said with a grin. "Luckily, the next two artists have studios in the same building, so we won't have too far to travel."

"On the minus side," she said, "it will be harder to run away. So, who's up next? Please tell me it's a performance artist. How awesome would it be if someone wants to sit in a box in the brewery for a month? Do you think my brother would go for it?"

"There's one way to find out. Unfortunately, our next up, Ms. Enid Combs, is a textiles artist."

"So knitting and weaving?"

She sounded genuinely excited about it, and he had to laugh. "I guess so, although I couldn't tell you what's so artistic about a sweater."

"My mother used to knit us sweaters for Christmas every year, I'll have you know," she said. "And I wore mine with pride. Lee, not so much."

"Oh yeah? Why's that?"

"Apparently, he thought the guys at school might beat him up for wearing something with a reindeer's face on it."

Finn grinned. "He might have had a point."

"He kept them, though," Adalia said, her voice softer, sweeter. "He kept them all. He showed them to me the last time we got together. They were all there in a box, every last one."

The love in her voice, the bittersweet melancholy, the sorrow of being on the outs with a brother she clearly loved...it moved him. *She* moved him.

"She must have been an incredible person," he said, and meant it. "I don't know what it's like to be loved like that."

He hadn't intended to say that. He hadn't meant to rip himself open for her. God, he was acting so pathetic lately, so soft, and for some reason it all seemed to come out in front of Adalia.

But her only reaction was to look at him and say, "She *was* incredible. And I'm sure that's not true. Family isn't always the people you're born with."

She was right, and besides, it wasn't like his parents didn't love him. He knew they did. But his father's way of loving was to push people into a mold he found pleasing, and his mother's love always came from a distance. They might think they wanted him in Charlotte, but he suspected he wouldn't see them any more often if he ever succumbed to their pressure and moved.

"Yeah," he said. "Lee doesn't sound so bad either. Maybe you should reach out to him. Tell him what happened."

From his peripheral vision, he could see her narrowed eyes.

"How did you know I *hadn't* told him?"

Oops, River was the one who'd said that. "River may have mentioned it," he admitted, not wanting to lie. "It's just…I didn't tell River about the Bev Corp sale when I should have, and it changed things between us. Our friendship still isn't the same. Maybe it's worth letting him in. Lee, I mean, obviously, not River."

She was silent for a long moment, and he was starting to wonder just how badly he'd blown it when she said, "It's not the same situation. If I tell Lee, it's basically the same thing as telling my father. They work together. He's basically in the man's pocket."

"Are you sure about that?" he asked, because he really did have a big mouth.

"You have a lot of opinions about people you've never met," she said sharply, the message obvious. *Stand down, idiot, or a bunch of eccentric artists will be the least you have to worry about. The Valkyrie in the car will burn you alive.* "I'm not some project, Finn. I'm not something for you to fix."

That wasn't what he was trying to do, was it?

No, he *did* want to help her, though—he needed to in some strange way. But she was right about one thing: he could be a little pushy at times. In business, it helped him get ahead, but this wasn't business, and Adalia wasn't the kind of woman who liked being told what to do.

"I know that," he said. "And I'm sorry for interfering. I guess I really am the sort of busybody who forms strong opinions about people he doesn't know. And isn't smart enough to keep them to himself."

"Busybody?" she asked, drawing his gaze, and he saw one corner of her mouth had tipped up.

"That's what you're latching onto?" he asked.

"Count yourself lucky."

"Oh, I do," he said.

They sat in mostly comfortable silence for another couple of minutes, until he pulled into the parking lot for the studios.

It was a large red brick building in the River Arts District, an intricate mural painted on one side.

"These are all studios?" Adalia asked in a small voice. She was watching the building with wide eyes, her hand gripped around the door handle but not moving to open it.

He reached for her other hand, realizing this was different for her than it was for him. The building was some kind of art mecca, and being here was loaded in a way a visit to the nutty goat whisperer hadn't been. "Yeah. Are you sure you're okay with this?"

She looked down at his hand on top of hers, but she didn't remove it. Glancing back at him, she said, "I wouldn't miss meeting Enid for the world. Let's go."

But she still didn't move his hand. It was almost like she was waiting for him to do something. Did she want him to kiss her? Would she be mad if he did?

Because she licked her lips, and he found his eyes following the progress of her tongue, his body reacting as if he'd seen something much more erotic.

Yeah, the whole *just friends* plan was suffering some setbacks.

You're being selfish again, a voice advised him. *You're thinking of what you want, not what she needs.*

And it was that voice that drove him out of the car. He went around to open her door, but she was already out.

"Why do you Southerners think a woman can't open a car door all by herself?"

She sounded a little pissed, but he had a feeling it wasn't about the door.

"Aren't you technically from the South?" he asked wryly. "Beau was a North Carolinian, born and bred."

"Sure, but I hardly knew him." She shot him a look as they walked toward the building, some of her sassiness reappearing. "I saved us last time, so you're in charge of the exit strategy when things inevitably go south."

"Is that so?" he asked, opening the door to the building.

She rolled her eyes as she walked through. "Yeah, that's so."

He looked at the directory, seeing Enid was located in a studio to the left, last door down.

"First floor," Adalia commented. "Easy getaway."

"If the other exit isn't blocked," Finn said, pointing to an exit sign on that side of the building.

"Good point. We don't know the lay of the land." She bent over the directory, studying it like it was a crib sheet for a test.

A woman walked past them, her dark, curly hair pulled back in a colorful scarf. Finn couldn't place her, but he knew he'd seen her before. She was lovely in a way that would have usually inspired him to angle for her number, but he felt no pull toward her. No interest. She glanced at him, an assessing glance, then continued on down the hall.

"Let's go," he said, reaching for Adalia's hand. When she gave it to him—acting like it was no big deal, this holding hands thing—he felt a surge of triumph in his chest, a feeling better than winning first place at last year's Brewfest.

They walked like that, hand in hand, until they reached the door at the end of the hall. It was open, albeit barely, communicating the message that the artist was prepared for visitors but perhaps didn't want to be disturbed by loud walkers.

"Ready to enter the lion's den?" Adalia asked in a near whisper. She said it close to his ear, near enough to press a kiss to his flesh, and he felt a pulse of longing that she'd do just that.

Just friends, just friends, he reminded himself.

"Yes, I think I'm prepared to meet a geriatric old knitter named Enid," he replied.

"That's what Dottie wants you to think," Adalia teased. "She's lulling you into a false sense of security."

Which was a fair guess, really. Dottie was known for her surprises.

"I'll go first," she said, still in that low voice. "Since you're our escape plan." She released his hand, the absence of it hitting him center mass, and stepped into the room. The little gasp she released upon entering the space had him assuming the worst, but when he followed her, he realized it had been a gasp of wonder.

Hanging from the ceiling were dozens of intricately knitted octopuses, each a bright burst of color. They were huge, probably two feet from top to bottom, and although

Adalia could walk under them without worry, he feared their trailing tentacles would catch in his hair. The walls were covered in enormous weavings, some of animals, some abstract pieces.

"She likes to keep people guessing, that Dottie," Adalia said in disbelief, shaking her head slightly.

A woman cleared her throat delicately, drawing their gazes to her. She sat behind a desk in the corner of the space, in front of a piece in progress—a half-formed whale.

"I was wondering if you were the people Dottie had sent," the woman said. It was the woman from the hall—the lovely one with the bright scarf.

"*You're* Enid?" Adalia asked. Clearly he wasn't the only one who'd expected a geriatric old grandma. "Wait. We saw you leaving the knitting store the other day, didn't we?"

Finn nodded briefly, placing her, and pure wonder filled Adalia's eyes.

"Probably," the woman conceded. "I order most of my supplies online, but I like to support them. Most people call me Blue." She offered no explanation, not that one was required, he supposed. It was far from the strangest nickname he'd ever heard.

"Your work is amazing," Adalia said, her eyes darting around the room like she was a kid in a candy shop, which was a pretty good analogy, actually. "I know a few people who work with textiles, and my mom was a home knitter, but I've never seen anything so intricate."

"I'm Finn," Finn said, approaching Blue's desk. She stood up and shook his hand, her hand like Adalia's—callused in places from her work.

Adalia, as if realizing she hadn't introduced herself either, joined him at the desk and shook Blue's hand after he did. Her

171

eyes shining, she said, "Sorry, I guess I forgot to introduce myself earlier. I'm Adalia Buchanan. I'm your new biggest fan."

Blue smiled at her, a wide, disarming smile. Strangers didn't usually smile at you like that.

"Adalia," she said. "Dottie thinks the world of you. She tells me you're an artist too."

Adalia's whole face flushed, something Finn hadn't seen before.

"I used to be," she said. "Dottie's much too kind. I'm not here to talk about me, though. Finn's putting together an art show that will be hosted at my family's brewery, and I'm helping him organize it. We want you to be part of it."

She glanced at him, as if daring him to dispute the offer. Like he would. Even if the pieces had been knitted sex organs, he would have accepted Blue with a grin on his face. Anything to see that look in Adalia's eyes.

"It's going to benefit an animal shelter," Adalia said pointedly, as if knowing that might sway her. Finn wasn't the only one who knew how to push for what he wanted.

Blue smiled again. "I already told Dottie I'd do it. I could use the exposure. My pieces aren't your usual impulse buys."

"That's because people are stupid," Adalia said bluntly. "You're a genius."

"Will you be this nice to me if I learn how to knit?" Finn asked, quirking his brow. Adalia gave him a playful shove, but she didn't lean away afterward, her body pressing into his.

"Would you like to sit down?" Blue asked, gesturing to the chairs in front of her desk.

They lowered into the chairs and discussed the details of the show—how much space would be available to each of the artists (something they didn't know yet since Finn had only lined up a few people, but Adalia insisted Blue would have all the space she needed), who would select the pieces (Blue agreed to send photos of the selections she wanted to bring to Adalia, who'd make the final choices), and the possibility for future shows. Finn was still running with the idea that they'd do it twice a year. The pieces that didn't sell would be put on display at the venue until they sold or the artist requested them back.

Finn glanced at his watch, aware that they were coming up on the time they needed to visit the last studio, a sculptor.

"Does that mean you need to leave?" Blue asked. If anyone else had asked him that, he might have assumed they were annoyed, but she seemed incredibly Zen, like she did yoga in her sleep and dosed her coffee with chia seeds. Realizing he'd internalized Adalia's 'Who are you?' game, he couldn't help but smile.

"Yeah, we have one more meeting. But we're excited to have you on board." He gestured to Adalia, who was still almost bouncing with excitement in her seat. "Obviously."

"Let me just steal one more second of your time." Blue gestured for Adalia to follow her, and Adalia jumped out of her seat like a jack-in-the-box. Finn felt his smile spread a little wider. They followed Blue to a door at the far right corner of her studio, and she opened it, revealing an open space with a cement floor, surrounded by windows.

"I know you said you're not doing art anymore, Adalia. Or at least not right now, but I wanted to invite you to use this space. I lead yoga classes in here, but it's empty more often than it's full. You're welcome to come to my classes too."

To his surprise, Adalia didn't say anything. She just stood there staring at the space, her eyes wide. He wanted to know what she was thinking, but it would seem wrong to ask. Like he'd be interrupting something important. So he didn't. Neither did Blue.

Finally, Adalia looked up at them and smiled. "I guess we'd better get going. Thank you, Blue. You're amazing."

Blue hugged her, which was again something Finn wouldn't have expected from a stranger, and when they left, Adalia sought out his hand and held it. There was no playfulness to it this time. It was as if it really meant something.

"What do you think?" she finally said. "Is the next surprise going to be a good one or a bad one?"

"Definitely bad," Finn said. "Dottie likes to keep us on our toes. We're going to see a Mr. Fred Wilcox, sculptor. I'll bet they're sculptures of human anatomy, based on nude models volunteering from an old folks' home."

"Oh, I hope so," she said, "that sounds amazing."

"You *would* think so, you deviant," he said, giving her hand a squeeze.

But when they reached the studio in question, they found a different sort of surprise. The door was closed, but one of the sculptures sat outside of it. It was an enormous piece incorporating found objects like glass pebbles, buttons, and sections of chain-link fence. The sculpture was strange and glorious, and Adalia's eyes filled with tears as soon as she saw it. This was her preferred medium, he remembered. He'd seen a few of her mixed media pieces on Instagram.

Finn tugged Adalia's hand, still linked with his, and urged her away from the room, turning a corner.

"It's good," she said, a tear escaping her eye. "We need to go in there, Finn. We have to meet with him and ask him to be in the show."

He traced the trail the tear had left on her face and, not thinking, leaned in and kissed her cheek. She tipped up her face a little, as if inviting him to kiss her, something he intended to do when the time was right. Being friends was only a *just for now* plan, after all. But she was too vulnerable right now, and he refused to take advantage of that.

"No," he said. "We don't go in there unless it's what you want."

"I can't." Her voice cracked a little. "Not right now. But I meant what I said. His work needs to be shown. Isn't he waiting for you?"

"I have his number," he said, already walking away, Adalia coming with him. "I'll call him from the car."

"Thank you, Finn," Adalia said quietly.

But he wondered if he'd done the wrong thing again, and she only thought this was what she wanted.

CHAPTER
Seventeen

Adalia couldn't help feeling like she'd overreacted and looked foolish. But the sight of the mixed media piece had hit her square in the chest, resurfacing all the suppressed feelings of pain and betrayal. It was like she was back in that gallery, seeing her pieces with Alan's name on them all over again.

Slopping the paint on them, she'd felt a vindictive sort of fury, but there'd been a moment afterward, before the police cuffed her, where she'd looked at them and felt a well of sorrow open inside of her. Of loss. That feeling had risen up now too.

Alan had texted again last night, waking her.

You know I don't like to be kept waiting, Adalia. Call me.

Maybe it was time to tell Georgie that he was still bothering her, especially since the message sounded less wheedling and more demanding, but she didn't want to admit that she hadn't blocked him. Which was something she finally *had* done. It felt freeing, but the messages still hung over her.

The feelings inside of her seethed, but they settled some once she and Finn left the building.

She tried to convince him to go inside and meet with the artist by himself, but he just took a long look at her and shook

176

his head. "No. I'm not leaving you alone." Then he hastily added, "In the car. It might get too hot. I don't want you to end up like one of those dogs."

If it had been someone else, Adalia would have gotten defensive. She would have said that she didn't need a babysitter, thank you very much, she was just fine on her own. But this was Finn, and his presence tamed her anger and was like a balm to her pain. They both knew she could have rolled down the windows or opened the door. It wasn't that warm today. He was giving her an out.

He placed the call on Bluetooth as he pulled out of the parking lot. The sculptor was understanding when Finn asked to reschedule, especially since Finn told him that he had an official invitation to participate. The meeting would just be to discuss logistics and which pieces he'd like to include.

Adalia felt Finn's eyes on her as they reached a light, but she stared out the window, berating herself for her overreaction. The sculptor's pieces would be at the show. How was she going to handle it there? Finn didn't need a weepy assistant tailing him around. That would be a great way to drive off buyers.

Neither of them said anything when he ended the call, but he took her hand again, and she realized she was not only getting used to it but welcomed it. She was used to dating artistic types—men whose moods bounced around like a yo-yo and were emotionally draining. Finn was even-keeled and emotionally stable. She liked that she could rely on him when she was an emotional wreck, and while he had troubles of his own, he never made it seem like his dwarfed hers.

She'd been lost in her own thoughts for several minutes before she realized they weren't headed back to her car. In fact, he was heading in the direction of her house.

A.R. Casella and Denise Grover Swank

"Are you taking me home?" she asked in surprise. The thought of being alone in the empty house made her uneasy. It was too quiet just for her. Too lonely. Jezebel would be there, probably, but she wasn't much for company.

"No," he said, casting a nervous glance at her. "Unless you want me to. I thought we might head to my house and..." His words trailed off as if he'd decided that it was a bad idea halfway through the explanation.

"I'd love to see your house," she said softly. "I'm not ready to go home yet."

He squeezed her hand and shot her a warm smile that would have melted the iciest of hearts, but hers had already thawed to him. She couldn't believe she used to think he was full of himself.

He parked his car in front of a contemporary building with straight lines and asymmetrical windows that didn't look like it belonged next to the Victorians and Arts and Crafts homes around him. She loved it, though. It fit him.

"What made you buy this place?" she asked in awe.

"This is a well-established area that's been growing in value."

She turned in the seat to face him. "Come on, Finn. You did it purely for investment reasons? There wasn't some part of you that loved it?"

He smiled, his eyes lighting up. "Most people hate it. Are you telling me you don't?"

"What's there to hate?"

"It's been called an eyesore from time to time."

She could see why other people might hate it, even if she didn't agree. The house next to it was a two-story Victorian with pale blue siding, and the house on the other side was a bungalow.

"It's a masterpiece," she said in awe, studying it again. "Very Frank Lloyd Wright meets Mies van der Rohe." She shrugged when his brow rose. "I took an architecture class or two in art school."

He laughed. "I wish you'd been around when I showed it to my mother."

"Why, because my charming personality would have distracted her?"

"That too. Want to go inside?"

"Uh. *Yeah.*"

He hopped out of the car, and she was still studying the house through the car window when he came around and opened her door. She smiled at him as he offered a hand to help her out. Truth be told, though she'd teased Finn about it earlier, she liked his Southern gentleman vibe. Didn't matter that it would have annoyed her had someone else done it. Maybe she didn't mind with him because there wasn't an ounce of social obligation. It was like he really wanted to open her door.

"So what am I going to find in there?" she asked as they approached the front door. "Will it smell like a locker room, with clothes and dirty dishes lying around everywhere? Or will it be so uber neat I'll be afraid to touch anything?"

He grinned back at her. "You can touch things."

"Ah-ha!" she said, pointing a finger at him. "I knew it. Uber neat."

He unlocked the door, then pushed it open. "See for yourself."

Her stomach fluttered as she crossed the threshold into Finn's living room. The walls were painted light gray, and there was a black leather sofa in front of a big-screen TV. Several armchairs were arranged on either side. Two glass and iron end tables bearing lamps bracketed the sofa, and a matching coffee table sat in front of it. It looked sleek and contemporary, the decor matching the exterior, but there were well-placed accessories as well as several tapestry throw pillows that softened the vibe. It was clean yet inviting.

"You decorated this yourself, didn't you?" she asked, aching to take off her boots and curl her toes in the thick wool rug that anchored the room.

"Yeah," he said hesitantly. "Is it that bad?"

She turned back to look at him, surprised to see that her opinion mattered so much to him.

"No, Finn. It's that *good*." She gave him a huge grin. "Maybe you should become an interior designer."

He laughed. "I think I'll pass."

She headed into the kitchen at the end of the long, open concept room. The cabinets were a dark walnut, which was a nice contrast to the white quartz counters and stainless steel appliances. He had a couple of barstools at the island. The counters were bare with the exception of a very expensive-looking espresso machine and a stainless steel toaster.

"Well?" he asked as he followed her in. "What do you think?"

She shrugged but let a smile slip through. "It'll do." It pleased her to think of him living here—stretched out on the sofa, watching a movie or a game. Cooking in the kitchen. Hanging out with friends. But then it occurred to her that he would have brought his old girlfriends here too, and a sudden stab of jealousy caught her by surprise. She wasn't typically a jealous person, but she didn't like the thought of another woman with Finn.

"Can I see upstairs?" she asked, her voice lower than before, and she wished she could hit rewind and say it more playfully. She could see that Finn was reading all kinds of things into her husky tone, and the way he hesitated suggested they weren't entirely pleasant thoughts.

The sting of rejection stole her breath, but she told herself that it wasn't that he wasn't interested—he obviously was—but something was holding him back.

"On second thought," she said, opening the refrigerator door. "I'm hungry."

"You won't find much in there, sad to say, but we can order something."

He was right. All she found was a half-gallon of skim milk, a nearly empty jar of pickles, a carton of eggs, and a couple of takeout containers.

"Dottie doesn't bring you food?" she asked in disbelief.

He shrugged. "She doesn't have a key." A smile tugged at his mouth. "Besides, she's too busy feeding all of you ingrates."

"From the bare refrigerator, I take it you don't cook much?"

"I can cook the basics."

"Like eggs?" she teased.

"Scrambled eggs are easy."

"Finn," she said, shaking her head. "You're letting this gorgeous kitchen go to *waste*. I'm going to make you dinner."

"You don't have to do that, Adalia," he protested, but she noticed the gleam in his eyes. The thought pleased him.

"Don't you worry," she said. "This won't be me cooking while you watch a college football game on TV. You're helping."

He grimaced. "I have to warn you that I don't know the first thing about cooking."

"So you say, but I'm a genius, and I'm going to teach you. The real question is what to make?"

They settled on eggplant parmesan with roasted broccoli and a side salad with homemade vinaigrette dressing. Unfortunately, he didn't have any of the ingredients or most of the basic kitchen equipment. Adalia offered to take care of the equipment by picking some up from her house, but Finn insisted he wanted his own stuff.

"So we'll have them the next time we cook," he said.

Adalia ignored the flutter in her stomach at the thought of cooking with him again.

Don't get ahead of yourself.

So they made a Target run, buying Finn a cartful of kitchen essentials, from measuring cups to a decent set of pots and pans. She felt guilty when she saw the total, but he waved it off as if it were nothing and told her he'd been wanting to fill his cabinets with more than plates and glasses and the odd serving dish he could fit into his microwave, but he hadn't known what to buy.

They hit the grocery store next and got spices and pantry essentials as well as the ingredients for their meal and some extras. He picked out a couple of bottles of wine, and they checked out and headed back to his place.

Finn hadn't lied about not knowing how to cook, but he was a fast and eager learner.

"Maybe you should be a chef," she teased.

"I considered buying a restaurant once, before I met River, but I wasn't convinced it would pay off in the end," he said as he chopped broccoli. He paused mid-chop, giving her a sheepish look. "I didn't mean that to sound so pretentious."

"You weren't being pretentious. You were stating a fact." She hated that he didn't feel like he could be himself with her, that he had to watch his words, and she was determined to change that. "So I guess that means you don't want to be a chef?"

"'Fraid not. They work grueling hours and have to absolutely love cooking food."

"Are you saying you aren't enjoying cooking with me?" she teased.

He picked up his glass of wine and took a slow sip, then lowered the glass, never taking his eyes off her. "I'm loving every minute of cooking with you, Adalia."

Her breath caught in her throat. Yes, he wanted her, but he wasn't making any moves. Did he think *she* wasn't interested?

"You're a quick study and good with your hands," she said. "You're a natural."

She'd intended the innuendo, and he'd obviously noticed, because he picked up his wine and took a gulp. But when he set it down, he turned his attention back to cutting broccoli as if it had never happened.

Had Finn sworn off women?

The eggplant parmesan took some time to assemble before it went into the oven, but she'd planned it that way— wanting an involved dish so she could spend more time with him. They cleaned up the dirty dishes while the main meal baked, then set the table, chatting about everything and anything. Well, except for art, which both of them avoided mentioning by silent agreement. She loved his wit, and he gave as good as he got with her teasing. She couldn't remember the last time she'd had so much fun. Definitely not with any of her past boyfriends.

They'd spent so much time shopping and getting everything ready before they even started cooking that it was getting dark outside. Adalia had found a couple of candlesticks and taper candles in a cabinet while putting things away. She figured they were probably left over from a past girlfriend, but she didn't ask. Truthfully, she didn't want it confirmed. She just put them on the table and lit them before she could change her mind.

Was she trying to seduce Finn with food and candlelight? Maybe…

The timer went off, and she had him pull out the casserole dish and cookie sheet while she mixed the vinaigrette. They set out the food and sat down on opposite sides of the table.

"This looks so good, Addy."

"You helped make it too, but let's see how it tastes before we make any judgments," she said, slicing into the eggplant parmesan and lifting a piece onto Finn's plate.

He waited until she'd served herself before he took a bite, moaning with pleasure.

The sound blasted straight to her core, making her breathing shallow. Would he make that sound if he took her up to his bedroom?

"You like?" she forced out, in case he realized she wasn't acting normal.

"It's delicious. I think you should cook for me every night."

"You mean cook *with* you," she said. "You were a very active participant in this meal."

But she wanted him to be an active participant in another activity. She was going to need to splash cold water on her face if they kept up this dance of innuendo and attraction.

They discussed books and movies, and Adalia shook her head when he admitted he hadn't seen her favorite, the Keira Knightley version of *Pride and Prejudice*.

"How is that possible?" she demanded. "It's a classic."

"I think by definition, a classic is something at least a few decades old," he said, working on his second helping.

"Well, then it's the best version ever made."

"I'll take your word for it since I haven't seen *any* version."

"Then we must rectify that," she said. "I have a copy at home in my room."

He laughed. "You own the DVD?"

"I used to watch part of it every night before I went to sleep while I was in art school." She shrugged. "And for a few years after too."

A strange look covered Finn's face. Then his gaze quickly dropped to his plate. "You don't have to go home to get it. We can just buy it online and watch it."

"You'll watch it?" she asked in surprise.

"Yeah. If it's your favorite movie, then...yeah."

"What's *your* favorite movie?" she asked. "If you're watching mine, then the least I can do is watch yours."

He took a second to think about it, then said, "*The Bride of Chucky*."

Her jaw dropped and she scrambled for a response. The corners of his mouth twitched, and she threw her napkin at him. "You're the worst!"

His eyes twinkled. "I couldn't resist."

"So what's *really* your favorite movie?"

"*Fast Five*," he said unapologetically.

She shook her head. "What's that?"

"It's in the Fast and Furious franchise." He grinned. "It's a *classic*."

Since her napkin was gone, she considered throwing a piece of broccoli at him but reminded herself she was working on being a grown-up. "Well," she said coyly. "If it's a *classic*, I guess we have to watch it."

"But *Pride and Prejudice* first," Finn said. "I had a woman tell me I was like Mr. Darcy, so I want to see if it's true."

Adalia took a gulp of wine. She had a feeling it hadn't been intended as a compliment. Maybe he'd deserved it, but she suspected she wasn't the only one who'd misunderstood Finn. If he hadn't discovered her secret, she might never have learned that there was more to him than his button-ups and docksiders, than his ambition and drive. So she was grateful he'd seen her that day, because it had allowed her to see him.

CHAPTER

Eighteen

Finn's house had always felt a little lonely. He'd had out-of-town friends come to visit and locals over for dinner. Plenty of women had spent the night. But it had always felt a little big, a little empty. His mother hadn't just found the style obscene, she'd considered it a strange choice for a young man like him, a bachelor, to buy a house large enough for a family. She'd clearly perceived it as a worrying development in her plan to get him to move back to Charlotte. Her disapproval had stayed with him, though, making him wonder if the purchase had been a mistake.

But the house didn't seem too big with Adalia in it. Shopping with her, making dinner with her…he didn't want her to leave. Which was why he'd suggested the movie, but the moment she asked if he had any blankets they could share, he worried it had been an impulsive mistake.

All night long, he'd been fighting the temptation to pull her to him and kiss her. To take her hand and lead her upstairs.

Because this was kind of a date, wasn't it? When was the last time someone other than Dottie had made him dinner? And she kept making those innuendo-laced comments that were driving him nuts. And when she'd talked about watching her favorite romance movie in bed…it had planted an image in his head of Adalia in *his* bed. Now he couldn't stop thinking about it.

Part of him wondered why he was hesitating. Yes, Adalia was wounded, but she was also a fierce Valkyrie, very capable of knowing what she wanted and reaching for it. If she wanted him, shouldn't he just consider himself the luckiest man alive and roll with it?

He had to conclude that Adalia's past wasn't the only speed bump. He knew how to charm women, but he didn't know how to keep them around. No, that wasn't precisely true…he'd just never been this worried about messing things up. Maybe it went back to that fortune-teller. She may have said he and Adalia were meant for each other, but she'd also said Adalia would be leaving something behind. He didn't want that something to be Asheville. Or him.

Of course, he wasn't sure he believed in fortune-tellers. But he couldn't help feeling a little twinge of superstition about the whole thing.

"Are you sure you want to watch this?" Adalia said, misinterpreting his hesitation. "It *is* profoundly moving. You may never be the same."

Didn't he know it.

"A deal's a deal," he said, retrieving a fuzzy red blanket from the chest beneath the TV. "Just don't renege on your part of it. *Fast Five* is *also* profoundly moving. The cars are unbelievably fast."

"Oh. My. God. You just made a dad joke," she said in mock horror. "I now have doubts about this entire enterprise." But even as she said it, she snuggled onto the couch.

Finn lowered down next to her, keeping a little distance between them, but she instantly snuggled closer, pulling the blanket over both of them. Her side was pressed up against him, her warmth suffusing him.

It was so distracting, it took him a solid five minutes to find the movie and set it up. (They really had made about a dozen different versions.)

At some point during the movie, Adalia's hand landed on his thigh. It happened organically. She'd raised her hand to point at the screen, accusing one of the characters—Finn had no idea what his name was, something British that ended with "ham"—of being a bounder and a cad, and when she'd lowered it, it had landed on Finn's leg. She hadn't moved it, and several of his brain cells had fled from *Pride and Prejudice*. He also had to concentrate enormously, and shift the blanket, to avoid embarrassing himself.

When the heroine visited Mr. Darcy's enormous estate, Adalia poked him. "Pay attention, this is the good part."

A grin crossed his lips. "What? She's going to look at him differently because she realizes he has a big house?"

"Oh, don't you besmirch Elizabeth Bennett that way," she cried out. "Besides, it's not just a big house—it's Pemberley! But that has *nothing* to do with why she changes her mind about him."

"Oh yeah?" he asked, giving into temptation and putting his hand on top of hers. "Maybe you should give me some tips? Like I said, I've been told I'm like this guy, and from what I can tell, he's a bit of a jackanapes." Which was another word she'd used for the Ham guy.

Adalia surprised him by reaching for the remote and turning off the TV. It took a moment for his eyes to adjust, her profile swathed in shadow now. Her lips came into focus first.

"You can start by kissing me, you jackanapes. How long are you going to keep a girl waiting?"

He opened his mouth to explain, to tell her what he'd been thinking, but they'd all be the wrong words, so he let himself do what he'd wanted to do all night. What he'd wanted to do since that day at Dottie's. He kissed her.

It was a soft kiss first, exploratory, but Adalia lifted that hand on his leg—the one that had maddened and delighted him—and grabbed a handful of his shirt, pulling him closer, and something inside of him shattered. He opened his mouth and she did the same, and as they were tasting each other, breathing each other in, she straddled his lap.

Groaning, knowing Adalia was feeling his arousal, which had been there since the first act, he wove one hand through her curls, bringing her closer yet, and let the other slip under the hem of her shirt, touching the soft skin of her back as their mouths moved together, tilting for better access, never satisfied. Adalia rocked against him, the sensation maddening.

She started ripping at his shirt buttons, making a little sound of protest in her throat, and he broke away for a moment, already missing the feel of her, and unbuttoned a few before pulling it over his head.

"Hey," she said, her voice husky. "I was supposed to do that." Her hand tracked to his chest, tracing the muscles. "Don't you punch numbers all day? How does a guy like you get a chest like that?"

She said it teasingly, her fingers tracing the ridges of muscle.

"I get some of my best ideas in the gym," he said, sliding his hand under the hem of her shirt again, lifting it up slightly.

"Fair is fair," she said, grabbing the hem and pulling her shirt off. She wore a lacy yellow bra—a sunny blast of fabric—and he took a moment to just take in her beauty, her curls all mussed from his touch, her eyes bright and glimmering even in the dark, her breasts cupped in yellow lace.

"You're gorgeous. If I had even a slight bit of talent, I'd paint you."

She smiled, fingers still exploring him, and he leaned in to kiss her neck and started trailing a line of kisses down to her breasts. She wove her fingers through his hair, gripping—maybe the longer hair hadn't been such a bad idea—and said, "Maybe we can get Blue to knit me."

And suddenly they were both laughing, their chests pressed together, Adalia cradled to him.

When had this ever happened?

Never. He'd never laughed with someone when he was this aroused. But it only made him feel closer to her.

He leaned forward and kissed her again, wanting to show her how much she affected him—how much this meant to him—but the doorbell rang.

Which might have been fine if River hadn't shouted out, "Finn? You in there? I see your car."

"Shit," Adalia said, "shit, shit, shit."

She grabbed her shirt and shoved his button-down at him, and even though he absolutely did not want River to see them like this, he couldn't help but chuckle a little.

"What are you laughing about, you ingrate?" she said in an undertone.

"Don't you suddenly feel like you're a high schooler and your dad just walked in?"

"Trust me when I say we're both lucky River is *not* my father."

191

"For any number of reasons," he said as they both pulled on their shirts, and they laughed again. A helpless, semi-hysterical kind of laughter.

"Finn?" River shouted again.

"Be right there!" he called back.

"Any other evidence?" Adalia asked in that same urgent almost-whisper, poring over the room like a forensic examiner at a crime scene. Finn did the same. There wasn't, not really, but there were a dozen little things that would stand out to his friend: the single fuzzy blanket, discarded on the couch, the smell of eggplant parmesan that hung in the air, the two wine glasses on the coffee table. Those damn candles centered on the table.

But there was no way they were going to strip the whole house of any sign they'd been on a date, or a sort of date, and truthfully he didn't want to. He wanted those things to stay after Adalia left, because they were the things that made his house finally feel full.

His glance fell on her again, on the beautiful mess of her hair and her swollen lips.

"Do you have a hair elastic?" he asked softly.

"Oh my god, I've got sex hair, don't I?" she asked.

The way she said it, so blunt and forthright, like everything she said, sent a zip through him that made him tempted to forget all about River banging down his door. But then she was throwing her hair up into one of those inadequate little buns that let the tendrils spill out, and he shook some sense into himself and made his way to the door, flicking the light on when he got there. Blinking in it like a bat thrown into the midday sun.

When he opened it, River immediately peered past him, his gaze finding Adalia.

"There you are," he said. "You weren't answering your phone, and Georgie got worried."

"The battery died hours ago," Adalia said, collecting her bag. Something wrenched inside of Finn at the realization that she'd be leaving. He'd guessed that, of course, but part of him had hoped she wouldn't. Now that their couch frenzy had come to a crashing halt, he realized they'd leapt into things way too fast. But he would have liked to finish her movie, even if it drove him utterly crazy to be under that blanket with her.

"Sorry," River said, making a face, "but you know how she gets. Plus, she thought it was just a coffee thing. I guess the two of you had talked about doing dinner tonight." His gaze drifted to Finn's shirt, and a quick glance revealed he'd messed up and missed a button, giving the top half a crooked look. It was the kind of thing Finn would never have overlooked under normal circumstances. Their eyes met, and Finn knew he'd be having a conversation about this sooner rather than later.

"It was just coffee," Adalia said. "But then it became a meeting thing, and a dinner thing, and a movie thing." Her gaze darted to the couch, to that mussed blanket, before searching out Finn's.

He mentally filled in for her: *and it became a kissing thing too.*

"So," River said, clearly uncomfortable, "do you want a ride home?"

"Can you give me a lift to Bessie?" Adalia asked. "I left her outside the coffee shop, and I worry that she might get stolen."

She glanced at Finn as she said it, and he knew she was messing with him, so he messed back.

"You're right, that car has a big 'Steal Me' sign on it. You don't want to take risks."

"Um, sure," River said. "Why don't I go out to the car and wait for you?" Too Finn, he said, "We'll talk later."

Obviously. Finn nodded. "Later."

As soon as the door closed behind him, Adalia gave Finn a severe look, like she was a teacher and he was an errant pupil, and just like that, he was turned on again.

"Don't you dare say that was a mistake," she said.

"I wouldn't think of it," he said, pulling her into his arms. "Although I do think we were moving too fast."

She scowled at him, her lips making a pretty pout. He wanted to kiss them, so he did.

She pulled away, but only slightly. "Why'd you make such a big deal of the 'just friends' thing if you felt like this?"

He could tell his answer meant something to her, so he decided to be honest. As if he could help himself.

"After the whole Alan thing…I wasn't sure you were ready to date. I didn't want to be just one more guy who was asking something from you. I thought you needed a friend more than you needed…well, this. And if that's still true, then we can take an even bigger step back. We can forget this happened. We—"

"Finn," she said, her tone serious but not cutting, like he'd worried it might be, "I'm a big girl. You don't need to worry about what I'm ready for and not. And I absolutely do *not* want to forget this happened."

"Good," he said, "because I don't either."

River honked the horn, and Adalia rolled her eyes.

"I guess I have some 'splaining to do."

"Are we telling them?" he blurted out.

"Not yet." She pulled a face. "If you can bear to keep quiet about it, of course. I'd rather figure this out before we bring anyone else into it."

"So we're going to be furtive," he said, his voice husky to his own ears.

"Very," she said with a grin. "Do you have a trench coat?"

"I thought we were talking about being spies, not flashers," he said, running a finger down her cheek and then cupping her chin.

Kissing her one last time.

She said goodbye and walked out, closing the door behind her, but he stayed put, watching from the window by the door as she got into River's car. Watching as it pulled away.

And then he was left in a house that suddenly felt emptier than it ever had before.

He sucked it up and brought his laptop to the couch—wanting to sit there so he could be closer to the memories of the night, to the feel of her. He added some finishing touches to his proposal for Gretchen, feeling increasingly good about it. He'd look it over tomorrow and then send it along Monday. If she decided to move forward, he'd talk to River and Georgie and some of the other brewery owners to see if they'd be willing to participate in the beer festival. He couldn't think why they wouldn't—it really was a win-win for everyone involved, sore feelings or not.

An ad popped up on his computer, and an idea suddenly struck him. The perfect date for him to bring Adalia on. If she'd agree. If he could manage to keep it a surprise.

Care to play hookie on Wednesday? he texted. *I have an idea I think you'll like, but it'll take an indeterminate amount of time, and I have to be in Charlotte tomorrow night.* He'd arranged to talk to the robotics people on Monday morning in Charlotte, so he'd agreed to have Sunday dinner at his parents' house. No doubt his mom wanted to interrogate him about the woman he'd mentioned to his father.

Although he had zero interest in actually taking a job with the robotics start-up, he was interested enough to have a conversation with the team. What little he'd been able to learn about the company through online research had sparked his imagination. He could have suggested Tuesday for the date, but Gretchen would probably want to talk through the proposal once he finished, and he'd need to get started on follow-up.

Somewhere in there, he needed to make more arrangements for the show. Hopefully with Adalia. They'd need to select more artists, and another meeting with Jack was in order at some point to iron out ideas for the event.

He realized belatedly that it was eleven o'clock, not really an appropriate time to text for anything but a booty call, and he immediately texted back: *Sorry it's late. I didn't realize it was this late until I sent the message. This is NOT a booty call. I have an idea I think you'll like, although I'll say no more.*

Still no answer, so he decided that she maybe, probably, was asleep. And would wake to a flooded phone. Oh well, too late to withdraw the messages. So he added a *good night, sorry for blowing up your phone*, because why not at that point, and set down his phone.

He turned on the TV, intending to watch something to calm his racing thoughts, and saw *Pride and Prejudice* was still on the screen, paused where they'd stopped it.

His lips tipped up at the memory of Adalia's excitement when she'd said this was her favorite scene. Which was why he found himself watching the end of the movie by himself. And he was glad he did, because Mr. Darcy's line about being bewitched, body and soul, sent a wave of recognition through him.

It was exactly how he felt.

CHAPTER
Nineteen

River was staring straight out the windshield when Adalia got into the car.

"I'm nearly thirty years old," she said, irritated. "You didn't need to go out on a search and rescue mission for me. I can take care of myself."

"I told her I found you," he said, picking up his phone and handing it to Adalia. "But I think this is between the two of you."

He was right, and even though Adalia didn't want to talk to her sister at that precise moment, she placed the call anyway.

"Georgie, it's me," she said when her sister answered.

"What were you thinking, Addy?" Georgie asked in an accusatory tone. "No one knew where you were!"

It only took a millisecond for Adalia to revert to her teenage self, being mothered by her "perfect" older sister because their mother was gone. "Gee, I didn't realize I still had a curfew. Am I grounded now?"

River shot her a glance. Adalia was sure he didn't appreciate her talking to his girlfriend that way, but too bad.

Georgie had been her sister long before River had come onto the scene.

"Addy," Georgie said with a sigh. "I know you're a grown woman used to living in New York City and answering only to yourself, but with everything else going on…"

"What? You think I'm so upset I'll do something stupid?"

"Well, no…but something bad could have happened *to* you."

"It's Asheville, Georgie. Not Gotham. I'm perfectly safe."

"I still worry about you, Addy. As your big sister, it's my job."

Releasing a sigh, Adalia ran her hand through her hair, forgetting she'd pulled it back. "Look, I'm sorry, Georgie," she said in a softer tone. "You're right. I'm not used to anyone caring where I am and what I'm doing."

And if that didn't sound pathetic…

"Well, that's changed," Georgie said, her voice breaking. "You have people here who love you and care about you— me, most of all—and I worry. *We* worry."

Adalia suspected River hadn't shown up because he was worried—more like he wanted *Georgie* to stop worrying. Still, she had to admit it was nice having someone care about her. In New York, days might have passed before someone thought to ask if something was up. Well, except at the end when Alan had become more controlling. By then her friends had grown accustomed to her disappearing.

She pushed away the memories of him and, worse, of what she'd been like with him. "I know, and I love you too. I didn't mean to upset you. I'll try to do a better job of making sure my phone's charged. Okay?"

But that was easier said than done. Her phone was the worst, with an old battery that needed constant recharging.

"Thank you." Georgie paused. "So you spent the day with Finn?"

Adalia heard the unspoken question in her sister's voice, but she wasn't taking the bait. "We had a lot of work to do for the art show."

She was proud of herself for not sounding defensive. Given what Georgie had said about him, it was clear she didn't approve, but she also didn't want to act like she was ashamed of her association with him. Or that she agreed with Georgie's assessment of his character. Because even though her sister was often right, on this one issue she was very wrong.

"Yeah, I'm sure you did…" Georgie said, but the way she left it hanging promised there would be more interrogations in the future.

"I'll call you tomorrow, okay? But not too early," Adalia said. "I plan on sleeping in." Or maybe seeing if Finn was interested in coming over for brunch, but she wasn't sharing that tidbit either. She quickly hung up and handed the phone back to River.

He shifted on his seat as he turned onto the road where her car was parked. "I know she seems overprotective," he said tentatively. "She just cares about you."

"I know, and I appreciate it, but…"

"I get it. Nothing like your sister's boyfriend showing up to bust up your…?" He shot her an inquisitive look.

In return, she gave him a pointed glare, but her teasing tone softened it. "Et tu, River?"

He chuckled. "Sorry, but at least now I can tell Georgie I asked." He pulled up next to Bessie. "For the record, I'll be following you home, otherwise your sister will kill me. And she may have a point. Your car looks like it needs to be pushed to your house."

She rolled her eyes as she opened the car door. "It's a classic."

But the word classic reminded her of Finn and their nearly perfect night. No man had ever offered to watch her favorite movie before.

What if she went back to his house to finish what they started?

The idea sent a wave of heat to her core, but River was going to follow her home. While it would be hilarious to drive to Finn's house, taking River back to the place he'd just left, it certainly wouldn't be covert. Besides, Finn thought they were taking this too fast, which was likely due to the whole Alan thing. The reason annoyed her—she didn't want Alan to have any control over her life—but she kind of liked the idea of going slow. She'd never hesitated to jump into bed with a guy if she really liked him, but Finn was different. What they had felt special. If she were honest with herself, that scared her a little—okay, *a lot*—but she also believed in taking risks and going for what she wanted. Or at least she used to before her arrest.

When she got home, she parked in the driveway and gave River a wave as she unlocked the door and went inside.

Dottie had left a note that said she'd dropped by with more food, and Adalia plugged her phone into the charging cord on the counter, then opened the fridge to see if there was any dessert.

"Ah-ha!" A plastic storage container marked "sassy" held a slice of what looked like lemon raspberry cake. She'd just grabbed a fork to eat it straight out of the container—*sorry, Jack, not sorry!*—when her phone dinged multiple times with all the messages she'd missed. Shaking her head, she walked over with the container to read her sister's texts.

Still, it wasn't Georgie's texts that caught her attention. It was a text from an unknown number: *You seriously blocked me? I've tried being nice, Adalia, but if YOU can't be nice, I'll have to take this to the next level.*

The next level? What did that mean?

She wasn't sure, but it was clearly a threat, which made her uneasy. She turned off her phone and put the cake back in the fridge, then hurried upstairs and took a shower. She hated being subjected to the stench of Alan on the heels of her night with Finn, and she was desperate to wash it away.

Sleep was slow to come, and despite what she'd said to Georgie, she was up by nine, itching to head to Dottie's garage—or even the shed out back—except she didn't want to paint. The mixed media piece she'd seen the day before had stirred something in her, and she might have considered doing something about it, only the memory of Alan's texts held her back. Not for the first time, she wondered what he'd done to her ruined pieces. They would have been released to him, right? Or maybe they'd just been thrown away.

What did he want from her, anyway? Money? Validation? It was probably time to talk to Georgie again, tell her that he was being more persistent than expected, but she didn't feel like having that conversation just yet.

Needing a boost, she lay around the living room, watching half a dozen episodes of *Friends*, debating whether she should call Finn and invite him over for brunch...and maybe something more.

Then she remembered she'd turned off her phone last night like a coward. She headed back into the kitchen and unplugged it, watching the percentage instantly drop from

100% to 98% when she turned it on. Multiple texts from Finn popped onto the screen.

A warm glow filled her chest, but then she realized it was after eleven a.m. and she still hadn't responded. Did he think she was blowing him off? She quickly sent him a text.

I can't wait to hear about your idea. We can hatch an elaborate plan to get me out of the brewery. I'll tell Georgie I have to go to the bathroom and sneak out the back door to play hooky... No. That's too simple. Maybe we can come up with something involving that trench coat. Or, you know, I could just take the day off. ;)

Then she added:

Sorry I'm just now responding. My phone was off.

He didn't respond immediately, and she worried she'd pissed him off. Alan hated being ignored—case in point, his last two messages. She hadn't responded to his initial overtures, which he'd probably thought were sweet, so he'd started rolling out threats. She knew Finn wasn't like that. Still, she was nervous until she saw the bubbles in the text box a couple of minutes later.

I tried not to respond immediately so I wouldn't look too eager, but this was as long as I could hold out.

I suppose I shouldn't have confessed that, huh?

She laughed to herself, then saw he was still typing.

Maisie wants to meet at the rescue at one to discuss the show. You up for going with me? I think you'll like her.

She would have been up for going to the city dump if it was with him. Finn was exactly what she needed this morning.

As your assistant, it seems like a given that I should go with you. Plus, puppies? Can we go sooner?

He immediately sent back: *Who said you were my assistant? More like co-chair, and how about I swing by and pick you up so we can get lunch before we head over?*

She was still in her pajamas, so she started typing—*Give me a half hour*—but then she deleted what she'd written and sent: *I'm not dressed yet, so give me time to put on some clothes. A half hour?*

He started typing, stopped, and then started typing again. For as much time as he was taking, he could have written a novella, but when he finally sent the text all it said was *Okay*.

She laughed again. Before last night she would have presumed he hadn't caught her innuendo or wasn't interested. Now she suspected he was imagining her naked.

She very much liked that.

She was putting on her ankle boots when he knocked at the door. When she yelled for him to come in, he opened the door, but he stopped in the entryway when he saw her sitting on the sofa, tugging the zipper on her boot. He just stood there, staring, uncharacteristically not saying a word.

Oh, God. Had she chosen the wrong thing to wear?

She'd put a lot of thought into her outfit, deciding on jeans since she hoped to play with some of the dogs…and also because they hugged her butt pretty well. The ankle boots because they were cute and easy to walk in, and since the air had a chill today, she'd put on a black long-sleeved T-shirt and a khaki jacket—both washable and practical for playing with dogs. But she was starting to think Finn didn't have a single dressed-down look in his wardrobe. He had on a pair of chinos, a pale blue button-down dress shirt, and loafers.

She got to her feet and took a step toward him. "Should I have dressed up more?" She thumbed toward the stairs. "I can go change."

He seemed to shake himself out of his stupor. "No, Addy. You look amazing."

He glanced down at his outfit, as if realizing why she'd asked, and…had Finn Hamilton just blushed? "My mother refused to buy me jeans when I was a kid. I guess it kind of stuck."

"You don't have any jeans?" she asked, genuinely shocked. "Are you Amish?"

"No, I do have some," he said quickly. "It's just not my default. And no, I'm not Amish, as far as I know."

She smiled and closed the distance between them. "Well, you're lucky that I like your one look."

And, because she could, she pressed a kiss to his lips.

She started to pull away, but he wrapped an arm around her back and tugged her closer, deepening the kiss.

When he leaned back, he cupped the side of her face and stared down at her with gleaming eyes. "While your text this morning has been driving me crazy, and I can't stop thinking about you naked, if we don't go now, we might not be able to fit lunch in before we need to be at Maisie's."

"I would say we should skip lunch and/or Maisie's," she confessed, giving him a wicked grin, "but one, I haven't had anything to eat today, and two, *puppies.*"

He laughed. "Maisie doesn't always have puppies. Sometimes she only has older dogs she's struggling to adopt out.… In fact, be prepared for her to try to convince you to foster a dog." He slid his hand down to her upper arm and squeezed it. "Be strong."

She gasped. "Oh, my God. Those poor dogs."

He grinned. "Maisie can sense weakness from a mile away. You're a goner. But you should probably wait until Jack gets home before you commit to anything." He glanced around. "When does he get back, anyway?"

"Late tonight, I think." She'd thought about calling him, hoping he'd maybe open up about whatever was going on in his life, but that would have required her to do the same. Shaking it off, she said, "But we're moving off-topic. I was promised there'd be lunch? I have to warn you that I'm not some delicate eater who picks at my food."

He laughed. "I went on a date with a saladatarian once. Trust me, I'm good with that."

"That's not a thing," Adalia said bluntly.

He shrugged it off. "I don't disagree, but the fact remains that she only ate food in salad form. Fruit salad. Chef salad. Pasta salad. I never knew there were so many types."

"Please tell me you left early."

His grin wicked, he said, "Would you have? I spent an hour and a half asking her questions about it, and she was more than happy to answer me. Turns out she was writing a book proposal on it. She was certain it would be the next health craze."

"Guess what I'm ordering for lunch?" Adalia teased.

"You would," he said, pulling her to him. He kissed her in a way that told her what she already knew—he might think the slow plan was best, but he didn't necessarily want to follow it. Neither did she. And yet it had sounded pretty nice when Finn wasn't in front of her. When he wasn't kissing her with the same kind of fervor with which Mr. Darcy had taken Elizabeth Bennet's hand. (A person didn't watch or read Regency stories for the steam factor, although Adalia had learned that touching a person's hand could look sexy as hell.) But something held her back, and she was the one who stepped away.

She reached up and caressed his cheek. "While part of me is very much on board with forgetting all about our plans, the other part of me wants to go slow." She kissed him one last time, just because she wanted to. "Now let's go before I change my mind."

She picked up her purse and flounced out the door, fully aware that Finn's gaze had zeroed in on her butt.

Good.

CHAPTER

Twenty

"Are we seriously going to Big Catch?" Adalia asked, giving him a little shove. "Why didn't you say anything?"

Because he still wasn't sure it was a good idea. But he was proud of what he'd done there, and it was, ironically enough, one of the few places in town where people didn't give him funny looks or throw rolls at him. River wasn't the only one who'd quit, but the workers who'd stayed were happy with the deal—he'd negotiated for them all to get a nice salary bump, and Bev Corp had a much better benefits package than he'd been able to afford.

The mural was coming along nicely outside. The artist hadn't finished yet, but she'd covered up the STDs slogan with a rushing river. The hull of a boat had just been started within it.

"I wanted you to see it, and I guess I wasn't sure you'd be up for going," he blurted out.

"Of course I want to see it," she said. "If only so I can lord it over River."

"For my health and well-being, *please* don't do that," he said. River had texted him to ask about his intentions (again), but truthfully his friend hadn't given him a hard time. *I've never seen you look at anyone like that*, he'd written. *I won't say Georgie isn't worried, but then again, she's worried about everything when it comes to Adalia.*

Which was maybe just the way of things with siblings. Finn had felt some of that same worry about River and Georgie getting together, so he didn't hold it against her.

"We'll see," she said, eyes twinkling. "How does this work with our whole plan to keep things covert?"

She said it like it was a naughty word, and it took everything in him to keep walking forward rather than back.

Take it slow, Finn. Don't scare her off.

"Nothing strange about two co-chairs having a business lunch together." He patted his messenger bag. "I even brought some more artists' portfolios for us to look at. I figure it'll save us from scheduling in-person meetings with another Stella."

"Oh, is that what's in there? I figured you were just into man purses." She laughed, and it was such a happy, carefree sound, he immediately wanted to hear it again—even if it was at his expense.

"I prefer the term bro bag."

She laughed harder, and he felt that familiar warm glow she always seemed to inspire. "You would," she said. "Do business colleagues hold hands?"

"Frequently." He reached for her hand and squeezed it.

They stepped into the brewery, which had been designed to look like the interior of an old boat. The inspiration for it was the Vasa Museum in Sweden—an entire museum centered around an ancient ship, perfectly preserved, reminiscent of the Vikings and Valhalla. The foyer was bustling, several people waiting on benches or milling about outside, but the hostess, Claire, broke away from the stand to hug him.

"We miss you and River around here." She shot an assessing look at Adalia, her gaze lingering on their linked hands. Finn wasn't much of a hand-holder usually, but Adalia brought it out in him. "Come on back. We have a table set aside for y'all."

A red-faced man on one of the benches got to his feet, his expression sour. "Why are they getting seated? They just got here, and we've been waiting for half an hour."

So much for the whole friendly vibes idea. The guy looked sort of familiar in an *I've seen you around town* kind of way, but Finn didn't know him personally. Recognition flickered on the man's face, and if anything, his cheeks got redder.

"Hey, aren't you that jerk who sold this place to Bev Corp? You *ruined* this place."

Finn had learned how to cut these conversations short quickly—be polite, take what they dished out, move on—but Adalia cut in before he could say anything.

"If you're so unhappy with the new management, why have you been waiting so long to get a seat?"

The man just stood there for a moment, mouth open, as if considering whether to make an ugly reply. Finn sincerely hoped he didn't. He didn't want to make a scene, but he wasn't about to let someone insult Adalia.

Finally, the guy shrugged. "They still have the same chef. He makes the best hot wings in town."

"Fair enough." Adalia shot Finn a wicked grin. "Why don't you get your hot wings to go and head down to

Buchanan Brewery. There's no wait, and our beer's even better."

"You're one of Beau Buchanan's granddaughters?" the man asked with interest.

"Sure am," she said, "and our brewery's the best in the city!"

A couple who'd been making beleaguered sighs while they waited for their table exchanged a glance and headed out the door, bound for Buchanan, if Finn had to guess.

Claire shot Adalia a dirty look, like maybe she suspected her of having written the STD graffiti, but she led them to their table—a nice, *covert* booth in the back— without further comment.

The expression on Adalia's face suggested she was enjoying herself immensely.

"Nicely done," he said. "Although I'm starting to think I shouldn't have brought a competitor through their doors."

"A competitor? You say that like you still have a stake in the brewery." She must have seen something on his face, because some of the joy slid out of her expression. "Do you?"

"No…" Except that wasn't quite true. He didn't want to lie to her, though he wished he'd talked to River first about the work he was doing for Bev Corp. "Well, not really."

She tilted her head. "What does *that* mean?"

"I've been doing a little consulting work for them. Helping them find more of a niche in the community."

She gestured at the crowded room. "Doesn't seem like they're hurting."

"No," he said honestly, "that's never been a problem here. There's a tasting room on the floor below us, and that's usually full too."

"So what's the problem?"

"The problem is one of reputation," he said. "Most of the customers are tourists. They'd like to do better with locals, and they don't want to be the bad guys in town."

She raised an eyebrow. "Kind of like someone I know."

Finn just shrugged, knowing it was true.

A server Finn didn't recognize came by with food and beer menus.

"Have you been here before, folks?" he asked, his tone bubbly.

Adalia shot Finn a challenging look. "No"—she looked at the server's name tag—"Bryan, we haven't. What's the origin story?"

The guy gave her the long-suffering smile of someone who'd been asked that question often. "Well, the place was started by Finn Hamilton, a local entrepreneur, with River Reeves as the brewmaster. They say it was named after Finn's stories. He always embellishes them like a fisherman exaggerates the size of his catch."

Adalia burst into laughter. "So, this Finn guy likes to embellish the size of his...catch?"

"Very funny," Finn said, winking at her, "but there's no need for embellishment." Turning to Bryan, he added, "Still, you might want to rethink the way you phrase your story."

Poor Bryan fidgeted in place. He seemed to have caught on to the situation, but it was clear he couldn't decide whether to acknowledge it.

"Um. Do you need a minute with the menus?"

"Nah, that's okay," Adalia said, handing them back. "My colleague here is *very* familiar with them."

The mounting evidence that Finn was, in fact, the Finn Hamilton seemed to fluster Bryan even more, so Finn put him out of his misery.

"I'll have a Blue Whale IPA, and a Lake Trout Lager for the lady. We'll both have burgers."

Bryan practically launched himself away from the table.

"I think you frightened him half to death," Finn commented.

"We'll tip him well," Adalia said. "I guess I should have mentioned the fact that while I'm not a saladatarian, since it doesn't exist and all, I *am* a pescatarian."

"Oh shit," Finn said, getting to his feet. But Bryan had pulled off an admirably quick retreat and was nowhere to be seen. Settling back down, he shrugged. "We'll break the news to him when he brings our drinks."

"So, you were saying?"

Her teasing had taken on a slightly antagonistic edge, and he suspected it had something to do with his partial revelation about Bev Corp.

"It's not what you're thinking," he said. "I'd never do anything to hurt River and Georgie, not again, and the art show has nothing to do with Bev Corp. It's a completely separate project."

A corner of her mouth tipped up. "For a man in search of his next big idea, you sure have a lot going on. So what are you doing for them, *Big Catch*?"

Oh, God. The way she said that, her gaze raking over him…the last thing he wanted to talk about was work. He wanted to convince her—and himself—the slow approach was not working, and they should take this back to his house, or hers, but first he needed her to understand.

He told her about his ideas for Gretchen, Bryan arriving with their beers sometime in the middle of their conversation.

When Finn told him one of the burgers would need to be switched to a veggie, Bryan apologized to *him*. If that wasn't confirmation enough that someone had confirmed his identity to Bryan, the server called him Mr. Hamilton. And sir.

Adalia grinned at him the whole time, her eyes bright with repressed laughter.

"Hey," he said when Bryan walked away. "It's not like I *asked* him to say that. But I'm not going to lie—it feels better than being called a jerk."

"Fair enough."

He finished up his spiel about the beer festival right after Bryan brought out the burgers, practically bowing as he backed away, and Adalia thought for a minute, tapping the side of her glass in a way that increased Finn's suspense.

"This is good. Similar to our Hair of Hops lager but different," she said. "River's super talented."

"No kidding," he said. "So, what's the verdict? Tell me what you think."

"You need to talk to him sooner rather than later. He's going to flip if he finds out from someone other than you." He'd rested his hand on the table, and she put hers over it. "And no, I'm not going to tell him. I'm not sure they'll go for it, but I think they should. You're right. It's a win-win."

He released a breath. "Thanks. I was planning on telling him as soon as Gretchen gives me an idea of whether they want to move forward with the event. I figured…"

"No need to cause trouble if it's not going to work," she finished for him. "Practical. You're good at this, you know."

He met her gaze. "It's what I like best. Figuring things out. Troubleshooting. The day-to-day stuff doesn't interest me as much."

She was quiet for a moment, and he was about to shift the conversation when she said, "You would have sold the brewery a long time ago, if it weren't for River."

It wasn't a question. She'd seen it in him somehow. He found himself thinking again about Lola, and the tarot cards all lined up in a neat row.

"You're right," he said simply.

She moved her hand off of his. For a moment, he regretted its loss, but she lowered it onto his thigh instead, the heat instantly driving him mad. "What are we doing on Wednesday?"

"I'll never tell," he said, leaning into her touch. "Well, except for on Wednesday morning, when it will, of course, become need-to-know information."

"You *are* being covert. Now, let's see what you have in that man purse."

"I thought you'd never ask."

———————————

Based on the portfolios he'd compiled, some handed to him by Dottie, the rest found through his own research, they decided to invite three of the artists to participate in the show, to visit five others, and to (hopefully) forget the last one, whose realistic clown paintings would probably haunt Finn for the rest of his life. Had Dottie known about his irrational fear of clowns?

They drove over to Dog is Love, talking about the show and hypothesizing about the models used by the clown artist. Did he travel from circus to circus? Were they based on people he didn't like? When Finn pulled into the lot, ten minutes late—lunch had taken longer than he'd thought, partially because Bryan had brought over his origin story speech at the end of their meal and asked Finn to both edit and sign it—he saw River's car.

"Well, there you go," Adalia said, grinning. "You need to talk to him, and the universe delivered. I'm sure Dottie would have something to say about that."

Except he suspected it wasn't a coincidence at all. Maisie must have been desperate enough to duck River—or at least being alone with River—that she'd changed her meeting with him to coincide with Finn's visit. And she'd neglected to tell Finn, fearing (correctly) that he'd cancel. He was tempted to just pull out of the lot and leave, but if he did that he'd have to explain to Adalia, and she might feel compelled to say something to Georgie, and then…

"It's not a coincidence, is it?" Adalia said. He started to say something, but she raised a hand. "Say no more. I can tell you're on the verge of telling me what's going on in there. But I'd prefer to keep it a horrible surprise."

"Well, I'm not inclined to argue with that."

He went around to open her door, and she hooked her arm through his like they were about to go on a picnic.

The front door was open, since they'd come during the shelter's regular hours, and an older bearded guy sat behind the desk, eating some sort of smelly cheese Danish.

Seeing them, he swallowed thickly.

Finn introduced himself, thought about shaking the guy's hand, thought about the Danish, and settled for a nod.

"Maisie's already back there with River," the guy said. "They're in the visiting room. Do you need me to show you back?"

Finn grappled with his conscience. Maisie obviously didn't want to talk to River alone, and part of him thought he should go back there and save her. But another part of him genuinely believed that she was avoiding the inevitable. That her hesitation to talk to River, and maybe even divulge her secret, was causing both of them pain. Besides, he believed in River and Maisie's friendship—even knowing what he knew—and it was never going to get back on track if they didn't talk it out.

"Actually, maybe we could look at the adoptable dogs first?" He shot a glance at Adalia and gently pulled her to his side. "This one's thinking of becoming a foster mom."

CHAPTER
Twenty-One

The man got up and walked around the desk, licking his fingers and thumb, and Adalia resisted the urge to cringe. Was that a wise idea in a place like this?

"I'm Dustin, by the way," he said, leading them to a side door. "Are you sure you don't want to head back and see Maisie? She seemed pretty insistent that I send you back as soon as you got here."

"No," Finn said, but Adalia caught the glance he shot to the closed door in the back before he headed for the door marked *Kennels*. "I promised Adalia she could see the dogs first."

"Okay…" Dustin said, sounding like he wasn't sure that was a good idea.

"You don't need to show us around if you're busy," Finn said. "I know my way around."

Dustin appeared reluctant, but his gaze drifted longingly to the Danish on his desk. "If you're sure you don't mind…"

"Not in the least," Finn said, already opening the door.

"But try to hurry," Dustin said. "Maisie really wanted you to join her."

Finn didn't answer, and instead ushered Adalia into a large room with multiple kennels on one side and lots of windows on the other. The fans on the ten-foot ceiling were circulating the air, but the room still stank of dog.

Barks and howls filled the space, and the first kennel held a large lab mix who was adding to the chorus. He jumped up, the metal door clanging under his paws.

"Oh, that poor dog," she said, reaching toward the door.

"Be careful," Finn said, pulling her hand away. "Some of them are biters." He released her, nodding to the door. "But this one seems to be okay. Maisie labels the ones that you need to be careful with."

She looked up at him, her eyes narrowing. "Why didn't we go back to the room with Maisie and River? What's going on?"

"I thought you didn't want to know," he challenged with a small smile. "I thought you wanted it to be a horrible surprise."

"Well…the fact that you're avoiding it like it's a smallpox plague has me intrigued. You don't tend to shy away from conflict."

He grimaced. "River was supposed to come see Maisie this morning, but she obviously rearranged her schedule so that we'd be here when he showed up."

Her brow lifted. "And you didn't know she'd rescheduled?"

"Not a clue or I wouldn't have agreed to come. Which is why she purposely kept it from me."

Adalia looked at the door to the lobby, worry starting to brew in her chest. "Should I be concerned?" Her gaze lifted to Finn's. "Should *Georgie*?"

"No." He took her hand and held it against his hard pec. Maybe she shouldn't notice something like that at a time like this, but sue her. She had hormones. "River loves Georgie," he continued. "I would never be part of anything that would tear them apart."

When she made a face, he added, "Again."

"So what's going on?"

"River and Maisie have been friends for a long time, and they've always been tight. They used to hang out all the time, and the three of us got together every week for Taco Tuesday."

"But he doesn't do that anymore," she said. "At least Georgie never mentions it, and I know she would."

"You're right." He dropped her hand and walked past several of the kennels.

The dogs leapt in their cages, eager for attention, and while Adalia felt compelled to give it to them, this conversation was too important for her to let it go.

"Georgie wouldn't forbid River to see his friend," Adalia said defensively. "She's not the jealous type."

"I know," he said, his mouth twisting to the side. "Or at least I know Georgie's not the reason they haven't gotten together."

"River?" she asked, giving it some thought. "Did he stop meeting you two weekly after he and Georgie started seeing each other? Partially because he was pissed with you?"

"The weekly Bro Club dinners? Yeah, that had something to do with it."

"Bro Club dinners?" she teased. "Really?"

He smirked. "That's what Maisie called them, and it kind of stuck. As a joke."

"But he stopped seeing Maisie?" That bothered her more than she cared to admit. She understood why he'd shied away from Finn for a while, but had he really just abandoned his childhood friend? If so, it didn't say much for his character.

Finn grimaced again. "This is not my business to tell."

He was protecting someone. River? Maisie? *Georgie?*

"Were River and Maisie ever more than friends?"

"No, Addy. If they were, I would tell you. Honest." His expression said he meant it.

"But something's going on, otherwise we wouldn't be hiding back here. We'd be with River and Maisie."

"They had a fight," Finn blurted. "No, not really a fight, more like a misunderstanding. I advised Maisie to talk to him about it, but apparently she doesn't *want* to, otherwise we wouldn't be here right now. We'd be at my place or yours watching *Fast Five*."

She grinned. "We never finished *Pride and Prejudice*."

He grimaced. "I might have finished it without you."

She gave his shoulder a playful shove. "You cad."

He laughed and captured her hand in his.

They looked into each other's eyes for a moment, and Adalia was astonished that she was in this place with him, not the dog rescue—okay, yes, the dog rescue—but in this state of happiness. Of *easiness*. She'd never felt this way with anyone before, and while she reveled in it, she was still scared. She'd given far too much of herself to Alan, and look where that had gotten her.

Finn is nothing like Alan. Alan isn't even fit to tie the shoelaces on his dockers.

Are those laces even real, or are they just for show?

She laughed, and Finn's eyes lit up.

"Something funny?" he asked.

"I have sad news for you: there's no way we're moving on to your *Fit and Fabulous* movie without finishing *Pride and Prejudice*. Together. It's not my fault you cheated and watched the rest without me."

He gave her a mock glare. "Excuse me, it's *Fast Five*."

"Well, the deal was we'd watch them together, so we'll just have to pick up where we left off."

His eyes darkened. "Exactly where we left off?"

A spark of desire ignited in her core, but she ignored it—and his question—as she turned to face the next kennel. A red Siberian husky lay on the concrete floor, staring up at her with a look of resignation.

"*Finn*," she cried out as she squatted next to the dog.

He moved closer. "The sign on the door says his name is Tyrion."

"Does it say why he's here?" she asked, staring into the dog's soulful eyes.

"I guess he was returned."

Anger burned in her blood as she stood, glaring up at him. "Returned? What kind of monster would do that?"

He gave her a half shrug. "Maybe he was in a foster home and something came up."

"Whatever it was broke him," she said, close to tears. "We can't just leave him here."

"Let's talk to Maisie."

"We'll have to stop hiding first," she countered with a stern look.

Taking her hand, he tugged her to a cage closer to the door. "Adalia, meet Cinnamon."

He was trying to distract her with an adorable little terrier mix, jumping up against the door, but Tyrion still lay on his side, his eyes mournful, and she felt close to tears.

Finn offered her an understanding smile. "A lot of the dogs are scared—like Tyrion—and they have trouble snapping out of it here in the kennels. It may actually distress him more if we hang out outside of his kennel. If you want to visit with him, we can have Maisie bring him to the playroom after we talk to her."

She held her hand up to Cinnamon, and the little dog sniffed it and then licked her through the cage.

"That means he likes you," Finn said, pressing his chest to her back.

A wave of heat washed through her. If he was still trying to distract her, it was working in the most delicious way. "Do you lick too when you like someone?"

He groaned and took two steps back. "You're determined to torture me," he said, his voice tight, but his eyes were dancing. "And no, I don't typically lick people when I first meet them."

Adalia spun around and advanced on him as though he was her prey. He backed up into the wall, his eyes hooded as he watched her.

"I should hope not," she said in a husky tone, placing her hands on his chest. "I only lick people who are very special to me." Holding his gaze, she lifted onto her tiptoes and lightly ran her tongue over the hollow of his throat. Then, before he could get his arm around her, she backed up out of reach, flashing him a wicked smile.

He watched her, a war waging in his eyes, and she almost felt guilty about teasing him. It hadn't been a premeditated move. It had been completely natural—organic—like everything with him so far.

"I like you, Finn," she said, all teasing gone. "I've never known a man like you. You make me feel like I can just be me." And wasn't that a revelation. Plenty of guys had been interested in her for her body, and Alan had been in it for her art, but she'd never been involved with a man who was this interested in her as a person. Her mouth lifted into a crooked smile. "I'm sort of sorry for what happened just now, but not because I regret doing it. More like I'm sorry if I'm making this harder for you."

He slowly shook his head. "Don't stop being you, Addy. I love that you're so spontaneous. You bring it out in me too."

Smiling, she took his hand and squeezed it.

"I'll try to behave," she said in a teasing tone.

"God, I hope not," he said, pulling her to his chest. He kissed her, and she grabbed a handful of his shirt, clinging to him as his mouth devoured hers. She pressed into him, needing more, and he responded in kind, sinking a hand into her hair, tilting her head to give him better access.

"Well, *this* is awkward," a woman said in a dry tone.

Finn lifted his head to face the woman who stood in the doorway. She was about medium height and had a head full of curly red hair, the look in her green eyes alternating between irritation and amusement.

"Is this the new make-out spot and someone forgot to tell me?" She cast a glance over her shoulder, into the lobby. "River, you'll have to bring Georgie. Maybe we can book appointments."

"Maisie," Finn said, gently releasing Adalia and taking a step toward his friend. "It's—"

One brow lifted higher than the other as the red-headed woman gave him her best schoolteacher glare. "Not what it looks like? If that's true, then I'm super curious what it is."

River appeared behind her, a dark look in his eyes. "Maisie, let it go."

"Obviously, this is inappropriate," Finn said, holding his hands up. "I apologize for any—"

"Whatever," Maisie said, rolling her eyes and turning around. "We have things to discuss. After you two wrap things up here, meet us in the playroom." Then she shoved River into the lobby and shut the door behind her.

Finn spun around to face Adalia with a questioning look in his eyes. "Addy, I'm sorry."

She clenched her hands at her sides, her irritation rising. "Don't you dare say you're sorry for that. I'm not. Was it embarrassing? Sure. But I still don't regret it. Do you know why?"

He cracked a grin. "No, but I can't wait to hear."

Jabbing her finger into his chest, she kept her gaze on his. "Because what we have is raw and it's real. And every time you kiss me, it makes me want to know you even more. Mentally, emotionally, and—" she paused and licked her bottom lip, "—carnally."

Finn sucked in a breath.

"Granted," Adalia said with a grin, "the location could have been better. But we'll be more careful next time." Then she walked past him, making sure her butt swayed with her gait. She grabbed the doorknob and glanced over her shoulder, not surprised by the direction of his gaze. When his eyes lifted, she grinned. "Or maybe not."

CHAPTER
Twenty-Two

When Finn and Adalia walked into the playroom, the tension was almost palpable. Although there was a small table surrounded by four rickety-looking chairs, Maisie and River were both standing, almost on opposite sides of the room. It took everything in Finn not to grab Adalia's hand and declare they were heading back to the new make-out spot. But Maisie shot him the kind of look that would pin a butterfly in its box, and he knew better than to try. River just seemed frustrated, which suggested that Maisie still hadn't leveled with him—because if she had, he would be more upset.

"Where's Hops?" he blurted out. It was a stupid thing to say, really—he'd known the Hops thing was a ruse, and Maisie had clearly known too.

"Miraculously improved," Maisie said with a tight smile. "But River came over anyway so he could discuss the art show with us."

River clearly wanted to object, and it was obvious he would prefer it if they both got lost. But wishes were horses, and they were all out of hay (or something like that—Finn's maternal grandfather had basically only spoken in colloquialisms, but they'd gotten jumbled in his old age. He'd been by far the most relatable person in Finn's family).

"Well, hallelujah!" Adalia said brightly, lowering herself into one of the empty chairs. Finn shrugged and sat next to her. "So tell me, Maisie, how does a person go about becoming a foster parent for the shelter?"

"Oh, so you noticed there were dogs back there?" Maisie asked, her lips curling up a little at the corners, softening the remark.

"Of course! He used the dogs to draw me back there. Then he had his wicked way with me," Adalia said with a straight face, then burst out laughing—probably at Finn's strangled expression. He could practically feel River's gaze shifting from Maisie to him.

"It wasn't *quite* like that," he said.

But Maisie laughed too, and she finally left her position by the door and sat down across from Adalia.

"If you're serious about it, you can fill out an application at the front desk before you leave. Spoiler alert: I'll approve it. We're always in need of new fosters." She tilted her head. "But you're living at Beau's old place, huh? With Jezebel around, we'll need to get you one that doesn't scare easily."

Adalia laughed. "You're not scared the dog would go after her?"

Maisie just gave her a look.

"Touché. That's okay. I wouldn't want a wimpy dog, anyway." Her eyes softened, and Finn knew she was thinking of Tyrion, of the deep sadness in his eyes as he lay on the floor. Something about that dog had spoken to Adalia, like maybe she saw the brokenness she felt reflected back to her.

She glanced back at him, and he took her hand under the table. River and Maisie could probably see what he was doing anyway, but hell, that ship had sailed.

"What about Jack?" River asked, the first time he'd spoken since they'd entered the room. "Shouldn't you ask him before you bring home another pet?" To Maisie, he said, "Jack's back from Chicago. He's living at the house too."

Maisie's only response was a terse nod. Her gaze still on Adalia, she said, "One of them's caught you, I can tell. Want to give me a hint?"

Adalia smirked. "Let's just say I'm a *Game of Thrones* fan, even though the last season was a major letdown."

Something lit in Maisie's eyes, and he knew Adalia had her on the hook. "Ah, Tyrion. Certain dogs don't do well in the shelter. He needs to be with people. I tried taking him home with me, but my old man isn't a fan."

"You live with your father?" Adalia asked, her tone more curious than judgmental.

"That's what she calls her dog," River answered, finally approaching the table. "Einstein's twelve, and he's what you might call set in his ways." He glanced at Maisie, as if asking for permission to sit. Emotion warred in her eyes, but she gave him a slight nod.

"Tyrion's been returned three times, you know," Maisie said, her focus back on Adalia. "Trust me, I want to get him out of here. You saw him. But I also don't want him to get attached to someone only to be let down again."

"Three times?" Finn blurted out. "What's wrong with him?" He hadn't noticed any special markings on the kennel, but the last thing he wanted was for Adalia to take a biter home with her. Especially a biter the size of that dog.

But suddenly everyone at the table was scowling at him.

"He's perfect," Adalia insisted.

Maisie, speaking at the same time, said, "Nothing." The two of them exchanged a smile, then Maisie added, "Huskies are adorable puppies, but they get big fast, and they're more work than people think. They need a lot of exercise, plus they shed enough to make a fur coat. Several times over. And they're notorious runners. Tyrion ran from his last home enough times that they just gave up."

Would it really be a good idea for Adalia to bring home a canine escape artist when she already had a cat that went on walkabouts?

But Finn saw the look in Adalia's eyes—she didn't care. She needed to bring that dog home to heal something in herself.

"If he wanted to stay with me, I would never bring him back," she said simply. "Never."

Maisie gave her a weighing look again and then nodded.

"Maybe you can text Jack?" Finn suggested.

"You're going to ask him over text if he wants to foster a dog he's never met?" River asked dubiously.

"Why not?" Adalia said. "He just moved in with a sister he'd never met. It'll be a year of firsts for him."

Maisie snorted, her eyes sparkling. "I think I like you."

"Well, good," Adalia said, sending a look at River akin to a dare. "Because I like you too."

River held up his hands. "Text him. I know when I'm beat." He glanced at Maisie again. "And I know better than to stand in the way of a person and their soul companion."

"Soul companion?" Adalia asked, already pulling out her phone. Her eyes flicked to Finn, and he felt his heart start racing.

"That's what I've always called them," Maisie said softly. "Pet seems demeaning to me."

Some of the tension in the room had eased, like a balloon with a slow leak. Maisie wanted to harden her heart to River, that was clear, but it wasn't working. Not with him around, anyway.

Adalia fired off the text so quickly that Finn felt borderline sure it just read: *You're okay with me fostering a dog, right?* She certainly hadn't typed enough to have warned him about the shedding or the running away.

Then again, maybe Jack shouldn't have taken off abruptly if he hadn't wanted to come back to a depressed husky. Finn still didn't totally trust him after what he'd overheard on the phone the other day, although he realized there could be dozens of different interpretations. It had only been a one-sided conversation, after all, and Adalia hadn't seemed overly concerned.

"Should we talk about the show while we wait for him to respond?" Finn proposed. Then, because Maisie clearly didn't know the deal with Jack, he added, "Jack's been doing a lot of work organizing Buchanan's events, but he's out of town this weekend. We'll loop him in when he gets back."

"Sure. Whatever." Her gaze shot to River, and she said, "I've been thinking about what you said, Finn, about coming in to tug on some heartstrings—and purse strings—opening night. I'm down. And I'd be happy to bring a litter of puppies for people to play with so we can really turn the screws."

So she'd decided she wasn't going to ignore River for…well, however long it took to get over unrequited love. Well, unrequited romantic love. He knew River loved Maisie, but he saw her as family. Always had. Something Finn might have—gently—told Maisie a long time ago if he'd realized how she felt.

Adalia gave a little huff of a laugh. "I was thinking about that, actually. I've been doing photo shoots with Hops and Jezebel to promo River's new beers. What if I take photos of the adoptable dogs? We can display them in the events hall. Maybe raffle them off, and the funds for a particular photo can go to help that dog."

Finn squeezed her hand. "That's a great idea."

Maisie grinned. "We'll need to use a bucket of treats, especially for the surlier ones, but I like the way you think. People have trouble ignoring sad-eyed photos. As they should."

Adalia brightened even more, like a dimmer lamp turned up on high, and Finn wanted to photograph *her*. He wanted to always remember how she looked in this moment, when she was letting her creativity, her passion, freely flow. When she wasn't trying to shut it down.

She glanced at him. "Maybe I can even see if Blue will knit one of them. That would be beyond incredible. You know she could do it."

"Blue Combs?" Maisie asked.

"Yeah," Finn said. "Do you know her?"

"She's good people." She smirked. "I set her up with this enormous Flemish rabbit someone had brought to the shelter. I usually only take in dogs, but I couldn't turn him away. He had to stay in this playroom until Blue took him home, because I was worried how the dogs would react."

"She *would* have a giant rabbit," Adalia said fondly, and Finn had to laugh.

"If you keep talking about her like that, I might get jealous," he said.

"Maybe you should," she said, nudging him.

River shot them another look, but he didn't say anything. At least he didn't look pissed. Finn got the impression he intended to leave them to sort this out—whatever *this* was—and he appreciated it. It was a trust he didn't deserve.

Maisie studied Adalia for a moment, then said, "Maybe the three of us could meet for a drink sometime. You, me, and Blue, I mean—not these losers."

River's gaze shifted to Maisie, and Finn saw a gratitude in his friend's eyes that he keenly felt too. If Adalia was going to stay in Asheville, and oh God, he wanted her to stay, she would need to make connections. To grow roots, as River would say, and Maisie, despite whatever she might feel about Georgie, was offering that.

"I'd like that," Adalia said.

Her phone buzzed then, and she jumped a little before she bent over to check it.

"Ha!" She set the phone on the table and turned it so they could all see the screen.

He could see Adalia's text, which, sure enough, read: *I want to foster a dog. You down?*

Jack's reply was beneath it: *I'm gone two days, and now you're getting a dog? Sure. Why not. Make sure Jezebel doesn't eat him.*

"Welcome to Winterfell, Tyrion," she said, grinning.

"Why not King's Landing?" River asked.

"Duh. Huskies prefer the cold."

"Who's volunteering to restrain Jezebel?" Finn said. "Because, *not it*. I still have scars on my arms from when I tried two months ago."

"Oh, you'll do it," Adalia said. "You *know* you will."

She was right. He'd do it for her, and much more than that too. And a part of him was terrified at the thought.

CHAPTER
Twenty-Three

"Welcome to your new home, Tyrion," Adalia said, as she opened the back door to Finn's fancy car, which now had tufts of hair all over the leather.

Would Finn be upset? She mentally shrugged. *Love me. Love my dog.*

Then she realized she'd said the L word, which was problematic, even if it was only in her head. That was leapfrogging many steps ahead, but she really liked him. She could see it might be a possibility in the future.

Out of self-preservation, she considered telling him to go home, that she wanted to get Tyrion acclimated to his new home alone, but most of her wanted him there. She liked the bubble of happiness that surrounded her whenever he was close.

The dog jumped out, sniffed the grass next to the driveway, and promptly lifted his leg.

"Well, he's not running yet," Finn said, walking around to her side of the car. "I take that as a good sign."

"The leash probably helps," she said. Maisie had warned them both to keep a good hold on it in case he decided to bolt.

Finn started to shut the door but noticed all the hair on the seat and swept it out, grinning. "Maybe we should save it for Blue. She could knit a second Tyrion out of his own fur."

Adalia's heart burst open and, keeping a firm grip on the leash, she walked over and lifted onto her toes to kiss him.

"Not that I'm complaining," he said, his eyes shining, "but what prompted that? So I can be sure to do it again."

"Just you being you," she said, patting his chest. "Thank you."

Grinning, he started to say something, then stopped and shook his head. "I'm going to stop while I'm ahead. The only responses I can think of are Mr. Darcy responses. They'd make you think I'm as conceited and full of myself as you did when you first met me."

"Oh, I wouldn't assume you're too far ahead." They both laughed, but Adalia didn't want to just laugh him off. He'd said something real. "I'm sorry if I ever made you feel that way."

"It was partly deserved," he said. "I fully admit that."

She studied him in amazement. How many men had that level of self-awareness? How many *people*?

His expression shifted, and he cast a glance at the dog, who was still sniffing around with interest. "You ready to bring him inside?"

Biting her bottom lip, she was silent for a moment, then said, "Maybe we should stay out on the front porch for a bit. Let him get used to me."

He laughed. "You spent an hour with him in the playroom at the shelter. You're stalling."

"I just don't want to scare Tyrion. Jezebel is like a banshee with claws."

"Jezebel *is* a banshee with claws. And besides"—his gaze dropped to her side—"I don't think any adjustment period is required. He already seems taken with you."

Tyrion sat at Adalia's side, patiently waiting.

She leaned over and rubbed behind his ears, staring into his eyes—an arresting mix of yellow, green, and one patch of blue. "Don't worry, big guy. Finn will protect us both."

"I should have stopped by my house and picked up my leather jacket."

She gave him a hopeful look. "It's not too late."

He laughed again, but it had a nervous edge. "Maybe we should call Dottie. Without Jack's sorcery at hand, she's our best bet for taming the beast."

Pushing out a sigh, she considered it. She had hoped to be alone with Finn for a while before he left for Charlotte, but then again, she'd just brought home a nervous, unsettled dog. Did she really want to ignore him to make out with Finn?

Did it make her a bad person that she had to give it a half-second of thought?

"That's probably a good idea, don't you think?" she asked hesitantly.

His eyes softened. "Yeah. It actually is. Let the record show I came up with it."

She shook her head, laughing. "Duly noted. Point to Gryffindor."

"What makes you think my house is Gryffindor?" he asked, his brow raised.

"After the whole Big Catch sale, I can see how some people might peg you as a Slytherin, but you're a Gryffindor, through and through." She patted his chest again. "Courageous. Chivalrous."

"Courageous?" he asked in surprise.

"Anyone else would have tucked tail and run, but you're still here, Finn, trying to make things right. That's courage."

He was silent for a moment, and she started to worry she'd said the wrong thing, but then the now-familiar teasing look filled his eyes. "What are you, a Hufflepuff?"

"God, no," she snorted, scrunching up her face. "I'm a Ravenclaw. Now let's call Dottie."

Dottie, of course, agreed to come over right away.

Adalia and Finn waited outside with Tyrion, who continued to walk around and sniff the yard, peeing on several things in what Finn assured her was an encouraging development.

The frizzy-haired neighbor from a few houses down was walking down the sidewalk and did a double take when she saw the dog. Her eyes lifted to Adalia's in horror. "You have *another* pet?"

"Yep," Adalia said, puffing her chest with pride. "This is Tyrion. He's part dire wolf."

The woman's eyes grew wide and she hurried off, casting backward glances at Adalia and the dog.

"I'm not sure you should have provoked her," Finn said, shaking his head with a grin. "River's phone's about to blow up with people petitioning to remove the wolf from the neighborhood. You better hope he doesn't give them your number."

"I can take it."

Dottie arrived a few minutes later, wearing a flowing multicolored kaftan, her lavender hair wrapped in a bright blue and white turban. She held out her hands as her gaze landed on the husky. "What a darling!"

"Dottie," Adalia said, "this is Tyrion."

"Such a strong name for such a handsome dog," Dottie said, crouching down to pet him. He instantly started wagging his tail. "I'll go find our sweet girl so your boy can get to know his new home. I'll let you know when it's safe to come in." She rose up spryly, as if crouching at her age weren't a near-wondrous feat, then headed up the porch steps.

"Sweet girl?" Adalia snickered under her breath.

"Dottie always seems to see the best in people…and animals."

There was no disputing that.

They chatted about the show for a few minutes—Finn asked if she'd be willing to make a couple of artist visits while he was out of town, and she agreed. But when Dottie didn't reemerge after ten minutes, Adalia made a show of looking at her watch.

"What do you think? Has Jezebel murdered her?"

"Probably not," he smirked. "But the last time Dottie was given full run of this house she nearly burned it down. Maybe we should go in and check."

"Good idea. It's one thing for Jack to come back to a new dog, and another to come home to a new dog sitting in a burnt-out house."

They took Tyrion around to the back yard, tied his lead to the tree by the bench, making sure he had plenty of shade, then went in through the back door.

"I'll go first," Finn said, motioning for her to get behind him.

"See, I told you that you were courageous," she teased. But she didn't object. She didn't feel like getting clawed any more than he did.

Dottie was standing in the middle of the kitchen, holding a smoking oversized cigar. An open can of sardines sat at her feet at the center of a three-foot-diameter circle she'd drawn in chalk. Several multi-colored crystals had been spaced out along the line.

"Um, Dottie…" Finn said, his hesitation apparent, "this looks…interesting."

Adalia shot him a huge grin before turning back to Dottie. "What do the crystals do?"

"The energy from the blue and yellow crystals is intended to draw Jezebel to the center of the circle, while the purple, black, and clear ones will keep her there."

"Why didn't we use this setup in June when Jezebel was on the loose?" Finn asked, glancing down at his arms as if he could still feel the cat's claws.

"I've been reading up on it, dear," Dottie said patiently, "in case Jezebel lost her way again. I confess, I never expected to use it in the house."

"Are you planning to catch her?" Finn asked.

"I was thinking we'd draw her into the circle, then bring in your newest guest while she's safely inside," Dottie said.

"And the crystals will keep her there?" Finn asked.

"That's the plan."

"Sounds foolproof," Adalia said, but she had to admit that as much as she encouraged Dottie's kookiness, she was worried about how the cat would react to Tyrion. He already seemed scared, and she didn't want to traumatize him any more than necessary. Nor did she want any of the humans in the room to lose an eye.

"I need to find the dear and send her toward the circle with the sage," Dottie said, glancing around. "Now where did she wander off to?"

"I know how to draw her," Adalia said, glancing out the back window to check on Tyrion. He looked content enough, but she didn't want to leave him out there any longer than necessary. She grabbed an oven mitt from a drawer and put it on the kitchen table. That done, she started adding things to the blender: frozen strawberries, frozen peaches, orange juice, and a generous squeeze of honey.

"Um, Adalia," Finn said. "Are you making the cat a *smoothie?*"

"I know it sounds nuts," Adalia said, "but every time I make a smoothie, she's on the blender like I'm chopping catnip. No interest in margaritas, though. Go figure."

"She's definitely Jack's soul companion, not yours," Finn said with a small smile. "I'm not sure what that says about him."

She nudged him. "Anyway, one time I caught her licking the container, so I figure we can use the smoothie to subdue her, too."

"That's what the crystals are for," Dottie said.

Adalia grimaced. "Maybe we should have a backup plan. Finn, get a laundry basket from the basement."

He hurried off, and when he returned with the white plastic basket, he looked so triumphant she was tempted to pull up "Eye of the Tiger" on her phone. "Got it," he said, "and may I state for record that I feel much better about trying to trap her with this than with that flimsy nylon collapsible carrier I used last time. Now how does a smoothie draw a cat?"

"Not just *any* cat," Adalia said. "Watch and learn." She pressed a button on the blender, creating a loud grinding sound, and seconds later, a black streak shot into the kitchen, jumping up on the counter. Jezebel started attacking the blender, screeching and hissing, her paws flying.

"What the hell?" Finn shouted as Adalia backed up out of reach of the cat's claws.

Adalia donned the oven mitt and grabbed the electric cord, trying to pull it from the wall, but Jezebel took a swipe at her.

"Trap her, Finn!"

Finn rushed forward with the basket but tripped on a crystal and missed. The basket hit the blender, tipping the appliance over onto its side. The lid popped off, and smoothie shot all over the counter and walls while Jezebel continued attacking the blender as if she were in a fight for her life. The machine slid across the granite counter, spreading the strawberry concoction all over Adalia's and Finn's chests and faces…and everywhere else.

Adalia burst out laughing, trying to reach the cord again, but slipped on the wet floor and fell, her butt cheek landing on a crystal.

"Oww!"

Finn reached for her, concern in his eyes, but she waved him off and got to her feet, determined to shut off the blender before the cat managed to reach inside and hurt herself. Ignoring Jezebel's frenzied clawing at the small appliance, she got a good hold on the cord and yanked.

As soon as the blender stopped, Jezebel halted her attack and became completely complacent, looking at the blender as though wondering how she'd gotten there. She jumped off the counter and landed in the center of the circle, sitting on her butt in front of the sardines.

Finn sprang into action and slammed the basket over her. Instead of fighting him, she lay down and licked her paw and sniffed the sardines, totally calm.

"See?" Dottie beamed, clapping her hands. "My plan worked."

CHAPTER
Twenty-Four

Finn was going to be late for dinner with his parents, and he had half of a fruit smoothie on him.

Too bad he still didn't want to leave.

They'd brought Tyrion inside, and the dog had instantly gotten to work licking up the splatters of smoothie that covered the kitchen like a Jackson Pollock painting, tail wagging the whole time. Only when the kitchen floor had been licked clean did he approach the laundry basket that was now bucking and weaving under Finn's hand, Jezebel hissing and spitting like a possessed thing.

"Let them smell each other, dear," Dottie said. "The animal world is primal. That's how they'll know they're friends."

Which was well and good for her to say. Finn didn't want to lose a hand.

Except Tyrion took one sniff of Jezebel and immediately backed up and lowered to the ground, head between his paws. Another growl from the cat, and he turned over onto his back, revealing his stomach. He had at least sixty pounds on her, but he was acknowledging her dominance.

"Smart man," Finn said. "He knows she's in charge."

"Smart man, indeed," Adalia said, raising her eyebrows.

Dottie gave them the satisfied smile of a cat drunk on milk (another of his grandfather's favorite sayings). "Oh, the energy pouring off you two. Red and purple and green."

"That's a lot of colors, Dottie," Finn said. "I think all of those blended together would be black."

"You and River," she said, tut-tutting, "you boys are both such literal thinkers sometimes."

"Returning to the situation at hand," Finn said. "Can I let her out?"

Jezebel was still bucking against her containment, but she'd stopped hissing and spitting—or maybe she hadn't stopped, precisely, but it wasn't quite so loud.

Tyrion whined a little and edged farther away, as if asking him to stay put.

"That settles it," Adalia said with a smile. "You live there now. That spot is your new home."

She was teasing, obviously, but a part of him remembered what his house had felt like the night they'd cooked dinner, the feeling of fullness. Of possibility. It had almost been like—

The plastic laundry crate cracked loudly, and Jezebel burst out of it, her mouth wide open, her needle-sharp teeth bared, and lunged at Finn's hand.

He screamed and leapt backward, only to realize that of course he shouldn't leave Adalia and Dottie and Tyrion at her mercy.

But she didn't even bother with Tyrion, who'd rolled even further onto his back, displaying every bit of his belly, as if to assure her he would never think of challenging her. She merely sniffed in an aggrieved manner, jumped back onto the counter, and started licking up the splashes of smoothie Tyrion hadn't been able to reach.

"Well, I guess the smoothie wasn't such a crazy idea," Finn said.

"Yes," Dottie said, "our combined approaches really did the trick. I expect the two darlings will get on quite well when all is said and done."

Adalia, who'd been watching with wide eyes, burst into laughter, bending over with the force of it. "Your face," she said to Finn between puffs of air. "And that scream."

He felt his face flush. "Yeah, yeah. Laugh it up. Your hand wasn't in the danger zone."

But that just made her laugh harder, so much so there were tears running down her face, and then he was laughing too, and Tyrion eyed them curiously from his position on the ground, as if wondering what kind of a funny farm he'd stumbled into this time.

"Yes," Dottie said in a satisfied tone. "I'm very happy with the energy in here."

So was Finn.

Three hours later, he rolled into his parents' driveway, wishing he could have stayed with Adalia, feeling a strange ache like he already missed her. Was that a thing? Missing someone after only a few hours apart? Maybe he just felt a little uneasy about what had happened right before he left— Adalia had gotten multiple back-to-back text alerts on her phone, and after checking them, she'd hurried him out like she feared he'd give Tyrion fleas. He couldn't help but wonder if it was Alan again. But surely she would have told him if that creep was still bothering her?

He shot off a quick text: *Hope Tyrion is still doing okay.*

He tapped the side of the phone with his finger. He was tempted to type out something about the texts she'd received just before he left. But that would be weird, right? They probably weren't at a point where he could just flat out ask her.

Three dots appeared, indicating she was typing something, and then a photo of Tyrion came through, Jezebel perched on his back.

The dog looked, understandably, nervous.

Adalia: *I'm afraid to make any sudden moves in case she snaps. Guess Jack's not the only cat whisperer.*

Finn: *You said he's coming back tonight?*

Adalia: *I just heard from him. He's taking a red-eye again, the psychopath.*

That brought out a smile, but a quick glance up at the house revealed his mother was peering at him from behind the living room curtain. She'd never been the sort to come out running and sweep him into a hug. She wasn't like Dottie. Still, he knew she wanted to see him. This was her way, even if it wasn't the approach he would have preferred.

Finn: *Duty calls. Have fun tonight.*

Adalia: *Thanks. Dottie's going to make me dinner. River and Georgie are coming over too. Hope you have fun too.*

Another three dots showed up, but this time she didn't write anything. He wanted to wait for her reply to come, but his mother was still staring out at him, probably wondering why in the world he was making them wait when he was already forty-five minutes behind schedule.

He tucked his phone into his pocket and got out of the car, his mother disappearing behind the curtain instantly.

No one opened the door for him, even though they clearly knew he'd arrived, not that he was surprised. Proper etiquette required him, as the visitor, to ring the bell, which he did.

His mother answered the door then, taking him in from head to toe before she leaned in so he could kiss her cheek.

"You haven't cut your hair since the last time I saw you," she said.

It had been before the article. Before his fight with River. Before Adalia. It felt like a lifetime ago.

"I know," he said, touching it self-consciously. "I need to look for a new stylist. Sorry I'm late."

"That's okay," she said, smiling a little. "Don't tell your father, but I like the curl. It reminds me of how mine looks naturally."

He wouldn't know—she flat-ironed or curled it every morning, and had for as long as he could remember. It was part of the performance she put on for the other ladies in her circle, part of what he thought of as the show. And he hated it.

But he didn't hate her, so he just said, "Thanks, Mom," and followed her into the house, shutting the door behind him. "I'll get my bag later. I know I got here late."

"It's no trouble. Just wash your hands and join us in the dining room. Your father didn't want to keep our guest waiting, so we've already sat down for some wine and appetizers."

For a moment his mind hung on the wine part—had his parents ever actually tried Big Catch beer? He genuinely didn't know. Then the rest of her statement filtered in.

"Guest?"

"Oh, didn't we tell you?" She shook her head a little as if to say, *Silly me, those memories keep slipping out of my head*, but he knew better. This was an intentional type of not telling that meant he absolutely did not want to meet their dinner guest.

Because the last time he saw his father, he'd admitted that he was interested in a woman, and his father was not the kind of man who enjoyed allowing people to choose for themselves what he could instead choose for them.

But it was too late to leave—wasn't it?—and he really did want to take the meeting with the Charlotte Robotics guys, so he washed his hands like a good, obedient son. Before he left the bathroom, he snuck a peek at his phone.

Adalia had finally written her message, although he had no way of knowing if it was the original message she'd intended to write: *Wish you were here.*

He replied before leaving the bathroom: *Believe me, so do I.*

She'd said River and Georgie were there too, along with Dottie. They'd probably hand heaping dishes of food around family style, and he was sure someone would throw a treat or two to the dog and even the cat.

That kind of scene would never, ever happen here.

Sighing, he left the bathroom—staying in there for the next two hours wasn't really feasible—and headed into the dining room. Just as he'd expected, his father sat at the head of the table, a beautiful woman in the chair next to him. Her blond hair was long and wavy and very orderly, which only made him miss the wild mass of Adalia's short curls.

"Ah," his father said, "look who decided to make an appearance."

"Hi, Dad," he said, turning on the charm. His mother wasn't the only one who knew how to act when the occasion required it. "And who's this?"

"This is Charlotte Davis. She's Bud's daughter. She just moved back home from Chapel Hill, and Bud thought she might appreciate meeting some young people. Since you were already coming to town for the meeting, it seemed just the thing."

Bud was the one funding the robotics start-up. So his dad wanted to set him up with a Charlotte so he would move to Charlotte, where he could work at Charlotte Robotics. When he crafted a life plan for someone, he was really thorough.

"Pleased to meet you," he said, nodding.

She smiled at him and lifted a hand, holding it up toward his mouth. Did she think he was going to kiss her hand?

Finn shook it instead.

He expected her expression to turn peeved, but her smile just seemed a little more fixed. A little more plastic.

"Pleased to meet you too, Finn. I've heard a lot about you."

"All good stuff, I hope?" he asked, only then realizing that the table had been set in such a way that he had no choice but to sit next to her. He circled around it and took his seat, pouring himself a liberal amount of wine.

"I read the article in *Fortune* with great interest," she said.

"Oh?" he asked. "Are you in the industry?"

She made a face that suggested he might as well have asked if she starred in pornographic movies. "No. I've never been to a brewery, but I admire that you were able to read the market well enough to cater to the lowest common denominator."

Ouch. It was an insult wrapped in a compliment, which confirmed everything he'd suspected about her. No wonder his father had hand-selected her for him. "Not a fan of beer, then?"

"Oh, you're too funny," she said, laughing, and touched his arm. He inched away, wondering what he'd said that was humorous. "You're wasted out there with the hillbillies."

Hillbillies? Who *was* this woman?

"Finn, would you like any of the goat cheese crostini?" his mother asked brightly. "I can ask the server to bring the plate back out."

His parents always hired a server when they hosted anyone outside the family for dinner. Even one person. It had always seemed crazy to him. Wasn't a private chef enough? Did they really need a person to carry things from one room to another like they lived in a castle instead of an oversized house?

"No, Mom. That's not necessary. Why don't we just move on to the next course?"

The sooner they could get through this nightmare, the better.

By the time they got to dessert, Finn was seriously contemplating staging an accident for himself. Dessert fork in the eye, maybe? Even though he'd disagreed with pretty much everything Charlotte had said, openly, she'd written off his responses as jokes. According to her, he was the most hilarious man alive—and judging by the way she kept finding excuses to touch him, she was interested despite his "provincial" background.

"Finn, Chef made your favorite dessert," his mom said, "chocolate soufflé." Which would have been great if it had been his favorite and not something he'd complimented once after getting tired of the silence at the dinner table. His mother had latched on to the comment, though, and he hadn't had the heart to correct her. Plus, he could tell this was her attempt at an apology. While his mother preferred it if everyone liked her, she didn't actually like everyone back, and he could tell she did not share his father's approval of Charlotte. (And in all honesty, his father probably approved more of Charlotte's looks and her father's connections than of any sort of sparkling personality on her part.)

"That's great," he said, "but I'm actually really tired. I think I'd better go to bed early tonight. Get a fresh start in the morning for my talk with Bud and the team."

"Oh, my father will *love* you," Charlotte said. "He has a great sense of humor just like you do. But are you sure you need to go to bed? I was hoping to lure you out for a nightcap." She put her hand on Finn's leg, and he jerked away so vehemently, he almost fell out of his chair.

"Is something wrong?" she asked.

"Yes, yup," he said, springing to his feet. "I have a medical condition that requires me to get at least ten hours of sleep a night." He glanced at his watch. "It'll be a close one tonight. Take care, Charlotte. See you in the morning, Mom and Dad."

His father was scowling at him again, a look that had become very familiar, during this meal and over the course of a lifetime. But if he wasn't pleased, it was a problem of his own making for trying to set Finn up—and with Charlotte, no less—just days after he'd told him about Adalia. His mother wouldn't have okayed this ludicrous setup if she'd known about Adalia, but then again, she likely didn't know. Neither was exactly the sharing type. Maybe he'd have a talk with her over breakfast.

Finn hurried away, waving at Charlotte, who was muttering something about him being "so brave."

He didn't feel very brave. He wouldn't dare leave his room until he saw her drive away. In retrospect, he should have noticed a car was parallel parked near the driveway—a sporty silver Mercedes-Benz.

In the safety of his room, he pulled out his phone and texted Adalia.

I think my dad just tried to set me up with a human robot (literally...her father is funding Charlotte Robotics and her name is Charlotte. Coincidence? I think not.) Okay, maybe that's not nice, but neither is she. I deeply regret coming home.

Those three dots appeared again, then disappeared, then reappeared.

He started to type out an explanation of what had gone down—how he'd told his father about Adalia, and then his dad had tried to manipulate him into doing what he wanted, and...

Her message appeared before he finished, and he deleted the essay he'd written.

Adalia: *I always deeply regret going home. Want to watch the end of Pride and Prejudice with me? We can video chat so I can see the tears you will inevitably shed at the end. You will, of course, have to pretend you didn't finish it the first time.*

Finn found himself smiling as he wrote his response: *I do want that. So much so that I skipped the chocolate soufflé for dessert.*

Adalia: *Amateur move. You should have grabbed it and run.*

And Finn finally let himself write what he'd wanted to write earlier: *I miss you.*

CHAPTER
Twenty-Five

So introducing Tyrion to his new home hadn't exactly gone as planned, but Adalia had learned a lot about Finn from his reaction to the whole disaster. He'd seen the humor in it, just like she had, even when the smoothie had sprayed all over his expensive clothes and shoes. She'd laughed at him— hysterically, in fact—and he'd just grinned back, his eyes sparkling.

It was like he was too good to be true.

And even though he'd warned her early on that he wouldn't be able to stay long before he left for his parents' house in Charlotte, he'd seemed reluctant to leave. Selfishly, she would have kept him there if not for the texts that had popped up on her phone.

The first two, from Lee, had set her heart racing.

I've heard something that I need to talk to you about.

Then: *This is IMPORTANT, Addy.*

What was he talking about? Had he found out about her arrest?

Still, she might have ignored that and called him later, if not for the message that had arrived moments later from an unknown number: *I've only just started, Adalia. Deal with me or deal with the consequences.*

Had Alan talked to Lee? She had to call her brother. *Immediately.*

Finn had clearly wanted to know why her phone was blowing up, and why she suddenly had the crazed look of Jezebel going after that blender, but she didn't want to involve him any deeper in this mess. He'd done enough for her, and she didn't want him to see her as some wounded bird. So she'd kissed him goodbye and shoved him out the door, telling him she couldn't wait until their Wednesday mystery date.

Dottie left moments after Finn, saying she'd be back with dinner, but she had to run home to get a special cake plate to celebrate Tyrion's first night home. Did she intend to make the dog a cake? How did she manage to constantly have so much food, all of different varieties? She was like a human house elf. It was slightly worrying, being alone with Jezebel and Tyrion, but it gave Adalia the perfect window to call her brother. Putting Tyrion on a leash, she took him out back and sat on the bench, her fingers shaking as she pulled up his name.

"Addy," Lee said when he answered. "Are you okay?"

Her heart skipped a beat.

"I'm sitting in Grandpa Beau's back yard," she said, as though it was an adequate answer.

"Why did you really leave New York?"

A lump filled her stomach. "Lee…"

"The truth, Addy. Not the bullshit you keep feeding me." He sounded pissed, but she heard the undercurrent of worry under it.

"Did he call you?"

"Your *boyfriend*? The one I told you was bad news from the beginning?"

"Congrats, Lee. You were right," she said, her voice breaking. "How does it feel to have all the answers?"

He paused. "I don't have all the answers, Addy," he said with a heavy sigh. "I hardly have any of them." Then, to her surprise, he added, "I'm sorry if I made you feel like I thought I did."

Funny how she was seeing both sides of Lee in a span of seconds. She'd known the authoritarian Lee most of her life. He'd always been so eager to please their father, and their father, of course, encouraged it. But something had changed between Adalia and Lee before she left New York, like he'd started to consider her a person, not just his baby sister.

She had invited him to a small show that included a few of her pieces. In truth, she'd done it to stick it to him, to make him feel guilty for inevitably saying no, but he'd surprised her by coming. They'd gotten dinner afterward and talked all night, and after that, they'd started getting together once a week or so, always without Victoria, much to Adalia's relief. She'd discovered a Lee who was a little more like her and Georgie, a little more like their mother. He had a sense of humor and a warm heart, but make no mistake, he still had an authoritarian streak a mile wide. She'd opened up about Alan, and he'd told her under no uncertain terms to break up with the creep. Immediately. That very day. And when she'd tried to explain why it wasn't that easy, he'd insisted that she was making excuses. He'd refused to discuss Alan again until the jerk was in her rearview mirror.

"Why didn't you call me?" he asked. "We were talking. Getting closer."

"It's hard to feel close to someone when they keep giving you ultimatums."

"I was only trying to look out for you, Addy. That man was bad news. The call I just had with the asshole only confirms it."

Her heart sank. "What did he tell you?"

The call disconnected, and she was sure he'd just hung up on her, but a video call from him showed up on her screen. She sucked in a deep breath and answered.

His worried face appeared on the screen. "This seems like a face-to-face discussion. I was two seconds away from booking the next available flight to Asheville, but I didn't think this conversation could wait that long."

"What did he say?" she repeated. It had to be bad if Lee was willing to come to Asheville to sort things out. Despite being one-fourth owner of the brewery and the house, he hadn't been back since the reading of Grandpa Beau's will.

"That you vandalized an art gallery, and if I don't pay him two hundred thousand dollars, he's going public."

Tears stung her eyes. "You didn't agree to pay him, did you?"

"Addy, what the hell happened? I've done a quick search online, and there's no mention of you doing anything of the sort, but he insisted it was true, and if I don't pay him for the damages, the gallery will sue Buchanan Luxury. That lowlife actually threatened our family business."

Hadn't she wondered about the damage to the gallery? She'd been so furious, so distraught…surely she'd hit the floor and walls with paint. They would have had some say in whether charges were brought against her. Alan must have convinced them not to go the criminal route, for fear she'd release her side of the story, but that didn't mean they weren't interested in some sort of restitution. She closed her eyes. Why wouldn't this just go away?

A.R. Casella and Denise Grover Swank

"Addy," Lee said insistently, "just tell me what happened."

So she told him everything, from how Georgie and River had paid her bail and arranged for her to fly to Asheville the day after the incident to how Georgie had gotten Alan to back down. Several times, her brother looked like he wanted to interrupt, but he remained silent.

"I thought that was the end of it," she said when she finished. "But he's been sending texts."

"What kind of texts?" he asked in a deep voice.

"The first ones were flattering, like he was trying to get back into my good graces, but they've gotten more threatening over the last few days. I tried blocking him, but he texted from an unknown number."

"Have you responded to any of them?"

"No. Georgie thought he'd quit it if I didn't respond."

"Even after he started to threaten you?" he asked in disbelief.

"She doesn't know about that part," she admitted.

He was silent for several seconds. "Why didn't you tell me?" he asked, sounding hurt. "After all of our conversations before…" He swallowed thickly. "Addy, I hate that you didn't feel like you could call me." He paused, his eyes tearing up. "I hate that you were in trouble and you didn't feel safe asking me for help."

She didn't know what to say. She knew he needed to hear that he was wrong, that she *did* trust him, but they both knew it would be a lie.

"I understand why you didn't call me from jail," he continued. "And I understand why you didn't tell me you were going to Asheville until well after the fact, but I don't get why

I'm just now hearing all of this, months later and under duress at that."

"Because," she said, "if I told you, it would be the same as telling Dad. And Victoria." Then a new thought hit her. "Oh, my God. Is she listening to all of this?"

He made a face. "No. She's with her mom and sister getting mani-pedis." His jaw set. "And telling me isn't the same as telling Dad."

"Oh come on, Lee. We all know you'd do anything to stay in his good graces. I figured you'd tell him the first chance you got." Which meant this very conversation could get back to him. But what could he do? Her father had no power over her…except that wasn't true. It still hurt her when he lashed out, when he treated her like she was nothing more than a minor inconvenience or disappointment, like a latte being delivered with the wrong milk.

"Addy…" Lee started, then stopped. "Okay, we'll address the stuff about Dad later. And we *will* address it. But right now, we need to figure out what's going on with the gallery. With your permission, I'd like to call them and hear their side of the story, because this reeks of a scam. If they'd wanted you to pay for damages, they would have sought *you* out. Stansworth's threat to go public is empty. He got the charges dropped because he doesn't want anyone to find out what he did, but he's obviously still looking for a payday. My guess is he's broke. Who knows what he told the gallery."

She nodded, tears stinging her eyes again. "Okay."

"I wish I were with you right now," he said, his voice rough. "I wish…" He cleared his throat and swiped at his eyes. "I'm here, Addy. I'll help you through this. Thank you for telling me the truth."

"What about Dad?"

His jaw twitched. "He won't be hearing about it from me."

"And Victoria?"

He took longer to respond. "This is between you and me. And I guess Georgie." Then he made a face. "And her new boyfriend."

So his attitude toward River still needed a little work, but that was a conversation for another day. "I don't feel right having you call the gallery," she said. "I'm a grown woman. I feel like I should handle this myself. Be a grown-up, like Dad is fond of saying."

"Dad's wrong. You *are* a grown-up, Addy," he said. "And sometimes, you need to let other people help. I'll call the gallery and let you know what they say, but I might not be able to get a hold of anyone until tomorrow."

"Thanks, Lee," she said with a soft smile.

"That's what big brothers are for. Let me do my job." He cocked his head. "Is that a dog I see next to you?"

She lowered the phone to give him a full view of the quiet husky. "This is Tyrion. He's a foster dog from the animal shelter that will benefit from the charity art show Finn Hamilton and I are putting together. We're hosting it at Buchanan Brewery."

"A charity art show? Tell me more," he said fondly, without further commenting on the wisdom, or lack thereof, of someone in such an uncertain situation fostering a dog.

She told him about working with Finn, keeping her romantic feelings out of it. Lee asked questions, smiling when she told him about the woman with the goats.

"I miss you, Addy." Her surprise must have shown on her face. "You have a *joie de vivre* most people lack, and it's contagious. Don't ever let anyone take that from you, okay? Not even Dad. *Especially* not Dad."

That was probably the nicest thing he'd ever said to her, and instead of coming back with some smart-mouthed retort, she said, "Thank you."

"I love you. I don't say it enough, but I'm determined to change that. With both you and Georgie."

Her jaw dropped, and she was about to ask him if he'd had a recent *It's a Wonderful Life* experience, but then she heard Victoria's voice in the background.

"Lee! Where are you? I need you to unbutton my jacket so I don't mess up my nails."

He made a face. "I've got to go so I don't have to explain why I'm talking to you. Yeah, I know. It's sad that I would have to explain why I'm talking to you. I'll call you tomorrow."

Her screen went blank.

Tyrion rested his chin on her lap, looking up at her.

She rubbed his head. "I know it's been a lot. Jezebel. Finn leaving. My distressing call with my brother. It's never a dull moment with me. I hope you can get used to it."

He reached up and licked her chin.

"Yeah, yeah, I love you too. No need to get sloppy about it."

———

Dottie texted soon afterward, saying that she'd invited Georgie and River to join them for dinner to celebrate the new addition. Adalia brought Tyrion back inside and settled down on the sofa to read a book, the dog lying on the floor next to her. It was a struggle to focus, her conversation with Lee running through her head on repeat, and when Jezebel started slinking toward them, looking every bit the panther advancing on her prey, she lowered the book onto her chest.

"Don't do it," she warned.

But Jezebel wasn't about to start listening now. She leapt into the air, landing on the dog's back. Adalia flinched, but Tyrion didn't react at all as the cat kneaded his fur like he was a blanket, then curled up on top of him. It was a miracle.

When Finn texted her later, she snapped a photo of the cat on top of the dog, knowing he'd appreciate it as much as she did. She told him about the spontaneous dinner party, then stopped midway through typing *I miss you.* It was too soon for that, right? But she'd promised herself she'd do things differently with Finn, so she told him the truth—she wished he were here.

Her heart filled with happiness when he said he did too.

Dottie showed up with a feast, which did indeed include a separate cake for the animals, followed by Georgie and River, who had brought Hops to meet his new cousin.

Jezebel seemed to have grown bored with the whole new-member-to-the-household situation and hid in the living room, leaving Hops and Tyrion to get acquainted. After the humans and the dogs ate, they all headed out to the back yard. Tyrion seemed comfortable enough that Adalia let him off his leash, even though she worried he'd jump the back fence and run off. But he was too content, romping with Hops, playing fetch with a dog toy Maisie had sent home with him, to pay any attention to the fence. Finally, he got tired and lay at Adalia's feet.

Adalia had loved every minute of the evening, but her mind kept drifting back to Alan's behavior and the way Lee had stepped up to help. She was dying to tell Georgie, but she knew it was best to wait. Her sister looked too content, sitting on the bench next to River. They really were in love, and Adalia couldn't be happier they'd found each other. But seeing them together put a strange ache in her chest.

"Where's Finn?" River finally asked, and Georgie's head jerked up. "I figured you would invite him too."

"In Charlotte," she said, tossing the toy into the yard and watching both dogs run after it. "Dinner with his parents."

River cringed.

"Yeah," she said with a soft laugh. "That's exactly how he seemed to feel about it."

Georgie looked away, her lips pressed together firmly, which suggested her feelings about Finn hadn't changed. But they would. Adalia would help her see the man that she saw— the man who'd sparked such deep feelings in her, such joy, that she was beginning to feel the itch to create again. To pour herself into something. But it wasn't the shed or even Dottie's garage that called to her. It was the space behind Blue's studio—with its high ceilings and all those windows. The sculptures she could create there…

When they all said goodnight, Georgie gave Adalia an extra-long hug before patting Tyrion on the head and saying, "Goodbye, nephew," to which he replied with an atonal howl that made everyone laugh. They all left, and Adalia was once again alone with Tyrion. (Jezebel was hiding in parts unknown.) She headed up to her room, where she made a bed for Tyrion next to her own.

As she was getting ready to crawl into bed to watch a movie, she heard the ding of a text. She leapt for her phone, her stomach doing excited somersaults when she saw it was from Finn and not Unknown Number. He said he was regretting his trip, and she started to reply with a joke, only to stop and respond in a more serious vein, letting him know she understood. Then she moved them both on to something else. He helped drive away her dark thoughts and frustrations, and she wanted to do the same for him.

They set up a screen share on their laptops and stayed up late into the night, watching the end of *Pride and Prejudice*. She could have sworn he teared up at the end when Mr. Darcy told Elizabeth that she'd bewitched him body and soul and professed his love, but he vehemently denied it. After the movie, they talked about everything and nothing until both were heavy-lidded with exhaustion.

"You need to get some rest, Finn," she said softly, deciding to do the selfless thing and call it a night. "You need to be on the top of your game for your meeting. We can't have you showing up looking like a zombie with half a brain."

"And you need to go to work," he said.

"That too." She smiled. "Good luck with your meeting tomorrow."

"I'll let you know how it goes."

It was such a simple promise, but it had a deeper meaning. This was important to him, and he wanted to share it with *her*.

She quickly hung up before they both changed their minds.

As she drifted off to sleep, she realized she'd just wished him luck on a project that would likely take him from her. But she wasn't sure she was selfless enough to actually have meant it.

CHAPTER
Twenty-Six

Finn hadn't wanted to like Bud, and truth be told, he didn't. The man had all the charm and warmth of a block of unshaped granite, and his bald head was just as shiny. But he didn't need to like Bud. Bud was just the money behind this enterprise. And Finn *did* like the people he was funding. In a weird way, Sean and Mo reminded him of himself and River— two young guys with a vision and the determination to get them places. They'd met at MIT and instantly bonded, Sean from New Jersey and Mo from a first-generation Afghani family based in Charlotte.

Their ideas for the company had first been cooked up at a frat party that both of them had found so objectionable, they'd retreated onto the back porch (in thirty-degree weather) rather than stay inside.

"I don't know how I ended up having a scientific mind," Sean said. "I come from a family of artists. My older sister even went to the Lanier School of Fine Art."

Where Adalia had gone.

"Oh? When'd she go? A friend of mine also went there."

"I was an oops baby," Sean said. "She graduated probably fifteen years ago."

Which meant she hadn't overlapped with Adalia.

"Did she happen to know Alan Stansworth?"

Sean made a face that spoke volumes. "According to her, he made sure all of the girls knew him. She's got some stories about that guy." Then a panicked look crossed his face. "I hope he's not like a family friend of yours or something. I mean, I'm sure he's fine. Some people just have a creeper vibe without being actual creepers, so…"

Finn lifted a hand. "Nope. We're on the same page. My friend had similar things to say."

Mo gave Sean a look as if to say, *Don't blow this*, which made him smile again. Yup, a bit like him and River, except these guys were legit geniuses. The inventions they'd made— and would make—would change the world. He had *ideas* for them. His mind was firing on more cylinders than it had since those early days with Big Catch.

At the end of a two-hour meeting, they broke for fifteen minutes. Then the guys came back and offered him the job, Bud smiling congenially like he thought he deserved credit for both the offer and Finn's existence.

But they needed a CEO who would be there, boots on the ground. They needed someone in Charlotte. They needed someone who would devote themselves to Charlotte Robotics, and only Charlotte Robotics.

Finn's home was in Asheville. His life was in Asheville. *Adalia* was in Asheville.

And a little part of him wasn't so sure he wanted to sign one hundred percent of himself over to something new. It was exciting now, but at some point it would just be a business to run, right? Besides, it was hard to ignore the fact that his father had set all of this up, down to the horrible nondate with Charlotte last night. He wasn't going to dance like a puppet just because Machiavelli had chosen a nice pair of strings.

"I'm sorry," he said, surprised by how much he meant it, "but I don't see this working out. I'm not interested in relocating right now."

"Think about it," Mo urged him. "We could really use someone like you to get us off the ground."

"Yeah," Sean said, tapping the table. "If you're not willing to flat out take the job, do you do consulting?"

"Now, now," Bud cut in, "no need to undercut his job title before he even accepts the position," he said with a wink. It was obvious he thought Finn was feigning disinterest in order to negotiate a higher salary or a better company car. (Bud had mentioned three times that he'd bought a Mercedes for everyone in the family for Christmas last year.)

But Sean's words had struck a chord with Finn. *Consulting.*

Could he do for Charlotte Robotics what he was doing for Bev Corp? Of course, their need was greater, its scope many orders of magnitude larger, but maybe…

"Let me think about everything and get back to you," Finn murmured, his mind churning.

Bud, who'd chosen the seat next to his, slapped him on the back so hard he nearly fell off his chair.

"Good man! Now what say you we get lunch? My lovely daughter tells me you made quite an impression on her last night, but she mentioned something about a sleep condition?" He raised his eyebrows but thankfully didn't give Finn a chance to explain. "Lunch is probably more your meal, I'd guess. Charlotte can be here in fifteen minutes. There's a Bavarian place down the way that serves an excellent cut of meat. Only thing on the menu!"

Mo and Sean exchanged a look that suggested they realized lunch with Bud and Charlotte was not a universally appealing notion, but neither said anything. They wisely recognized who was feeding them. No rescue was coming from that quarter, so Finn decided it was time to put this whole medieval matchmaking effort to rest once and for all.

"My girlfriend would probably never forgive me if I went to a place like that," he said, slapping Bud on the back. "Go figure. She's a pescatarian."

Probably Adalia would object to being called that—the "girlfriend" part, the pescatarian label was factual—but he decided he liked the sound of it.

Bud didn't, judging by the way his face went red.

"Well," he sputtered, "this is highly irregular. Your father assured me that you weren't spoken for."

Spoken for? What was this, *Fiddler on the Roof*?

"My father isn't the greatest authority on my personal life," he said, getting to his feet. "But he *does* employ one of the best private chefs in the city, so I hope Charlotte's evening wasn't totally wasted."

He grinned at Mo and Sean, who looked like they were fighting smiles of their own. "I'll be in touch. I'm not sure if I have a future with your company, but it's abundantly clear that *your* future is bright. You've got a good thing going on here."

Then, because he didn't want to totally burn a bridge, he offered Bud his hand for a shake. The man shook a little harder than was strictly necessary, but Finn didn't hold a grudge against his would-be father-in-law.

"Enjoy the meat!" he said on his way out.

Finn found a little restaurant for lunch, choosing a Mexican place (both to ensure he didn't accidentally run into

Bud and Charlotte and because it reminded him of Adalia), and finished his proposal for Gretchen. He sent it over and asked her to call him to discuss it, preferably later that evening or tomorrow because he had a personal commitment (i.e., date) on Wednesday.

By the time he paid the bill, the first irate text had arrived from his father: *You told Bud you have a girlfriend?*

Yeah, he answered, *because I kind of do. Which you knew. Mom knows too, by the way, because I told her this morning. I like Mo and Sean, but I don't see this working out. For what should be obvious reasons.*

And others he didn't feel like discussing.

Call me before you make any hasty decisions, his father said. *There could be a real future for you there, with or without Charlotte. I just wanted to make you understand you have options, Finn. Across the board. Your vision is too limited sometimes.*

I like these particular blinders, he said.

His father sent another message that he ignored in favor of writing a text to Adalia: *Interesting meeting. Not going to take the job, but there might be some other opportunities with them. If my father's friend doesn't have me drawn and quartered for being disinterested in his daughter.*

Adalia wrote back immediately, like she'd been waiting: *I wouldn't like you as much if you were drawn and quartered. Messy. Try to avoid it.*

A smile tugging at his face, he wrote, *I'm looking forward to our mystery date, but any chance you want to get together tonight? You still owe me a viewing of Fast Five.*

Adalia: *Can't. I'm having dinner with Jack, a family/housemate thing, and tomorrow night I'm getting that drink with Maisie and Blue. I visited two of the artists this morning, BTW. One was brilliant, and I'm pretty sure the other runs a cult out of her garage. More on that later. I think we have a good roster, maybe just one or two more.*

267

Disappointment tugged at him, but then he saw those three telltale dots.

Maybe I can come over after drinks? she wrote. *Tuesday night could lead in to Wednesday?*

He needed to put his phone down for a second so he could get himself back under control. Good God, when had any woman ever affected him like this?

The server shot him a concerned look, like maybe he thought he was having some sort of episode, and hurriedly wrote out the bill, slapping it on his table. The jarring sound helped him pull himself together.

What a scandalous suggestion, he wrote. *Also, yes. Oh God, yes. I can't wait to see you.*

Even though he wasn't seeing her tonight, he found himself driving a little faster than usual on the way back to Asheville.

He'd only had a few minutes to unpack his car—an easy thing since it had just been an overnight trip—and order takeout when his phone rang.

He knew Adalia had plans, but he fumbled it out of his pocket, only to see it was Gretchen. Since he'd already made a fool of himself in his haste to answer the call, he did.

"Do you think they'll go for it?" she asked, no preliminaries. "River left without even taking a meeting with us. And the temperature on the ground has been decidedly cold."

"There's only one way to find out," he said. "But yeah, I don't see why not. It would be to everyone's benefit. If you're agreeable to the proposal, I can make the initial contact with River and Georgie. You might want to use someone else to approach the other brewers, but I knew them personally."

"A lot of good it did you last time," she said. Though her remark was tongue in cheek, it still stung.

"Fair enough. Let's see if I learned my lesson."

Because he really, really hoped he had. He'd changed, hadn't he? He *felt* like he'd changed, but the measure of a man was in what he did more than what he said or felt. *Act like an ass, and you better start braying, because you've become one*, his grandfather had once said to his father, which had made a seventeen-year-old Finn burst out laughing.

"Okay," she said. "Yes, talk to him. If Buchanan steps on board, it'll help ease the way for the others."

"Thanks, Gretchen. I think this is going to work."

A pause, then she said, "I think it will too. You're good at this, and I don't say that lightly. Let me know how it goes."

After they hung up, he texted River, asking if he could get together tonight or sometime tomorrow. Of course, right after he sent the first message, he realized River was going to think he wanted to talk about Adalia, which he didn't really, or at least not in the same conversation in which he pitched the Bev Corp event. So he added, *Not about Adalia.* But he also didn't want to give River the impression he wasn't serious about Adalia, so he added: *Not that I haven't been thinking a lot about Adalia, because I have, but it's not about her. It's a business thing. Georgie should probably be there too. Nothing horrible. I promise.*

What about tomorrow night? River asked. *You can come over for dinner.*

It might infringe on his tentative sleepover plans with Adalia, but this was important too. Hell, maybe she'd want to join them at River and Georgie's place.

Sounds good.

Finn set his phone aside, not wanting to badger Adalia while she was doing the whole brother-sister bonding thing with Jack, and he found himself thinking of what she'd said a couple of days ago. Something about him being a creator too,

269

only he created businesses. He hadn't given it much thought at the time—he'd never *felt* creative—but maybe she'd seen something in him he hadn't seen in himself. Gretchen had said, *You're good at this*. And Sean, earlier, had asked him about consulting.

He took out his laptop and started working, and before he knew it, it was after midnight.

CHAPTER
Twenty-Seven

Finn's texts had made Adalia feel like she was floating in a happy bubble, but the bubble burst midafternoon when Lee texted saying he'd gathered some information and wanted to video chat with Adalia and Georgie so they were all on the same page.

Okay, she'd texted back, *but give me a few minutes to catch Georgie up to speed.*

Hurry. My window of availability isn't very wide.

Meaning Victoria and/or their father might swoop in at any moment. Lee was like a prisoner in some ways, but she couldn't feel too bad for him given it was a prison of his own making.

After Adalia's meltdown the week before, Georgie had moved her desk out to a small room beneath the stairs—too large to be just a supply closet but not quite large enough to be anything else. Adalia fondly called it her cupboard under the stairs. Right now she felt reluctant to leave its safety, but she forced herself to get up and head to her sister's office, clutching her phone in a death grip.

Why was she so nervous? Georgie knew about the whole Alan mess, so this wouldn't come as a total surprise. Still, she knew Georgie would be hurt that she'd held back.

Adalia stopped at the partially open door and knocked on the wood trim. Georgie was staring at her computer, her brow furrowed, but she glanced up and smiled brightly when she saw her sister.

"How's Tyrion?" she asked, pushing her chair away from her desk a few inches. "He's such a sweetheart. Hops was so worn out he didn't ask to go out in the middle of the night. We'll have to set up another playdate soon."

Adalia's eyes bugged out. "Puppies need nighttime bathroom breaks?"

Tyrion had slept through the night, climbing up onto the bed next to her at some point and cuddling with her. The dog was a furnace. He'd definitely come in handy when it got cold.

She walked into the office and sat in a chair in front of the desk. "I guess it'll help break you in for when you and River make gorgeous babies." She made a face. "Can I talk to you for a moment?"

Georgie gawked at her, seemingly stuck on the making babies comment.

"Surely you and River have discussed babies."

Her face turned an adorable shade of pink. "Sort of…"

Adalia gave her a stern look and lowered her voice. "Do I need to give River a talking-to about his intentions?"

Georgie laughed, but it sounded forced. "I know he's saving for a ring, although I have no idea how since the brewery's still not making a profit and he refuses to accept the full salary in his contract. I suspect that's why he's looking into setting up an online class to teach hobbyists how to make beer or improve their technique."

Adalia's brow lifted. "That's actually a great idea. Is he doing it under the Buchanan umbrella? It could be a huge draw."

Georgie nibbled on her lower lip. "We haven't talked logistics. He only mentioned it last night, but he said he's been thinking about it since he was still at Big Catch."

"Maybe we should tell Lee about it. He'd probably be interested, being that he's one-fourth owner and all," Adalia said. Georgie gave her an odd look, as if she'd just spoken complete nonsense, and she supposed her sister had a point. Lee had made it clear he had zero personal interest in the brewery. "Or maybe we can talk about that later. Either way, Lee wants to have a video call with us. Is this a good time?"

Georgie's mouth dropped open. "Why does he want to talk to us?"

Adalia steeled herself with a deep breath. "Georgie. Alan's been sending me more texts."

Before her sister could respond, she told her about the threatening messages and then Alan's attempt to extort Lee by threatening Buchanan Luxury.

Georgie's face lost color. "What?"

"Lee said things weren't adding up, so he was going to call the gallery to get more information. Now he wants to video chat with us both."

Georgie gaped at her for a second before shaking off the surprise and shifting into efficient big sister mode. She turned to her computer and tapped on her keyboard, and within seconds, the call was going through. After shifting the monitor to face the visitor chairs, Georgie got up and shut the door.

"Hey, Lee," Adalia said when he answered, her stomach twisting with nerves.

"Is Georgie there?" He was wearing a dress shirt and tie and didn't look nearly as relaxed as he had the day before. Was it the environment he was currently in, or did he have really bad news?

"Present," Georgie said, taking a seat in the chair next to Adalia's. "I hear I've missed a few things."

"As have I," he said curtly, "which is why a group chat seemed prudent."

"Maybe we should bring Jack in," Adalia said dryly. "For the first time he can be on our side of one of these video chats."

Lee's brow lifted. "*Jack knows?*"

Adalia heard the accusation in his voice loud and clear. How could she tell Jack—a brother she'd only just met—before she told Lee? "Calm down. He doesn't know."

"Addy said you were calling the gallery," Georgie said, moving the conversation along with her usual efficiency.

"Yeah. I spoke to the director this morning. Apparently there was some damage to the walls and flooring. They're seeking reimbursement for the damages."

"But that asshole stole her work!" Georgie protested, her face turning red.

"They don't know the full story," Lee said, "but they do know things aren't adding up. One of the staff members was there that night, and she thought she heard Addy accuse Stansworth of stealing her work, but before she could intervene, Addy was trashing the pieces. Of course, the staff member called the police, and we know the rest. Stansworth assured them the sculptures were his work, and turns out we're not the only one he's pressing for money. He insisted their insurance reimburse him, claiming the crime was committed on their property, which makes them liable. I guess he came to them with this whole sob story about Adalia being a mentally disturbed former lover who did it out of revenge. That's his story for why he dropped the criminal charges and asked them not to file any. He claimed he'd pay for their damages…*after* he was reimbursed by the insurance company."

"They're going to pay him for my work?" Adalia asked, feeling violated all over again. She'd destroyed her sculptures—pieces she loved—so he couldn't profit off her work, but he'd found a way to get paid anyway. And she was furious too, enough to raze a mountain. How dare he act like she was mentally unstable when he was the one who'd driven her to the brink?

"No, not yet. They've been stalling the insurance company because of the discrepancies in his story. They've actually been trying to find Addy, but they had no idea how to reach her since she didn't leave a forwarding address and Alan claimed he didn't know how to get in touch with her. They didn't realize she had ties to us."

"So they do want to take action against me," Adalia said.

"Maybe not," Lee said, rubbing the back of his neck. "The gallery director wants to talk to you. She wants to hear your side of the story."

"Is that really a good idea?" Adalia asked. "Don't I need an attorney?" She turned to Georgie.

Georgie gave it a moment's thought, then said, "If their attorney isn't present, then I think it would be fine, but I would want to sit in on the call." She nodded to the computer screen. "And Lee too, of course."

"I can see if they're amenable to a group video chat," Lee said, "but I think it would send a better message if you go in person. The good news is the director genuinely seems interested in discovering the truth about what happened. I got the impression she thinks Stansworth is shady."

"What if they don't believe the pieces were mine?" Adalia asked.

"I already told them I have photographic proof," Lee said. "I took photos in the studio when I dropped by for a visit a few months before you went to the gallery."

"But it was Alan's studio," she said, feeling sick to her stomach. "He can just say I was posing with his art."

"And welding something onto one of the sculptures?" Lee said.

It wasn't really proof, and they all probably knew it, but it was something. It was definitely something.

Georgie shot her a look she didn't need to be a mind reader to understand. Her sister had lied to Stansworth, saying she had photos of Adalia sculpting the pieces. It had been a lie, so far as they knew. If they had opened the conversation to Lee months ago, they might have worked through this a whole lot sooner.

She nodded, feeling unsettled, wishing Finn were here to hold her hand and reassure her that everything was going to be okay.

When had she become so clingy? The fact that she felt like she needed him left her more unsettled.

"Thanks, Lee," she said. "You have no idea how much I appreciate this."

"I'm gonna nail this bastard to the wall." He shot a glare at his older sister. "Which is what should have been done in the beginning." He glanced to the side and made a face. "Gotta go. I'll get in touch after I make the arrangements."

Before they could respond, he disconnected the call. He hadn't asked about their schedules—in his usual Lee way, he'd assumed they'd be able to drop everything and hop on a plane at a moment's notice. Then again, he wasn't wrong, at least not about her. And a quick glance at Georgie told her what she'd already known on some level: her sister would make the time for this too.

The two sisters were quiet for a long moment. Then Georgie asked in a soft voice, "Do you think Lee is right? That I should have handled it more aggressively from the beginning?"

"Aggressive isn't your style," Adalia said.

"Which is why I wonder if we should have gone to Lee in the first place."

"For what it's worth," Adalia said, taking her sister's hand, "I wouldn't change a thing. Going aggressive in the beginning would have been a mistake, and I wasn't ready for it. But Lee is a good backup team."

"More like cleanup."

"No, backup. We both went with the approach we thought would work best, and *you* got him to drop the charges. That was no small thing."

Georgie nodded, but she didn't seem fully convinced.

Adalia squeezed her sister's hand. "I love you. I'm glad I'm here with you."

"I love you too." Georgie studied her for a moment, her expression changing. "You look happier. Does that have anything to do with Finn?"

The corners of her mouth ticked up. "I wondered how long it would take for you to bring that up again."

Georgie hesitated. "Maybe I was too harsh. Finn seems nice enough, but I worry that loyalty isn't his strong suit. Just be careful with your heart, okay?"

It wasn't much of an improvement on Georgie's previous assessment of Finn, but Adalia had to admit her sister had a point. Was the Big Catch situation a one-off, or was Finn capable of doing something like that again, but with her this time?

"Thanks for the advice," Adalia said with a small smile. "I bet River appreciates having the wisdom of a much older woman at his disposal."

Georgie gasped, then playfully swatted Adalia's arm. "Ugh! He's only three years younger."

Laughing, Adalia shook her head. "I'm teasing, but you make it much too easy. There's something else I wanted to mention," she said, getting to her feet. "I'm going out for drinks tomorrow night with Maisie and an artist I met last week, Blue Combs. She's amazing. Would you like to join us? We could both use a girl's night out."

Georgie looked excited at first—obviously she needed a night out; the woman even dreamed about work—but it quickly faded. "I can't. For one thing, I'm not Maisie's favorite person."

"Why?" Adalia asked. "Does it have anything to do with the tension between her and River? It was thick enough to gag on yesterday."

Georgie hesitated, then said, "I don't know this for certain, but I'm fairly sure Maisie has a thing for him."

"They've been friends forever," Adalia protested. But she thought back to the meeting—to the hostility Maisie had shown toward River before she softened at his mention of her dog. It made sense.

"Which makes it hard," Georgie said. "Especially since River has no idea."

Did Finn know? She suspected he did based on the way he'd acted at the rescue shelter. After seeing River's car, he'd avoided the back room like a vampire at the entrance to a garlic festival.

"You said for one thing," Adalia said. "What's the other?"

"Finn's coming over for dinner tomorrow night."

Adalia felt like her world had turned slightly lopsided. "What?"

"You didn't know? I thought you might be coming, but Finn told River it didn't have anything to do with you. He said it was a business thing."

Which meant Finn wanted to discuss the beer festival with them. She understood why he'd want to do that alone, but a part of her wished she'd found out from him instead of Georgie.

"No...but he knows I have plans tomorrow night," Adalia said, a little discomfited although she couldn't put her finger on why. When had he set this up, anyway?

Georgie studied her again. "This is what worries me. I get why you like him. Finn's a fun guy, but I'm just not convinced he's dependable."

Adalia wanted to laugh off her sister's paranoia, but she'd trusted Alan too, in the beginning, and look what had happened there. Of course, Finn was nothing like Alan.

If Finn let her down, it would crush her so much more.

CHAPTER
Twenty-Eight

Finn had spent most of his day in virtual meetings with Sean and Mo—guiding them through his idea and how it would work on a practical level—so there hadn't been much time to process what this dinner with River and Georgie could mean.

Why had he agreed to talk over dinner, anyway? He regretted it the moment River opened the door to his loft apartment. Not because of the smell—it smelled amazing, like an Italian restaurant—but what had he been thinking? If Georgie and River balked at the idea of the beer festival, would he have to sit through dinner and dessert, awkwardly staring at them across the table? Or would they maybe kick him out? He hadn't eaten lunch, and he was starving.

Of course, going hungry was hardly his biggest worry. His friendship with River was already strained, and if he wanted things to work out with Adalia, he needed to improve her sister's impression of him, not worsen it.

River clapped him on the back. "Come on in. Georgie and I made lasagna." Hops had joined them at the door, wagging his tail wildly. He had an old black sandal clenched in his teeth.

"Whoa, is that *the* sandal?" Finn asked, surprised by how big Hops had gotten, although he was still very much a puppy.

"He used to hump it, and now he carries it around like a chew toy. Admittedly, we did get him neutered, so not much humping goes on around here anymore."

Finn had to bite his lip. If Adalia had been here, she would have made an off-color joke. God, he wished she were here. He'd texted her earlier to let her know about the dinner. He'd ask if she'd be up for joining them after her girls' night, in the event that River and Georgie didn't throw him out the moment he mentioned Bev Corp, but she'd been noncommittal. He suspected she didn't want anything to interfere with her bonding time with Maisie and Blue, and truthfully he was okay with that. He wanted her to stay in Asheville, and that meant she needed reasons to stick around. Maybe he was arrogant, but he wasn't arrogant enough to think he was enough.

Rather than make that joke for Adalia, he lifted up the six-pack he'd brought, realizing he probably should have asked what to bring. "I didn't know we were having lasagna. I guess I should have gotten wine instead."

River tilted his head. "Not Big Catch?"

"The new guy's stuff isn't in bottles yet, and I figured it might be a little weird to bring you your own beer. I got the new brown ale from Perplexity."

A neutral place they both liked well enough. It had taken him a solid five minutes in front of the cooler case to choose it. Which probably should have told him how nervous he was about this dinner.

Georgie emerged from the bedroom, giving him a speculative look that did nothing to ease his mind about the evening ahead.

"Why are you guys standing by the door?" she asked. Which was when Finn realized he still stood just beyond the door. He took a deep breath, steeling himself like he was a vampire entering an Italian restaurant, and finally stepped inside, closing the door behind him.

On his way to the kitchen, he took a look around the place. He hadn't been there since Georgie had officially moved in, and it looked different in a dozen subtle ways, plus one big way: she'd updated the living room furniture with a nice transitional set in light tan, with several dark brown and light beige throw pillows. A fluffy throw was draped over one edge of the sofa.

"It looks great in here," he said, setting the beer down on the counter. "You did wonders with the place, Georgie."

River, following him in, huffed, "How do you know it wasn't all me?"

"Oh, I know. Your old coffee table was something you literally grabbed off a street corner."

"Waste not, want not."

"Thank you," Georgie said simply, her tone letting him know that flattery would get him nowhere. "Would you like something to drink?"

"I'll just have one of these," Finn said, grabbing one of the bottles. Except then he realized it might be construed as rude to choose the Perplexity beer over all of the Buchanan brews they inevitably had on hand. He glanced at River. "Unless there's something you'd like me to try?"

"I made you try all of our new stuff at the launch," River said.

"Yeah, twisted my arm," Finn said with a faint smile. River had poured him a flight, and it had felt like old times. But his friend had been pulled away quickly, leaving Finn in a room full of people he'd pissed off, who hadn't hesitated to tell him so. He couldn't even count the number of times the *Gazette* article had been mentioned. Then he'd spilled his drink on Adalia, and…

"Let's all have one of these," River suggested, interrupting his circling thoughts, which had already found their way to Adalia. River handed Georgie a bottle of the Perplexity and then took one for himself.

"A brown ale," Georgie said, scrunching her nose. "I think Beau Brown is the only brown ale I like."

"Try it," River said. "We can use the Georgie Scale to rate it."

"You have your own scale?" Finn asked, wondering how he'd rate on it. Probably on the *Take it back to the store* side.

"Yes," River said proudly, "and a palate to go with it. She might not have been a beer drinker for long, but she's a good one. The Georgie Scale has helped inspire all of our new beers."

"You puff me up too much," Georgie said, giving him a little shove, but it was obvious she was pleased. "Why don't we all sit down? I just took the lasagna out, but it needs to rest for fifteen minutes."

They headed over to the new seating arrangement—Finn opting for a chair while they both sat across from him on the sofa. If he had to be in the hot seat, at least it was comfortable.

Hops followed them into the room and, after a moment of what looked like nerve-wracking indecision, surprised Finn by settling at his feet rather than near the couch. He'd take it as a much-needed sign of encouragement.

Georgie sipped the beer and tilted her head as if considering the taste.

"So, what do you think?" he asked.

"I'm surprised by how much I like it," she said. "Not too bitter like some." Shooting a smile at River, she said, "I declare this a seven on the Georgie Scale."

"A rare honor," River said. "Nice pick, Finn."

Silence hung in the room for a moment, but it wasn't the comfortable kind of silence he used to share with River. Because they were both waiting for him to explain himself.

"So…" He took a breath, then said the words guaranteed to put a scowl on River's face. "Bev Corp wants to foster a little more local goodwill. I've agreed to help them." Realizing they might misunderstand and assume he'd gone to work for them, he clarified, "Purely as a consultant."

"Is this business conversation about Bev Corp?" River asked, glowering at him. "Because if so, I can tell you right now I pass."

Georgie just looked at Finn, that weighing look again—as if she was trying to see what River and Adalia saw in him. He suspected the fact that she kept looking at him that way meant she had yet to figure it out.

"Please hear me out," he said.

River nodded, but he managed to look pissed about it.

"I don't want the other employees at Big Catch to have to keep dealing with fallout from the sale. They don't deserve it. They're just doing their jobs. Plus, I came up with an idea that should benefit everyone…and Bev Corp wants to move forward with it. They're going to hold a beer festival with heavily discounted tickets for locals, and all of the local breweries can have tents free of charge. There'll even be best-in-category contests"—he held up a hand, anticipating their next objection—"juried by outside judges. I know there are a lot of beer festivals in town, but they're going to put a big push behind this one. This will be incredible publicity for everyone, not just them. It's a good opportunity."

"I don't want anything to do with them," River said, overlapping with Georgie, who said, "You suggested this?"

"Yes, I did," Finn said. "I get how you feel, River. Trust me, I do. But I wouldn't have suggested this if I didn't think it would help everyone. If I didn't think it would undo a little of the damage I did." He paused, considering his other motivation, the one he hadn't shared with anyone yet. He glanced at Georgie, whose study of him had intensified, if anything. "I've suggested they do it in January. There aren't a lot of beer festivals at that time of year, and everyone's looking for something to do. I figured it could be a practice run for Brewfest."

Neither of them said anything for a moment, and he wondered if they really would ask him to leave.

Finally, Georgie shook her head a little. "If we don't get on board, this might not happen," she said. "Am I right?"

"It's possible," Finn acknowledged. "It would send a message to the other brewers, and the community has been known to stick together." He almost said "our" community, but he knew how that would be received. He'd relinquished his part in it months ago.

More silence, then Georgie said, "You have a knack for getting people to do what you want, don't you?"

The words dug in deep. It wasn't a compliment, and they all knew it.

Glancing at River, whose face was unreadable again, Finn said, "This isn't about me. It's about making things right. This might be a little thing, but it's better than nothing."

It was true, but it wasn't the full truth. He also hoped it would help change the way people perceived him. He really had felt like he was part of the beer community in town, but many of the people he'd counted as acquaintances and friends had turned their backs on him. Sure, Bev Corp wasn't likely to advertise his involvement, but there was no stopping word of mouth. People would know. It would help, although how much, he didn't know.

"We'll think about it," River said.

Georgie shot him a look, like maybe she was surprised that he'd said it, or maybe it was his tone that surprised her. He clearly meant it.

"But I have to warn you," River said, "the rules of parley have been broken. You mentioned Bev Corp in my apartment, so now you have to talk to us about Adalia."

Finn's gaze shot to Georgie, who did not look amused. "Um, what do you want to know?"

"As you probably know, Adalia's going through a lot," she said, "and she needs the people in her life to be there for her. Especially when things get rough."

What did that mean? Was that Alan guy still bothering her? She hadn't wanted to watch a movie over video chat the previous night, but she'd insisted it was because she was tired after her dinner with Jack—and because they'd stayed up way too late the previous night—and he'd believed her. Was something else going on?

"Is Alan still bothering her?" he asked.

Georgie shot another look at River. "Maybe I've said too much. Adalia's the person you should ask about this."

Finn wanted to push for answers, but he knew better. Georgie's opinion of him had soured further, and if there was more to the Alan story, he'd prefer to hear it from Adalia. In person. So he just nodded, taking her up on her challenge. Because it *had* been a challenge.

"I don't have any intention of going anywhere. If you hadn't heard, your sister and I are meant for each other. Dottie's psychic said so, and I don't argue with people who can read the future." His words were tongue in cheek, but he tried to communicate with his eyes that he sort of believed it, however crazy it sounded.

"So Dottie keeps saying," Georgie said.

Which meant they'd talked about him. He wanted to know what had been said, but that was the people-pleasing part of him kicking in, and at the end of the day, he didn't need Georgie to like him. He could live with her tolerating him, so long as she wasn't actively pushing her sister away from him.

"Shall we eat?" River said.

As fast as possible. He wouldn't ask Adalia to join them. Although part of him thought it would help, having her here, he didn't want her to feel uncomfortable.

The lasagna was delicious, and some of the awkwardness leaked away over the course of the meal. Georgie laughed at one of Finn's stories, and they all hypothesized, with no small amount of trepidation, what Dottie was planning for the company Halloween party. Although Jack was handling most of the brewery events, he'd agreed to let Dottie take the lead on employee events.

The Halloween party was her favorite, but there was always some sort of fallout. One year, Lurch had superglued a wig to his head as part of his costume and proceeded to wear it around for two weeks afterward. And people still talked about the year Dottie had run a haunted house out of her bungalow. One of the rooms had been haunted by "bad decisions," and everyone who entered was reminded of all the mistakes they'd made (from the perspective of a former staff member, Josie, who'd been hidden in the closet). Most of them were minor complaints, like finishing all of the half-and-half in the staff fridge and putting the empty carton back in, but Josie knew plenty of gossip too, and had exposed an affair between two staff members.

Hops had further de-escalated the situation by settling down on top of Finn's feet and refusing to move.

After dessert—salted caramel ice cream from one of the local ice cream shops—Finn said goodbye to Georgie, who'd warmed toward him a little (or maybe just thawed), and River offered to walk him out.

"I wasn't aware this was a date," Finn said as they headed for the door.

"Do you think I make lasagna for just anyone?" his friend quipped.

Finn stepped outside, and River joined him, shutting the door behind him. "Is this where you tell me that Georgie hates me?" he asked. "Because I kind of already got that impression." Before River could object, he added, "Not that I blame her. I realize I haven't made a great impression."

"She doesn't hate you," River said. "She just worries about the people she cares about. And I won't lie to you, she's especially worried about Adalia. You really should talk to Addy. I'm sworn to silence, but I think she could really use the support."

"Thanks, man," Finn said, clapping him on the back. "I intend to. We're going to spend the day together tomorrow."

River smiled. "Huh. So she's not actually visiting a goat farm to look at paintings of murderous farm animals."

Finn laughed. "No, we did that last week, but Adalia's got a real talent for description."

"I haven't said this to Georgie in so many words," River said, studying him, "but I think Aunt Dottie's right about you two. I've never seen you like this with anyone else."

"Thanks, River. That means a lot."

"And about the Bev Corp thing?"

"Yeah?" he asked cautiously, still worried River would explode. He wasn't quick to anger, but by God, when someone finally managed to burn up the last of his long fuse...

"It kind of kills me to say so, but it's a good idea. I think we'll probably do it."

Finn checked his phone as soon as he got to his car—no messages—and although part of him thought he should wait to text Adalia, they had promised to check in with each other. He wrote: *I'm not dead, so there's that. It's possible they might go for it. I hope you're having an epic time and you don't see this until later.*

He paused, tapping the side of his phone with his thumb, then added, *Well, if you're doing karaoke like you did with your brother and sister, maybe don't announce that you're single.*

Adalia had told him about that, but he would have known even if she hadn't. It had ended up in one of the local blogs the next morning.

He was about to stow the phone away when her response came: *Oh yeah? Does that mean I shouldn't let the strapping man across the bar buy me a drink?*

He thought for a moment, then responded: *Only if you can guarantee you'll throw it in his face. Are you still thinking of coming over later?*

This time the three dots appeared and lingered for a while before she answered.

Not sure, she finally said. *This might turn out to be a late night. You know, late for a Tuesday, and I want to be 100% for our mystery date. Where should I meet you in the morning if tonight doesn't work out?*

He couldn't help but wonder if the Alan situation had something to do with her reticence. But he just said: *Text me later if you want to come over. If not, meet me at my house at 10. Dress like a tourist.*

If she came at ten, he'd have plenty of time to talk to Gretchen.

Her reply made him groan. *We're already doing role-playing? ;) Count me in.*

CHAPTER
Twenty-Nine

Adalia put her phone down, only to catch Maisie grinning at her. "I'd ask who you're texting, but it's obvious from the look on your face."

"It isn't so obvious to me," Blue said, giving a playful smile. "Unless it's Finn Hamilton. I noticed the way he was looking at you when you came by my studio last week."

Adalia took a sip of her lemon drop martini, lifting her eyebrows.

"You should have seen them at the shelter on Sunday," Maisie said. "I'm thinking of renaming the kennel Lover's Lane." She waggled her eyebrows, making them all laugh.

"I like him," Blue said. "He doesn't know much about textile art, yet he didn't try to pretend otherwise. You wouldn't believe how many people do. He let you take the lead."

Adalia felt her cheeks flush. "I like him too."

And she did. A lot. But this Alan thing had her on edge and questioning everything.

"Why does his name sound so familiar?" Blue asked. "It's been bothering me since I first got his message about the show."

"You probably heard about him from the sale of Big Catch Brewing," Maisie said, sipping a margarita. "He became public enemy number one in Asheville after that."

"Because he bought it or sold it?"

Maisie laughed. "I guess you don't pay much attention to the brewery scene."

Blue's mouth twisted to the side. "Not really."

Resting her elbows on the table, Maisie leaned closer. "Finn started Big Catch with my friend River. They met at a beer festival five years ago and became instant friends. River and I have been close since we were teenagers, but it was the first time I'd ever seen him click with anyone else like that." She glanced down and started playing with the straw in her drink. "Until he met Georgie, anyway."

"My sister," Adalia inserted. "She and River live together now. That's how I met Finn."

Blue nodded. "So what happened next?"

Maisie was still staring down at her drink, stirring it a tad aggressively, but she looked up at that. "Finn had the money. River had the talent. They started with nothing and created this amazing brewery. I just so happened to have a front-row seat since I was part of the Bro Club."

"Bro Club?" Blue asked, her eyes twinkling.

"I came up with the name," Maisie said, her lips tipping up just a little bit. "They hated it at first, but then they got used to it. I tend to have that effect on people."

Adalia tried not to look too eager for information, but she was desperate to hear an outside opinion of Finn. Georgie obviously didn't care for him, but Adalia didn't think she really knew him. Her dislike was born from what she perceived as his betrayal of her boyfriend.

"Finn really screwed up with the whole Big Catch sale," Maisie said, "but honestly, I'm surprised River didn't see it coming. It was obvious Finn's heart wasn't in it anymore. But then, River has blinders on sometimes." She looked like she wanted to say more, but instead she took another sip of her drink.

"How did he screw up?" Blue asked, glancing between both women.

"He lined up a big buyer and signed on the dotted line before he said anything to River," Maisie said. "In his screwed-up way, he thought he was doing River and the other employees a favor. He'd negotiated for them all to get better benefit packages and raises, but he miscalculated. Finn's all about the bottom line, and River's all about relationships."

"What do you mean by that?" Adalia asked, trying to keep her question light.

Maisie looked her in the eye. "Finn's an entrepreneur. He's not interested in the day-to-day work of running a business. That's why I was kind of surprised that River was so blindsided. Sure, Finn handled it all like an idiot, but it was a long time coming. Finn had gotten bored and was only hanging on because of their friendship. That's Finn's deal— he makes something out of nothing and then moves on to do it all over again. Before Big Catch, he did the same thing with a little software company in Charlotte."

Adalia tried to hide her dismay. Was that what was happening between the two of them now? Did he see her brokenness as a project?

"But to answer your question, Blue," Maisie said, thankfully turning her attention away from Adalia. She'd been looking at her with eyes that saw way too much. "The brewing world in Asheville is super tight. When Finn sold out, half the town hated him. River included. Finn holed up and avoided just about everyone and everything for a few months. But now he seems to be emerging and trying to find a new place for himself."

"Like with the art show," Blue said, giving Adalia a warm smile.

"Yeah," Adalia said, forcing a smile of her own. There was no doubt he'd been inspired to create the charity art show because of her. Would he move on once he thought she was whole?

Would she stop being *interesting*?

"Obviously, Finn screwed up," Maisie repeated, "but he's a solid guy. I mean, he could probably sell ice to a polar bear, but he's got a really good heart." She gave Adalia a pointed look. "If you break his heart, I'm gonna have to hurt you."

Adalia forced a laugh, but it sounded tinny. "What about you, Blue?" she asked, knowing better than to ask Maisie. "Got anyone special in your life?"

Blue smiled, but it was no more genuine than Adalia's laugh. "Nope. No one. I might go online again, but I've been taking a sabbatical from love and devoting my energy to my art."

"Now, I hear a story there," Maisie said, leaning closer. "Do tell."

Blue laughed, but something shuttered in her eyes. "Not much to tell. I just happen to be unlucky in love."

"You sound like you've been hanging around Dottie," Adalia teased. "Just don't let her convince you to go see her tarot card reader."

"Lola?" she asked with a grin. "Too late."

"She keeps trying to get me to go too, but I've learned my lesson when it comes to Dottie's mumbo jumbo," Maisie said. "She convinced me to let Josie read my palm at the Buchanan Brewery holiday party last year." She turned to Blue. "Josie is as eccentric as they come and used to be one of their employees. *Anyway*, let's just say it was a *big* mistake."

"Does that mean you don't have any of her crystals?" Adalia asked.

Maisie gave her the side-eye. "Well, let's not get *too* crazy. Every girl can use a good self-defense weapon."

She reached into her purse and pulled out a large pink crystal.

Adalia laughed and pulled out a matching pink crystal from her own purse.

"Huh," Blue said. "Pink crystals have great loving energy. I wonder if that's why she chose them for you."

Maisie huffed. "Well, mine certainly hasn't brought me any luck in love."

"And mine hasn't brought *Finn* any luck," Adalia said, partly because it was funny, and also because she wanted to turn the conversation away from Maisie and her secret. "I hit him with it the first time we met."

They all laughed as Adalia told them about her less-than-promising first encounter with Finn. Then the women exchanged Dottie stories, Adalia relishing all of them. She loved Dottie, and it warmed her heart to know so many other people did too.

"I really should be getting home," Adalia said as she pulled some cash out of her purse to cover her portion of the bill. "I'm a dog mom now. And while Tyrion's with a sitter, I've got those new mom nerves."

Maisie laughed. "Please tell me you didn't hire a babysitter. You *can* leave dogs alone, you know."

"I didn't go *that* far," Adalia said, "but I did give my brother explicit instructions to call or text if he had any problems." She held up her phone. "So far no texts, but I don't want to push my luck."

"I had a good feeling about you," Maisie said, only her teasing tone was gone.

"Back at ya," Adalia said.

"I'm so glad we did this," Blue said, reaching for her purse. "We definitely need to do it again."

"Let's get together at my house sometime," Adalia said. "Then I won't have to get a sitter. And if you have a taste for beer, I have access to a free stash. River always brings over the new stuff he's working on."

"Sounds good to me," Blue said.

"It's a date," Maisie said.

Adalia waved goodbye and headed out to Bessie. As she got into her car, she briefly considered going by Finn's. But Maisie's assessment of him had left her unsettled. In one breath, she had said that Finn had a short attention span and never stuck around anything for long, and in the next she'd threatened Adalia with bodily harm if she broke Finn's heart.

She was more confused than ever.

She couldn't help thinking that just seeing him would alleviate some of her concerns, but she didn't want to be one of those insecure women. Besides, if she stopped by, she was worried she'd lack the willpower to leave later. As much as she wanted to sleep with him, she wasn't ready. Not yet. She felt too unsettled. She had no rule about when to sleep with a guy, but she knew the sex with Finn would be special. And besides, she had Tyrion to think about now.

The house emanated a warm glow when she pulled into the driveway, and she liked the thought that Jack and Tyrion were inside. It made the house feel fuller and more welcoming, more like a home. Only they weren't inside. She found Jack on the back porch, tossing a toy for Tyrion to chase.

"Have a good night?" he asked, sounding subdued. He'd been like that since he'd come back from Chicago, leaving Adalia to wonder what or who he'd left behind. Because he still hadn't offered that information. During their dinner last night he'd insisted he was single, so she had to wonder if he was suffering from the pangs of unrequited love, like Maisie.

"I did," she said, sitting on the bottom step.

Tyrion came running and nearly toppled her over as he raced in tight circles, as if his excitement was so great it needed to be released physically. She laughed and rubbed his neck and head as he showered her face with kisses. "Did you miss me, boy?"

"He's a good dog," Jack said. "I'm glad you got him."

"Yeah," she said softly. "Me too."

Turned out, all teasing with Maisie aside, she was one of those dog people she'd always made fun of. She'd purchased a kennel, food, treats, and a few toys for him on her lunch break on Monday (putting a good dent in her already threadbare bank account), after going to see the artists in the morning. And she'd stuck around to play with him for a bit before heading back to the brewery. She'd come home for lunch again today, plus she'd left work over an hour early so she could spend time with Tyrion before she left to meet Maisie and Blue.

Her branding and marketing plan had been more effective than she'd expected. She'd made a couple more posts this week, photographing customers and asking them what they were drinking and why, and now people had started spontaneously posting their own Buchanan stories and tagging the brewery. Georgie had taken notice and asked her to keep it up.

She nodded to the porch railing on the other side of Jack. Jezebel sat there quietly, watching them. "Do you happen to be Dr. Dolittle? Because that cat is *never* this calm with anyone other than you."

He smiled. "I think she's stalking me like prey."

"I don't think so. She would have attacked by now. In fact, she doesn't even hiss at you. Like ever."

Jack released a long laugh, and Adalia felt good that she'd been the one to instigate it. He needed to laugh. She might not know what troubles were weighing him down, but she understood what it was like to have them.

"Speaking of wild beasts, I hear you're embarking on a safari tomorrow," Jack said in a teasing tone. "I had no idea Asheville was populated by murderous goats."

She shrugged. "Just goes to show you never know a place until you live there." She couldn't remember exactly what her cover story had been, so she improvised. "Someone needs to corral them so they don't terrorize the population. I'm just doing my part to make the world a better place."

"And are you going with a special someone?" he asked, his brow raised.

"Maybe…" she said in a mysterious tone, but her mood shifted as her gaze landed on the shed. She still hadn't used it, and she hadn't been to Dottie's place either. The call of Blue's studio had grown stronger. She'd considered asking her earlier if her offer to use it was still good, but she hadn't felt comfortable bringing it up in front of Maisie. There was safety in a text.

She grabbed her phone out of her pocket and sent Blue a message before she could change her mind.

Is your offer to use your studio still good? I'd be happy to pay you rent to use some of the space.

Blue responded right away. *Yes! Want to come by tomorrow?*

Part of her longed to say yes, but the pull to Finn was stronger.

Can we make it Thursday? I have the day off tomorrow, but I have a date.

Ooo, an all-day date with Finn? Thursday it is!

Was it an all-day date? She couldn't say without knowing what he had planned, but she knew she'd missed him the past two and a half days. Absence really had made her heart grow fonder, even if she was scared about what that might mean. Even if she now had doubts.

She hung out with Jack a little while longer, then headed up to her room to get ready for bed. Tyrion didn't even bother with his pallet on the floor, jumping onto the bed with her. She lay in the dark, suddenly feeling lonely for Finn, so she set up her laptop to watch *Pride and Prejudice* as she went to sleep.

But fifteen minutes into the movie, she grabbed her phone and decided she wasn't going to let fear ruin what she had with him. She'd told herself she wouldn't hold back, for better or for worse, and she didn't want to start. Life was about taking risks, and Finn was a huge one. The payoff would either be the best relationship of her life or a heart ripped to shreds.

I miss you, Finn. I can't wait to see your face tomorrow.

Then she turned off her phone, and dreamed of him.

CHAPTER

Thirty

Finn was wearing jeans and an I Love New York T-shirt. Sure, they weren't in New York, but it was his idea of what a tourist would wear, and he figured it might get a smile out of Adalia, who was, after all, a New Yorker.

After getting home last night, he'd spent several hours stewing, working in fits and spurts. He was worried about Adalia without knowing *why* he should be worried. Because she hadn't told him what was happening. It was her right not to say anything, of course, but he'd thought they were getting closer. The fact that she hadn't shared her problems with him indicated he might be wrong, that she didn't trust him. Then she'd sent him that text about missing him, and most of the worry had eased. Most, but not all.

He'd decided not to mention Alan right away. Today would be about them, not about the past. They needed to discuss the past at some point, though—he suspected it was the only way they'd be sure to have a future.

His bell rang at ten on the dot, and he all but lunged for the door, which he'd been watching like an expectant dog. What was happening to him?

He opened the door, and the answer to his question stood on his stoop, dressed in an I Love New York T-shirt that matched his, down to the color (black), jeans, and…

"Is that a fanny pack?" he asked, his mouth twitching with a barely restrained smile.

"That's what you focus on?" She feigned anger. "You said tourist, and I delivered. Now, can we address the fact that we match? Is Jack spying for you or something?"

"No, this is a delightful coincidence," he said. Although he wasn't so sure that was true. The matching shirts made him think of Lola again, of the cards she'd pulled for both of them.

"We're going to look ridiculous," Adalia continued with a smirk, "and I totally love it. So is the mystery finally over? Are you going to tell me what we're doing?"

"Actually…" he said, pulling the blindfold out of his pocket. "I thought we could keep it going awhile longer."

She raised her brows. "Kinky. I like it."

Oh God, the thought of Adalia wearing that blindfold in his bedroom did things to him…but he was determined to deliver on his promise of a mystery date. He knew she'd love their destination, and he selfishly wanted to be the person who took her there for the first time.

Of course, there was a chance she'd already gone with Georgie, but he didn't think so. Adalia had told him that she'd spent her first few months in Asheville as a complete hermit, not engaging with anything outside the brewery or her house.

"You can put it on in the car," he said, his voice husky.

But she took it from him and secured it around her eyes, then tilted her head up, waiting for a kiss.

Finn had never seen anything more beautiful in his life. He watched her for a moment, soaking in the sight of her, trying to commit it to memory, and then he realized he was being an idiot and drew her to him. It was a slow kiss, a claiming kiss. And she leaned into him like she didn't want to let go—like she really *did* trust him. They tilted their heads, trying to get closer, closer, until there wasn't any closer they could get from just kissing, and they were breathless from trying. He was the one who finally pulled away.

"You're the most beautiful woman I've ever seen," he whispered into her ear. Whispered because it would have felt wrong to say it louder, for some reason, like it might break the moment.

She nudged the blindfold down. "Well, that's saying something."

For a second, he didn't understand what she meant, but then he realized she was talking about his past. About the fact that he'd dated a lot, and usually not for very long.

The trust between them had been punctured.

"I guess," he said. "You should know…this is different for me." He wanted to tell her that he'd never felt this way about another woman, but he saw something like fear in her eyes.

"Thank you. I should have just said thank you. Let's go," she said, the blindfold still pulled down a little, like she wasn't willing to relinquish control again.

He grabbed his bro bag, which made Adalia smile a little, and they headed out to the car, Finn coming around to open the door for her.

"Where's your car?" he asked.

"It's a nice day, so I walked, although I felt guilty about not bringing Tyrion. He loves walks."

They got settled in their seats and he started the drive in silence. He was the one who broke it, although the question he asked was not the one on his mind.

"Did you have fun last night? Maisie's good people, and I know you were excited about hanging out with Blue."

"Yeah, I did," she said, her posture relaxing—or so he thought from his peripheral vision. "Although it came as something of a disappointment that she didn't bring her giant rabbit."

"Naturally. Did she show you a picture?"

"I insisted on it. Get this, his name is Buford. She made a knitted doppelganger of him too, and he sleeps with it. How cool is she?"

He grinned. "I'm glad we met her. She's going to be a great addition to the show. I like that we're going to have so many mediums represented in one place."

"Yeah, me too," she said, her tone thoughtful. He wanted to ask what she was thinking about, but she beat him to it and asked him about his dinner with Georgie and River.

"They made lasagna," he said, straight-faced.

She scowled and nudged his arm, her hand lingering on his bicep. "You know that's not what I meant."

"Didn't Georgie tell you anything?" he asked.

"She may have texted me this morning, but I wanted to hear more about it from you."

"Okay," he said, glancing at her, "but we're getting close. Can you slide your blindfold back up?"

She gave him an intent look before tugging the blindfold into place.

"This better be worth it," she grumbled, but she sounded intrigued.

"I hope you think it is," he admitted. "Because otherwise I have a feeling you're going to make *me* wear the blindfold on the way home. And before you say it, yes, I will absolutely wear it for you on another occasion if you want me to."

"That was exactly what I was going to say," she said with a little laugh. "But you're not getting out of telling me about last night."

"Honestly, it went a lot better than I thought it would. River told me in confidence that he thinks they're going to go for it. Which will make a big difference in terms of who else agrees to participate."

"Yeah, Georgie confirmed it. I'll be honest, I know I encouraged you to tell them, but I wasn't sure how it would go. River, like, super hates Bev Corp."

Hearing her confirmation bolstered something in him, and he felt more confident about his new plan. His new direction. He *was* good at this, at helping businesses troubleshoot and grow and change. He was eager to tell Adalia about it, but not yet—he wanted this moment to be about her, about them.

"I won't say that's not good news. I'm happy it all worked out. I really think it will be to everyone's benefit."

She still had the blindfold on, but he felt her eyes on him, as if they were seeing through the fabric and skin, into his brain or maybe his heart.

"Georgie told me what you said about holding the festival before Brewfest. Did you do this for them?"

It would be easy to say yes—to pretend that his only motivation had been to help the friend he'd hurt. But it wasn't the full truth, and he didn't want to lie to her.

"Partly," he said. "And partly because I want to repair my reputation. But I also like doing a good job. The idea came to me, and it was a good idea. I knew it would work."

He pulled through the gates, joining a line of cars. Not too bad today, but it was a popular tourist attraction, so the fact that it was a Wednesday was basically meaningless.

He shot a glance at Adalia, but that blindfold made it impossible to read her expression.

"We're here, aren't we?" she asked.

"We've reached our destination, yes," he said. "But we'll be in the car awhile longer. Then I'm going to have to lead you on foot."

He pulled up to the red-suited attendant, who greeted him, scanned the tickets on his phone, and wished them a good day, all without reacting to the fact that Adalia was blindfolded in the passenger seat. He supposed they'd seen all kinds.

"The suspense is starting to eat at me, Finn. I assume it's some sort of attraction. Is it a zoo? No, a beer museum!" She paused. "A giant ball of yarn?"

Finn laughed. "Is that what comes to mind when you think of Asheville?"

His heart was beating a little faster in his chest now. He was pretty sure she didn't know, that it really would be a surprise.

She kept spouting off ideas, each a bit more ridiculous than the last, as he slowly navigated the road.

"Area 51," she said as he pulled into the parking lot.

"That's in New Mexico."

"Nevada, actually," she scoffed. "But you know what I mean—an Area 51-type place."

"That you can buy tickets to go see? I'm actually sorry that's not what we're doing. I'm tempted to turn right around and find us some aliens."

"Don't you dare!" she said, laughing. "Then I'll never know, and it'll drive me crazy. Oh hey, you parked the car. Is this the walking part?"

"It is indeed. Wait for me. I'll come around and get your door."

He did, and she took his hand as she climbed down, hanging on to it.

"Admit it," she said, leaning in to him as he closed the door. "You just insisted on the whole blindfold thing so I'd have to hold your hand."

"I don't think we need an excuse for that anymore," he said. "We can't seem to stop."

She tripped a little on a twig in the paved parking lot and then gave him a playful shove. "Hey, you're supposed to be my eyes."

He started describing the terrain to her, careful not to give anything else away. "We're stepping onto a gravel path through the woods. There are pines on either side of us. Up ahead, there's a big group of tourists. We'll say it's a family reunion. Or wait, it's more complicated than that—they discovered after their father's funeral that he had a secret family. This is the first time the two sides have met."

"So he's dead?" she asked. "Man, your 'Who are you?' stories are always such downers."

"Well, maybe they don't mind so much since he was two-timing them both, but this is their chance to get to know each other outside of him. To be a family again."

She was quiet at that, and it occurred to him that maybe he'd strayed a little too close to her own experience. To her situation with Jack and her father.

"Or not," he said. "Maybe…"

But a screech cut him off. He turned to see a woman with aggressively dyed purplish-reddish hair barreling toward him down the twisty trail, dragging a short man with watery eyes and newsboy cap. The man looked reluctant, as if he'd prefer to be back at the hotel reading a newspaper.

"Bernard, he's kidnapping her! Someone call the authorities!"

Bernard ducked behind her as she got closer, but the big group of people in front of them came to a halt and turned back.

"Hey, she's blindfolded!" one of them shouted.

A big muscle-bound guy pushed his way through his group, gunning for Finn and Adalia. He wore a CrossFit T-shirt that didn't bode well for Finn if he hoped to retain his nose in its current shape and size.

"Miss? Are you okay?" he asked, his eyes shooting murder at Finn.

"Haven't you heard anything about Stockholm syndrome?" Dyed Hair asked, and Adalia snorted in amusement. "Even if she says yes, we can't take her word for it. Could be he's brainwashed her. On *Private Eyes* last week, a woman did *unspeakable* things for the man who'd kidnapped her."

"Are you sure that wasn't a porno?" Adalia asked. She made no move to slip the blindfold down.

The woman's eyes narrowed. "It's the story that keeps me interested, not the sex. Are you here against your will? Hop twice if the answer's yes."

"How would that be any different than if she actually said yes?" Finn asked, genuinely curious. But he also wanted to de-escalate the situation. "Maybe you should take your blindfold down, Adalia."

"Not on your life," she said in an undertone. "You told me it was going to stay a surprise until the end, and I intend to hold you to it."

"Are you being kidnapped or not?" CrossFit asked. He sounded kind of sulky about it, like maybe he'd hoped to make it into the paper.

"Hop if you need to communicate without words," Dyed Hair shouted, as if she feared she hadn't been heard the first time.

"This is most definitely not a kidnapping," Adalia said. "And you all are kind of ruining our weird sex thing."

Finn bit his lip, trying to hold back laughter.

"I knew it was a sex thing!" Dyed Hair said, but she hung back, no longer looking like she was going to barrel into him. Finn had a feeling she was staying behind them on the trail because she intended to watch Adalia's feet the whole way.

CrossFit stared at Adalia with new appreciation, as if the knowledge that she wasn't in mortal peril freed him to view her as a sex object.

"Move along," Finn said, his tone hard.

CrossFit shot him another dirty look, but he rejoined his family reunion or whatever he had going on and kept walking. Good riddance.

Adalia had a huge grin on her face. "Was that part of the plan?" she asked as they resumed walking. "Because if so, well done."

"No, there are some things in life too perfect to be planned."

Like stumbling into Dottie's art studio and seeing Adalia, really seeing her, for the first time.

Would this have ever happened if that hadn't? He'd like to think they would have connected anyway, but who knew. There was a bit of magic to falling in love, it turned out.

The thought caught him off guard. Was he in love with Adalia? It was too soon, wasn't it?

They reached the end of the path, and he led her across the street and through yet another gate. The house stood before them in all its enormity and grandeur.

"Are we here?" she asked, her voice a little hoarse.

"We're here." And he reached into her mass of curls and gently loosened the blindfold, pulling it away.

She gasped, taking in the enormous stone mansion, which looked like it belonged in another era. That was what he'd always thought about the Biltmore Estate, that it was a place out of time. For a moment, she just looked at it, soaking it in. Then she turned to him with tears in her eyes.

"You brought me to Pemberley."

And in that moment he knew, with certainty, that he loved her.

CHAPTER
Thirty-One

Adalia wrapped her arms around Finn's neck and kissed him. Perhaps she should have known there was an enormous mansion sitting on the edge of Asheville, as if airlifted from Regency England, but she hadn't. She'd spent the last months in a cave, letting time go by without making anything of it. But she was making something of it now, and she didn't intend to stop.

Finn cupped the back of her head, kissing her softly, *adoringly*, as if he were marveling that he could. When had a man ever made her feel like this? Like she was someone special?

He pulled back slightly. "I considered suggesting we dress in nineteenth-century outfits so we could pretend we work here, but one, I suspected it would have given away the surprise, and two, a lot of people would probably have tried to ask us questions. I know we'd have fun coming up with ridiculous answers, but I kind of want you to myself today."

"We'll do it next time," she said, grinning from ear to ear as she pulled back and lifted a hand to his face. "Okay?"

He smiled back, his eyes alight with happiness. She could tell he was pleased he'd surprised her, that she hadn't known. "Deal."

She kissed him again, so full of joy it felt like it needed to bubble over.

Tomorrow. It could bubble over tomorrow in the studio. She couldn't wait to see what form it took. If the paintings that had come out of a place of rage and sadness had been good, what would her work look like now?

A thin sliver of fear poked at her. Would her feelings for Finn make her work better...or had adversity actually made her a better artist?

Stop sabotaging yourself, said a voice in her head, one that sounded like her mother. *Let yourself be happy.*

"The sad part," Finn said in a grave tone, even though his eyes still twinkled, "is that we now have to wait in line for half an hour before we can go in." He nodded his head toward the line of people waiting in front of the entrance.

Pulling back, Adalia crooked her arm, offering it to him, then said in a British accent, "We should proceed to the queue without delay, should we not, Mr. Hamilton?"

He laughed. "So we're doing this part without the costumes?"

She lifted her brow and gave him a stern look.

Linking arms with her, he said in what sounded like a cross between an English and a Southern accent, "Yes, Miss Buchanan, let us go. Posthaste."

She burst out laughing as they started to walk across the massive front lawn. Could it be called a lawn when there was a fountain in the middle of it? "Is that your version of a British accent?"

311

"You might find this shocking, but we didn't have international accent classes in business school."

"Well, they obviously *should*," she said, nudging her shoulder into his arm. "Think how useful it would be to speak to a French businessman in English with a French accent."

He shook his head, his lips twitching. "Or perhaps he might find it slightly insulting?"

"Why, Mr. Hamilton," she said, leaning away and feigning a look of reprimand. "Are you being contrary with me?"

He glanced down at her. "Never, Miss Buchanan." Something shifted in his expression and he said with a seriousness only slightly undermined by his accent, "I never want to be contrary with you."

She studied him for a second, and some of the uneasiness she'd felt about him, about *them*, faded. Funny, how she'd mostly forgotten about it over the past ten or fifteen minutes. Then again, when she was with him, she never felt distrustful. It was only when she was away from him that the doubt began to seep in.

Coming to a stop, she dropped his arm, placed her hands on his chest, and stretched up to kiss him. "Thank you for this. All of it. I never want to be contrary with you either." Then, feeling a little wicked, she added, "Unless it's fun."

"Oh, behave," he said, his eyes full of mirth. He reached for her arm, gently tucking her hand over his forearm again, and they walked in silence for a few seconds. Something between them seemed to have shifted slightly, like they both felt more settled and secure.

She dropped her accent and asked, "Have you been here before?"

"When I was a kid, but I don't remember anything about it except that my mom got me ice cream for not touching anything inside. I've been back once since moving to Asheville, for a meeting with several other brewers, but I didn't get a tour of the entire place." He squeezed her hand against his side. "I'm glad I'm doing it with you."

This was getting too sappy for her comfort, so she lifted her chin and said in her British accent, "Can we take a stroll around the gardens later, Mr. Hamilton?"

"We can do anything you like, Miss Buchanan," he responded in his British/Southern hybrid.

They played 'Who are you?' while they waited in line, skipping over the CrossFit guy's family reunion, and Finn determined that a man with bushy sideburns close to the entrance was an ax murderer.

Adalia grinned, shaking her head. "Why would an ax murderer be going into the Biltmore?"

"I'm sure there are a dozen places to hide bodies in there," he said with a serious face. "Perhaps somewhere in the dungeon."

She took a step back and gave him an inquiring look. "You think they have a dungeon?"

"All these old mansions do," he said matter-of-factly. "Or maybe he's here to check out the dungeon to use for his next grisly murder."

"You *do* realize that your stories just keep getting worse and worse, don't you?" she teased. "Should we be concerned about going into a house with a dungeon an ax murderer is scoping out for his next crime?"

"Don't worry," he said with a smug smile. "I'll protect you."

She nudged her shoulder into his arm again. "Maybe *I'll* be the one protecting *you*."

He laughed. "I believe that you could. We can protect each other."

"There's an ax murderer here?" asked the fuchsia-haired woman with the *Private Eyes* addiction. She and her husband had filed in behind them, and the woman had been keeping an eagle eye on Adalia. Apparently she'd been listening in too. "You have the police on speed dial, don't you, Bernard? Keep your hand over the button."

Adalia leaned closer to Finn. "Look what you've done," she whispered in a mischievous tone. "You're scaring the other tourists again. If we get kicked out before we even get in, I'll never forgive you."

"Then I'll sacrifice myself to make sure you make it in, Miss Buchanan," he said in his fake accent.

"I should hope so," she said. "But I don't want to see it without you, so you better do some smooth talking if a security guard shows up."

A man in front of them turned around and lowered his voice. "They have hidden doors, you know."

"What?" Adalia asked.

"Hidden doors," the man repeated slowly. "Someone could stash a body literally *anywhere*. I saw it on the news. The big plant room. The pool table room. The dining rooms. They're everywhere." His eyes grew wider as he spoke, although from his tone, it was unclear whether he feared that the mustached man was truly a murderer or if he'd been considering the possibility of hiding a body himself.

"Robert," the woman next to him snapped. "Those doors lead to *other rooms*. You can't very well hide a body in the butler's pantry."

Adalia leaned closer and said in a near-whisper, "I don't know. I've seen enough true crime Lifetime movies to know it's actually possible."

The man's mouth formed an O, and he turned to stare at the front of the line. "Which guy did you say was the ax murderer?"

"He's already gone inside," Finn said.

The man and woman whispered between themselves—something about visiting the shops and gardens before circling back to the house—and left the line a couple of minutes later.

Finn leaned into her ear. "We're two people closer to the entrance now. I'm not sure if I should be impressed by your skills or frightened of them."

"It was an unintended consequence." She glanced up at him, their faces inches apart. "And you should be both."

A slow smile spread across his face. "Did you really learn that watching Lifetime movies?"

She lifted a brow. "I'm a woman of mystery, Mr. Hamilton. Stick around and find out."

"Trust me," he said in a husky voice. "I intend to."

A shiver ran down her back, pooling in her core. If she didn't want to see the house so very much, and with him, she would suggest that they skip the line and return to his place to do scandalous things.

They played 'Who are you?' with a few more people, Finn making his characters more and more ghastly. Adalia knew it was because of her earlier statement, and she loved it. She'd only told a few other people about her game. A few had called it ridiculous, others had made a half-hearted attempt to play, and one person had even called it mean-spirited, which wasn't at all her intent. They weren't talking about the people they chose, not really. It was about imagination. About *creating*. And she did think Finn was a creator, whatever he said. He liked building something out of nothing, or using an existing foundation to make a much taller building. She even saw it in his approach to the game. He seemed to get more into it with each new round.

They finally made it inside, and Adalia was instantly blown away by the architecture and grandeur. A staff member was taking photos of the visitors, which they were told they could pick up later (probably for an obscene price), and Adalia and Finn exchanged a look and shrugged.

They posed pointing at each other's shirts, making wide, cheesy grins.

"Make sure they can see your fanny pack," he said through his smile.

"Only if your bro bag is on full display," she insisted.

The attendant gave them the slip of paper to claim their photos, and they moved along.

When she discovered there was a traveling *Downton Abbey* costume exhibit, she was giddy with excitement. The house was memorable all on its own, full of paintings and sculptures, of design choices both inspired and hideously ugly, but she eagerly sought out the costume displays, Finn watching her with a strange look on his face. Almost like he was trying to soak in her reactions to everything. To soak *her* in. She read every placard from the costume exhibits aloud to him, and since she'd seen every season of *Downton Abbey*, she explained the context for each particular costume.

"That's the dress Lady Sybil wore when she seduced Tom the chauffeur…"

"Sounds like a soap opera," he said with a grin.

"That's because it was," she said, giving him a playful whap. "A glorious one with fancy costumes and stodgy accents."

There was no dungeon, of course, but there was an underground bowling alley and pool, plus a basement kitchen. They kept pointing out locations someone could use to hide a body.

"That cabinet looks big enough," Adalia said, pointing to one in the kitchen.

"It would have to be a small woman," Finn said with a contemplative look. "It's too small to fit a man's body."

The family behind them looked startled, and the mother steered her tandem stroller in a wide arc to get around them.

"I bet I could stuff *your* body in there," Adalia said, trying to stifle a smile.

"Really?" he said with a grin. "Too bad we'll never know since it's roped off."

She gave him a playful look. "Rules are made to be broken, you know…"

He grabbed her wrist and tugged her away. "Did you learn that on Lifetime?" he teased.

"I'll never tell. Maybe I'll subject you to a marathon weekend. I hear there's a *Women Who Kill* theme this weekend."

"I need to draw the line somewhere," Finn said. "My bro purse is already threatening my man card. I'm worried the manly police will show up at my front door and demand I turn it over."

Laughing, she pulled him to a stop. "I'm not sure if you've heard," she said with a sly smile, "but I'm pretty talented with Photoshop. If they peel your man card out of your tightly clenched, manly fist"—she picked up his hand

and playfully kissed his knuckles—"I can just make you a new one."

"Thank God I have you in my life," he said, his eyes dancing. "I'll never have to worry about my Photoshop needs ever again."

"I'll still have to charge you," she said, lifting her shoulder into a shrug. "A girl's gotta make a living."

"Of course," he said, still grinning. "I wouldn't dream of asking for a discount."

She was still holding his hand, so she lowered it and laced their fingers together. They finished the tour like that, stopping at the booth to see the photos they'd had taken at the beginning.

"We don't have to see them," Adalia said as they waited behind an Asian couple who were arguing in a different language. "Everyone knows this is a huge rip-off."

"No way," he said, holding her in place with their still-linked fingers. "I want to see them." He was still smiling, but there was a seriousness in his tone that told her this meant something to him.

When they got to the counter, she burst out laughing. "We look like an '80s ad for tourism to New York."

"Exactly. I'm getting this one framed," he said.

It was a joke, to be sure, but she found herself wondering if he would. And if they'd look at it from time to time and remember this day—not as part of an almost forgotten past, but as part of a beginning. Their beginning.

They drove to the other side of the grounds and had lunch in the stable café, discussing the exhibits while Finn looked up George W. Vanderbilt on his phone and told her facts about the bachelor who had built the nearly 179,000-

square-foot house, then married several years after its completion.

When they finished their leisurely lunch, they wandered the gardens, strolling hand in hand as they discussed the garden layout and their own gardening experience, or lack thereof. (Finn had apparently killed no fewer than fifteen shrubs before giving up on his front yard.) She told him about a show on Netflix they should watch about large garden designs to help inspire his selection of the next plants he would kill.

Finn found a bench under a long pergola, and they took a seat. He wrapped his arm around her back, and she rested her cheek on his chest, neither one of them speaking for a couple of moments as they watched butterflies dancing around a planting of chrysanthemums.

"This has been perfect," she said with a sigh. "Thank you for my day at Pemberley. No one else would have made it this special."

He kissed the top of her head. "We'll do the costumes next time."

Sitting upright, she turned to face him. "You'd really do that? Look ridiculous in a period costume for me?"

A smug look filled his eyes. "I don't know about *ridiculous*. I think I could pull off a morning coat."

She laughed and gave him a soft kiss. "Yes, Finn. You definitely could. But right now, I'm more interested in what's underneath this ridiculous shirt." She placed a hand on his chest, her grin spreading. "And yes, you pulled off this ridiculous look too, but with great power comes great responsibility, which means we have to burn it when we get you home. Like *immediately*."

"Miss Buchanan," he said in his cheesy accent, but he sounded slightly breathless. "Isn't it improper for an unmarried woman to be alone with a man in his home? He could do unscrupulous things."

She gave him another gentle kiss, but this time she ran her tongue over his bottom lip. "One can only hope."

CHAPTER
Thirty-Two

Before they went any further, he should ask her about Alan Stansworth. Because he wanted so badly for her to trust him. He *needed* it. But the way she was looking at him...

"Race you to the car?" he asked.

Instead of answering, she started running, laughing hysterically while she did so.

He raced after her, laughing too, feeling exuberant in a way he'd only felt with her lately. They ran past a bunch of tourists who looked at them quizzically, not because they were running—locals came out here to run—but because they were running in their jeans and I Love New York shirts, bro bag and fanny pack bouncing. They passed the *Private Eyes* woman from earlier, whose eyes bulged at the sight of them.

"Now he's chasing her," she shouted. "*Do something,* Bernard!"

Her husband had a look of alarm, but he didn't attempt to follow them, and neither did she.

It was then Finn realized that some of the looks might not be because of their outfits. He hadn't outpaced Adalia yet, which made it look like she was running and he was chasing.

Adalia seemed to figure it out too because she was laughing harder, the sound drifting back to him.

They made it back to the car, breathless, and she panted out, "We'd better go… She's totally going to call the cops this time."

A uniformed police officer walked past them, hurrying off to destinations unknown, or possibly to the woman with the dyed hair, and Finn and Adalia exchanged a look. He unlocked the car, and she bit her lip when she heard the click, as if trying to suppress yet more laughter.

They climbed into the car all casual like—*nothing to see here, officer*—and then exchanged another look, grinning. And oh God, he couldn't ruin the moment by asking her something that would upset her. Not now. Not yet.

"Go," she said, and he didn't make her say it again.

They were quiet on the way back to his house, but every so often he looked over, and whenever he did, she was staring at him, lips parted, eyes full of wanting. And oh, how he wanted her. It had never been like this.

Then she slowly slid the blindfold out of her fanny pack and slipped it into place, tying it behind her head.

"Adalia," he said, his voice coming out so husky it sounded like a stranger's.

"I'm a big believer in finishing what you started, Finn," she said.

He sped the rest of the way home and parked in the drive.

"I do believe it's time for you to show me to your bedroom, Mr. Hamilton," she said, slipping into the British accent she pulled off all too well.

He opened the door so fast it nearly hit the almost-but-not-quite-dead shrub by the driveway, and he was circling around the car to open her door when he saw a familiar figure loping down the street. No, make that two. A small black figure preceded the much larger rusty-red and white figure.

"Jezebel?" he asked, baffled. "Tyrion?"

Adalia must have heard her dog's name through the window, because she immediately exited the car, the blindfold hanging loose around her neck.

"Tyrion," she shouted, running after him. The dog turned as soon as he heard her call his name, but he didn't race back to them. He whined and glanced up ahead at Jezebel, who was still prancing jauntily forward. The sleek black cat slowed at the sound of his whine and glanced back, hair bristling a little at the sight of them. But she stopped.

"Does she think he's her dog?" Finn said in an undertone.

"Shhh," she said, pressing a finger to her lips. "It sounds crazy, but I suspect they're working something out."

More whining followed, answered by a couple of meows and shrieks, and then Tyrion bustled up to Adalia, tail wagging, as if he were a child who'd been given permission. She wrapped her arms around him, hugging him with abandon, and Finn felt it down to his heart.

"What are we going to do about Jezebel?" he asked, really hoping she didn't expect him to tackle her.

"Let's see if she follows," Adalia said.

It seemed highly unlikely to him—when had that cat ever followed anyone, even Beau?—but Adalia had her hand on Tyrion's collar, so they weren't likely to lose him, anyway. And Jezebel…well, she'd shown she could very easily survive on her own when she had a mind to. If she stayed out, she'd come back, lured by sardines and crystals.

"Okay," he said, "let's give it a try."

They headed back toward his house, and sure enough, Jezebel trailed behind them, making a big production of every footstep, as if she were being dragged against her will. But she came, nonetheless.

"I've never seen anything like it," he said.

"I know," she said. "Thank God you saw them when you did. I wonder how they got out in the first place. It's only three thirty. I guess Jack might have come back home to let them out, but it's strange that he didn't call."

"You can check your messages when we get inside," he said. Which was when he realized that she might not want to come inside anymore. She would probably want to bring them home. "If you still want to come inside," he amended.

"You'd be okay with me bringing them in?" Adalia asked, her tone dubious. "Jezebel is like a poltergeist—she might never leave. And Tyrion sheds enough fur to make a coat. Your house is much too nice to be covered in fur."

"Yeah, I'm okay with it. More than okay." Besides, if they continued seeing each other, Tyrion would be spending plenty of time at his house. He knew Adalia wouldn't want to leave him on his own for any length of time, especially after this.

"I know this wasn't what we were planning…" she started as they reached the house.

"No, but life has a way of keeping things interesting for us," he said. They stopped in front of the door. "I've taken in a foster for Maisie before. I have a water bowl in the closet, plus there's some meat in the fridge and a few tins of sardines for Jezebel."

She gave him a look, and he felt himself blushing a little. "I got some after she ran away a few months ago. I figured River might be more willing to forgive me if I caught her and brought her home."

She nudged him a little with her shoulder. "That worked out for you pretty well, now didn't it?"

"Yes," he said honestly. "It did."

"I think they'll do okay without food for now. They always eat breakfast late, but maybe we can give them something later."

Did that mean she intended to stay for a while?

He unlocked the door and opened it, waving for Tyrion to go in, but he stood to the side until a streak of black shot through the opening. Tyrion padded in after Jezebel, then looked back to see if Adalia would follow. Which she did. Finn shut the door behind them.

By the time he'd turned back around, Tyrion was curled up on his couch, Jezebel perched on the back of the cushion above him. Both appeared as comfortable as if they'd lived there their whole lives.

Adalia gave him a slightly worried look, as if she thought it might shatter his psyche to see them curled up on his sofa, and he found himself laughing again.

"I don't care if they shed," he said. "They make vacuums for a reason. Why don't you check in with Jack to see what happened? I'll get some things ready for them."

But she groaned as soon as she pulled her phone out of her fanny pack.

"That's probably why he didn't say anything. My battery's dead. Again."

And no wonder. Her cell phone dated back to the first generation of portable phones.

"I'd tell you to plug it in," he said, "but there's no way I have a charger for that. If you know his number, you can call him on my phone." He pulled it out of his bro bag and handed it over. "Or call Dottie and ask her to pass on the message."

"Thanks, Finn," she said, leaving her hand on his for a moment. "For everything. Maybe you can give me a tour of the upstairs once they're settled."

She winked as she said it, and he felt at once turned on and amused—she'd said it like a mom talking in code around her toddler.

"I'd like that," he said.

She sat next to Tyrion to make her calls, and he found a couple of old dog dishes in his closet, along with a rope chew toy Maisie had told him to keep, making it clear she fully intended to guilt him into taking another foster. After filling one of the dishes with water, he found himself questioning the likelihood they would share and got them another Tupperware full of water. He could hear Adalia on the phone, but he didn't process what she was saying until he came back in with the water bowls.

"I'm not sure," she said. "But it may be after dinner. They're safe."

He lowered the bowls and the chew toy, which Tyrion and Jezebel promptly ignored, and looked at Adalia as she said goodbye and hung up the call.

"Dottie had Jack's number. He feels insanely guilty," she said, massaging the area between her eyebrows. "I don't know why he was home—something about a phone call from Chicago—but he says he'll explain later. Anyway…I guess he let Tyrion out, and Jezebel shot out the back. Tyrion started howling, then jumped the fence to follow her. Jack's been roaming the neighborhood for the last hour with pockets full of treats."

It occurred to Finn that it might be of some significance that Adalia had called Dottie for the number instead of Georgie. Was it because her sister would have advised her to go home? But he didn't have much time to consider it. She reached out and patted Tyrion, who leaned into the caress. "He's a loyal dog. I admire loyalty. Even if it's to Jezebel."

She bent down to kiss Tyrion's nose and then stood from the sofa. "They look like they're exhausted by their adventure," she said. "I think we can take that tour."

She held out her elbow like she had at the Biltmore, and he took it.

"I always prefer to start a tour in the master bedroom, don't you?" he asked.

"I like the way you think."

They walked up the stairs together, sides pressed together, and his heart pounded madly as he led her to his room. How many times had he imagined this? Well, he'd never imagined it quite like *this*, but in a weird way, it felt right. Because it was their kind of chaos.

He opened the door to the room, only then remembering that he probably should have warned her. Because across from them hung the painting he'd pieced together with glue. The cracks only made it more beautiful.

He'd kept the painting because she'd given it to him, however spitefully.

Because he couldn't bear to throw anything of hers away.

Because, even though it radiated pain, it was stunningly beautiful.

He hoped it wasn't weird that he'd kept it. He hadn't hung it there at first. Not until they'd become closer. Ultimately, though, it had called to him, as if insisting to be seen. Her light—even her vindictive fury—*deserved* to be seen.

Now, he realized he'd fallen a little bit in love with her that day, seeing her create and destroy. And he'd fallen in deeper every day since.

He glanced at her, worried. "Adalia…"

But something flickered in her eyes, and she walked inside the room, tugging him after her by the loops of his jeans, and closed the door.

"We'll have to burn it later," she said.

For a moment he was confused. Did she mean the painting or his shirt? But then she ripped off his shirt and threw it to the ground. Her shirt followed it, her bra a bright neon pink this time, and then their mouths met—no longer gentle, like they'd been earlier, but consuming each other. He pulled away to finish undressing her. Then he looked at her for a moment, marveling at her beauty, her curls wild, her eyes bright with mischief and joy, and marveling, too, at the fact that this was finally happening. That it felt the way it did. He tried to take off his own pants, but she pushed his hand away.

"I get to do that," she insisted, her eyes burning. And she slowly undid the button and the zipper, pushing down his pants and his boxer briefs, freeing him. She gave him a wicked look as she stroked him and said, "Big catch indeed."

Then she reached down and found the blindfold among the clothes they'd shed.

Before she could put it on, or suggest he did, he said, "No, not the first time. I want to see your eyes."

CHAPTER
Thirty-Three

Adalia's head rested on Finn's naked chest, his arm wrapped possessively around her. He was still catching his breath, as was she. Her finger traced the outline of his pec, then slowly slid down his abdomen.

He grabbed her hand firmly in his and lifted it to his lips, lightly kissing her knuckles. "Give me a chance to recover."

Laughing softly, she looked up at him. "Just exploring."

He shifted slightly onto his side so he didn't have to crook his neck to look into her eyes. "There's plenty of time, Addy," he said. "I plan to spend many hours exploring you."

It could have been a line. By all accounts, he'd had a variety of women in his bed. Then again, she was no prude. There were a dozen or so names on her own list. But this was different for her. So much different, and unless he was a really great actor, she was pretty sure it was different for him too.

"I like the sound of that," she said softly.

He leaned down to kiss her, and she wove her fingers into his hair. A quick, errant thought flitted through her head—any children they'd have would have curly hair. But she was getting ahead of herself, *way* ahead of herself, and suddenly he was pulling her closer, shifting her so she partially lay across his chest.

She lifted her head and gave him a sly smile. "I thought you needed to recover."

"I do, but if you keep kissing me like that, I might change my mind."

Her smile spread. "You say that like it's a bad thing."

"Oh, it's anything but." He lifted a hand and tucked a stray curl behind her ear, then turned serious. "Addy, I need to ask you about Alan. Has he been bothering you?"

She sucked in a breath, his question stealing some of her joy. The last thing she wanted to do while she was naked and still slick with sweat from their lovemaking was think about Alan, let alone talk about him. She would need to tell Finn something if she had to go to New York—she didn't want to lie about that—but she didn't want to let Alan taint this moment, or her relationship with Finn.

She started to pull away, but he held her close. He looked at her with entreaty in his eyes. "Adalia. You can trust me."

That should have been reassuring, but it only made her doubts resurface. While she knew logically she could likely trust him, her heart had been so battered it refused to open up all the way. At least not here. Not now. Not when she was already so vulnerable.

"I know," she said, breaking free. Sitting up, she scanned the room for her clothes. "I was thinking about staying so we could cook dinner together."

He sat up too, his eyes narrowed. It had escaped neither of them that she'd avoided answering his question. "I'd love for you to stay for dinner, but you don't have to cook. We can get something delivered. I just want to be with you."

"I like to cook," she said, getting out of bed and making her way to the closet. He had multiple dress shirts lined up and sorted by color, because of course, and she grabbed a light blue long-sleeved one and slipped her arms into the sleeves. "Don't worry, you'll be cooking too."

He studied her with hooded eyes as she buttoned the middle two buttons, leaving the top gaping down to below her cleavage.

"You're wearing my shirt." His voice sounded slightly strangled.

"Is that not okay?" she asked, giving him a coquettish look.

He got off the bed, slowly advancing toward her as though she were his prey. "It's more than okay. Do you have any idea how sexy you are right now?"

"What?" she asked, trying to sound offended. "I wasn't sexy in my I Love New York T-shirt and fanny pack?"

"Addy, you'd look sexy in a chicken suit." He wrapped an arm around her lower back and tugged her to his chest. "That wasn't a challenge, by the way."

She laughed. "Are you sure?"

"Definitely." He lowered his mouth to her neck, kissing his way down her chest to where the shirt gaped. "In fact, if you never wore anything but this shirt, I'd be a very happy and very turned-on man."

Closing her eyes, she released a contented sigh. Finn had a way of making her feel like the most beautiful woman in the world. But when she opened her eyes, she saw her painting on the wall. She'd been caught off guard when she'd walked in and seen it hanging on the light gray wall next to the window, and then Finn had kept her distracted. But now it was there, right in front of her.

He'd found a way to repair it, and seeing it now, whole again, she was taken aback by the fury in the strokes and colors. It felt like she'd painted it years ago. Had it really only been a little over a week? She vaguely remembered telling him it was his, but she'd presumed he'd throw it away. Not piece it back together. Definitely not hang it up on his wall. His bedroom wall.

"Why did you keep it?" she asked, her voice strained.

He lifted his head, standing upright, the look in his eyes telling her he not only knew what she was talking about, but was terrified to tell her. It took him a few seconds to finally answer. "Because it's beautiful, and it's part of you. I couldn't bear to throw it away."

It was the perfect answer, only he'd barely known her then. So why had he *really* kept it? She started to ask him, but then Tyrion started barking and Jezebel released a screech.

"Oh crap," she said, then bolted down the stairs.

Tyrion barked at Jezebel as she attacked one of the sofa pillows, which was now on the floor and in shreds. The cat continued to attack it with a vindictive fury, as if it were stuffed with mice, ignoring Tyrion, who was circling her like a distressed schoolteacher would a disobedient student.

Finn was seconds behind her, wearing the boxer briefs she'd stripped off him less than an hour before.

"Jezebel!" she shouted, clapping her hands at the cat, but Tyrion's barking drowned her out.

"Maybe you should take Tyrion and I'll take Jezebel," he said as he stood behind her, lowering his hands onto her upper arms.

She glanced over her shoulder at him. "And ruin that gorgeous body? You don't have any clothes on! She'd skin you alive! At least I'm partially covered."

He glanced down, looking into her eyes. "Who knows what offense that pillow caused her. No way am I risking that she takes offense to your beautiful legs. Besides, Tyrion needs *you*, not me."

The cat was still attacking the pillow, batting it across the room into the kitchen. Good. There wasn't much in there to damage.

"Let me try to settle Tyrion down first," she said. "Then we'll address Jezebel."

"Okay."

Adalia squatted next to the husky and wrapped her arms around his neck, burying her face into his fur. "Tyrion. You can stop barking. You're okay, and Jezebel's fine too."

The dog stopped barking and licked her cheek, his eyes so soulful they almost looked human.

"Good boy," she said, squeezing him tighter, then loosening her hold. She stood and caught Finn watching her with a lust-filled gaze. The back of her shirt had hiked up, she realized, giving him a view of most of her bare butt.

"Focus, Finn," she teased as she leaned to the side and kept her hand on Tyrion's head.

"You make it damn near impossible," he said, his boxer briefs not hiding his arousal. He took a step toward her.

But Jezebel's hissing redirected their attention.

The cat had shoved the remains of the pillow against the sliding glass door, and was now attacking her own reflection in the glass.

"What do you want to do about her?" Finn asked.

"My magic touch with beasts stops with Tyrion and you," she teased. "Jack's the one who's good with Jezebel."

Jezebel was launching into full-on attack mode on the glass, getting progressively more pissed that the other black cat was still fighting her.

"Do you want to call him?" Finn asked, his disappointment obvious.

She understood why he was disappointed. She couldn't greet Jack at the door dressed in Finn's shirt and nothing else, and if she got dressed again, some of the magic would be gone. "What about the sardines?"

He gave her a long look. "What's your level of tolerance for the smell of rotten fish?"

She cringed. So far her cat had torn up his cushion, there were two big tufts of white fur on the couch, plus about a thousand small strands, and now his house was going to stink like a barge. "I'm sorry. It's just that you mentioned you had them…"

Was this fate's way of trying to tell her to go home? Maybe she should. Jack had sounded off on the phone, like something else was up with him besides losing their pets.

Grinning, Finn said, "I'm willing to sacrifice my olfactory nerves if it means you're going to cook in my kitchen wearing my shirt."

And she was lost. "Open the can, Finn. We have some cooking to do. Maybe we can use the blindfold next time."

The remark brought to mind what he'd said earlier. He'd wanted to look into her eyes, and he had. When had a man ever looked at her like that while he was inside her? It meant something, and it both terrified and delighted her.

He released a groan and closed the distance between them, not stopping until their chests were pressed together, his mouth hovering over hers. "Do you have any idea what you do to me?"

She grinned. "That's a two-way street. Now someone needs to open the sardines." She took a step backward. "Not it!"

He laughed. Pillow stuffing was strewn from the living room to the kitchen, and they were about to unleash an unholy stink in his immaculate house, yet he was laughing.

"Again," Finn said, walking backward and giving her plenty of opportunity to enjoy the view of his broad shoulders and the well-sculpted chest and abs he hid under his business shirts. "It's a sacrifice I'm willing to make."

Sure enough, he opened a cabinet and pulled out a tin of sardines.

"Maybe I should sign Tyrion up for some dog training classes," she said distractedly. "If he escapes, then I can train him to come when I call him."

"Good idea," he said as he opened the can. The smell immediately permeated the room. "And maybe we can tame Jezebel. Might be a good project."

Something about the way he said it prodded her insecurities.

"You said you've fostered for Maisie before," she said carefully. "Why did you just foster?"

"Having a dog didn't seem to fit. I worked long hours when I owned Big Catch, and I did a lot of traveling."

"How long did you foster?"

"A month," he said in a tight voice. "A corgi named Kiki."

She'd had Tyrion for less than a week, and if Maisie called and said she was on her way to pick him up, she'd take him and go into hiding.

How had he given up his dog after a month?

Seeing her painting in his room had jarred loose some of her all-too-familiar insecurities, and finding out he'd had a dog for a month and then just given her away only made it worse. She could see that he didn't want to talk about Kiki, so he hadn't given her up glibly. Still, her doubts had been let out of their cage, and they were no more willing to go quietly back in than Jezebel would be.

Things had been so perfect with Finn, and she couldn't help wondering when the bottom would fall out, because it always, *always* did.

CHAPTER
Thirty-Four

Finn still had groceries from the last time he'd gone shopping with Adalia, and they managed to throw together a meal that incorporated rice, pinto beans, and a suspicious jar of mint jelly that Finn's (now-deceased) grandmother had sent him in her yearly Christmas basket five years ago. (It hadn't expired—miraculously it wouldn't for another two years.)

She hadn't put on any other clothes, and neither had he, and the whole process of cooking had been like a dance, leading up to what was sure to be an epic round two. (She had loosely tied the blindfold around her neck as a tantalizing hint of what was to come.) Jezebel and Tyrion had put the whole pillow misunderstanding behind them and were having a *Lady and the Tramp* moment with some of the shredded chicken he'd set out for them, which was sort of gross but also kind of adorable. So he wasn't sure why something felt off.

It had happened after they came downstairs, he knew that much. Had it been his question about Alan? Sure, he probably shouldn't have mentioned her ex-boyfriend while they were lying together naked, but he'd felt so close to her in that moment. He'd felt like he could finally vault over the final obstacle wedged between them. But he'd thought wrong. She still hadn't answered him. He'd tried to subtly (and not so subtly) nudge her back toward the question several times during the dinner preparations, but no dice. He'd even asked her whether she'd made up with her brother Lee. She'd said yes and promptly changed the subject.

Now, as they sat down to dinner, he thought it was probably time to adopt a more direct line of questioning. Glancing at her through the candlelight—he'd left the candleholders out after their last dinner, and sap that he'd become, he'd even bought new candles for them—he felt a strange combination of emotions. He was happy, certainly, but that happiness was tinged with the fear that it might be taken away at any moment.

Was she trying to keep him at arm's length?

"So…" he started. Then, because there was no good way of bringing up the man who'd trampled her heart and stolen her sculptures, he took the direct approach. "What's going on with Alan? He's been texting you again, hasn't he?" The look on her face made it clear that she intended to shut down this line of conversation quickly, so he said, "Please, Adalia. I want to know what's going on. I want to help you. I think I *need* to."

But it was clear he'd said the wrong thing, again, because she had an almost panicked look in her eyes now.

"There's nothing for you to worry about," she said. Then she took a big bite of the dinner, made a face, and set down her fork. "Turns out there's a reason people don't combine these particular ingredients."

He wanted to press her, but he suspected she'd react badly. That she'd lash out or maybe leave, and he didn't want that. But the mystery of what had happened with Alan weighed on him, like that Greek guy who'd had to carry that huge round rock around on his back. No, it was a globe, wasn't it? Anyway, it wasn't good. A little more of the spell from earlier lifted. The world was creeping back in, and he didn't like it—even if he was the one who'd triggered it.

Did Alan want her back? The text Finn had seen the other week certainly suggested it. He didn't think Adalia would ever consider that, but if not, what was going on?

"You know," Adalia said, her voice slightly playful again, though it felt a little forced, like she was auditioning for a part. "You owe me for sending me to that stained glass artist on Monday. She's taken it upon herself to send me daily horoscopes by text. Apparently, I'm at risk of being eaten by wolves today." She waggled her brows up and down.

"Ha," he said. "Thanks for meeting with them. Speaking of which, would you be interested in taking on a bigger role for the show? I know we were going to do this as co-chairs, but I'm going to have less time coming up than I originally thought, and I was wondering if you'd like to be *my* boss."

She had a crestfallen look, and it occurred to him that he hadn't offered her any compensation for her time. While he hadn't planned on taking a salary for himself, it wasn't rational of him to expect Adalia would continue donating her time, especially with an expanded role. He'd planned for that, but he hadn't said anything about it to her.

"I don't expect you to do it for nothing," he said hurriedly. "I was thinking we'd build in a stipend for you. If you're willing. I know you're working on the branding stuff for Buchanan, and it's totally fine if you don't want to do it or don't have time. I can find someone else to take point."

"Why aren't you going to have time? Did you decided to take that job in Charlotte after all?" she asked, her face unnaturally pale. She cinched the shirt closed, as if she no longer wanted to be revealed to him.

"No," he gushed out, horrified.

He was going about this all wrong. He hadn't even told her about his idea yet, and he'd meant to do that first, before bringing up the show. Except he was nervous, and his brain was skipping around, and it had skipped right past the point.

"You see, you inspired me. You and Sean and Mo, the guys from Charlotte Robotics, and even Gretchen from Bev Corp. I realized that I don't want to work at just one company. You told me I was a creator, and I couldn't see it at first. But you were right." He smiled a little. "You're right a lot of the time. The part I've always liked best is creating—building a company up and helping it be all it can be. So why not do that all the time? I'm going to start a consulting company, right here in Asheville, and it looks like Charlotte Robotics is going to be my first client. Well, them and Bev Corp, I guess."

But he didn't see any relief or excitement in her eyes. Her expression was guarded in a way it hadn't been since they first met.

"So you *are* working for them?"

"No, not in the way you're thinking," he rushed to say. "I'm not taking the role they offered me, but I'm going to generate a launch strategy for them. They won't be my only clients, though. I'm going to find office space here in Asheville, and hopefully I can recruit another couple of consultants to join me."

"So…all of that buildup for the show, everything you said to convince me to participate, and now you're not going to have time for it anymore. Just like that?"

He didn't miss the bite behind her tone.

"I wanted to do it for you," he blurted out, and before the words were out, he knew he'd ripped an even bigger hole into the bubble they'd been in today. So he tried to talk fast and seam it up. "No, not just for you. I think the show is going to be really great, and I've loved working with you on it—I've never had more fun in my life—but let's be honest, I don't have the expertise to push it to the finish line. You're a better fit. I think I've always known that on some level. But I still want to do this with you. I just won't have as much time to meet with the artists."

"And here I am, little old Addy, with tons of free time on her hands." She pushed back in the chair, crossing her arms over her chest, and while he was no body language expert, it seemed fairly clear as far as signs went. "I didn't know you felt *sorry* for me, Finn. I don't need people fighting my battles or inventing jobs for me. Whether or not you realize it, I can take care of myself. But the last thing I'd do is let down Blue and the other artists, so sure, I'll do it."

Silence hung between them for a moment, but only because Finn couldn't think of a single way to improve upon it. He hadn't intended for her to think any of those things. He'd wanted to let her know how much she meant to him—how much he respected her opinion and vision. Instead, she thought he was some micromanaging jerk.

And isn't there a grain of truth to that? a voice in his head argued. *What kind of nutjob sets up a charity art show so he'll have an excuse to talk to a woman?*

Except that wasn't the full story either. It was part of it, he wouldn't deny that, but he had thought of the art show because he believed in Adalia, and because she'd made him appreciate art in a way he had never experienced before. She had broadened his horizons and challenged him, and he'd wanted to pass that favor on to other people.

Finally, he found words. "I've never once felt sorry for you. You're not the kind of person I *could* feel sorry for. And no, Adalia, I don't want to fight your battles, but I would like it if you'd let me be a part of them. If I could maybe fight by your side." He paused. "I'd like to at least *know* about them."

For a moment, conflict raged in her eyes—he'd gotten through to her, whether she wanted to admit it or not—but then they hardened. "Well, we all want something, Finn, but that sure as hell doesn't mean we're going to get it."

She got up and made for the stairs, then turned back around and blew out the candles before stomping her way upstairs, her perfect butt taunting him with every step.

Jezebel stalked toward the table, leapt onto Adalia's chair in one perfect, fluid movement, and studied him with something like distaste. She was Beau Buchanan's cat, and it almost felt like Adalia's grandfather was taking him to task for screwing up, a thought that gave him the chills. He shook it off, telling himself he'd been listening to too many of Dottie's superstitious notions lately.

"I know," he said. "I said the wrong thing." Her look sharpened. "Okay, the wrong things, plural. No need to rub it in."

Except it might not matter what he said. Maybe he'd been right in the beginning, and Adalia wasn't ready for another relationship. For all he knew, she wasn't over Alan. Maybe they really were communicating. The thought made him want to crush the guy—not literally, Finn wasn't that kind of person—but he would savor revealing Alan Stansworth's sins to the world.

Finn knew how much it could hurt to be seen.

His heart ached in his chest. Should he go up after her? Talk to her?

But he'd said his piece, and ultimately, he hadn't expressed himself badly.

If she decided to think the worst of him, the way almost everyone had decided to think the worst of him, he couldn't do anything about it. He'd done everything he could to prove himself to her, and if that wasn't enough...

Jezebel hacked as if she'd eaten poison, and he saw that she'd tried some of Adalia's entree. Was it some kind of sign that the first dinner they'd cooked together had been delicious, while this one was inedible? The cat gave him a withering look of judgment, then slunk off as Adalia came back down the stairs. She had her clothes on, although she was carrying the fanny pack instead of wearing it—almost as if that bit of tongue-in-cheek fun was too much for such a weighty moment.

"You might want to get your clothes on," she said. "I asked Jack to come over to help with the menagerie. I don't want to *inconvenience* you."

Her words were barbed, but he saw it for what it was—self-defense.

He stood from the table, and from the meal he hadn't tried (not that he was keen to taste it at this point), and even though he knew she would likely turn him away, he went to her and wrapped his arms around her. There was a certain vulnerability to be in only boxer briefs while she was fully clothed. It made him a bit uncomfortable, but that was the point.

"I didn't mean to hurt you," he whispered. He wasn't sure why he said it like that. Maybe the words just felt like they should be spoken in an undertone.

The cat had slunk over to join the dog on the couch, and she and Tyrion were lying together in apparent harmony, grease-stained faces on the cushions. If Adalia saw, she'd likely worry about the furniture, but he thought it was kind of sweet. Like a lion lying down with a lamb. *Focus, Finn.*

At least Adalia hadn't pulled away.

"The last thing I would *ever* want to do is hurt you. But in case you haven't noticed, I sometimes speak a little faster than I think. Can we please talk about this? The company, Alan…all of it?"

He pulled back to look at her, and there were tears in her eyes. One of them tracked down her cheek, and he traced it with a finger.

"Oh, Addy, I didn't mean to make you cry."

"I know you didn't," she said with a trembling smile. "You're just that good at it."

"It's about the last thing I'd like to be good at," he said, cupping her cheek.

"I know, you goof. I'm kidding. I'm sorry too. It's amazing that you're doing this…the consulting thing, I mean. It's a natural fit."

Why did it sound like she thought that was a bad thing?

"Let's talk this weekend," she added. She must have seen the alarm on his face, because she bit her lip and looked down. "I need some time to think."

"Whatever you need," he said, pulling away. But her words had dug in under his skin. He knew he'd be interpreting and reinterpreting them tonight. Tomorrow. Every day and night until she agreed to see him again. "I'd better get dressed before Jack gets here."

He took a step toward the stairs, but she tugged him back by the arm and kissed him. A sweet, simple kiss that confused the hell out of him.

"It was a beautiful day, Finn," she said.

There was something sad about the way she said it, something that made him think he was maybe already turning into a memory for her. Something in her rearview mirror as she went on to do the great things he had no doubt she would accomplish.

He found himself thinking again about Lola and the cards she'd drawn for him and Adalia. She'd said someone from the past would come back into their lives, causing them heartache, and help would come from the last person they'd expected. He'd thought he would be that person for Adalia...but what if he was wrong?

And who was supposed to help *him*?

CHAPTER
Thirty-Five

Jack pulled into the driveway just as Finn disappeared from view. Adalia stepped outside and stood on the porch, quickly closing the door behind her.

"Did you bring the cat carrier?" she asked the second he got out of the car.

He gave her a weird look as he pulled out a pet carrier and shut the car door. "Yeah. And I hurried, just as you requested. Is everything okay?"

"The deal was no questions, Jack," she snapped.

Instead of getting pissed, he looked perplexed. "I take it you want me to deal with Jezebel since you seem to think I have some spell over her."

She lifted her arms out at her sides. "My arms aren't exactly prepared for a wrestling match with that cat. Now come on," she said, reaching for the door handle. "We have to hurry."

Surprisingly, he didn't press her. He just followed her in and handed her the leash she hadn't noticed he was carrying.

The truth was she didn't want to see Finn again. At least not right now. She knew she'd have to see him eventually, but it couldn't happen this weekend like she'd suggested, because even now she wanted to sweep all of her fear and anger and worry under the rug and pretend like everything was okay. And if she saw him too soon, she'd do just that. Lord knew, she'd almost relented when she pulled him back and kissed him.

Seeing him again was inevitable. She'd agreed to help with the art show, and unlike him, she was going to finish what she started.

Jezebel was sitting on the back of the sofa, but she slowly turned her head toward Jack and watched him, as enthralled as though he were a snake charmer. He had the carrier in his hand, but instead of lifting it to scoop her inside, he calmly reached for her and cuddled her to his chest.

"Wow," Adalia said. "I'm not sure whether to be impressed or terrified that she's about to slash you across the jugular."

He flinched. "Let's not press our luck. Open the door."

Adalia didn't need to be prodded to move quickly. She could hear sounds upstairs. She hooked Tyrion's leash onto his collar and opened the door, stepping out onto the porch as she heard Finn's door open.

Jack walked out past her, snuggling Jezebel to his chest while holding the carrier in his free hand. Adalia reached for the door, preparing to close it behind her, just as Finn came into view, his face hopeful when he saw she hadn't left yet.

She pulled it shut with more force than necessary. Maybe that was harsh—okay, it was—but her heart was already begging her to stay and she could feel her willpower draining away.

How was it possible to hurt this much when they'd barely begun this thing between them?

Thankfully, he didn't follow.

Adalia reached for the car's passenger door but quickly changed her mind after Jack gently released Jezebel into the car. The cat hopped onto the passenger seat and stared haughtily up at her. Then, when Adalia didn't immediately stand down, she hissed.

"I'll walk."

Jack studied her in his quiet way, as if trying to gauge what variety of craziness was going on.

"Look, you may feel like staring death in the eye and laughing while you drive home that feral cat who has free rein of your car, but I choose life." She flashed him a peace sign. "See you at home."

"Okay," he said and got inside.

She took off walking in the direction of their house, but before she could stop herself, she cast a glance at the front of the house. Sure enough, Finn was standing in the window, the look of hurt in his eyes so painful she wanted to forget everything and go in there and comfort him. Which only made her madder.

She didn't head directly home. She wasn't ready for the questions in Jack's eyes. He'd want to know what had happened.

What *had* happened?

She was sure she'd known Finn well enough to judge his character. Sure, before they'd spent all this time together, she'd believed the stories about him, although she had to admit they'd been colored by Georgie's disapproval. But the more time she'd spent with him, the easier it was to accept there were two sides to every story. That people were complex organisms who did things they thought were for the right reasons. And whether they were right or not depended on the vantage point.

That was why she'd let him explain, hoping she'd misunderstood. That she hadn't been just another project. And while he hadn't outright admitted it, he *had* admitted he'd never been all that invested in the art show. Not really. He'd done it for her.

I didn't mean to hurt you.

She believed that. He truly hadn't meant to hurt her, which in a way made it so much worse. She had thought he was as excited as she was to showcase the artists they'd chosen. She'd believed him when he'd said they were doing this as a team. But then he'd bailed. Granted, it was for the right reasons, but he'd given it up so quickly. So decisively, with absolutely no regret other than the fact it had hurt her.

How long until he moved on from her?

She couldn't fault him for starting a new business, in fact, she was excited for him. A consulting business gave him endless opportunities. He could stay in Asheville, which meant that he wasn't set on changing *everything* in his life. Maybe he was even looking for a long-term relationship. But their…entanglement hadn't started out like a real relationship, had it? Sure, they'd known each other for a while, but he'd never shown any interest in her until he'd walked in on her destroying her painting.

A painting he'd repaired and hung on his wall without telling her.

She walked several blocks past the Buchanan house, then decided to turn around and head back home. Her cell phone was dead, and the last thing she needed was for River and/or Georgie to show up at Finn's house looking for her.

Jack was on the front porch reading a book with Jezebel curled up on his lap.

"Aren't you worried about losing your manhood?" she asked as she cautiously climbed the porch steps.

"She's sweet," he said, stroking the top of her head as she purred.

"That cat knows how to purr?" she asked in disbelief.

He made a face, his gaze still on the book. "You all keep saying she's the devil, but she's not so ferocious once you get to know her."

Adalia gaped at him, sidestepping them both. "If you say so."

"Decide to take a walk?" he asked, finally looking up.

"Yeah. I thought Tyrion might need to walk off some energy."

"Tyrion, huh?" He hesitated, then asked, "Want to talk about it?"

"No," she said decisively. "Definitely not."

"Fair enough." She started for the front door, and he said, "Sorry about letting Tyrion get away. Maybe we should look into putting in an invisible fence. I can probably install it. We'll just need to train him."

She turned back to him, horrified. "You want to shock my dog?"

"It wouldn't hurt him. Plus, he's smart. He'll learn quickly." When she didn't respond, he added, "It's better than risking he'll get loose and be hit by a car or taken by someone who wants a husky."

While she knew he had a point, she was in no frame of mind to consider it. "Yeah. I'll think about it."

She went inside and plugged in her phone, restless. And then she found herself going out to the shed, pulled by some magical force as if she had no free will to refuse. Tyrion followed her and sat by a tree as she opened the doors and stared into the studio created by the people who cared about her.

Finn had been one of them. There was no denying he cared about her, but she still couldn't help thinking it was because he'd seen her at her worst—destroying her art, getting drunk at the Mexican restaurant. He'd seen her exposed and vulnerable, a state she didn't allow many people to see. Not even Alan until she'd destroyed her own work.

Why would Finn stick around someone in her situation if not because he wanted to fix her? Because there was no doubt in her mind that's what he'd been trying to do with the art show. This shed too. He'd tried to smooth out the cracks of her life as he'd done with the ripped seams of the painting.

You couldn't build a relationship on that.

She grabbed a canvas and set it on the easel, then set up the paints and the brushes before smearing a line of red on the canvas.

The rip in her heart.

Using her palette, she added blues and greens and black, painting her pain and disappointment that one more person had hurt her.

She poured her heart onto the canvas, only becoming aware she was crying when Tyrion nuzzled her leg, whining. Setting down the brush, she squatted next to him and gave him a hug.

"I'm okay." It was partially a lie, but he'd never know.

From her squat, she looked up at the painting, feeling the urge to slash it to bits so that no one would ever see it, let alone be able to repair it. Especially since it felt like she'd cut her chest open and attached her heart to the canvas. It was raw and real, and it made her feel more naked and exposed than any other painting before it.

351

She stood and touched a corner, fresh tears filling her eyes. Finn had been wrong, so, so wrong. He couldn't fix her. No one could.

No one but her.

The first step was to acknowledge that she was an artist. Art ran through her veins along with her blood. She could no more live without it than she could live without oxygen. Denying it was denying part of herself, and she'd never heal until she accepted it.

Which also meant no more destroying it. She could hide it, but to destroy it would be like slashing her own heart.

And as much as painting had purged her troubled mind, it wasn't enough. It had been a stopgap over the last few months, but it would never be enough.

Wiping her cheeks with the back of her hand, she smiled down at Tyrion. "How about we take a drive?"

She ran upstairs and put on a fresh T-shirt and a worn pair of overalls, wrapping a large headband around her head to keep her hair back. Then she ran downstairs and grabbed her phone and called Blue.

"How was your date?" Blue asked, her excited tone knifing into Adalia.

"I know I said I'd drop by tomorrow, but can I come by today instead? Like, now?"

Blue must have heard the desperation in her voice because she didn't ask any more questions. "I'm still at the studio," she said. "I'll wait for you."

"See you in a few minutes."

Adalia grabbed her charger and her purse, then headed out the front door, Tyrion's leash in her hand.

"Will you be out long?" Jack asked, looking up from his book. Jezebel was now draped over his shoulders, licking her paws.

Adalia cocked her head. "Do we have some kind of witchery in our bloodline?"

He chuckled. "She's a good cat. You all are just overreacting."

"You've seen her at her worst, Jack."

He reached up to pet the back of her head. "She just needed someone to understand her."

"I'm not sure you should say that so openly," she said, descending the steps. "Some people might think you're a hellcat too." She opened the passenger door of her car and let Tyrion in. "I have no idea when I'll be back, but I brought a charger for my phone. I'm going to see my friend Blue." A partial truth, but it was all he really needed to know.

She closed the door on her dog and started around to the driver's side.

"Addy," he called out. "You can talk to me, you know. I'm a good listener, and I know how to keep my mouth shut."

"Thanks. I might just take you up on that, but I have something I really need to do first."

She drove to Blue's studio, her heart a jumbled mixture of anticipation and grief. Blue met her at the door before she got Tyrion out of the car.

"I hope it's okay that I brought him. I've been gone all day, and I didn't want to leave him again."

"That's okay," Blue said with a soft smile. "I'd ask you about what happened, but the look in your eyes suggests I shouldn't."

Adalia headed toward her, leading Tyrion on the leash. "I'll tell you, just not now, okay?"

"I understand," she said, stepping out of the doorway and letting Adalia and Tyrion enter. "You have the look of an artist with an idea that needs to be let loose."

She nodded. "Something like that."

Blue showed her around, then gave Adalia a key to the space. "I had this made after you and Finn came by. I was hoping you'd want to work here."

"Thanks, Blue," Adalia said, taking the key and clenching it to her chest. "I'll be happy to pay rent and utilities."

"We'll talk about that later," Blue said, taking a step backward. "Right now I have to go meet this guy from a dating app I signed up for."

"Oh, you took the plunge."

"Yeah, I got to thinking about it after I had drinks with you and Maisie. It was time."

"Are you getting a drink?" Adalia asked, glancing at the clock on the brick wall that read 7:30.

Blue grimaced. "Dinner. First date."

"Amateur mistake," Adalia said, itching to start working. "Always go for a drink or coffee first."

"Yeah, I hope I don't regret it later." She left, waving as she headed out the door.

The space felt huge, cavernous. It was getting dark outside the windows, and while she preferred natural light to the industrial lights overhead, it wasn't going to stop her.

Taking Tyrion with her, she went to the back door, propping it open, then found a dumpster and climbed inside, thanking the stars above that it was a trash receptacle for artists who produced little actual waste garbage, and had thrown out assorted items she could use. Empty paint cans, a pallet, some broken pieces of pottery, along with multiple other pieces of junk. It took several trips to drag inside everything that called to her.

Then she loaded Tyrion up in her car and drove to Buchanan Brewery. She snuck in through a back door, and luck was on her side for once, because she didn't see anyone. She raided discarded bottles and boxes, along with a few other items left over from a batch of beer River must have made that morning.

Her stomach rumbled, so she detoured to a drive-through and picked up a sandwich for herself and a burger for Tyrion, and took everything back to the studio.

After she brought her latest haul inside and fed Tyrion and provided him with a clean bowl of water, she stared at the pile of stuff she'd pulled together, realizing why her preferred medium was to work with discarded items. Every person important to her had left her: Georgie when she went to college, then Lee. Her mother, through no fault of her own. Boyfriends and friends. She had never been the person to leave someone behind. She was always the person left. She could fast-forward the inevitable with Finn and take control of her own life.

She could leave first.

She felt a freedom she'd never experienced before, even if her heart wept at the thought. She loved him, of that there was no doubt, but sometimes love wasn't enough. Sometimes it was flawed.

Maybe Adalia was meant to live her life alone, and she needed to learn to be okay with that. Because in the end, there was one love that meant more than the others—self-love.

Maybe that had been her problem all along.

Grabbing the pallet, she dragged it into the middle of the room, then seized one of the metal poles while Tyrion watched with a puzzled look.

"Better settle in, boy," she said, picking up a piece of wire she'd found in the dumpster. She didn't have all the tools she needed, but she could get started. "We're going to be a while."

CHAPTER
Thirty-Six

Finn couldn't stop thinking of the look on Adalia's face as she shut the door—literally—between them. It had looked like her heart was broken. But why? He'd bumbled his explanation of the consulting company, but surely that wasn't what had pushed her away. Or at least it wasn't the only thing that had.

Which made him think it had to be wrapped up in the Alan thing. Something he didn't even know about and, it seemed, wouldn't.

Finn had promised himself he wouldn't text her until the end of the weekend. That he wouldn't be that guy who refused to give her an inch of space when she'd asked so clearly. In the meantime, he poured everything he had into work. Because any time he had a spare moment, he thought of her. Or the fact that he was still finding stray Tyrion hairs in the house, and each time he did, it felt like his heart had lodged in his throat.

Actually that happened a lot—every time he saw her painting, heard about the Biltmore on the radio, ate anything in his kitchen, saw those candlesticks...the list went on. It would have been easier to put away the things that reminded him of her, but he didn't want that. It would have been like burying his heart.

Other people in his life texted—River, to confirm he had the go-ahead for the Big Catch beer festival and ask why Finn hadn't been around; Dottie, to say she'd had an alarming dream about him and would like him to come for tea; Maisie, to say she *knew* something had happened, and he'd better text or face the consequences; his father, to say that this wasn't quite what he'd had in mind when he'd suggested Finn get together with the Charlotte Robotics folks. But he didn't answer any of them. He couldn't. In a weird way, it felt like if he answered them, it would be real. He would be acknowledging Adalia wasn't coming back.

By Sunday night, he'd stopped being able to convince himself any news would be good. And that was when she finally texted.

Finn, I know it's shitty not to talk about this in person, but I think we need to take a big step back. You were right in the beginning. I'm not ready for a relationship right now. There's a lot I need to take care of before I'll be ready for that. Maybe it would be best if we communicated through Dottie for art-show related matters for now.

And there it was. His heart, which hadn't been doing so great, seemed to burst into pieces. The worst part was that he couldn't argue with her, not really. He'd thought all along that he should give her some space, and fool that he was, he hadn't stuck to it. But he did allow himself to speak his mind, to say: *I could support you through it. You don't need to be alone to work on yourself.*

Those three awful dots appeared, then reappeared, then disappeared, like a magic trick designed to mess with him.

But she didn't say anything else. And he didn't say anything else. For once, he did the smart thing and shut off the phone. And sat there with these feelings—these awful, heart-wrenching feelings.

Had he ever made a woman feel this way? Most likely, and the knowledge didn't sit easily. Maybe he deserved to feel this broken. Maybe he'd casually and unwittingly caused more pain than he realized.

That night, he found himself watching *Pride and Prejudice* by himself, something that both wrecked him and made him feel closer to her.

The next morning he texted Dottie to say if the invitation were still open, he would very much like to come over for tea, and she immediately responded to say the invitation was always open, and anyway, she'd been expecting he would come today.

Of course you were, he responded, smiling a little for the first time since Wednesday.

When he arrived that afternoon, there was no room to park in the drive, because River's car was there, with Maisie's Jeep next to it. Were they having a party? He wasn't so sure he wanted to see them yet—especially River—but before he could seriously contemplate turning around, Dottie came out the door.

"Dear, don't even think of it," she called out.

And he couldn't exactly leave with her looking at him like that.

He got out and met her on the stoop, and she wrapped her arms around him and held him close. Finn hadn't grown up in a family of huggers, but *he* was a hugger, and he melted into her embrace.

"Go on inside," Dottie said fiercely. "I've called an emergency meeting of the…what is it you call yourselves? The Bro Club."

"You didn't need to do that," Finn said. But it struck him that she'd asked River and Maisie to come, and they had. In the middle of the day. On a Monday. He had a flexible schedule, but this would have taken some doing for them. That meant something to him.

"Oh, but I did," she said. "There's no emergency like an emergency of the heart."

It was the kind of thing she said that would usually have River and Finn exchanging fond but beleaguered looks, but it felt weightier today. Truer.

His gaze shot behind the house, to the shed where he'd seen Adalia that day, and he nodded.

Dottie ushered him inside, pushing a piece of clear quartz into his hand.

It had been a while since she'd foisted a crystal on him.

"What's this one for?" he asked.

"Healing," she said.

He stuck it in his pocket. Because he wasn't going to lie and say he didn't need that.

There was a rumble of conversation in the kitchen, and when they stepped in, Maisie and River got to their feet.

They didn't look so antagonistic now, so maybe something had been settled between them, or maybe Maisie had gotten used to pretending again.

"I told you there'd be consequences," Maisie said, giving him a fake punch on the arm. "You just didn't realize you were going to be ambushed with a teapot and a spread of finger food."

Indeed, Dottie had pulled out all the stops. It looked like the kind of tea that would be served in one of those Regency movies, which made him feel a little pang. Adalia would have gotten a real kick out of it, but she would never have shown up, knowing he was present.

River patted him on the back. "Take a seat. Tell us what happened."

"You're not pissed at me?" he asked in wonder. He'd figured he would be. That he'd be mad that Finn had managed to bungle things so badly with his girlfriend's sister, but there was no judgment on River's face.

"You look like someone just drowned your puppy," River said.

"Hey," Maisie griped. "Not cool. Use a less disturbing analogy next time."

They sat again, across from each other, and Dottie took the chair next to Maisie. He sat down next to River, looking down at the cup of tea in front of him. The leaves in the last one had shown Dottie that he was destined to fall in love with Adalia, or so she'd implied. What would this cup tell her?

"Well?" Dottie prodded gently. "You're not usually at a loss for words. Tell us. We're here to listen."

"And to help," River said. "You're not the only one who looks—"

Maisie shot him a warning look, and River finished with "—like someone peed in your cornflakes."

"You just said that to bother me," she muttered, and River tilted his head and smiled. Finn was caught up on the implication that Adalia was feeling this way too. That maybe he hadn't imagined the despair on her face as she walked out his door.

"Children," Dottie said severely. "Focus. And take some petit fours. They aren't going to eat themselves."

Because there was no denying Dottie, they all took some food from the spread. Finn had lost his appetite, but there was something about Dottie's food. It was more healing, he would guess, than the crystal that was now lodged in his pocket.

"Now, Finn, we'd like to know everything."

So he told them about last Wednesday, skipping over the sex, although Dottie gave him a knowing look when he said they'd "hung out" at his house for several hours, and ending with a detailed description of the argument they'd had, followed by her hasty retreat and the text he'd received last night.

"She didn't tell you anything about Alan?" River asked.

"No," he said, feeling that strange sinking sensation in his gut again. "Only the initial story, but Georgie made it sound like something else was going on. That he's been bothering her. I…I have to wonder if she still has feelings for him. The text that he sent her a couple of weeks ago was an attempt to wheedle his way back into her good graces."

River snorted. "Oh, she has feelings for him all right. She hates his guts, and with good cause."

Something loosened in Finn at that. At least she wasn't thinking about forgiving the man for what he'd done. At least she hadn't left him because she was in love with someone else.

"So," Maisie said, her tone blunt. "Maybe you can enlighten us about what's happening? You clearly know, and Finn needs to know too. Because I know people, and Adalia is *not* acting in her best interest here. She's miserable over this. You're not doing her, or her sister, any favors by keeping quiet."

River sat with that for a moment, thinking, and then nodded. And Finn felt such a surge of relief that he popped a red petit four in his mouth. Then swore because it was the spiciest sweet he'd ever consumed. He gulped hot tea, revealing the first leaves at the bottom.

"Oh, you got one of the negative-energy-flushing ones," Dottie said encouragingly. "That'll help you."

He sure hoped so, because it felt like the roof of his mouth had been burned off between the "sweet" and the hot tea. Maisie glanced at her plate, scrunched her nose, and moved one of the red cakes back onto the serving platter.

"Alan stopped trying to charm her," River said. "He started sending threatening texts."

A surge of fury shot through Finn, but River lifted a hand as if to say he wasn't done. "He actually called her brother Lee, threatening to sue the family company if Lee didn't pay him two hundred thousand dollars. But Lee knew better than to pay up. He called the gallery, and it turns out Alan's trying to get them to pay restitution for his ruined pieces. We're guessing Alan is in debt and he saw Adalia as his payday. He had some BS sob story for why she destroyed the pieces, but the gallery director knew things weren't adding up. Adalia and Georgie are flying up to New York to meet with her on Thursday afternoon. I think their brother Lee is joining them."

Adalia hadn't told him any of that, which felt like a sucker punch. Had he gotten it all wrong? Did she not care about him after all? Those feelings were twined with anger—fury—toward Alan, the man who had hurt her. He had abused his power, his position, to seduce a student and then steal her art…what kind of person would do that?

The kind of person who'd done it before. How many other people had Alan Stansworth wronged? How many other artists had he siphoned talent from, like some sort of energy vampire?

They were all looking at him, waiting for a response, so he collected himself enough to give them one.

"I didn't know any of that," he said in a strangled voice.

"A woman's nothing without some fire in her belly," said Dottie, reminding him that he was still very much feeling that petit four somewhere in his esophagus. "She has her pride. You caught her at a very personal moment in my art studio— *two* if you count the time she told you about Alan at the restaurant. She wants to be seen as a worthy person in her own right, not a collection of problems."

The way she said it made him wonder if she'd spoken to Adalia, if maybe those were Adalia's own words she was speaking to him.

She nodded in a way that told him he was onto something.

"But I've never seen her that way," he said honestly. "I only want to help her because I care about her. Because she matters to me."

"I know that, dear, and I truly believe she will come to that realization too at some point. It's no mistake that Lola pulled the same draw of cards, in the same order, for both of you. You and Adalia belong together. Cosmically." She paused and took a sip of her tea. "You had good reason for passing some of the management of the art show on to her, but it seems to have ignited some worry that perhaps you aren't the type to stick around."

"But that's business—that's not a person," Finn sputtered. "There's a big difference."

River leveled him a wry look. "Doesn't always feel like business."

Which meant he'd made a similar mistake. Again. And didn't that burn. Almost as badly as the red petit four. He popped a green one into his mouth.

Mint. It reminded him of the atrocity he and Adalia had made for dinner that last night. He'd thrown the jar of mint jelly into the trash, only to fish it out, empty it—gagging at the smell—and recycle it out of guilt.

"I don't know what to do here," he admitted, glancing around at each of them.

"Give her some space," Maisie said. "I think she'll come around eventually."

Dottie tilted her head. "Yes, I agree. But I also think she might require a sign that you haven't given up. That she matters to you regardless of whether you're together. That she matters to you as a person."

"Of course she does," Finn said. He shot a glance at River. "I'm in love with her."

His friend nodded, and Maisie said, "Yeah, we know."

"And you must find a way to show her," Dottie said.

"Like Darcy!" he said in a gush.

"Say what?" Maisie asked.

"Like Mr. Darcy in *Pride and Prejudice*. He and Elizabeth Bennet weren't together, but he made a grand gesture by helping her family deal with a scandal."

"Finn, my bro, you need to get out more," Maisie said. But her smile suggested she was totally aware of the plot of *Pride and Prejudice* and that she maybe, sort of, approved of his line of thinking.

"Do you know what you're going to do?" River asked. "We're here to help if you need us."

"Are you going to tell Georgie?" Maisie asked pointedly.

River winced. "Not unless there's something I need to tell."

"I have an idea," Finn said. He took another sip of tea, somewhat surprised to discover he'd reached the bottom of the cup.

"Oh good, let me take that," Dottie said, and she did.

A smile curved her lips as she studied the bottom, which looked like nothing but a mess of soggy leaves to Finn's eyes. "Yes, I think everything will work out just fine."

He sure hoped so. Because he couldn't bear to lose Adalia for good.

CHAPTER

Thirty-Seven

Adalia had comfortably lived in New York City for over a decade, but now that she was back, she was anxious. It wasn't just the situation that had brought her there, it was the realization that it no longer felt like home.

Ultimately, the gallery director had given them the choice of a remote meeting or a face-to-face, and Lee had come down hard on them to make the trip. So they had. And now Adalia couldn't stop tossing and turning in the hotel room she shared with Georgie. Based on the occasional sighs she overheard, her sister wasn't having an easier time of it.

Finally, Georgie cleared her throat and said, "Addy, are you awake?" in a stage whisper.

Adalia threw a pillow at her. "Does that count as a yes?"

She expected her sister to roll over or maybe ask if she wanted to turn on the TV, but instead she said, "Addy, I think I may have made a huge mistake."

"For the tenth time," she said, her tone soft even though her words were not, "I think we handled this as well as we could in the beginning. I feel so much more capable of handling it now."

Alan was still sending her texts, but his threats felt hollow now that Lee was in direct contact with the gallery. Maybe he'd heard from the gallery that his account had been disputed, because in his last few messages he'd gone back to calling her baby and begging her to at least talk to him, which she'd also ignored.

"No," Georgie said. "I mean by discouraging you with Finn."

Adalia's heart stuttered. The last thing she could handle right now, the night before her meeting with the gallery director, was talking about Finn. She opened her mouth to say so, but the words wouldn't come out.

"I don't know what happened between you two," Georgie continued, "but I was wrong, Addy. He's good for you. You seemed so happy with him. Happier than I've ever seen you. And River says you're good for him too." She stared at her across the small distance between their beds, her eyes pleading. "Can you tell me what happened so I can help you work through it?"

Adalia shook her head. "I think I have to do this on my own."

"Sometimes it's okay to let people help," Georgie said softly. "It doesn't mean you're weak. It only means you're blessed to have people care about you."

Adalia changed the topic after that, asking if Georgie was interested in watching *Golden Girls* reruns, and they both fell asleep listening to the theme song. She dreamed about Finn.

They met Lee for breakfast the next morning, sans Victoria, thank goodness. "Just stick to the facts like we practiced," he said, his expression grave. They'd already ordered food, although Adalia wasn't so sure she could eat.

"And if they don't ask something, don't volunteer the information."

Adalia nodded, fingering the short strand of pearls around her neck. Georgie had insisted she wear it along with the dark gray sheath dress she'd borrowed.

Georgie, who sat next to her in an equally "serious" navy blue dress, nodded. "Agreed. Just stick to the facts."

Adalia frowned. "You both look like I'm about to march off to my execution, and I feel like I'm already dressed for the funeral." She tugged lightly on the pearls. "Are you sure these are necessary?"

"They make you look more mature," Lee said, then quickly added, "Not that I'm suggesting you're not. But you're trying to make an impression here. We have to make sure it's a good one."

"You thought I'd show up in my overalls and headband?" She was teasing, sort of, but that was her outfit of choice in Asheville now, since she spent most of her time working in Blue's studio…well, now partially her studio too, since she'd pinned Blue down on paying her fair share for the space.

Now that she'd cut back at the brewery and was only working the part-time hours the position required, she was constantly at the studio with Tyrion, working on her sculptures. Or digging through dumpsters or taking Bessie to the junkyard or flea markets. Of course, she had to work around Blue's yoga classes. She covered her work with sheets before visitors came to the studio, and Blue, genius that she was, had apparently incorporated them into her classes, telling her students they represented the unseen baggage they were carrying.

Her art had helped fill the Finn-shaped void in her heart. Somewhat. But she still missed him like crazy. She'd had a week to figure out there was no way Finn had only spent time with her because he was on some one-man mission to fix her. He'd truly enjoyed her company—both in and out of his bed. Altruism didn't spark the heat she'd felt between them. Nor did it make two people laugh so hard they doubled over with it.

She'd tried not to show Georgie how much her words last night had affected her, but they'd dug in deep.

Sending him that text last weekend had been the coward's way out. But while the act of texting such a thing rather than communicating it in person was wrong, she stood by the message. She needed time to sort herself out. She'd come to Asheville broken, and Finn deserved someone who was whole.

The sad part was she'd never believed in soul mates—in two people who belonged together, cosmically speaking—but now that she'd lost Finn, she wondered if she'd been wrong. Maybe it didn't matter. She couldn't help thinking she would have lost him eventually anyway.

Georgie quickly veered the topic away from the meeting, and they had an agreeable meal. Maybe Adalia's siblings were just trying to keep her calm, but she hoped the laid-back vibe had something to do with the phone call Georgie and Lee had last week, which supposedly had nothing to do with Adalia's legal issues.

Soon it was time to go, and they walked the two blocks to the gallery.

A younger woman who looked slightly familiar met them at the door and led them to the director's office. On the way,

Adalia searched for any lingering evidence of her attack, relieved when she saw no splashes of red paint.

"Adalia," the older woman said as she got to her feet and walked around her impressively clean desk for such a small space. "I'm Henrietta Higgins, the director of the gallery. Thank you for agreeing to this meeting. We're very interested to hear your version of events." While she wore a severe business suit and her hair was pulled back into a bun, she had friendly eyes.

"That's why we're all here," Lee said in his best stick-up-his-butt voice. There was a soft edge to it, though, like he wanted to sound both professional and approachable. Lee could act when he needed to. It was how he managed to spend so much time around their father without pissing him off.

"Please, have a seat." Henrietta gestured to three chairs that had been crammed into the narrow space in front of her desk.

The siblings all took a seat, with Adalia in the middle, and the woman who'd escorted them sat on a stool on the other side of Henrietta's desk.

"As I'm sure your brother has told you," Henrietta continued as she got settled behind the desk, "we're only interested in learning the truth. We'd already decided not to press charges."

Because Alan had made up a story about her being a sad-sack psychopath.

Criminal charges weren't the only danger, Lee had warned her. They could file a civil suit if they thought there was just cause.

"That's why we insisted on no attorneys being present," Henrietta continued. "To make this all less antagonizing."

The other woman remained silent.

"I understand," Adalia said, clasping her hands in her lap. "I'm eager to tell you my side of the story as well."

"Good," Henrietta said, her smile widening. "How about you start with what prompted you to come to the gallery the night you were arrested."

A bit of fire rose up in Adalia's chest. "Is that your polite way of asking why I came into your gallery and threw paint on the sculptures?"

Georgie gasped and Lee stiffened.

Sorry, sibs. Addy's tired of playing the sad sack role.

Henrietta's smile spread. "That's another way to put it, yes."

"Let me give it to you straight, Henrietta," Adalia continued. "Alan Stansworth is a thief. He instigated a relationship with me after he saw my work at a show about a year ago, taking advantage of his previous position as my instructor to exert authority over me. Then he stole my work by gaslighting me into believing he was putting several of my pieces in storage. I only figured out what he was up to when I showed up at your gallery and saw he'd attached his name to *my* work."

"So you resorted to destroying them?" Henrietta asked, her smile gone. "You expect us to believe that you would destroy over one hundred thousand dollars' worth of your own work to spite him? Why not just bring the issue to our attention so the situation could be resolved in a more civilized manner?"

That stung, because Henrietta was right. In hindsight, there were a half dozen better ways she could have reacted.

"First of all," Adalia said, "I had no idea my work was worth anything. Alan had convinced me it was mediocre at best but that I should 'keep trying.'" She used air quotes for the last two words. "Second, he'd been playing mind games with me for several months, building me up only to tear me down." She narrowed her eyes. "Like any good abuser would do."

Surprise filled the director's eyes.

"Yeah," Adalia said, her head held high. "At the risk of sounding like a hysterical female, I just accused the great Alan Stansworth of emotionally abusing me." She steeled her back. "Are you an artist, Henrietta?"

The director gave Adalia a weak smile. "While I love creating art, I don't have the talent to be *really* good." She held her hands out. "So I run a gallery. This way I can be surrounded by what I love. Even if I can't create it."

Was she suggesting she didn't believe Adalia had created the pieces because she'd destroyed them?

"Has someone ever claimed something of yours as their own?" Adalia asked. "Something that you poured your heart and soul into?"

Henrietta was quiet for a moment, then said, "No."

"Suppose you had a piece you were exceptionally proud of and someone else claimed it. How would you react?"

She took a breath. "I'd be upset, of course, but I wouldn't destroy it. I would rather it continue to exist apart from me than take it from the world."

This wasn't going at all like Lee had suggested it would. Then again, Lee and Georgie had expected Adalia to play the meek, submissive role they'd written for her. They hadn't expected her to hit the ground running.

"Fair enough," Adalia said, "but tell me, did you have a good childhood? Has life been good to you?"

"Adalia!" Georgie whisper-shouted.

"That hardly seems relevant," Henrietta said, clearly offended.

373

"Where does art come from?" Adalia asked.

"The artist, of course," Henrietta said.

"Of course," Adalia conceded, "but we both know it goes much deeper than that. Think of the great artists who have contributed breathtaking work to the world. Vincent van Gogh. Henri de Toulouse-Lautrec. Edvard Munch. Hell, even Caravaggio. They experienced great tragedy and emotional upheaval in their lives. And it showed in their work, because they put their *everything* into their pieces. Their art was their life. Their reason for living. For breathing. Their names have become synonymous with it."

"Several of those artists were mentally ill," Henrietta said in a dry tone. "Are you suggesting you have such an excuse?"

"Now hold on!" Lee exploded, scooting forward in his seat. "That question is out of line."

"She's the one who brought it up," Henrietta said.

"That's a fair question," Adalia said, holding up a hand. "And no, to the best of my knowledge, I'm not mentally ill, although I suspect I need a few years' worth of therapy. But that's my point. I have a deep emotional well to draw from, so when I put my soul into my work, it carries a piece of me. It's like little pieces of me are scattered throughout the world. And as long as I know they're out there, with my name on them, I'm good with that. But then Alan took parts of my soul and tried to claim them as his own. He'd already beaten me down emotionally and stolen my sense of self-worth. I couldn't let him take my work from me too."

She took a breath. "Was destroying them the logical thing to do? We all know the answer to that. Should I have tried to set the record straight instead? We all know the answer to that too. But that deep emotional well I mentioned is always there. It's not a spigot I can turn on and off whenever I create.

And when I saw what he'd done…I had to stop him. I had to reclaim myself."

"By destroying them?" Henrietta asked dryly.

"In my mind, they were already destroyed before I ever threw paint on them. Even if I'd followed the proper channels and managed to do the impossible and prove they were mine—because the photos Lee possesses were taken in Alan's studio, and we all know it would have come down to his word against mine—I still would have destroyed them."

Henrietta was stone-faced, but Georgie's eyes were glassy and Lee's jaw looked hard enough to crack granite.

The other woman, who had yet to utter a word, swiped at her eyes. "I believe her. I saw her that night. She was clearly upset."

That's when Adalia placed her. She'd been at the gallery that night. She was the one who'd called the police.

"She could merely be a woman scorned," Henrietta said.

"No," the other woman said softly. "She was reclaiming pieces of herself. Like Horcruxes."

"Except I didn't murder anyone," Adalia said in a light tone, only to be met with looks of horror from her siblings and weak smiles from the two women.

They were all silent for several seconds before Henrietta asked, "Why haven't you sued Alan Stansworth for stealing your property or tried to file charges?"

"Because I would have had to relive it all over again," Adalia said. "And frankly, I was not in a good emotional place for months after that."

"But you're better now?" Henrietta asked in a softer tone.

Adalia gave her a small smile. "I'm getting there."

Still, she had to wonder if she'd taken the chicken's way out by not pursuing a legal route. All she'd wanted to do was hide away and lick her wounds, but now she realized that she'd let him get away with it. Could she find the gumption to go through with the torture a legal case would ultimately bring her? Was it too late? The thought of fighting him should have felt empowering, but the prospect seemed exhausting.

Henrietta shifted in her seat, looking away for a moment, and when she met Adalia's gaze again, her eyes were friendlier. "I suppose I can understand why you did what you did, although I truly wish you hadn't destroyed them. The first time I saw them, they took my breath away. I feel like the world is a little bit dimmer without them in it."

Adalia's mouth parted in surprise.

"That being said," Henrietta continued, "I would love to discuss the possibility of showing a new collection." Then she added with a grimace, "Under your name, of course."

Adalia blinked. "I'd be open to a discussion."

"I have an available spot in February," Henrietta said. "I can hold it for you for a few weeks if you're not ready to give me a definitive answer."

The Brewfest competition was in March. Adalia didn't feel right about committing to something so big that close to the competition that sealed the brewery's fate. But when she turned to glance at Georgie, she found her beaming with pride.

"She'll have an answer for you soon," Georgie said. "She's working in Asheville now, so shipping will be a consideration."

"I'll see what we can do to help," Henrietta said with a small nod.

"Thank you for the offer," Lee said, "but there has been some interest from another gallery, so she'll need to take that into consideration as well."

Henrietta looked a little stricken. "I'm more than willing to negotiate, so feel free to let me know your terms before you make a final decision."

"I definitely will," Adalia said, struggling to keep a straight face. Lee had lied through his teeth, but he'd done it so well that Henrietta was none the wiser.

Lee got to his feet. "If there's nothing else, we'll let you get back to your day."

He led his sisters out of the office and out to the sidewalk. They walked a block without saying a word until he ducked into a coffee shop.

"You didn't do what we discussed, Addy," he said, his tone that of a lecturing teacher.

"When do I ever do as I'm told?"

"Do you realize it could have ended up backfiring?" he said, then took a breath. "But I confess, it worked to your advantage."

"And you got to use those negotiating skills Dad paid so handsomely for," she teased, but the momentary flash of pain in his eyes made her sorry she'd gone there. "I'm teasing, Lee. Thank you. For everything." She turned to her sister. "You too, Georgie. I couldn't have done this without either of you."

"We love you, Addy," Georgie said. "We wanted to help."

"Speaking of which," Lee said. The words seemed to spill out of him. "Are you interested in putting together an exhibit for Henrietta's gallery? Or having an exhibit at all? There's no shame in waiting a while if you need to. Or not doing it at all. Whatever you want, Addy. You don't need to prove anything.

We believe in your work whether you ever sell another piece again. But if you are interested, I can help negotiate the terms."

His verbal vomit reminded her of Finn, and the pain of losing him washed over her again.

"Thanks, Lee," she said, her voice tight. "That means more than you could possibly know."

"I'd like to see what you're working on," he said, "if you're willing to show me. Georgie tells me you're keeping it hidden from the world."

So they *had* talked about her, not that she could really blame them. It wasn't a huge surprise, and considering that Georgie and Lee rarely spoke at all, this was a good thing. She wanted her siblings to be close again. Even if they *were* discussing her.

"I'm not letting anyone see them yet," she said, "but I'm getting closer. And I promise to let you be one of the first." She'd even kept them hidden from Blue.

"Are you planning to come visit?" Georgie asked in a hopeful tone.

Lee's face went blank, although she thought she caught a glimmer of disappointment. "No. I'm much too busy here, and Victoria never wants to go to Asheville again."

"Come without her," Georgie said.

"Yes," Adalia added a little too quickly. "Please leave her at home."

He hesitated. "We'll see." He glanced at his phone. "I've got to get back to the office, but rest assured, Dad hasn't caught wind of any of this. Your secret is safe."

Adalia threw her arms around him, pulling him into a tight hug. "I love you, Lee. Thank you."

His Adam's apple bobbed. "Love you too. Now stay out of trouble."

She knew he was teasing by the gleam in his eye. "I'll try," she said with a laugh. "No promises."

Georgie gave him an awkward hug goodbye, and he hailed a cab and left. The sisters were silent for a moment. Then Georgie said, "We have a few hours to kill before we need to catch our flight. Do you want to go shopping or visit a museum?"

While normally she'd love to do either of those things, her stomach twisted.

"Can I take a rain check? There's something I need to do first."

An hour later, Adalia was sitting at a table at the same coffee shop, alone now—Georgie had left to go shopping. Already buzzed from her fourth cup of coffee for the day, Adalia waited anxiously, clutching cup number five.

The atmosphere in the room seemed to change the minute he walked through the door with an air of self-importance that she'd once mistaken as confidence. With thick salt-and-pepper hair and intense eyes, he was still handsome in a striking way, only it struck her as cold now. His gaze landed on her, scrutinizing her as he made his approach.

"Adalia," he said as he reached her table. "You always had a way of making things difficult. Couldn't you have picked a place closer to the art school?"

"I flew in from North Carolina," she said in a dry tone. "The least you could do was take the subway to meet me."

His nose wrinkled. "Subway?"

She'd purposely made the subway remark, knowing full well he refused to ride in anything so plebeian and full of germs.

He took the seat opposite her and gave her a once-over, his eyes filling with lust. Maybe he liked the businesswoman look she had going on. He'd always been after her to adopt a more "mature" style. "I've missed you, Adalia, and I've decided to be the bigger person and forgive you."

Her eyes flew wide.

"You're willing to forgive me?" she asked, keeping her voice neutral, not an easy task.

"I'm willing to put aside this misunderstanding and move forward," he continued. "Of course, there would have to be changes."

"Changes?" she asked, beyond curious what this delusional fool had in mind.

"Yes. We'd need to rebuild trust, of course, so there would be some harsh restrictions."

"Of course," she said in a reasonable tone. "First, you wouldn't be allowed anywhere near my work."

He blinked, confusion covering his face. "What? No." He pushed out a sigh. "Adalia, I can see there has been a huge misunderstanding about the gallery incident, so I propose that we use both of our names next time so there will be no hurt feelings."

"I'm sorry?" she said, fighting the urge to blast him. "You think I'm going to let you claim ownership of more of my work? There was no misunderstanding."

"Adalia," he said, his tone condescending. "We both know you couldn't have created those pieces without me. Me putting my name on them was no different than Michelangelo putting his name on work his apprentices had done."

"Only, Michelangelo actually did work on those pieces," she said, shaking her head as she reached for her purse. "Thank you for that. I needed to hear how you'd justified what you did, and now that I know, I look forward to never hearing from you again. We're done."

Panic filled his eyes. "You can't go." When she got up and started to walk toward the door, he grabbed her wrist and held her in place. "You're nothing without me, Adalia. Just a two-bit hack who didn't even have the talent to finish art school. Don't you even *think* of walking out on me."

He wasn't saying anything new, but this time she saw his words for what they were—a desperate attempt to control and use her. To bleed the talent from her so his own well wouldn't run dry.

"You know," she said evenly, "I almost feel sorry for you. You must really be scraping the bottom of the barrel to be threatening an art school dropout and a hack to create your art. Worried the world will figure out that I have more talent in my pinky fingernail than you have in your entire body? You know what they say—those who can, do, and those who can't, teach."

Anger flashed in Alan's eyes, and his hand tightened around her wrist, painfully twisting the skin. "You're just jealous of my talent and deluded enough to think you can be something without me. You'll be sorry, Adalia."

"I already am sorry, Alan, but I'm rectifying that now." She wrenched her arm free and took a few steps before turning back to face him. "Oh, and if you ever contact me again, I'll slap you with a restraining order so fast it will make your head spin."

She left him sputtering about her ingratitude while several customers clapped and cheered loudly. At the door, she turned back and bowed. Then she walked out.

CHAPTER
Thirty-Eight

Turned out it was hard work, ruining a man, even if he was the sort who'd left a long trail of destruction in his wake.

Sean had been all too willing to put Finn in touch with his sister, Sorcha.

Alan had put the moves on her *while she was a student*, plus she knew someone who claimed Alan had stolen his idea for a sculpture.

He'd followed those threads, with help from River and Maisie…and found more and more. Some of the people they'd spoken to had attempted to turn Alan in, only they'd encountered resistance from the school. Which made this an even bigger story.

In the meantime, Finn had gotten in touch with a reporter for *The New York Times*, a favor he had somewhat shamefacedly called in with the *Fortune* reporter who'd written about him. He hadn't given any names, but he'd explained that he knew of a prominent art professor in New York who had a long history of seducing students and stealing from them, and the reporter was on the hook. She wanted what he had.

The question was whether he should give it to her.

"No," Maisie said. It was their second Tuesday meeting since the revival of the Bro Club in Dottie's kitchen. This time they'd returned to the Taco Tuesday restaurant. Being there reminded him almost viscerally of Adalia, but then again, most things did. Besides, it actually *was* Taco Tuesday, and it felt good to be there with his friends, almost like old times.

"You can't just out him on your own. That's like mansplaining to the tenth degree. You've put together a pretty slick portfolio on the dude. Enough for that reporter to take it and run with it. I say you give it to Adalia and let *her* make the call. Show her you care about what she thinks."

He glanced at River, who shrugged. "My impression is that Adalia *does* want Alan to suffer consequences. Things went really well with the gallery, but they're not going to take any action against Alan. It would be the opposite of good publicity to admit they almost exhibited stolen pieces. Which is fine since they believe Addy, but I don't know…it's still not right. Apparently Adalia met up with Alan when she was in New York—"

Finn bristled, and River held up a hand. "Just for closure. He was totally unremorseful. She'd like to stick it to him, but she doesn't want to relive everything, or to get Buchanan Luxury rolled up in the mess. She and Georgie hate dealing with their father more than they have to. You've come up with a way to ensure Alan pays without mentioning her name. I think she'll go for it."

"Sure," Maisie said hotly. "But it needs to be her choice."

"You're right," Finn said. "I mean, Mr. Darcy just went for it, but then again, it was the nineteenth century. It wasn't exactly a banner time for women's rights."

"Man, you are taking this *Pride and Prejudice* thing *way* too far," Maisie said.

She had no idea. He'd actually read the book, something Adalia's mother had read to her when she was a kid, but he wasn't about to admit to that.

River just shook his head a little, a smile playing on his lips. "I never thought I'd see you like this over a woman. I have to say, it's kind of refreshing."

"You're only saying that because you've gone all cuckoo for Cocoa Puffs too," Maisie said. "Both of you have officially lost it." She said it almost fondly, though, without any noticeable strain of bitterness.

"It'll happen to you too," River said. Finn wanted to swat him, although he doubted Maisie would thank him for it.

Something flashed in her eyes, but she just said, "No, thanks. I've made a conscious decision to stay single. Two saps are enough for this group. Especially when this one"— she pointed at Finn—"is stuck in overdrive mode."

"Well, if you think I've already gone too far, wait until you hear my other idea," he said.

So he told them. Maisie thought he was nuts. River piled on and said he had more peanuts than a Snickers bar, to which Finn replied that he'd never thought they had quite enough. This led to a semiserious discussion about ranking candy bars, broken up when the server arrived with another round of margaritas. It was the same woman who'd waited on Finn during his last two visits, and she'd been eyeing him with trepidation, as if she feared he'd start dancing on the table, wearing the chip basket as a hat.

"Maybe I am nuts," he declared.

"Aha!" Maisie said, lifting her margarita up for a toast. "He finally admits it."

He clinked glasses with her and then with River, who added, "If it's nuts to love PayDays, then I'm nuts too. To being nuts!"

Finn took a sip and then shrugged. "Nuts or not, I'm doing it anyway."

"So when is this going down?" Maisie said. "I only ask because I want to hide from the shrapnel."

She said it glibly, and he was reasonably sure it was a joke.

"This weekend. I need to go to Charlotte first."

"Good luck," River said. They all knew he'd need it. Talking to his parents was almost always a recipe for frustration.

He went up to Charlotte on Friday, by which time he had even more ammo in his Alan takedown portfolio. Part of the reason his plan had taken so long to execute was because he was also working on his business. He'd managed to secure an office on the South Slope starting next month—an open, bright, loft-style space with a conference room—and he'd even interviewed a few candidates to join his team. One of them was probably going to work out—a recent business school graduate who'd already sold the idea for an app allowing people to trade their fresh garden produce. Another of the candidates had spent nearly his entire interview talking about how magnets could be used to communicate with the aliens. Finn had bitten his tongue, but he tried it on his fridge as soon as he got home. Nothing.

The Summer in January Beerfest he'd conceptualized for Bev Corp was also moving full steam ahead. Most of the other local brewers had agreed to participate, thanks in part to Buchanan Brewery's inclusion and, Finn suspected, some kind intervention on River's part.

Charlotte Robotics had already begun implementing some of the ideas from his launch plan. Sean and Mo were over-the-moon excited, and so was he.

According to Dottie, she and Adalia had finalized the lineup for the Asheville Art Display. She'd had an almost mischievous look on her face when she told him, as if she knew something he didn't. Which, to be fair, she usually knew plenty of things he didn't. She'd also mentioned that Blue was knitting Tyrion as a surprise for Adalia. God, she would love that.

Professionally speaking, it was the most exciting time in his life, but something was missing…or more accurately, someone. It gave everything a strangely hollow feel.

He spent the morning in back-to-back meetings with Sean and Mo and the rest of the staff at the Charlotte Robotics office. The work was both exhausting and invigorating. It helped that he liked them so much, that he was invested in their success.

At the end of the day, Sean asked if he could have a private word with him, and they stuck around the conference room to talk.

"Sorcha says you're looking to take that guy down," Sean said. "The pervy professor guy, I mean."

"I hope so," Finn said. "He shouldn't be allowed to get away with it. The art school either."

"Good. Sorch doesn't like to admit it, but the whole thing disturbed her. After going to Lanier she even talked about leaving art, doing something else entirely. But it didn't take." He smirked. "Art's in the blood, my parents say. You can't deny it because you *are* it."

"Yeah, I think that's how my friend feels," Finn said.

"Must be some friend," Sean said, clapping him on the back.

"She sure is."

Between what Dottie had said about the show and some cryptic hints from River, Finn suspected Adalia might have finally started working on her art again. He hoped so. He wanted that for her, as much as he wanted Hamilton Consulting for him. (He could already hear her teasing him—*you* would *use your own name*—which, in all honesty, was part of the reason he'd done it.)

He took his leave and headed back to his parents' house for dinner. It was already early evening, and his mother had suggested that he arrive by six o'clock for pre-dinner drinks and appetizers. Honestly. It was just three of them. What were they, the Vanderbilts?

But he needed to talk to his parents—to be straight with them about his intentions—and it would be best if he made a timely appearance. He'd texted his father beforehand to warn him, in no uncertain terms, that if there was another unscheduled guest, particularly if that guest was Charlotte, he'd speak in verse throughout dinner.

I'm pretty sure even Charlotte will notice that.

Grow up, Finn, his father had answered.

I'm working on that. Truth is, I need to talk to you about a woman. Might not go well if we have this conversation in front of someone you're trying to set me up with.

His father hadn't responded, which either meant that he had been planning another setup and would, hopefully, cancel it, or that he didn't wish to dignify the message with a response.

There were no unfamiliar cars in the drive, which he took as a hopeful sign.

His mother opened the door for him, like she usually did.

"Your dad says you're still seeing that woman you mentioned on your last visit," she said after he kissed her cheek. She led him into the living room, which was conspicuously empty except for a platter of various appetizers, some fizzy-looking drink and a tumbler filled with what appeared to be bourbon. "I know you care for bourbon, so I took the liberty of ordering for you," his mother explained. "Now, can you tell me about your friend?"

"Where's Dad?" he asked, surprised.

"At work," she said. "He's going to be there until at least six thirty. I figured it would give us some time to talk privately."

"Oh," he said, caught off guard. When had they ever had a private chat? His father was the sort who had an opinion about everything and never shied away from expressing it. It seemed unlikely that he was aware of this arrangement— unless his parents had decided together that his mother had a better chance of gently discouraging him. Neither of them would get very far if that was their aim, but he'd listen to what she had to say and hope for the best.

"Well?" she asked. "I'd like to hear more about this woman who's made such an impression on you."

He took a hefty sip of the bourbon, trying to find words for what Adalia meant to him.

"Her name's Adalia," he started, savoring the sound of it. "She's incredibly brave. She doesn't see it, but it's apparent in everything she does. In who she *is*. Most people try to hide their emotions, their worries and fears, but she pours herself into everything she does. She puts it into her art, for everyone to see. She's more herself than anyone I've ever known."

"So she's an artist," his mother said with a furrowed brow, as if he'd said she were an exotic dancer. "What about her family?"

A smile twitched on his lips. "Dad would approve of her father, I bet. He runs a luxury real estate company in New York. He's also a huge dick."

"Language, Finn," his mother said, but it lacked any heat.

"I'm in love with her," he said.

He'd expected surprise or maybe an objection—something along the lines of: *You don't know what love is until you've met someone with a solid investment portfolio and an heirloom set of pearls.* But she simply nodded. "I thought as much."

"Wait…what?" he asked, shocked. "I've barely mentioned her to you before today."

"When was the last time you ever told your father about a woman in your life?"

He honestly couldn't remember. Maybe never.

"And I can see it in your eyes," she said. An almost wistful look passed over her face as she took a sip of her drink. "You're not the only one who's ever been in love, although it might seem like it at the moment."

Another shockwave roiled through him. Was she talking about his father?

"I had a life before your father, you know. But there are many different considerations a person should make when choosing their life partner, Finn. Love isn't the only one that matters."

Ah, that sounded more like them.

"How about this?" he said. "She makes me want to be a better person. And without her, I'm not sure I would have ever figured out what I want to do with my life. I only hope I'm lucky enough to spend it with her."

She studied him for a moment before nodding. "Your mind is made up. I can't say I'm happy that you've decided not to come home, but I won't try to dissuade you. Come with me."

She set down her drink, but he took his tumbler with him. He figured he might need a little liquid courage.

His mother scowled a little, but if she objected, she didn't outright say so. She led him to her room—only hers, because his parents had kept separate rooms for as long as he could remember.

To his surprise, she led him to her jewelry box. He hadn't even asked.

She lifted a hand. "Your father didn't want me to wear my grandmother's ring, but it's a family heirloom, and when you're ready, it's yours to give to Adalia." Her mouth twitched with repressed laughter. "It sounds like it'll be *quite* interesting to see her match wits with your father."

Wouldn't it ever. Finn only hoped they both had a chance to see it.

CHAPTER
Thirty-Nine

Adalia's alarm went off on her phone midway through her adjustment of a spring connecting two parts of her sculpture, and she felt the all-too-familiar grip of indecision. Should she go to meet Blue and Maisie for their girls' night out or continue working?

There was no denying she was a woman obsessed. When she wasn't at Buchanan Brewery or working on the art show, she was at the studio. It was as if her soul had been starving for art all these months, and now she was gorging herself.

Only that wasn't the full story. Her art was helping her express and work through her emotions, just like it always had. It had brought her a rare sense of clarity about what she'd been through these last months. She'd gone through the loss of her mother, and while it had thrown her entire world off its axis, she'd reached a state of grace. She was grateful she'd had a caring, warm, loving mother, even if she'd lost her too soon. Her father would *never* approve of her—and while she'd always instinctively known it, now there was a peaceful acceptance. He was a bitter, narrow-minded man whose opinion no longer mattered to her. Her attitude would likely enrage him even more, which would have been the perfect revenge, but she found she no longer cared about that anymore either. Not with him anyway.

As for Alan, his betrayal still stung—deeply. The thought of toppling him from his self-appointed throne was tantalizing, but she just wasn't sure she could endure seeking revenge through the legal system. So she would move on instead.

But the loss of Finn…

She wasn't a fool. She knew the reason she stayed so late at the studio was to fill the time she wished she were spending with him. They'd only been together a short period of time, yet she'd never before known someone who got her so completely.

She regretted not being more open with him about Alan. If she'd allowed him to hold her hand through that ordeal, it would have made them stronger. She'd blown it.

She'd never been big into wishing for a wedding and marriage, but when she let herself daydream in her new game of 'What if…', when she looked into her perfect future, she saw herself with Finn.

But she reminded herself that her changed perspective didn't resolve all their issues. There was still the matter of his need for change.

One day the previous week, Dottie and Adalia had gone out to lunch to work out some logistics for the show. The conversation had somehow landed on astrology, although they'd gotten there by such a meandering path, she couldn't quite remember how.

"I've read my horoscope online from time to time," Adalia had admitted with a laugh. "Who hasn't?"

"Oh no, dear," Dottie had said with a wave of her hand. "Everyone knows those things are nonsense. I'm talking about *real* astrology. Have you had your star chart done?"

Adalia quirked a brow. "Are you really asking me that, Dottie?"

The older woman chuckled. "Fair enough, but you should consider it. I could set you up with my friend Ollie."

"No, thank you," Adalia said, holding up a hand. "Not after that disastrous visit to Lola."

Dottie frowned. "That was serendipitous, dear, not a disaster." She paused and leaned closer over the table. "Do you realize how rare it is for a fortune-teller to pull the same cards, in the same order, for two back-to-back clients?"

Adalia pushed her plate away, her stomach in knots. "Dottie…"

But Dottie forged on, not that she'd really expected her to give up. "You're a Sagittarius, Adalia, a fire sign. Bold and brave and full of life."

"I don't feel very brave," Adalia admitted, half under her breath.

The older woman reached across the table and covered her hand. "You are *very* brave. And full of happiness and light. Sagittarians don't cotton to lies and untruths. They're optimistic and bright, and you, my dear, are the epitome of your star sign."

Adalia sighed. "Dottie…"

"Gemini is an air sign. The twin sign. They're not called the twin sign without reason. They love to talk and sometimes they're too busy talking to really listen. They're change makers, partially because they're easily distracted and often grow bored." Dottie had given her a pointed stare then. "Do you know who's a Gemini?"

"Finn." Did it make her a stalker that she'd looked up his birthday after she'd broken up with him?

"That's right," Dottie said, "which is why his new career will be perfect for him. He'll have a constant stream of new clients and new ideas to feed his need for change."

Was Dottie confirming what Adalia had already suspected?

"But Adalia…" Dottie squeezed her hand tighter. "Once Geminis find the love they are destined to have, they hold on tight and don't let go. And they're extremely compatible with Sagittarians."

Adalia hadn't confessed her fears to anyone, so how had Dottie known?

Wait. Had she said *love*?

Adalia's eyes narrowed. "Have you been talking to Finn?"

Dottie held her gaze. "Yes, I've spoken to Finn."

"About me?"

"We've discussed you, but I've never once betrayed your confidence or shared anything that I think would hurt you."

Adalia didn't know exactly what that meant, but she trusted Dottie, as crazy as that seemed at times.

"Your life is your own to do with as you wish. But sometimes we shouldn't struggle against fate. Just keep that in mind." Dottie winked at her. Then she picked up her fork and said, "Are you sure you don't want to make a space for the goat paintings? Stella Price could bring some of her goats to the event. We'll already have dogs. A few more animals might make it feel like a petting zoo. Very festive."

"Maybe we should skip the goats," Adalia said, grateful for the change in topic. "At least the dogs are house-trained. Do we really want goats pooping in the brewery event space?

Not to mention, they might start eating the other artwork. Or the patrons' clothes."

Dottie got a faraway look in her eyes. "That might be interesting. A nude art exhibit."

"As open-minded as I am," Adalia said, "I think we should encourage people to wear their clothing, and to ensure it stays on, we should be safe and skip the goats."

Dottie made a face, then shrugged. "Perhaps you're right, but keep it in mind, will you?"

Adalia had promptly tried to forget the goats and their owner, but Dottie's words about Finn had stuck with her.

Was it a bad thing that she was thinking about going to see him?

What if he didn't *want* to see her? He'd be well within his rights. And what if he'd already met someone else? The thought made her physically sick. How could he date anyone else? Finn was *her* soul mate.

And now she was running late for her girls' night out with Blue and Maisie.

She quickly changed into a dress and flats, then headed out to Bessie to make the short drive to the Italian restaurant Maisie had chosen. She'd gone from the brewery straight to the studio to get some work in before seeing the girls, so she hadn't taken Tyrion with her. It felt weird to go out sans her sidekick, but Jack had assured her multiple times that he'd smother the dog with plenty of love in her absence. He'd said if she were this bad with a dog, he couldn't imagine how protective she'd be when she had kids.

Which had made her think of Finn, of course. Did he want kids? She was pretty sure she did.

It took her a while to find a parking place and then walk to the restaurant, and when she got there, Maisie and Blue were already seated with drinks in front of them. Another drink was on the table between them.

"I took the liberty of getting you a sangria," Maisie said, lifting her own drink. "They make the best I've ever had."

"No complaints from me," Adalia said as she took a seat between them. "Sorry I'm late."

"You're not late," Maisie said, checking her phone, then glancing up with a smirk. "You're exactly on time. If you were one minute later, I'd feel justified in giving you a hard time over that grease smudge on your cheek. But since you're not, I won't say a word."

"What?" Adalia reached for her cheek, but Blue pulled a tissue out of her purse and began to swipe at her face.

"Let me get it. At least I can see it."

"I take it that's from your artwork," Maisie said before taking a sip of her drink.

"Yeah," Adalia said with a smile. "Now that I'm sculpting again, I seem to be a woman possessed."

"Huh," Maisie said. "A lot like Finn and his new consulting company. Now that he has nothing else in his life, he's put every waking moment into setting it up." A strange look lit her eyes. "Well, almost every moment."

She wanted to ask what exactly that meant, but surely Maisie wasn't talking about another woman. She wouldn't joke about that. Deciding to shift the conversation completely away from herself, she turned to Blue. "How was your date?" She shot a glance at Maisie. "She met a new guy just before she came here. Just coffee this time. She learned the hard way to save dinner for the ones she likes."

Maisie grimaced and held up her glass. "Been there, done that. So spill it, Blue. How'd it go?"

Blue rolled her eyes. "It was a disaster. I realize this is Asheville and all, but this guy, Leo, took eccentricity to the nth level. He showed up wearing a tinfoil hat."

"What?" both women squealed at the same time.

"And it wasn't to fend off alien gamma rays, or whatever those things are supposed to do. He makes them and sells them on Etsy. As fashion."

"Sure, he might have them for sale," Maisie said, "but the real question is if people *buy* them."

"Do you have a link?" Adalia asked. "I really need to see this."

Blue ignored her. "That's not the worst of it. He said his underwear was made of tinfoil as well. And not just regular tinfoil. *Recycled* tinfoil." She gestured to the foil-covered leftovers a couple tables down. "Just think. That could be cradling Leo's balls in a matter of days."

"Yikes," Maisie said with a look of horror. "I really could have gone without that image in my head."

"Remind me not to use tinfoil in any of my future projects," Adalia said with a laugh. "I have no idea which pieces may have done the cradling."

All three women shuddered, then burst out laughing.

"I gave up on online dating a year ago," Maisie said. "I've decided to let it happen the old-fashioned way." She said it flippantly, but Adalia could see resignation in her gaze instead of the fury and sorrow she'd seen before. Did that mean that Maisie had made peace with the whole River thing? She hoped so, for all of their sakes.

"I'm about to give up," Blue said. "It's not like I really need a man. I'd just like to have someone to share my life with. I mean, someone besides Buford, of course."

Maisie didn't respond, and Adalia's heart ached. She didn't *need* Finn. She'd survived just fine without him, but she still *wanted* him. He'd made her life brighter and less lonely.

"We're a bunch of losers," Maisie said dryly.

They all laughed at that, then changed the subject to the art show. The conversation meandered while they ate, but it never stopped being comfortable and fun and warm, and Adalia felt like she'd known them for years instead of only a few weeks.

The bill came, and they were all reaching for their wallets when Maisie got a text that made her frown. "I need to head to the shelter. A new dog came in, and I'm at capacity." She put some cash on the table. "I'll probably end up bringing her home with me for the night, then look for a foster family in the morning."

"Do you have trouble finding foster families?" Blue asked.

"Sometimes," Maisie said absently as she refastened her wallet. "Some people end up keeping the dog, which means they're no longer available to foster, and others find it so devastating to give up a foster animal they can't bring themselves to take another." She glanced over at Adalia. "Like Finn."

She blinked hard. "*What?*"

Maisie grimaced. "I placed a corgi with him that had bladder issues, peed everywhere. He complained about her every time I saw him, so I thought he wanted out of the arrangement. I found a permanent home for Kiki. But when I told Finn…" She made a face. "I broke his heart. Sometime toward the end of his month with her, he'd fallen in love, and I hadn't realized it. But I'd already promised the dog to another family, one with a couple of kids, so we had no choice.

He told me he couldn't foster any more. He couldn't take the heartbreak."

Oh, God. Adalia knew she'd made a terrible mistake.

She set her money on the table. "I have to go."

"But you paid too much," Blue said. "Don't you want to wait for your change?"

"No," she said, picking up her purse and jumping out of her seat. "I have someone I need to see."

Maisie gave her an incredulous look. "The dog story was what finally did it?"

"What?" Adalia asked in confusion. "How'd you know I was going to see Finn?"

"Please…" Disgust washed over Maisie's face. "I've been trying to figure out a way to show you that you're throwing away the best thing that has probably ever happened to you without being that obnoxious friend who is always in your business. If I'd known the foster dog story would be the tipping point, I would have told you two weeks ago." She shrugged. "In hindsight, knowing how much you love Tyrion, I should have guessed."

Adalia stared at her in shock for a full two seconds. "Are you in cahoots with Dottie?"

"Is it *possible* to be in cahoots with Dottie?" Maisie asked. "She's a one-woman show, and we all just orbit around her."

"Why are you still here?" Blue said, giving her a soft shove. "Go! At least one of us should get the man of her dreams."

Adalia ran out the door, ignoring the dirty looks the customers and restaurant staff shot in her direction. She'd wasted enough time. It was time to go get Finn back.

CHAPTER
Forty

It took some of the wind out of Finn's sails to realize Adalia wasn't home. Somehow that hadn't figured into his plans. He'd driven to her house with purpose, but Bessie wasn't in the driveway. He'd gotten out anyway to check, since for all he knew Bessie might have finally given up the ghost and broken down.

Psyching himself up, he got out of the car and rang the bell, the Alan takedown file tucked under his arm. He waited a few antsy seconds. Rang it again. He heard Tyrion howl inside, as if picking up the pitch of the bell, but no one responded. It was then he heard a raised voice in the back yard. A man's voice. It was almost certainly Jack—*his* car was in the drive—but he felt a tingle of worry. Especially when Tyrion's off-pitch howl rose up again from behind the door.

What if Tyrion was carrying on not because of the bell but because someone was back there bothering Adalia?

Looking around for something to use as a weapon, he spotted a rain stick by the front door. He set down the file and grabbed it, something he immediately regretted when he started moving around the house with it, because it made a rushing noise that was sure to draw attention to him.

Still, it was better than nothing.

He rounded the edge of the yard carefully, catching sight of Jack from behind. He was standing by the bench, his posture rigid.

"I want to talk to my sister *right now*," he said. There was no mistaking the hostility in his voice, and Finn's heart started pounding double time in his chest. Something had happened to either Georgie or Adalia. He had to find out what and offer to help.

He ran toward Jack, the forgotten rain stick rushing in his hand, and to his shock, Jack whipped around, dropping the phone, and punched him directly in the face. He staggered back and landed directly on his butt, his hand flying up to his eye as the pain set in.

"Oh shit," Jack said, shaking out his hand. "It's you. I'm sorry. I saw someone out of the corner of my eye, running at me with a stick, and…"

But Finn was already climbing to his feet. "I heard you on the phone. Adalia, Georgie, are they okay?"

Jack's expression turned bleak. "They're fine," he said. "Give me a second, and I'll explain."

He picked up the phone and wandered off, talking in a hushed voice. Finn was tempted to follow him, to see if he and Jack had similar definitions of the word fine, but Jack was already hanging up and pacing back over.

"What happened?" Finn asked, carefully palpating his injured eye.

"Let's go inside and get you a bag of peas or something."

"What happened?" he insisted.

Jack swore under his breath. "I wasn't talking about either of them," he insisted.

It took a moment for the meaning to penetrate the fog of pain in Finn's head.

Oh.

"There's another secret sibling?"

"She's not their sister," Jack said harshly. "She's mine." He ran a hand through his hair. "But yeah, I need to tell them about her. I know that. I…didn't want to at first."

He tried to remember what he'd heard Jack say in that conversation he'd overheard a few weeks ago. All he could remember was Jack saying he didn't trust her. Presumably he'd been talking to his sister, so who didn't he trust? Adalia? A surge of protectiveness rose in him.

"Why didn't you say anything?" he asked.

"She's only seventeen. She lives at home with our mother."

The way he said it made it obvious the mother was the one he didn't trust—and it was also apparent why Jack kept going back to Chicago.

"You take care of her," he stated.

"Not enough," Jack said. "But I plan to do better. Come on. Let me get you those peas."

"No, that's okay," he said. "I need to find Adalia. Do you know where she is?"

Panic rippled across Jack's face. "You can't tell her. I need to be the one who does."

"I won't," Finn said, "and not just because I don't want you to punch me again." He managed a slight smile, which hurt like hell. "Believe me, we have plenty of other things to talk about. But you should tell her soon. Georgie too."

Jack nodded slowly. "I'm glad you're going to see her. She's at that Italian tapas place downtown with Maisie and Blue."

There were at least three restaurants that could loosely meet that description.

"Do you remember which one?" he asked.

Jack shrugged. "Nope. But let me get you those peas."

Since it really did hurt, and the gesture would clearly make Jack feel better, Finn just nodded. "Meet you around front?" he suggested. "I left something on the porch I need to pick up."

"Sure," Jack said. Then his gaze lowered to the rain stick. He picked it up, his brow furrowed, and said, "Here's your…thing."

"It's not mine," Finn said. "It was on your porch."

"Dottie must have left it here," he said, shaking his head a little, although his expression was fond. He lowered the stick and propped it against the bench. "She leaves things here all the time. One time I came home, and there was a purple ukulele sitting on the porch. She said she saw it and thought of me."

"And have you played it?"

Jack smiled. "Wouldn't you know it…I have. She was right."

They parted ways, and Finn circled around to the front, reclaiming the Alan file. Tyrion was still howling agitatedly, and a superstitious part of Finn worried that maybe Adalia really was in trouble. He was anxious to find her, but he'd said he would wait for the peas, and he didn't want to give Jack any reason to doubt or dislike him. He'd leave as soon as he had the peas, though, and he'd go to every single Italian restaurant in town if he had to.

Jack finally opened the door, a bag of peas in hand, but Tyrion charged him from behind, pushing him so hard he staggered through the opening.

The dog slipped past Finn and raced down the hill and then the street, moving at a speed that might have won him the Iditarod if he'd been born in a different state.

"Shit," Finn shouted. "Follow that dog!"

He and Jack raced down the street on foot—Jack with a bag of peas in his hand, Finn with his arms wrapped around the file.

Tyrion was so far ahead, Finn worried they'd lose him, especially in the poorly lit areas, but he continued to see a flash of white ahead, the tip of Tyrion's fluffy tail.

Then it dawned on him—Tyrion was heading in the direction of *his* house.

Jack was ahead of him, because he was apparently some kind of super athlete with a hell of a right hook. But sure enough, he slowed and then stopped as he reached Finn's house. The look on his face said he'd found Tyrion, so Finn let himself walk the rest of the way.

That was when he heard her—"I guess maybe you were right about that fence."

And he found it in him to run the rest of the way after all. Adalia was sitting on the steps, wearing a red sundress that made her hair look like a gilded crown. Tyrion sat at her feet, as regal and untroubled as if he hadn't just hurtled across half the neighborhood.

"Finn," she said, getting to her feet. Then she gasped. "Your eye."

Which was when he realized he was covered in sweat and one of his eyes was likely black and definitely swollen. This wasn't exactly how he'd envisioned his grand gesture.

"Your brother hit me," he blurted out, his mind firing at warp speed. Why was she here? And Tyrion…it was like he'd *led* Finn to her. It was something that shouldn't be possible, but he knew Dottie would say it was. That it was the same kind of impossible that had led to them getting the exact same tarot draw. And to Finn and River falling in love with sisters.

"What?!" Adalia barked, turning on Jack.

"It was an accident," Finn added, and Jack nodded and handed him the bag of peas.

"I'm going to bring the escape artist here home. Give you two some time to talk."

"No, you can leave him here," Finn said, then glanced at Adalia. "If you're okay with that."

Something glimmered in her eyes—could he dare to hope it was affection for him and not just the dog?—and she nodded.

"See you later," Jack said, nodding to them, and he took off, his pace unhurried now.

They both watched him for a moment. Then Adalia took the bag of peas from Finn's hand and gently pressed it to his eye. Her touch sent a wave of warmth through him. It didn't even matter that there was apparently a tear in the bag of peas, and the cold pellets started tumbling down the collar of his shirt.

"Hit you by accident, huh?"

"Let's just say you don't want to sneak up on that guy." He paused, still thrown off his game. Unsure of what to do next, he found himself asking, "Why are you here?"

"Because I realized something." She paused, lowering the rapidly emptying bag of peas. She gestured to him and Tyrion, peas flying out of the bag as she did. Then she noticed the leak and snorted as she lowered the bag to the ground.

He laughed with her, and dared to reach out and touch her hand. Weaving their fingers together, he squeezed her hand. "What is it you realized?"

"'The only thing that matters right now is the people in this room.'"

It was a weird way of putting it, what with the fact that they were outside, plus she'd said it with emphasis, as if the words were supposed to mean something special.

"You can't imagine how happy I am to hear you say that," he said. And because he couldn't avoid the temptation to tease her a little, he added, "Even if we're technically outside."

"It's from *Fast Five*," she said. "I needed to feel close to you… I've watched it at least five times."

He started laughing uncontrollably then, and the file slipped from his fingers, papers spilling onto the sidewalk. "Adalia. I've never seen it. I was messing with you. My favorite movie is *The Goonies*."

"Oh, you asshole," she said, but she was already laughing too, her eyes sparkling with it. "I kept trying to find all the good things in it because you said you loved it. It was a real struggle the first two times, but after that I kind of got to like it. You will always be the man who made me like *Fast Five*."

There were so many things he had to say, some of them scattered beneath their feet, but he pulled her to him and kissed her. It was gentle at first, but it turned fierce in an instant, Adalia pressing closer, slipping a hand under his shirt, laughing a little in her throat when a frozen pea tumbled against her hand. He slid a hand around to cup her butt, and she moaned in a way that made him want to forget all the things they'd left unsaid and carry her upstairs. They could talk later.

But then a car pulled into the driveway next door, and his octogenarian neighbors got out.

He pulled away, panting, and the woman, Phyllis, raised a hand in a wave.

"Hello, Finn," she said, acting for all the world like she'd caught him gardening instead of making out.

"Hi, Phyllis," he said.

"Beautiful night, isn't it? Ben and I just had dinner and dessert at that new restaurant downtown. What is it called, Ben?"

"I can't remember," he said, scratching his head. "Gumbo. Jumbo? One of those newfangled names."

"Amazing dessert," Phyllis gushed. "Out of this world. The dinner?" She lifted a palm out and shook it from side to side. "So-so."

"Well, goodnight, kids," Ben said with a wink, making Finn feel like they were teenagers caught necking in the park. "Have fun."

"Goodnight!" Adalia called out. "Thanks for the recommendation." Then she glanced back at Finn, giving him a wicked look. "'You know I like my dessert first.'"

Before he could comment, or maybe break it to her that there was no restaurant downtown named Gumbo or Jumbo and they had a needle-in-a-haystack chance of finding Phyllis's dessert, she said, "You wouldn't get it. *Fast Five* reference."

"That's going to be happening a lot, isn't it?" he said, laughing.

A little breeze picked up, and some of the papers flew around. "What is all of this, anyway?" Adalia asked. She stooped to pick one up, then stared at him with big eyes. "What did you do?"

"Nothing yet," he said quickly, silently thanking Maisie. "I…it didn't sit easily with me, knowing that he might get away with what he did to you. I had a feeling you weren't the only one, so I looked into it. He's sexually harassed or stolen from at least six other people at the Lanier School, and the school did their part in covering it up.

"Addy. It's your decision. Whatever you want to do. But there's a reporter for *The New York Times* who's interested in seeing these files. They wouldn't need to mention your name. You can make sure he gets what he deserves without involving your family."

Something rippled over her face. Then she steeled herself, and her expression shuttered. "You did this for me."

There was no denying it, so he simply nodded.

"I'm not going to ask them to reveal themselves if I won't do the same. I'll tell my story. They can use my name too."

"But your father—"

"Screw my father." Her eyes went from fierce to regretful in an instant. "I'm sorry, Finn. I'm sorry I nearly ruined everything. You mean so much to me. I just needed some time to put this behind me. And I…I guess I was afraid. I worried that I wouldn't be enough for you. That you'd want to move on from me like you did with Big Catch."

He reached into his pocket, his hand wrapping around the small box, and lowered onto one knee, the escaped peas mushing under him.

He heard a gasp, but he didn't look up as he took out the box and flipped it open. "Adalia Buchanan, 'you have bewitched me, body and soul. I love, I love, I love you.' Will you marry me?"

He finally looked up and saw the tears in her eyes. On her cheeks. She took his hand and pulled him up, then cradled his face and met his eyes.

"No," she said, and for a moment, it felt like the sidewalk would crack open and the earth would swallow him whole, but she added, "not yet. But I love you, you big idiot, and I do want to be your girlfriend." She motioned to the ring. "We'll get there. I know we'll get there." She smiled up at him. "And not just because that's the coolest ring I've ever seen in my life." It was a large ruby with two smaller diamonds bracketing it, the design from another era.

"I can live with that," he said, grinning back. He shut the ring box and pocketed it. She was right—he was nuttier than a Snickers bar for asking, but he'd needed to show her how much she meant to him. He'd needed her to know that he had no intention of moving on to someone else. Adalia was the one he wanted.

She kissed him this time, but it was a quick kiss, and she pulled back with shining eyes. "There's something I need to show you. I've been working at Blue's studio for weeks, but no one's seen my sculptures. I want you to be the first."

So she *had* been working again. She'd reclaimed the part of herself she'd cast aside, and she wanted to be with him.

He'd never felt happier in his life.

"I would be honored."

She gave him a playful nudge. "No need to sound like Mr. Darcy too. One person shouldn't be allowed to have everything."

"I know," he said, nudging back. "That's why I feel impossibly lucky right now."

She glanced around. "Well, don't feel too lucky. You must have left your car at my house, so we're stuck taking

Better Luck Next Time

Bessie. And to be honest, she's not smelling so great now that I've taken to raiding dumpsters for sculpting materials. Plus, we should really do something about this mess." There were peas and papers everywhere now. "You do have these electronically, I'm guessing?"

"Of course," he said, then shrugged. "The papers felt like a more dramatic gesture."

"Good call," she said. "Give me a second."

She headed toward Bessie, and Finn took the opportunity to pet Tyrion, who'd somehow known exactly where to bring him. Adalia returned with a plastic bag, and they hastily scooped the mess inside before tossing it in the trash bin.

Then Adalia took his elbow like she had that day at the Biltmore. "Let's go, Mr. Darcy. Dire wolf, heel!"

Tyrion fell in behind them, and they set off toward Bessie. As Finn entered the passenger side of that ramshackle car, which did indeed smell, he knew this was only the beginning of something beautiful. And it was the kind of beautiful he wanted to last his whole life.

EPILOGUE

"This is amazing!" Georgie exclaimed as she pulled Adalia into a hug. "Nearly half of the pieces have sold, and it's all gone so smoothly!"

Adalia grimaced. "I don't know about smoothly."

There'd been some last-minute glitches that had nearly made her pull her hair out. The pieces had been delivered a few days before the event, and a box of pottery had gone missing. The artist had been understandably agitated, but it was finally found in the brewery storage room two hours before opening night. It had been labeled *Y. East*—the artist's name—but one of the Buchanan employees had mistaken it for "yeast." The caterer had also flaked two nights beforehand, but Finn had worked his magic and found one last minute. And lastly, the zipper of the new dress Adalia had bought for the event had broken, leaving her with nothing to wear but a sundress. Blue had found her nearly in tears an hour before the opening night festivities started, and she'd run home to bring her a gorgeous blue dress that was sophisticated and classy, yet not as severe as something Georgie would have lent her.

"You should be proud of yourself," Georgie said. "You handled all the hiccups like a pro." She cracked a grin. "You better watch out, or Jack might worry about his job."

Adalia released a short laugh. "Uh. *No.* He can keep his job, thank you very much. I've agreed to co-chair the Art Display for the first year, but only because Blue is going to take over Finn's co-chair spot."

"Are you sure you'll have time?" her sister asked with a worried look. "You still need to finish your pieces for your own show in February."

Lee had worked out a deal with the gallery. They'd agreed to assist with the transportation costs, which would come out of her commission. He'd video called her while she was at home making dinner with Finn to give her the final details.

"What if the pieces don't sell?" she'd asked.

"They'll sell," Finn and Lee had said simultaneously, and they'd all laughed together.

Lee's expression once again serious, he'd added, "If they don't sell, then I'll pay for it myself, an offer I only make because I know it'll never happen." Which was a lie she didn't call him out on. She knew he'd do it anyway, for her. "I've seen your work, Addy. This is just the start of great things for you."

"Nah, I've already got plenty of great things." She glanced over her shoulder at Finn and winked.

"So cheesy," he said, shaking his head, but his grin gave him away.

To Adalia's surprise, Lee was fully accepting of Finn. Given his attempt to interfere with Georgie's relationship with River, she'd expected resistance, but then again, their situation was different. River technically worked for Georgie, and her brother wasn't the sort who understood mixing business with pleasure. Or pleasure with pleasure, given his choice of girlfriend.

"He makes you happy, Addy," Lee had said when she'd mentioned it during their now-weekly Sunday afternoon video chats. (She could only assume Victoria had some sort of recurring Pilates class.) "Anyone who makes you that happy is good with me." But there was something in his expression that raised her suspicions.

Her eyes narrowed. "You looked into him."

Lee shrugged. "I regret that I didn't do more about the Alan situation. Besides, it was only a small background check, nothing too in depth, so it didn't cost much."

It had taken a few seconds for that to sink in. "You hired a *private investigator* to do a background check? I thought you'd just Googled him!"

His eyes hardened. "No one's going to hurt you and get away with it, Addy. Never again."

To her surprise, Finn hadn't been offended in the least, and in fact, it had endeared her brother to him. "If I had a younger sister, I would have done exactly the same thing."

"You only say that because he approves of you," she'd said, hands on her hips.

He'd grinned. "What's not to approve?"

They'd been worried about the fallout of her name being in *The New York Times* piece about Alan, but so far, she'd mostly received support. Alan had been suspended from the Lanier School, and Lee was certain he'd be fired. Her father had sent her a letter—a literal, pop-it-in-the-mail letter, although he'd typed it rather than handwritten it—saying he wished she would have employed more restraint. And better judgment. She'd cut it into little pieces and incorporated them into a painting full of reds. This one she hadn't attempted to destroy. Several artists were joining forces for a civil suit, but Adalia had told the others she wasn't interested. She was ready to move on with her life.

And it felt *good*. Finn and Adalia were both busy, him with launching his consulting business, her with her art, but they tried to cook dinner together several times a week, switching between their houses, especially since Finn had admitted how much homemade meals meant to him. He often went with her to the studio space in the evenings and worked on proposals and whatever wizardry he came up with for his clients while she worked on her pieces, Tyrion always with them.

She was happy. No, it was deeper than that—she was content. So much so, she worried it was too good to be true. Finn had told her he'd always wanted to camp out in his back yard when he was a kid, but his parents wouldn't allow it. So she'd made it happen. And that night, as they lay under the stars in the back yard, she confessed to Finn that she'd never felt like this, and she was terrified it would be snatched away.

He'd cupped her cheek, and his blue-green eyes had searched hers. "I'm not going anywhere, Adalia. You're the very best thing that has stormed into my life. Why would I *ever* risk losing you?"

So here she was, at the end of an event that had been successful in every right. They'd sold every ticket. Maisie's speech had tugged heartstrings, and the guests loved the puppies. The last-minute food was delicious. The artists had all sold more pieces than expected. And Dog is Love had a few thousand more dollars to keep the lights on and give love to abandoned pets.

Finn was on the other side of the room, talking to a couple who were admiring one of Blue's unsold pieces, a

415

hanging octopus rendered in shades of blue and fuchsia. He looked impossibly handsome in his dark suit and tie. As if sensing her scrutiny, he turned his head slightly and caught her eye. A slow smile spread across his face—the one he brought out only for her—and her stomach somersaulted.

"Happiness looks good on you, dear," Dottie said, bustling up to her. "Now, are you quite sure you won't be attending the after-party? Stella was disappointed she couldn't bring the goats, so I promised her we'd have a petting zoo in my back yard. Lurch and Josie are setting everything up as we speak." Lurch and Josie were both ex-Buchanan Brewery staffers, and from what Adalia had seen at the couple of parties she'd attended with them, she suspected the party would rage well into the night. It was the kind of event she usually wouldn't miss for the world, but she had other plans.

Jack came up and hugged her. After sharing the news about his sister, Iris, with her and Georgie, he'd become much more open with them. He'd privately told her that her reaction to the news had been his favorite. She'd said, "I'd be happy to get another secret sibling every month if they all have a right hook like you do."

In truth, she'd been happy to learn his secret wasn't something sordid. His obvious affection for his sister only bolstered her opinion of him.

"Come on, Adalia," Jack said. "Stella stopped by earlier and she said her goats had formed a taste for Finn's clothes. She suspects he'll be down to his boxers within minutes of stepping into Dottie's back yard."

"Boxer briefs," she corrected, grinning.

He pulled a face.

Maisie came up to them then. There was dog hair on her green dress, something that made Adalia smile fondly as she reached out to brush it off. One of her volunteers had already taken the puppies back to the shelter, but Maisie had stuck around to "pull more heartstrings," as she'd put it.

"Four adoptions," Maisie said with a wide grin. "And I found a foster home for a senior dog too."

"That's certainly something to celebrate, dear," Dottie said with the smile of a carnival barker who knows they've caught someone's interest. "Why don't you head over to my house early for the after-party?" Her gaze shot to Jack. "Both of you. You can help finish the setup, and we can enjoy the back yard before the other guests show up."

Jack and Maisie exchanged a glance.

"Sure, why not," Jack said. "My little sister is in charge of this one."

Maisie's gaze shot to River and Georgie across the room, but she nodded without asking if they'd be leaving early too. Which was good. She no longer seemed intent on avoiding Georgie.

"Are you sure you want to miss the fun, Addy?" Jack asked one last time.

"Yup," she said. "I can undress my boyfriend just fine on my own. I don't need a goat to help."

Another wince, but a playful one, if that were possible. "Say goodbye to the bro for me," Maisie said with a wink. "I don't want to interrupt his sales pitch. Blue already has a box ready."

Adalia glanced back at Blue's exhibit as Jack, Maisie, and Dottie walked away, and sure enough, Blue was preparing a box with tissue paper that matched the piece, which was a sensible preparation because the couple did indeed buy it.

After that, the event closed down quickly, and before Adalia knew it, she was giving a closing speech. She thanked the Buchanan staff for helping make the night so successful and told them to head home and come back the next morning at ten to help clear the event space. The remaining pieces would be on display—and for sale—in the tasting room until the new year. They headed off talking and laughing, bound for Dottie's party, no doubt. Georgie and River gave her final hugs on their way out.

Finally, it was time to leave, and Adalia tugged Finn out to his car and made him get in the passenger seat.

"Do you trust me, Finn?" she asked once they were inside.

He turned serious. "Endlessly."

She opened her small clutch and pulled out the blindfold he'd made her wear to the Biltmore.

His breath hitched. "Is it a waste of breath to ask what that's for?"

Leaning over the console, she gave him a slow, provocative kiss, then pulled back a few inches and grinned. "Yes, but that's a hint."

He snatched the blindfold from her and slipped it on. "Why are you still parked? 'We talkin' or we racin'?' Go."

Laughing at the *Fast Five* reference—she'd "forced" him to sit through it five times, just like she had—she started his car and drove directly to her studio. After she parked, she led him to the front door and then down the hall to the space she subleased from Blue. Finn was an intelligent man, and she knew he likely realized where they were, but that wasn't the secret. Besides, they both loved the blindfold game.

Holding his hand, she led him to a small sculpture positioned on an overturned metal drum. She removed the tarp and tossed it to the floor.

"Okay," she said, "you can look."

He tugged the blindfold over his head and stared at the piece, his jaw dropping. "*Addy*. When did you find time to work on this?"

"It wasn't easy," she said with a wry smile. "What with you being underfoot so often. But I did some of it on weekends, and I've gone into work late a few days." He continued to stare at it, and her chest tightened. "Do you like it?"

His gaze shifted to her, and she saw her answer in his eyes.

She smiled up at him, tears pressing for release. "The piece I showed you before, the first one I made since the whole Alan debacle, represented what led me to you." She smiled. "Don't you see? That's my past, and this"—she gestured to the two-foot sculpture of an anatomical heart that sat on the metal drum—"is my present *and* my future." A tear slid down her cheek. "With you."

"Oh, Addy." Finn crushed her to his chest and kissed her so deeply it made her knees weak.

She pulled back and took his hand. "Let me explain it to you."

"Okay."

"Obviously, the heart is made of two different halves. One is rusted tin and the other is shiny but dented aluminum. That's us." Barbed wire was wrapped around both sides, but it was thicker on the rusted piece. There were multiple patches on both parts, representing their pasts. A heart locket she'd found in a flea market to represent her mother and a shiny silver business card holder to represent her father. On Finn's side, she'd embedded a metal key chain with a Duke insignia, and a few bottle caps from Big Catch, as well as small trinkets to represent the lives they'd led before they came together.

419

His hand squeezed hers. "*Addy.*"

She smiled up at him. "See the thin line of gold that binds them together? That's our love. And look at the bottom of the heart." She pointed to the tip. "The gold is spreading out from the seam, starting to cover the pain we brought with us."

The gold was partially covered a button with her high school logo and a piece of metal she'd embossed with the logo of the newspaper that had written the libelous piece about Finn.

"Addy," he said breathlessly.

"Come see the back." She tugged him around the drum. "Here the gold is streaking out through my interpretation of arteries, spreading through the heart, not only binding us together, but healing us as well." She gave him a worried look. "What do you think?"

"It's the second most beautiful thing I've ever seen."

She gave him a coy smile. "And what's the first?"

"I'm doing this all wrong if you even have to ask. You, Adalia Elizabeth Buchanan. You are the most beautiful thing I've ever seen. I wake up every morning grateful when I find you in my bed, and go to sleep at night deeply content when you're in my arms. Not to mention I spend fifty minutes of every hour throughout the day thinking about you."

She arched a brow, fighting a smile. "Only fifty minutes?"

He grinned. "I have to work *sometime.*"

Laughing, she wrapped her arms around his neck. "So you like it?"

"It's the thing I love second most." Then he added, "Spoiler alert: you're the first."

Her heart melted like butter. "Finn, I love you too."

"But you can't sell this, Addy," he said, an earnestness filling his eyes. "I'll buy it. Name your price."

Tilting her head, she gave him a dubious look. "What if I told you it was a million dollars?"

"Then I'll cash in some mutual funds," he said with a serious expression.

"You would do that?" she asked in shock.

A possessive look washed over his face. "If that's what it took to get this piece. Yes."

She kissed him again, slow and leisurely, then said, "It's your lucky day. I made it as a gift for you."

He sucked in a breath. "For me?"

"Yes. For you." She took the blindfold out of his hand. "And that's not the only gift I have in store, so you need to put this on, Mr. Hamilton," she said in her British accent.

Love and lust shone in his eyes. "I like the sound of that."

ABOUT
the Authors

A.R. CASELLA is a freelance developmental editor by day, writer by night. She lives in Asheville, NC with her husband, daughter, two dogs, and a variable number of fish. Her pastimes include chasing around her toddler, baking delicious treats, and occasional bouts of crocheting. *Any Luck at All,* co-written with *New York Times* bestselling author Denise Grover Swank, is her first book. You can find out more at www.arcasella.com

DENISE GROVER SWANK was born in Kansas City, Missouri and lived in the area until she was nineteen. Then she became a nomad, living in five cities, four states and ten houses over the course of ten years before she moved back to her roots. She speaks English and smattering of Spanish and Chinese which she learned through an intensive Nick Jr. immersion period. Her hobbies include witty Facebook comments (in own her mind) and dancing in her kitchen with her children. (Quite badly if you believe her offspring.) Hidden talents include the gift of justification and the ability to drink massive amounts of caffeine and still fall asleep within two minutes. Her lack of the sense of smell allows her to perform many unspeakable tasks. She has six children and hasn't lost her sanity. Or so she leads you to believe.

Made in the USA
Coppell, TX
05 March 2021